AFRICA RISEN

A New Era of Speculative Fiction

AFRICA
RISEN

EDITED BY

SHEREE RENÉE THOMAS,

OGHENECHOVWE DONALD EKPEKI,

AND **ZELDA KNIGHT**

TOR
DOT
COM

A Tom Doherty Associates Book • New York

AFRICA RISEN

Copyright © 2022 by Sheree Renée Thomas, Oghenechovwe Donald Ekpeki, and Zelda Knight

A Tordotcom Book
Published by Tom Doherty Associates
120 Broadway
New York, NY 10271

www.tor.com

Tor® is a registered trademark of Macmillan Publishing Group, LLC.

The Library of Congress Cataloging-in-Publication Data is available upon request.

ISBN 978-1-250-83300-6 (hardcover)
ISBN 978-1-250-83301-3 (ebook)

Our books may be purchased in bulk for promotional, educational, or business use. Please contact the Macmillan Corporate and Premium Sales Department at 1-800-221-7945, extension 5442, or by email at MacmillanSpecialMarkets@macmillan.com.

First Edition: 2022

Printed in the United States of America

0 9 8 7 6 5 4 3 2 1

Africa Risen is dedicated to the dreamers and the pioneers, to the unsung and unheralded, and to the meteoric rise of future newborn stars. This volume is also dedicated to you, dear reader! May your journey around the star we call sun continue to enlighten and encourage you. *Ashe amen.*

—Sheree Renée Thomas

Dedicated to my father, who is late but ever present in my mind and heart. To Dafe Ekpeki, for teaching me in words and deeds the value of striving to rise beyond our limitations and what we were either given or denied. For showing me that I, and Africa, like him, could rise.

—Oghenechovwe Donald Ekpeki

Dedicated to my Mother, Rochelle, and our ancestors who put down deep roots for us to flourish to this day.

—Zelda Knight

COPYRIGHT ACKNOWLEDGMENTS

TABLE OF CONTENTS

AFRICA
RISEN

INTRODUCTION

As the origin of humanity and home to the world's oldest civilizations, Africa is the origin story of storytelling. It is from its vast lands that humanity first sought to make sense of our world, the cosmos above and beyond us, the natural flora and fauna below. And it is from Africa, perhaps first known as Alkebulan, Af-ru-ka, Ethiopia, Ortigia, Corphye, Libya, among others, that the first humans emerged from stardust and traveled far, carrying their stories with them throughout the continent and on to other distant lands. These stories, first shared in mother tongues, took root in other nations and helped form other cultures. But many are still with us, while others too numerous to name, too old to be remembered, helped form the foundation from which an entire genre was later created: fantasy, which helped form the speculative fiction genre we think of today.

Until recently, the stories and literature of Africa and her diaspora were rarely discussed in the vaulted halls of the genre. For many years Black writers (and readers) of speculative fiction were discussed as dark matter, nonexistent, phantoms in a field that is full of ghosts. The pioneering works of writers such as Samuel R. Delany, Octavia E. Butler, Amos Tutuola, Ama Ata Aidoo, Ben Okri, Kojo Laing, Charles R. Saunders, Ngũgĩ wa Thiong'o, Steven Barnes, Jewelle Gomez, L. A. Banks, Eric Jerome Dickey, Tananarive Due, Nalo Hopkinson, Linda D. Addison, Nisi Shawl, Walter Mosley, Andrea D. Hairston, and others created a body of work that blazed a trail for new writers to come. Anthologies such as the groundbreaking volumes *Dark Matter: A Century of Speculative Fiction from the African Diaspora* and *Dark Matter: Reading the Bones,* edited by Sheree R. Thomas, as well as *Whispers from the Cotton Tree Root: Caribbean Fabulist Fiction* and *Mojo: Conjure Stories,* edited by Nalo Hopkinson, helped challenge the assumption of invisibility and created more space for new works from a variety of communities to find their way into the publishing world.

As newer audiences embrace storytelling from around the world, there is an excitement and openness to exploring rich tales that speak to the diverse cultural heritage that is born from not only Africa's broad and diverse diaspora, but from the continent of Africa itself, with its fifty-four nations, nine territories, and two independent states. Where before we spoke of dark matter, now Black writers from across the continent and around the world speak of black holes and wormholes, pathways and portals through time and space, wondrous mythologies and creations of new and old gods to reconnect the world to the origin, the source, the mother of all its stories. With this anthology, we hope to welcome readers to new tales and storytelling styles, inviting lovers of the speculative fiction genre to immerse themselves in a myriad of futurisms.

Fortunately today, there are more wonderful places where this work is supported. Presently, publishing African speculative fiction is less a project than a mission, a statement asserting not only the viability of the subgenre, but the necessity of pasts, presents, and futures for Black people. Independent Black-owned presses like MVmedia, Mocha Memoirs Press, and Rosarium Publishing have fostered countless careers. Short fiction magazines *Genesis, Omenana: Speculative Fiction Magazine,* and *FIYAH: Magazine of Black Speculative Fiction* have cultivated a plethora of voices in the genre, allowing authors to hone their craft with authentic stories rooted in their culture, struggles, and dreams. Multiple anthologies over the decades since *Dark Matter* have contributed to the proliferation of Black speculative short fiction, such as, but not limited to: *Dark Faith,* edited by Maurice Broaddus and Jerry Gordon; *Dark Thirst* by Omar Tyree, Donna Hill, and

Monica Jackson; *Dark Dreams* and *Voices from the Other Side*, edited by Brandon Massey; *So Long Been Dreaming: Postcolonial Science Fiction & Fantasy*, edited by Uppinder Mehan and Nalo Hopkinson; *Griots: A Sword and Soul Anthology*, edited by Milton J. Davis and Charles R. Saunders; the AfroSF series, edited by Ivor W. Hartmann; *Mothership: Tales from Afrofuturism and Beyond*, edited by Bill Campbell and Edward Austin Hall; *Trouble the Waters: Tales from the Deep Blue*, edited by Sheree Renée Thomas, Pan Morigan, and Troy L. Wiggins; *Obsidian's Speculating Futures: Black Imagination & the Arts*, guest edited by Sheree Renée Thomas with Nisi Shawl, Isiah Lavender III, and Krista Franklin; *Slay: Stories of the Vampire Noire*, edited by Nicole Givens Kurtz; *A Phoenix First Must Burn*, edited by Patrice Caldwell; *Octavia's Brood: Science Fiction Stories from Social Justice Movements*, edited by Walidah Imarisha and adrienne maree brown; *Jalada 02: Afrofuture(s)*, edited by Moses Kilolo; *New Suns: Original Speculative Fiction by People of Color*, edited by Nisi Shawl; *Imagine Africa 500*, edited by Billy Kahora; *Lagos_2060: Exciting Sci-Fi Stories from Nigeria*, edited by Ayodele Arigbabu; *Africanfuturism: An Anthology*, edited by Wole Talabi; *Dominion: An Anthology of Speculative Fiction from Africa and the African Diaspora*, edited by Zelda Knight and Oghenechovwe Donald Ekpeki; in addition to special volumes published by Black literary journals such as *Callaloo, Transition, Obsidian: Literature & Arts in the African Diaspora, Drumvoices Revue, The Black Scholar, Renaissance Noire, A Gathering of the Tribes, Anansi: Fiction from the African Diaspora*, and the *African American Review*, to name a few.

And the innovative work of Black comic book artists and cosplayers around the world cannot be overlooked in this journey. The accomplishments of the Sims family in creating *Brotherman*, Turtel Onli and Yumy Odom's pioneering work in creating the first Black Comic Book Festivals, the legendary Milestone Media, ANIA Comics Group, YouNeek Studios, Comic Republic,

Leti Arts, Kugali and the founders of the Black Comic Book Festival in Harlem—Jerry Craft, John Jennings, Deirdre Hollman, and Jonathan Gayles—the Megascope imprint, and Tim Fielder's *Infinitum* are all important figures and milestones among many in the comics community.

This anthology is inspired by this exciting growth and celebrates African and Afrodiasporic writers and the many stories they have to share with the world. It combines intergenerational voices, new and emerging as well as established authors, from across the globe, continental and diasporan. *Africa Risen* seeks to continue the mission of imagining, combining genres and infusing them with tradition, futurism, and a healthy serving of hope. Within these pages, you will be transported to the Black Fantastic and African Weird, tinged with Horror Noire, on a fantastical Pan-African journey featuring synthetic witches, goddesses, starwatchers, and much more.

We hope that *Africa Risen* inspires even more creative work, community-building, and scholarship in the field, as history has inspired us. As you read and explore these original stories, remember that this is a movement rather than a moment, a promising creative burgeoning. Because Africa isn't rising—it's already here.

—Sheree Renée Thomas, Oghenechovwe Donald Ekpeki, and
Zelda Knight

THE BLUE HOUSE

by Dilman Dila

A house loomed on the horizon, bright blue walls stuck out of gray rocks, barely discernible against the bare sky. Cana-B70 activated the telephoto in her eyes, and the lens whirred. Discs turned in her head with a scratching sound, prompting maintenance.sys to send yet another note to Katwe Garage. Her Outbox bulged, bloated with rejection. The lens failed to protrude. She launched the PhotoEdit App and zoomed in on the picture of the landscape, cropping out the house and ending up with a heavily pixelated image. The scratching grew louder as mem.sys scanned billions of media files in her drive to understand the house. It appeared circular, with a cone-shaped roof, much like the peasant huts in some of the photos she had, dated five hundred years ago. The late-afternoon sun bounced off its roof, and she thought she could smell the paint. In contrast, recent pictures of buildings had roofs that were too rusted to reflect any light, if any roof remained at all, and walls bled bare of paint. She searched the pixels around the house for evidence of a civilization that maintained the property. Nothing. Just bare gray rocks crowding an impossibly new house.

Perhaps it is a mirage.

Her system hung up. The discs stopped scratching, the gears in her belly ceased whirring, and the fans on her back froze. She had had a *thought*. . . . Mem.sys had not made calculations on image comparisons to associate the house with an illusion. It had received data from somewhere; *something* had whispered. She checked the address of the sender and found a strange program in a chip inside her head, Organic.sys, whose metadata identified it as a secondary operating system. It had become corrupted and, exactly fifty years, eight months, twenty-four days, six hours, forty minutes, and five seconds ago, had stopped functioning. Organic.sys sent another data packet to auto-correct "stopped functioning." *Died.* A memory purge had cleaned her system of the dead program, and yet, here it was, sending her data like a ghost whispering to a child.

Refresh.sys auto-started, the gears resumed their gentle hum, and Organic.sys auto-launched out of its grave. Security.sys tried to shut it down, but mem.sys overrode security, for it wanted to understand what was happening. The gears in her belly clanked and rattled as Organic.sys struggled to hold on to the thought, to nudge it back to levels that it told mem.sys were human. *Am I still alive?* Her power usage shot up and heat rose in her belly, making her insides hotter than the rock on which she stood. The fans on her back doubled their rounds per minute, and the liquid in her chest encasing CPU-3, the only processor still functioning, froze to keep it cool. Too late. Mem.sys closed Organic.sys, but CPU-3 overclocked, and shut down, plunging her into blackness.

Mercury dropped into the thermometer's bulb, triggering a lever to flip her battery switch, and she whirred back to life. Mem.sys revived her senses and she could see the sun going down, ice sheets forming on the rocks and beads of it sitting on her arm like little balls. The horizon was already too dark for her to see the strange building. She checked event.log to understand what caused the crash: A blue house, inexplicably new. An illusion? Organic memory detected. Power surge. CPU overload. Organic.sys had generated a record.log file, where it noted its thoughts.

The last line just before she plunged into blackness said, "If it's a mirage, shimmering in the heat wave, then I'm still alive."

She did not understand that line, or anything else in Organic. sys's log file. She was alive. She could see the sun go out, hear ice wrapping itself around rocks, smell the chill, taste the fear of dying alone, and feel the desperation to fix her withering body. Life. Was Organic.sys referring to its own death fifty years ago? Had the blue house triggered its resurrect? Why? To get answers she had to go into quasi-hibernation mode and launch Organic. sys without straining her processor, and the best time to do it was when in her tent. Not now.

The moon did not come and the night-vision mode gave everything a greenish hue, lending the rocks the look of sculptures in the photo captioned "New Art Museum." She analyzed images of houses at night and understood that, if it were inhabited, it would have lights, glowing in the dark, but the horizon was a sheet of blackness.

She climbed down the rock, testing each foothold for slipperiness, and mounted her bicycle-cart, which contained everything she needed to stay alive: a charger, a battery-powered thermal tent that supplemented her body heat, and a 3D printer she kept in the hope of finding cartridges of plastic filaments, or even bacteria-based ink, and printing out new parts to repair her body. She lined the tires with spiked rubber for a better grip on the ice, and then rode into the darkness.

She rode fast, anxious to investigate the house, for it might have cartridges. Perhaps it would be warm, for the data she had said houses became warm at night. She calculated that she would reach it before midnight, when temperatures dropped to negative one hundred. Her joints creaked as she pedaled, and again maintenance.sys auto-sent a note to Katwe Garage, reminding them that she needed oiling. The Outbox bulged with her solitude. It had been a very long time since she last encountered the carcass of another android and found recyclable parts and usable oil. The cart slid on the ice with a crunching sound, and she rode hard until the ice formed around the tires, trapping her. Then she put up the tent and settled for the night.

She initiated quasi-hibernation and launched Organic.sys. Nothing happened. The ghost did not whisper. Confused, she re-examined the log file, retracing the events that had triggered Organic.sys to resurrect. She had seen a building and had had a thought, that the house was an illusion, and she examined the photo she had taken of it, but now, instead of a circular blue structure she saw a grass-thatched hut in the moonlight, a little girl with a flaming torch running out of it and into the bush to harvest white ants. . . . That girl. She could not see her face.

Was she really examining a still image, or was this data from Organic.sys?

She realized Organic.sys had generated a file with a strange extension, .drm, which security.sys attempted to delete. Mem.sys overrode it, and opened the file, which turned out to be a video file. Its metadata identified it as a dream.

I've had a dream? She was in sleep mode, after all.

A quick scan told her that in the past, when all her systems functioned properly, Organic.sys had generated .dro files to imitate real-life dreaming. But unlike the artificial dreams, this one was not in a three-dimensional space. She could not view the girl's face from any angle. It was two-dimensional, like the images of a long-ago world that she stored in her Photos and Videos folder. She played the dream, then paused it at that moment when the girl came out of the hut, when her face was fully visible to the camera. Still, she could not see a face. Just a blank skin—no eyes, no nose, no mouth, no ears, not even a hairline, just a shiny metal ball on a neck. Though the video was paused, two holes appeared on the ball, imitative of eyes, and leaked rust that ran down like tears, creating a ghastly image. A lightning bolt of panic shot through Cana-B70, waking her up.

Nightmare, she realized. *I'm having a nightmare.*

A power surge. Overclocking. Processor overload. Overheating. Blackness.

When she auto-rebooted, daylight was breaking and the ice was melting. She stepped out of the tent. A hint of darkness lingered, mist enshrouding her camp, reducing visibility to only a few meters. Steam rose off the rocks like in the image of a kettle on a stove, an image from a time in the distant past that, without Organic.sys, she could not relate to. Then, like in the dream, it morphed from a static image into a moving picture, and she could not understand if she was experiencing the fragmented data stored in Organic.sys, or a video file.

A hand takes the kettle off the stove, and pours boiling water into a cup with a tea bag in it, and then the hand takes the cup to a face, but the face has no mouth to drink the tea. Like in the nightmare it has no features, just colored pixels. There is giggling, though. The person holding the camera, perhaps an elderly male, is saying something, and the person with the steaming cup, perhaps a little girl, is giggling. The colored pixels shimmer, and begin to bleed, and the video ends.

Is this a memory? Am I that girl?

Again, her systems froze, even though Organic.sys was not running. Security.sys searched for programs active in the background that could have caused the organic thought to occur, and it found a virtual library file that Organic.sys called upon to perform some activities. Assuming this the culprit, it shut it down. The system stabilized, and Cana-B70 went about her morning ritual.

First, she spread out the solar panels on her cart, unfurling them to cover an area four times the size of the cart, and then she hooked chargers into the tent's battery, and into the port on her lower back. Then she sat still on the bicycle's seat and waited for the juice to flow into her. A steady beeping marked the passage of time, growing stronger as the sun burst out of the mist. The last of the ice quickly evaporated, leaving a brazen sky overhead, bare gray rocks all around.

When her batteries were fully charged, the sun was at the ten o'clock position and already so fierce that she used both fans and liquid coolant to keep her internal temperature manageable, and she needed an umbrella that generated a cool micro-atmosphere. She then climbed the nearest rock, which was about eighty feet tall, and scanned the horizons for the house. Nothing.

Mem.sys then calculated that a large rock hid the house from her view, since she was now physically close to it. She preferred the other option, though, that it was an apparition, for it would be a clear sign, much clearer than the dreams, that the little girl who lived in Organic.sys was not dead. That she was still alive somewhere in there, and if she could find plastic filament for her 3D printer, or even bacterial ink, she could print out parts and revive her failing hardware. She climbed down from the rock, and rode her bicycle-cart in the general direction that she had seen the house.

She rode for about an hour, slowly, checking around every large rock, searching, and then she was going up a steep hill where the rocks were much shorter and packed close together in strange formations. At the top of the hill she found a plateau, and here the rocks were not haphazard acts of nature. They had been carefully placed together to form dry walls, the first sign of human civilization that she was seeing in nearly a whole year. An image in her archive compared them to the Great Dzimbabwe Monuments. Within the walls, flat stones had been stitched together to create artificial caves.

The caves had murals, which mem.sys compared to those in ancient sites with early human paintings. The drawings were of battle scenes. On closer analysis, mem.sys concluded they were made during an era they nicknamed The Great Burn, when the climate made the land uninhabitable. Whoever lived in these rock structures had been too poor to transform into androids, for the murals depicted people fighting humanoid machines. Yet the machines had identity. They had circles for eyes and a line for a mouth on squared heads. The people, in contrast, had no faces and their heads were smudges. They were stick figures, throwing spears and crude weapons at the refined metallic monsters, which were a foot taller than their tallest.

Faceless, like me.

Security.sys stopped the Organic.sys library file from launching itself, and the thought fluttered away like in the image of the frightened bird. A video image, blurry, and it implied that either security.sys had failed to stop the library file or fragmented memories from Organic.sys had seeped into her drives, corrupting her systems such that she could not separate thoughts and memories from stored media. In the image, a bright red bird sits on a windowsill, its beak pecking the pane, probably playing with its reflection. A girl, off-screen, laughs; the laughter grows louder as she runs closer to the bird. It leaps away with a shrill chirp, and the girl groans. Her image finally appears in the windowpane, and Cana-B70 should now see her face, but the file is corrupted and all she can see are colored pixels, the way they are in the TV news files with blurred faces.

What did I look like?

Security.sys fought a losing battle against Organic.sys, until mem.sys came in to support, for she did not want to shut down. She was in the only human ruins she had encountered in a long time, and she wanted to examine them thoroughly, to see if she could salvage anything to preserve her life.

While scrutinizing the depictions of battle on the cave walls, mem.sys found old files, bits of news talking about civil war. Some people had abandoned technology, which they blamed for The Great Burn, and turned to religion for salvation, and they fought those who put their faith in androids, accusing them of continuing acts that would anger ancestral spirits and ancient gods.

The caves were cool, and mem.sys concluded they had been built, cleverly, to keep the worst of the weather away. Each cave was big enough to hold several houses. In a mural, Cana-B70 saw structures like the blue house, cylindrical with a cone-shaped roof, confirming that the caves once contained villages that had all turned to dust.

She carefully searched the plateau. Perhaps there was something she could use, perhaps oil for her joints. Any oil would do.

A cylindrical rock stood in the middle of the plateau, with holes cut into the sides for a ladder. She climbed to the top, and found the blue house. It stirred strange feelings. Disappointment. Despair. It existed. It was not a hallucination. It confirmed that she was dead, that whatever human mind was left in her was long gone, and now she was all metal and electricity and ones and zeroes.

Am I? . . . I'm thinking. I'm feeling.

A power surge. A processor overclock. Overheating. Shut down.

She auto-rebooted when the sky had the deep purplish color of sunset. She had been out for nearly a whole day, a much, much longer time than ever before. Unlike previous incidences when she remained on her feet, she had fallen out of the umbrella's shade and lay in the sun, unable to cool down, until the shadow of the hut moved, and lengthened, and swathed her in a sweet coolness.

Mem.sys found comparative files that told her the hut, since it sat on a cylindrical rock in the middle of the settlement, had been of great importance, perhaps as the abode of their leader, or a place of worship. The walls were made of mud, the paint came from a plant-based dye, much like in the prehistorical caves. But, given its exposure to the sun and the weather, why had it not faded after all these years? The roof was made of polished stone slats. The door was wooden, but it showed no signs of aging, just as if it had been fitted yesterday.

The door was the same dimension as ordinary doors had been in the past, and so it looked like a rat's hole in the giant wall of the hut. It was locked. She spread her palm outward, as if waving a greeting, and activated x-ray vision to see what was inside, but the beams were like weak torchlight. She searched for the lock, hesitant to break it open and disturb whatever was inside. . . . Strange. No lock. No bolts. Nothing. The building was locked from the inside.

She stared at it in the dying lights of the sun, considering the implication. Whatever had built this house was inside. Was it still alive? Frantic, she unscrewed the door hinges, and then shoved the door inward to create just enough space for her to squeeze in.

A forest flourished inside. Plants smothered the wall, and crept up the central pillar. Plants! Trees in bloom. Undergrowth. Creepers. Flowers, in a myriad of colors.

Plants?

Had she ever seen plants, or was Organic.sys playing tricks on her, showing her memories that were dreams, when she was a little girl, running down a village path, shrubs whipping her face. She could smell the flowers just after a rain, their leaves sparkling. She stopped to pick a red one and sucked on the nectar, but there was an ant and she sucked it in too. She dropped the flower, laughing. She was now at a pond, strangely, in that weird manner of dreams, and could see her reflection, but again, there were no features on her face. No nose, no eyes, no mouth. Just flowers where her mouth should be, and the nectar flowing out like thick blood.

Overclock.

She wrung control of her system away from Organic.sys, and plunged back into the hut. Gears in every part of her body struggled to cope with the sudden outburst of organic memory. Security.sys fought desperately to shut down Organic.sys, but like an annoying weed it replicated itself and kept popping up here and there.

She realized that she had walked into the hut, and was in the middle, where a pond stood with the central pole jutting out. The water as clear as a mirror. Water. Not the deadly ice that formed every night. *Water.* Reflecting the sky. Not a ceiling. Strange. She looked up and saw that the stone slats were one-way mirrors, allowing her to see the sky just as if there was no roof.

A one-way mirror, like in the display window at the android shop. Her father had taken her to pick one for herself, and they could see the robots behind the glass, but nothing else inside the shop, just a reflection of the street. They wore masks, like everyone else, with tubes going into their noses to help with breathing. Her father had gotten a load of money about ten years ago, after a virtual reality puppet show he made became world-famous, enabling him to take them out of the village and into the city. The world was falling apart, but they had money, they could become androids and live forever. And there on the display window, with her father beside her, must have been the last time she saw her face. She must have seen her eyes then, looking back at her as she prepared to step into the shop and pick a new face, and she thought if she saw her eyes again in this memory she would recall what she looked like.

All she saw was a blankness, a plain metal sheet with worn-out edges, with splotches of rust where the paint had peeled off. Once upon a time it—*she*—must have been pink, sleek, reflecting everything around it—*her*—but now her face was white-ish, with two black disks for eyes, like the compound eyes of an insect, reddish rust running down her chin like tear tracks.

Error messages flashed in her sight. Overload. Overclock. Overheating. Something had snapped. Organic.sys had won the battle, and took complete control of her systems, preventing mem.sys from auto–shutting down. She could manually do it, punch the switch on her nape to save herself from a meltdown, but she had a good grip of her last memories as a little girl, and she fought hard to recall her face.

If she looked up, would she see her father again?

The discs in her head now emitted a tearing sound, like the pages she ripped off her schoolbooks to make aeroplane notes, to throw at her best friend two rows away; the tearing sound like the teacher's chalk scratching the blackboard. . . . Her father was a teacher before he became a virtual reality puppeteer, but what did he look like?

She stepped away from the pond, thinking she could smell the flowers in the hut, thinking she must fix the door otherwise the night ice would creep in and kill the forest. She walked to the door, but something was wrong with her left knee. A nut had jumped off.

She bent down to pick up the nut, and then noticed something that sent her over the edge. The pots out of which the plants grew, they were not made of clay. They were human skulls. No, not just skulls. Whole skeletons carefully arranged on the floor, just as if these people swallowed seeds—didn't her mother warn her not to swallow seeds or else they would germinate in her stomach and sprout out of her mouth and ears and nose and eyes? It happened to these people. The plants crept out of every hole in their skulls, out of their rib cages and their limbs, and blossomed.

Is this a shrine? A tomb?

Perhaps. They sealed themselves, swallowed seeds that would kill them so that their bodies would save whatever little there was left of life on the planet. And all these years, as the world burned during the day and froze in the night, their spirits kept the forest in the blue house alive.

She had to close the door, to keep the house sealed, to protect their dreams, but smoke now spewed out of her chest, and the fans on her back burst, and coolant liquid flowed out of holes in her body, thick, onto the floor. She collapsed onto her knees. . . .

. . . and she was a little girl with her mother, before her father became famous and moved them to the city. A huge storm was coming, stirring up a lot of dust in their courtyard, and Mummy had her baby brother in her arms, but she could not see her mother's face, nor her brother's. They were just plain metal balls, with flowers where eyes should be.

"Go close the door," Mummy said, as the wind whipped and slapped and brought in clouds of dust. She jumped off the mat, where she was making a doll out of maize cobs and banana fibres, and ran to close the door. . . .

. . . and Cana-B70 thought the girl's spirit had escaped from Organic.sys, and was going to close the door; that the blue house would be preserved as it had been before she broke in. With that thought there was a final puff and her processor smoked. The lights went out of her insectoid eyes and she knew there would be no auto-reboot. She just hoped the girl's spirit would close the door.

MARCH MAGIC

by WC Dunlap

Swamp waters soothe these old witch bones like Epsom salts. There is stories in these waters, buried deep in the thick mud, but rising like these moccasins twisting around my thighs. Snakes don't scare me none, no more than this here gator whipping me with its tail. These swamps long been safety-sheltering kin and kind running from the yoke and the whip. Nature loves a free soul. This here home. I could float here forever, but today there's conjuring need done.

The sun winks over the horizon, breaking the night. And I sigh, a subtle sound that moves through the swamp like a breeze.

Time to go 'bout the business of getting unstuck.

I've grown heavy from the decades—maybe longer—of stillness. My limbs curled around the branches of this lil' black willow, half-submerged in these healing waters. The gray coils of my hair, almost translucent in the rising day, twist with the fine tapered foliage of the willow. The yellow dust of delicate catkins covers my flesh. Cheek pressed against the cool bark, my skin is so thick and wrinkled you can barely tell my brown from the wood. But here I am. Here I always be. Black, Native, woman, witch, constant wader, leading my children to safety. Feels like never-ending work. But it's my purpose. Don't know no other way to be. They call and I come.

Gotta get moving. I blink, wiggle fingers and toes, but it takes the rest of my body a while to match the motion. I call the woodpecker to help—gentle now—he loosens flesh from wood so I can crack joints and stand on shaky legs. My feet sink into the soft wet earth until I get my purchase.

"Hmmm," I sigh with relief. Feels good to be moving again. I wade through waist-deep waters towards dry land.

Don't know what took them so long to call this time. And now it's troubling my waters. I can't see it yet, but I can feel and smell it—a nasty scent like kerosene oil, tobacco, and the musk of evil white men and dogs running through my swamp. A beast howls in the distance, a hell howl finna topple me over. The swamp moves beneath my feet, a nervous motion like a shudder. There are no dogs in my swamp, and I ain't too particular 'bout them who call themselves masters. Dead or alive, they still evil.

Not today, of all days, not today.

I raise tired, aching arms and the bent brown knees of the cypress roots emerge from the wetlands. More howls follow, so I raise the roots a little higher, and they surround me like palisades.

Now, where my demon killers at?

Suddenly, the soft purr of a car cuts through the hum of cicadas, its radio blaring through open windows:

"Today, August 28, 1963, an estimated two hundred thousand people will converge in our nation's capital to pressure Congress to pass a Civil Rights Act . . ."

I wade towards the noise and the moving headlights that cut through the morning haze. The car whips through my swamp on a path barely fit for a horse, never mind this modern thing. But it is as determined as these monsters busting through them gates of hell, thinking they coming for me.

"You can try!" I tell them.

The car parks at the edge of the waters. Five young Black men dressed in crisp dark suits and smelling like Sunday morning—oh, I love how we show out—step out of an old, rusted Packard. These the kind of men my swamp do welcome. They wait patiently as I make my way closer. I wave them forward, and they roll up trousers to haul this old body up to dry land.

"Morning, ma'am." The driver tips his fedora with a crooked white smile that breaks his deep brown face like the sun cuts through the night. He pretty—or it's been that long since I seen a man.

"Click off that noise." I point to the car radio, and the boy abides. "I don't need no voice box telling me why today so important."

"My name is William James, ma'am," the driver say. "You can call me Dubya. The Big Six sent us to protect the ritual."

"Hmpf," I grunt with hands on hips. "So, those ol' uppity preachers finally realize they need they roots now, huh?"

Dubya shrugs. "We was called just as you," he say. "We ain't exactly members of they congregations either, ma'am."

"How you get in this line of work then?" I ask him.

"Evil just happens," Dubya responds. The other boys shuffle nervously. "And if you survive it, you kinda called after that . . . I was ten."

Swamp mists rise with the day, and I squint to see these men clearly. They young. Boys really. Still scarred by that first battle. I smell it—fresh scabs.

And it's only five of them.

"This all who came?" I ask.

"Yes, ma'am. But we ain't exactly helpless." Dubya flashes a couple of gleaming silver knives under his jacket. He motions to his boys. One of them reaches into the back seat of the car and hands out shotguns to the others. "And we ain't shooting no ordinary bullets neither," Dubya reassures.

"Boogey man buckshot," says another with a grin.

Just then, something snarls not too far off. One of the boys steps forward, aims his shotgun into the shadows, and fires true. The smell of rock salt and the whimper of a dying beast follows.

Hmpf. They got heart.

"Alright then," I nod. "You can call me Mama Willow. All that ma'am stuff for white ladies and church ladies, and I ain't neither."

The boys laugh, but Dubya frowning.

"Now what's your problem?"

"No disrespect, Mama Willow, but are *you* all who came?"

He cute so I laugh, but the Black ass nerve.

I click my teeth. "Nigga, please. I called the coven."

And four Black women step forth from the mists.

From the North comes the Salem Witch, the New England debutante. A chill heralds her presence. She walks upon it as if floating on air, dressed in high-collared blouse and wool skirt snatched at the waist, glasses sliding down her sharp nose. Her face a mahogany-kissed cream, and framed by loose black curls that fall gracefully from a tight bun on top of her head. A delicate Celtic knot dangles from a thin chain around her neck. Ha—those ol' Puritans hung the wrong witches! Here be the blood of the right one—old magic from Irish ma fortified by the older magic of an African pa. She brings with her the warm winds and cold air of two lands—each striving for freedom with the tools of this world and the others.

I name her—"Glad Harvard could spare you, Siobhan."

She nods in deference and replies, "You call and I will come, Mama Willow."

The ground shakes with the pounding of boot and hoof. More beasts coming. The boys get a little nervous, I can tell.

From the East comes the Root Woman, red brown like Georgia soil. Her long limbs swing free from a light sheath, bare feet almost float through the mud. Watching her is like watching a seedling sprout forth from the dirt—glorious, earth-bending life that you just want to feed until it is a fruit-bearing tree. She whips her waist-length cornrows and the scents of cinnamon, clove, and whiskey fill the cold air brought by her sister. Dubya sneezes and finds himself unsteady on his feet. Her laughter is like the sound of backwater blues. She tugs on the pouch of powders 'round her neck and greets me with a mischievous smile.

I name her—"Hey there, Fox girl," and smile back. "I see you brought your bag of tricks."

She winks. And—ha—Dubya and the boys still trying to get themselves together.

We can smell the beasts and their masters strong now, like rancid meat, their scent threatening to overpower our magic.

From the South comes my Mambo. Cowrie-covered, she rattles as she walks, creating sparks that blaze in the cold, earth-scented presence of her sisters. Her full lips and wide nose announce the Africa shining through a pale complexion. She kisses me on both cheeks, and a trail of heat runs up and down my jaw. She holds my calloused, withered hand in both of hers, and fire straightens my crooked spine. Her touch is the embrace of a thousand spirits, writhing to burst forth and liberate they children.

I name her—"Caliste, I welcome you and the fourteen forty."

The stomps of angry boots and the bone-chilling rattle of chains join the growls of beasts.

"Nou goumen ansanm," she say.

"Yes indeed, chile."

From the West come the Preacher's Daughter. Blue-black skin shined with sweet, scented oils, thick coils twisted in two plaits that hang on each side of her head, dress falling way below the knee, a thin gold chain with a cross hangs from her neck. This one came for church. She follows my path through the swamp, the waters dancing around her, sprinkling us as she approaches. Her holy water revives. Her moisture brings the clarity of our victory. As she approaches, the peace of the Holy Spirit descends.

I name her—"You bring that gospel, Odessa."

She embraces me, drawing my tiny frame to her bosom, and I feel the power of the mighty outstretched arm.

The beasts appear through the trees, maws gaping wide like

gators, necks snapping back as chains held by hands not yet visible pull them to heed.

The boys fan out around us.

"There's only five of you!" Dubya shouts over his shoulder.

"We got a songbird with the King," I respond with calm. "Trust, we can do with six what Jesus did with twelve."

One of the boys encircles us in a ring of salt before lifting his rifle back towards the beasts. Another turns up the car radio:

"Go back to Mississippi! Go back to Alabama!"
"Go back to the slums and ghettos of our Northern cities!"

The so-called masters come into view—white rotting skin, empty eye sockets, mouths foaming with hatred. They cuss us, rancid spittle flying from decaying jaws. Hollow eyes pierce past the boys, and lock on we witches.

I join hands with my daughters as the radio booms:

". . . somehow this situation can and will be changed."

"This is blood magic," we witches speak as one.

"You got someone specific in mind?" Dubya shouts.

We pause, but then the answer comes, "A Jack of diamonds."

Dubya shrugs, his eyes focused on the haints. "Too late to back out now."

"And it won't last," we continue, "magic is fleeting."

"That would have been good information yesterday." Dubya snaps the shotgun.

"What is the power of two hundred thousand souls against three hundred and forty years of wickedness," we answer. "This is but a battle in a long war."

"We got you!" Dubya shouts.

The soulful voice of my sixth witch sings through the radio, each note a spell:

"Tell 'em about the dream!"

The King pauses, then begins:

"I have a dream . . ."

The demons and their beasts leap forward, the shotguns set off, and we witches begin to conjure a dream into reality.

IRL

by Steven Barnes

Three in the morning Pacific, and just since midnight the man called Shango had already voted on a terrorist attack in Tokyo, a burglary in Kiev and a particularly vile rape-murder in Colombia. As soon as the juries came in and the convicted were dangling, Shango jumped to alt-Earth and the Void Kingdom of Oyo, just to check in.

The Void-world of spires and golden domes, flying dragons, magicians and knights in hybrid Zulu-Japanese dress and armor seduced him as always. In Oyo, modeled after a fantasy Nigerian kingdom, he called himself Shango, the man-myth ruler of that ancient land. After a time there slaying the ungodly and commanding his troops, Shango felt the stirring of hunger and reached out, probing for the Realsoy sandwich he'd made earlier and abandoned once voting on the Sri Lankan matter had concluded. When blind fingers could not find it, with an irritated sigh he lifted his goggles.

The kingdom's glamour dissipated like morning mist in the light of dawn. Instantly he was awash in food wrappers and dirty dishes. His IRL bedroom. *In real life*. He hated that term. The Kingdom of Oyo *was* real life, not this reeking shithole. Shango glimpsed himself in a mirror: a brown-skinned seventeen-year-old round of face and body, X'd with the black bandolier of a Tesla haptic vest. Hulking bad posture and pimply skin. He ravaged his synthetic soy burger for a minute then pushed it aside, and dove back into VR world.

"I've got you," he crowed to Ponty Pool, the guy riding the white stallion opposite him in a European-style joust. Jousts looked cool.

"This ain't nothin'! I got *your* flabby ass, Shango . . ." Ponty's voice was deep and synthesized. God only knew how it sounded in real life. Or what he looked like. And when it came right down to it, who cared? Ponty was a friend, an equal with his own kingdom, not a vassal. In the Void, they were godlings. Real life sucked.

The door to his bedroom slid open. The man shuffling in looked a bit like Sam Jackson in *Django Unchained,* but shorter and with no sense of personal force or malevolent mischief. A black nimbus cloud of chronic fatigue hovered over him, the kind of physical depression that drags a man down and drowns him. "Please, Garrett. I need to sleep."

Shango *screamed* at him. "Don't call me Garrett, asshole. Ess. Aitch. Ay. En. Gee. Oh. Understand? Will you get out of here?" A sudden stab of pain from the haptic vest, right in his breastplate. "Dammit, you made me lose." Ponty had just skewered him. Ouch!

"Please try to be more quiet," the old man said, beaten before the words were fully formed.

Shango sneered in response and fluttered chubby fingers dismissively. "Yeah, right. Whatever. Just get out."

And his father vanished, like the miserable little rabbit he was.

"Asshole," Shango said.

"Who, your dad?" Ponty asked through the earbuds.

"I hate him. He brought the damned Spider in here."

Sisyphus Bunghole, Canadian, vassal and herald in his joust, broke character. "Shit, man, isn't that kind of harsh? I mean my brother got it, masks and everything—"

Shango flinched. Yeah, yeah, the pathogen they all called "Spider" for the web of veins that popped up on the faces of its victims shortly before death was hugely infectious. His father had

been an asymptomatic carrier, and his mother had had an un-
diagnosed immune issue that collapsed her systems before the
medications could kick in. The doctors had explained all of that.
His father had explained it. Shango didn't care: Dad had brought
it home, Mom had died.

"Yeah, well . . ." He could hear the gears turning in Ponty's
head, trying to find the right thing to say. "Screw him." And they
virtually high-fived each other, whether it made sense or not.

They were more than vassals or allies. They were his boyz, and
understood.

Their pod's living room was cleaner than Shango's personal
space, but possessed an odd and familiar sense of abandonment. It
had been that way, more or less, since Mom had Spider'd out, died
drowning in phlegm. Garrett's father, August Frost, was bundled
up in masks and gear, bent and shuffling as if the memories and
regrets weighed on him like concrete blocks chained around his
neck. Their pod was just one of thousands in the *favela* rimming
the San Fernando Valley, no better, no worse than those of other
families stacked against the hills in cargo crates, manufactured
homes and revamped tractor trailers. If desperation were a dis-
ease, it seemed the whole world was infected. He could not find it
within him to blame his son for escaping any way he could.

Especially since Désirée.

August called out "goodbye" to his son, not expecting an answer. Not even sure Garrett would hear him. Perhaps in memory
of a time when it still mattered.

Shango, Lord of Oyo, was enmeshed deep in his world. Glorious,
grand, beautiful, a land of stately pleasure domes and comely,
grateful maidens eager to lose their virtual virginity in his virtual bed.

Then came the staccato buzz of the *Lone Ranger* theme, his tripwire alarm. He'd requested his system alert him if certain games came online, especially legal games connected to any of his friends or rivals. A case finally emerged from the chaos.

His Kiwi buddy Ponty Pool barked laughter. "See this fool Dominex77? Xerxes is backing him."

Xerxes again, the bastard. They'd both arrived in VR land about four years ago, but whoever hid behind that moniker had somehow managed to build a better team, meld with bigger allies and wedge his way into the big leagues.

"What's the crime?"

"Stole some meds, man. Team Medicorp! *Roof!*"

"Xerxes will be Team Bic. Take him down!"

Shango engaged. Images flowed. He paid a little money to promote people moving sideways against Xerxes' cryptocurrency holdings, distracting him while they plotted a "guilty" verdict for his vassal Dominex.

"Can you get on the jury?" Sisyphus Bunghole asked.

"Naw. They capped that shit at twenty kay. But if we can find a juror . . ."

"Aw man! That's tampering. Get your ass banned."

Shango's grin widened. "Not if you can afford the wergild. Dark web, baby!" True. If you had the connections, and had the money, you could find people to fix anything.

"Dark web." His avatar shifted white, and he searched the index to find a publicly registered voter on the Dominex case, an industrial espionage case. It wasn't hard if you had access. The trick was avoiding any statement that could get you bounced out of the Void. Ah . . . Lupin434 seemed to be active, had voted in a dozen capital cases in the last week, but had modest holdings. Shango scribbled *bribable?* on a virtual notepad.

He reached out with a PM. Lupin434's avatar was the Monkey Punch cartoon, rakish jaw line, red tie and blue suit.

"I can't talk to you about things directly," Shango said. "But

I think you'll agree that we need to respect corporate profits, right?"

"Ah . . . yes?" The answering voice was hesitant, but not hostile. Shango's reputation had preceded him.

"Excellent. To cement our new friendship, I just gifted you five shares in Medicorp."

Lupin's avatar didn't shift. The cartoon capered, then leaned closer to an imaginary camera to speak through animated lips. "Isn't that illegal if I'm on the jury?"

"I'm not an attorney, or connected with that case in any way." That exchange was a little like a drug dealer asking *Are you a cop?* in an old movie. "Now now . . . technically it's ok. Just . . . vote your conscience and remember that if you can't do the time you shouldn't do the crime."

In other words, *If you vote to convict, I'll remember and gift you again in the future.*

A dozen calls like that and he was in good shape, and Dominex was well and truly screwed.

Corporate justice often ran parallel to governmental. For years, crimes against corporations had been the realm of corporate judges and lawyers. But in recent days, nations had been outsourcing justice to the Keiretsu courts. The circles of cooperating companies promised true democracy. Rather than a jury of twelve, they created simulations in the Void. If you robbed a bank in real life, and chose to be tried in corporate court . . . or if the offended corporation cared enough to exert pressure on the city or state in which the crime occurred, the procedure begun in 2030 was simple: In the Void, a virtual community bank would be robbed. Players had the chance to sit on a jury to hear the case. *Thousands* of them at the same time, depending on the timing. And the way they voted translated directly to the sentence of the IRL offender, up to and including death by hanging.

Private prisons, private executions . . . the cities and states were outsourcing justice more and more all the time, and the corporations were soaking up that responsibility eagerly. Eventually . . . there would be no cities or states or nations of any power and authority at all.

The corporations would rule absolutely. And few world citizens would really notice what had happened, until it was too late. And hell, did it really matter anyway?

"Verdict just came in!" Sisyphus Bunghole crowed. "Twelve thousand eight hundred 'guilty' to eleven hundred odd 'not guilty' votes. Take *that*, Xerxes!" Excellent. Lupin and the others had done as expected: reach out to their friends to encourage a "guilty" verdict, in a branching cascade. People jumped on the bandwagon, and pretty soon what started as a bribe became an avalanche, hitting Xerxes' vassal right in the giblets.

They virtually high-fived.

And as might have been anticipated, his vid rang. The voice on the other end was synthesized but surprisingly melodious. Imperious. The avatar was lean, burnt umber and bald with a variety of painful-looking piercings.

Xerxes himself. Wow. *That* was fast.

"Is this Shango77?"

"That would be me."

"Show me your real face."

Shango giggled. That was a pretty transparent ploy. The one intimidated into showing his real face lost the status war. "Nah, don't think I will. Stings a little, don't it?"

A pause. *"I knew him."*

"IRL?"

The avatar looked exactly like the ruler in *300*, right down to the sneer. *"There is no 'real' but here. My vassal has been ruined. You wish war? You challenge me?"*

"Go piss in your mouth, dipshit." That was Ponty! Christ, he'd forgotten to make the call private?

During the pause that followed, you could almost hear the angry electrons buzzing. *"You may regret that."*

And the avatar dissolved.

"What an asshole," Ponty said. "Are you sure no one knows who he is?"

"We've tried," Sisyphus said, "but he's careful."

"Yeah. Well . . ."

Shango giggled. "'Piss in your own mouth'? Sounds like he really loved that one."

"Well," Ponty explained patiently, "he's a butthole."

The western boundary of Oyo abutted the Kingdom of Xia, which was allied with Xerxes' faux Persia. But while certainly hostile, Xia was not a current danger to Shango's holdings. There were no troops massing at the border or armadas blocking their harbors or flocks of winged Chinese dragons masking the sun or anything of that nature. So he just raised the height of the wall between the Sea of Sorrows and the Mountains of the Moon and called it a day. The afternoon had waned. Shango was commanding the Northern armies in a mighty battle to increase his holdings, taking an ambitious knight down a peg or two without utterly destroying him. You *needed* aggressive allies. Just also needed to keep an eye on them.

"Hah hah! That's it! How you like me now?"

"M'lord, I think we have them on the run . . ." Cricketboy27 said. Cricketboy had been one of his first vassals, and a staunch ally.

"What the hell?" A tremor like a localized quake. At first he thought his haptic suit was malfunctioning, then lifted his goggles to find his father shaking his shoulder.

"Hey! What the hell!" He knocked his father's hand away,

whipped off his VR rig and looked up. August Frost looked gut-shot, seemed to have aged five years in five hours. The part of his mind that registered that odd fact wasn't connected to his heart. He barely noticed.

"What the fuck, man! Don't ever interrupt me! I'm right in the middle of . . ."

His father's heavy lips opened and closed. Opened and closed in silent pantomime. He looked as if he wanted to say something important . . . but then changed his mind and shuffled away, husked.

"Goddam idiot," Shango growled.

"What was that?" Ponty asked.

"My old man. Some shit."

"What a loser."

Shango laughed raucously, played awhile, but a thread of disquiet niggled at him. He frowned. "Doesn't usually get home this early. Idiot probably lost his job."

"Aw, crap! Hope not. How you gonna pay for your rig?"

Shango played some more VR, but couldn't commit, couldn't quite sink into the illusions as he wanted. Finally he could no longer ignore a sick, spreading sensation in his gut. "Something's wrong."

The sliding door to his room was still open, and if he pivoted at his desk, Shango could look straight down the hallway to his father's bedroom door. It was closed. The night trembled with a muffled, distant sorrow. He tried to ignore it, but couldn't.

"Hey, man, we need a decision," Ponty said.

"Take over. I need to check some stuff," Shango said.

"Got it, m'lord."

Shango walked down the hall. Past the living area neither of them had used since Dad had brought the Spider home, and Mom had died of it. It was twilight, and the view off the narrow balcony, the San Fernando Valley's vast honeycomb of modular box-homes, no longer seemed the ugliest thing in the world.

The twinkling lights made it seem almost festive. Rumor was that Steven Spielberg had smoked a joint lying upside down on the hood of his car not far from their pod, and thereby received the inspiration for the *Close Encounters* Mother Ship from just this view. That . . . would have been almost eighty years ago.

His toes tugged at the shabby carpeting beneath his feet, thinking for the first time that his own room was really the best appointed in the entire house. Sure, it was cluttered and shit, but . . . it was almost as if his father neglected his own needs to give his son all the good he had to offer. All he had denied himself since Désirée's death.

The closer he got to his father's door, the louder the sobbing became. Deep, rending, heartbreaking cries that took Shango aback. He paused. All of the anger and contempt that had festered within him for years just . . . drained away.

"Désirée. Désirée," his father groaned. "What am I going to do? What happens to Garrett if I go away?"

Shango slid the door open. His father was huddled in the nook between bed and bureau, knees up, crying. He'd never seen his father like this, and it spun him badly.

"Dad?"

His father looked up with haunted, red-rimmed eyes.

"What . . . what's wrong? Why are you home in the middle of the day?"

A trembling mouth could not answer.

"Did you get fired?"

He shook his head. Shango sat beside the sobbing man. "There . . . was an accident. A month ago. A guy named Fumio Hiyashi fell into one of the crushers."

Shango . . . *Garrett* . . . vaguely remembered his father trying to tell him something about what had happened in the recycling center where foods like Realsoy were synthesized from yesterday's garbage. Garrett hadn't cared then, and couldn't make sense of it now. "I'm . . . sorry? Why?"

"Now, it looks like sabotage, Garrett. And they think I did it."

Stunned silence. Garrett's brain wasn't working right. He felt as if he was floating up above himself.

"That's not possible," Garrett said.

"I know. It looks like I sabotaged a Nabiscorp subsidiary for the Yamaha Keiretsu. Check our account." He handed Shango the black plastic rectangle of his communicator. Shango's eyes widened when he touched the app.

"Holy shit! How'd we get an extra thirty kay?" The flash of delight swiftly turned to alarm. When had they ever had that much money all at one time? "But . . . the account is frozen?"

There followed a shocked moment of silence, as if the universe itself was waiting for something to happen.

"You see it?" His father seemed astounded to be believed.

"They framed you. And the Board froze your account. Dad . . . corporate sabotage leading to death? They'll *hang* you."

His father nodded. "I have no enemies. I don't matter. I have no idea at all what is happening to me." His pinkish tongue darted out, licked his lips, slipped back into his mouth. "I . . . if something happens to me, Garrett, it will happen fast. You know that. I've already talked to Aunt Lydia. You'll have a place."

Wha? Although they rarely spoke, since Mom's death his father was the last constant left in his life. Wouldn't it be good to be rid of the old bastard?

Absolutely nothing inside Garrett agreed with that. He found no joy, no hate within him to relish the collapse of the man he had blamed for his mother's death. But if there was no hate, what remained . . . ?

"Dad . . . no. There is a way to deal with this . . ."

"No. There isn't. *Shango*." His father smiled. God only knew why he'd chosen that moment to use the virtual name. It felt almost like a goodbye. "We don't have time. Maybe a day. I have to . . . get things in order before they come for me. What I want you to know is that I'm sorry. So sorry. For everything."

The words hit like hammers. "You've never said that before."

A wan smile. "I didn't think I had to. There were so many things I wanted to say to Désirée and never did. Thought I'd have time. And I was wrong. When she died, all of those words just . . . froze inside me. In my chest." He thumped his breastbone. "Now . . . let me try to handle what I can. I'll have a little advance notice about the trial. I have to testify."

Confused and depressed, Garrett slunk back to his room.

"What was it?" Ponty Pool asked.

"My dad," he said. "Someone framed him for negligent homicide."

"Holy shit. What are you gonna do?"

"Get the guys. Get a search. We're looking for an industrial accident. Death. This took money, either virtual or IRL. The event was a month ago. We need to find the analogue."

Over the next hours, he researched, looking for a corporate trial with similar circumstances to his father's. On his screen, Sisyphus' avatar was rolling his rock and Ponty's was doing a silly dance. Both were working hard, engaged in the game.

"I think I found it!" Sisyphus said. "A game called *Vista Summers*."

That's what the Keiretsu did: create a virtual game that mirrored a real-world offense, invite players to judge and then apply real-world justice based on how the players voted. He, Ponty and Sisyphus all joined *Vista Summers*. It was a life sim, a full community with a *favela* just like the one he lived in, with a recycling center like his father's. And there, as they watched, a virtual animation of a man fell into the gears of animated trash-crushing machinery.

"Shit," Garrett said.

The prosecutor was talking in a cadence that sounded oddly like a carnival barker's. "And we have in sidebar the security footage, the bank records, the accused's own words . . ."

Garrett fast-forwarded through it.

"What do you think?" Ponty said.

"I think this was all put together in the last five hours."

Sisyphus stopped rolling his rock and turned, animated face astonished. "How is that possible?"

"Someone with power, and money, and a master of cyber-space."

"That . . . would be expensive. Your dad has enemies like that? I mean real-world expensive."

"No," Garrett said slowly. "But I do."

"Xerxes?" Ponty whispered.

"I think so. He told me that I'd be sorry."

"I thought he didn't know who you were!"

"He found my dad, I guess," Garrett said.

They studied the computer screens. After a time, Sisyphus Bunghole had an idea. "Try advertising a public speech. Dump enough money in promotion, give perks to people sympathetic to your dad's position . . . recycling workers who have dealt with industrial accidents, maybe. You might change some minds or siphon off some votes."

"Clock is ticking. Let's do it!"

The crowd roared as Garrett, in golden armor, stepped out to greet his followers. "It's Shango! King of Oyo!" His avatar stood on a virtual mountainside, like Moses on Sinai. "Yes, it is I, my friends and subjects. I am here to say that it is a great injustice, that an accident, without malice, should be treated as such, and not the same as deliberate murder . . ."

He gave that speech a dozen times, but streamed each to a hundred vassals with instructions for each of *them* to stream to a hundred friends. And every so often, one of those who shared it would receive a reward. Not too often, not too infrequently . . . just enough for a peasant to think he might become a knight, or a farmer to think he might rise to merchant, or no, to royalty.

The minutes ticked past as he pontificated. He concluded his final speech:

"—And I wanted to say that any of you who vote acquittal will have free passage in my kingdom for a fortnight!" Cheering, and streams of thousands of hearts and applause signs, and oaths of fealty.

His father's negative numbers began to drop.

"Do an analysis," Garrett asked.

"I did, m'lord," Sisyphus said. "The trend lines are positive, but there is pushback. Man, you *really* pissed someone off."

"Look. The poor bastard in the game has a legal defense lawyer. Maybe you can contribute to the fund? You're fucking *rich*, dude!"

In game coin, yes, he was. "I'll try."

A flurry of efforts began to drain his bank. The first thousands of credits worked fine, but he rapidly reached a point of diminishing results, where the more he spent, the less the trends changed.

"Shit shit shit!" Garrett screamed. The numbers were still climbing. Slower now, but he had to reverse them.

"Running out of time, man," Ponty said. "Look at the safeguards. They aren't taking your money."

"Why not?"

"You don't wanna hear it."

"Tell me."

"Well . . ." Ponty said. "The Void isn't just about games, or even the justice system . . ."

"Are you off in conspiracy land again?"

"Hey, you asked. I can shut up."

"Go ahead."

"Those Keiretsu were more powerful than most governments, man. They use the Void to push back against governments. And that means it's possible that whoever is swatting your dad would *want* the perception of chaos. People will blame the people they can see: governmental leaders. They won't blame the faceless corporatists who really control things. That means that . . ."

Garrett heard it in Ponty's voice: the thing he didn't want to say openly, across a public line. And there was no scrambler that could possibly guarantee anything they said couldn't be unscrambled.

But the implication was there. The corporations and Keiretsu had motivations other than justice. Maybe they wanted chaos. Maybe hatred of the established symbols of power. Or maybe they were playing some other game he'd never understand, a war above his level entirely. Somehow, in some way . . . Garrett had stuck his father's head in a bear trap.

The positive numbers were declining, the negatives on the march.

"What if you paid his wergild?"

"What?"

"You know. If you're rich enough you can pay a fine instead of going to jail, or being executed."

"Shit! I have money . . ."

"That won't work," Ponty said.

"Why not?"

"Because let's say you negotiate a million credits to get this guy off. All that would happen is that your dad would have to pay a million credits. Got a million?"

His stomach sank. "IRL?" Garrett felt utterly crushed. He'd pushed the right buttons and become a god in his domain, not merely king. Surveyed all that he had built in four years. It was meaningless. All his wealth was in the Void . . .

A sudden thought came to him. "The Keiretsu. Anyone with the power to do all this, this fast, has access to real power. But he also has underlings, and the Keiretsu probably respects that base. That's probably how he attracted their attention, created his alliance." His brain was starting to race, getting ahead of his mouth. "Who are his partners?"

Ponty mulled it over. "Ummm . . . a couple of food companies, a transportation firm, an energy conglomerate . . ."

"Fire sale," Garrett breathed.

"What?"

"Dump everything I have. Buy all their outstanding debt. The small companies."

"You can't hurt Xerxes like that . . ."

"Yes, I can." Excitement stirred within him. "I know this bastard. I've watched him for years. He wouldn't have aligned with a larger organization if he didn't need them. And he wouldn't care about his vassals so much if his position didn't depend upon their health. Crush a few of them, control them, and his enemies will smell blood in the water. And attack. A feeding frenzy. I'm not the only person who hates him."

"But he's richer than you."

"Yes, but he wants to live in the Void. As long as I don't care, I can buy faster than he can stop me, for a couple of hours anyway. I'll run out of resources, but I can *hurt him*. And others will see the opportunity and try the same thing. And his masters will watch. And he'll have to put all his attention there for a while, and as he does that . . . we can act."

There was an unspoken reality: What if Xerxes wanted to hurt Garrett more than he wanted to protect his kingdoms and position? In that case, Garrett would bankrupt himself for nothing, and his father would die. But if Xerxes panicked, even for a few minutes, it was just possible . . .

For a couple of hours he would seem as rich as Xerxes . . . and that would be a glorious thing.

"You'll never get full value on a fire sale."

"I don't give a shit!" Garrett was shocked at the sound of his own voice. "*I* did this! It's my father."

"Yes, m'lord Shango."

Over the next hour he watched the screens, as everything he had built for the last five years went up in flames, and he gained controlling interests in the smaller companies, rocking their stock and making immediate mischief. As he did, he sent out encouragement to his vassals to join in the fun . . . and tell their friends.

And they'd tell two friends, and they'd tell two friends, and so on, and so on, and . . .

It was indeed a feeding frenzy. Chaos, in real time, like throwing all your money in the air and hoping that the crowd gathering to scoop it up would trample your enemy.

Boop. His avatar, an African warrior in red robes, popped into view.

"You have an offer to purchase your shares in AgriTech3000," his avatar said.

"Declined."

Three minutes later, another *boop.*

"You have an offer to purchase your shares in Viral Dynamics. It is very generous."

"Decline all offers in the next two hours."

"The value of your holdings is crashing."

"I don't care."

He watched the monitors floating in his virtual world. This little corner of the Void was rocked by his insane tactic. Not illegal, but unheard-of. Throwing his money away to destabilize a company just long enough for other, larger predators to sniff an opening and move in. Other Keiretsu had to see the confusion, and would send *their* vassals in to amplify the fun. He wasn't just playing with his own money anymore. Now the big boys were having fun.

And oh, the fun. The virtual bloodletting as his insane action triggered a cascade of more careful attacks. It was quite possible that no one had ever cashed out five years of careful building in such an orgy of spending and deliberate but legal sabotage. When he was able to forget the damage he was doing to his virtual world, it was even entertaining in a masochistic way.

He was down to 20 percent of his prior holdings when Sisyphus yelled: *"Not guilty! The verdict just came down!"*

"Yessss!" Garrett screamed. So Xerxes had been distracted long

enough for "Shango's" earlier, saner machinations to do their work.

All the adrenaline of the last hours hit him, hard. Garrett sagged back in his chair, hyperventilating, and just a little scared of himself.

He was a bad, bad man . . . but a good son. IRL.

"And . . . you're broke, m'lord Shango," Sisyphus said. "The other knights have broken rank. I think the kingdom is lost."

"I can build that again."

"I know, but . . ."

"I . . . don't suppose you'd want to help me?" he asked the Canadian vassal, almost shyly. "I threw all your work away." The joy was receding. What had he done?

"I don't know. M'lord Shango, can I speak directly?"

"Shit, Sissy. It's just a game."

"That's it. It's just a game. It's kind of easy to forget that. You remembered. I'm . . . proud to serve you, m'lord." And then Sisyphus Bunghole did something Garrett had not expected. The avatar shimmered . . . and his face appeared. His real face. A white man, middle-aged and balding with a fringe of pale hair. The wall behind him was covered with expensive-looking books. The ceiling was high and hardwood, with pricey appointments. Damn, Sisyphus was *loaded*!

His disembodied head bowed. "My name is Quenton Wilson, and I am honored to serve you."

Garrett smiled. He wanted to return the favor, but realized Sisyphus didn't want that. In the real world, he might well have been an executive. In the Void . . . he lived to serve. "Well done. We will rebuild."

On another day, in another time, he might unshield his own face. That wasn't what his vassals wanted, or they'd have built kingdoms of their own. But one day he would find a way to thank them that they would understand. It might take some major event on

Sissy's part. Some grand promotion. He found himself yearning to be seen.

Ponty Pool had been watching the whole time. "You're broke, my man."

"Yeah, I know."

The New Zealander's avatar smiled. "I hate to admit it, mate, but you've got balls of steel. I . . . uh . . . I kinda figured you'd crash, and sold short on your holdings. Made a mint."

Shango laughed harder than he had in a very long time. "Good for you."

"I kinda think you deserve a finder's fee. We'll work it out . . . it would be enough to help you take over New Sao Paulo." Huh. That was the kingdom next to Ponty's. A bankrolled warlord might very well be able to take it . . . and then Ponty would have an ally and friend right next door, a buffer against barbarians.

"We will have that discussion, sir."

Ponty saluted him. "Balls of steel," he repeated, and signed off.

He was about to turn off his computer when a message popped up. *Xerxes.*

"What do you want?"

"I know what you did, and now I know who you are."

"I know what you did, too."

"I'll have you banned from the game, mudak. *You hurt some of my people, and—"*

"You listen to me," Garrett snarled. "You came after my father. To do that, you had to frame him for an industrial accident. He could have been executed for it. That's attempted murder. *Real world.* I may not be able to find you, but do you think the corporations can't? You'll lose everything."

A pause.

"What do you want?"

"You leave me and my father and my friends alone. If we come into conflict in the game, we'll deal with that. But IRL . . . I swear to God. You can't erase what happened. You can't even be sure they aren't looking into it now."

"*Yebat.*"

The line went dead. Now that was interesting. Wasn't "yebat" a Russian curse, roughly equivalent to "fucker"? Was "mudak" Russian too? A quick search said it was. Was Xerxes Russian? In a moment of passion, had he finally dropped a clue to his origins? Hadn't there been a back-traced echo from Kiev, not six weeks ago?

Oh . . . this could be very, very interesting . . .

Garrett punched up his own personal stats. It wasn't pretty. Rebellious provinces were breaking away. Funded by his own jewels, armies were on the march.

"Bad formations there. And . . . fighting everyone at once? Xia . . . you should have promoted better generals."

And his expression changed to a grin. He'd been on top so long that he'd forgotten the real fun: building. Creating.

"Go ahead. Have fun. Oyo is finished, but the king will return."

He levered himself up out of the chair, his bulky weight ungainly. Stripped off his haptic suit and waddled down the hall to his father's room. Knocked.

"Dad?" No answer. He opened the door. No one was in there. Mystified, he turned and looked out on the balcony. His father was sitting out there, smoking a cigarette.

August Frost turned as Garrett stepped out.

"Dad?"

His father took another drag, exhaled slowly, watching the plume dissipate like a ghost in daylight. "I just heard the verdict."

"What was it?"

"Not guilty."

Garrett pulled up a chair, sat. "Kind of nice out here."

His father laughed. "Oh, bullshit. It's awful. The world we're giving you is just . . . terrible. I can't blame you for not wanting any part of it."

Garrett was wondering: *Should I tell him?*

"So . . . who is Shango?"

"King of an old empire." He shrugged. "Ruled until his palace was struck by lightning. Then they made him a god."

"Huh. Ain't that some shit. Tear you down, and then build you up."

"Circle of life."

They chuckled at that, breaking the tension.

"There are a lot of things I never said to you, Shango. After your mom died I just . . . crawled up my own ass."

"How's the view up there?"

A pause, and then they both laughed again. But this time, it was as if a dam had broken, and they guffawed at the lame joke until they were both crying. Together. For the first time, ever.

In real life.

THE DEIFICATION OF IGODO

by Joshua Uchenna Omenga

One night, Oba Igodo awoke to a voice that seemed to come from the stones of the wall.

'Why remain a king, when you can be a god?'

The voice spoke only once, but it echoed ever after in his head. The sleep fled his eyes. Silence took over the night as he pondered over the words and wondered at the daringness of the voice. And in his mind came memories of how he had delivered Igodomigodo from peril.

Before he was born into Igodomigodo, it was a troubled land without a name. It was a land ravaged by famine as brigands pillaged farmlands and carted away crops. There was sadness in every face, and people died before their time. Laughter was scant in the land. Mothers despaired with each birth, for the children they brought forth were ravaged by hunger or carried away by marauders to unreturning lands. No help came to the land from men or from the gods, for the chieftains of the land were weak and her gods had forsaken her.

Igodo's father was a poor man, but renowned for charm-making. At his death, he had nothing to bequeath his son except the power of his charms. Igodo was raised by his uncle and apprenticed to a hunter under whom he became distinguished in hunting. He dwelt chiefly in the forest and knew the ways of wild animals more than the ways of men.

One day, while Igodo was in the village to fetch supplies, the marauders came on their usual plundering. People fled before them, but not Igodo. He hunted after the marauders unaided and overtook them and took from them all they had plundered from the people.

The people rejoiced in his triumph and detained him in the village. In days that followed, they sought his aid against the assaults of the marauders. And each time he came, he triumphed over the marauders and recovered their loot. Stories began to circulate that the land was no longer undefended. Attacks on the land lessened, until enemies turned to friends, and strangers no longer entered freely into the land as in the days of its vulnerability. Farms became secure and crops flourished undisturbed. And smiles crept onto the faces of the people.

The people began to call the land Igodomigodo, for the land was delivered by the might of Igodo. They persuaded Igodo to forsake his dwelling in the forest and live in the village. They cleared a large and choice land for his compound and erected for him a magnificent building and fenced his compound with bricks of mud. When at last he consented to dwell in the house they had built for him, they flocked in his compound with tributes of yams and goats and palm wines.

With peace and abundance, Igodomigodo grew and expanded. The people perceived the need for a king, as in the kingdoms in their tales. They thronged into Igodo's compound and in a united voice, begged him to be king over them. Igodo accepted their proposal with secret joy, for the praises of the people had entered his head and he had begun to glory in his own excellence. At his coronation, he took the title of Oba, king of the people. And for a time, the love of the people for Oba Igodo bloomed.

But in proportion as he was loved and revered, Igodo's heart began to grow haughty within him. He looked upon the prosperity of

Igodomigodo, listened to the laughter of children, perceived the peace and freedom of the people, and recalled that none of these would be but for him. Had he not saved the people of Igodomigodo when no man or deity could save them? And Oba Igodo began to demand more from the people of Igodomigodo than they were willing to offer. His utterances became laws which the people must obey or be chastised.

The people of Igodomigodo could no longer see in their king the benevolent man who had brought them peace and security. Oba Igodo frequently descended on his subjects, and for errors that tongue would have righted he addressed with sword. Many disapproved in their hearts, but none dared to condemn aloud. Igodo mistook the silence of the people for approval, and sought continually more than the people could give.

Still, he was not content to be merely a king. Had he not done for the people more than a king? And then had come the voice whose echoes continued in his head long after the words were spoken:

'Why remain a king, when you can be a god?'

The words of the strange voice validated what he had been brooding upon. After days of pondering, Oba Igodo made up his mind to be more than a king. He declared Babura, festival of deification.

Babura was celebrated only when the people desired to create a new god by elevating an ancestor into godhood. No living man had memory of the most recent Babura, for the people had lost touch with their gods. Much of what was known about Babura came from the mythmakers. It was said that during Babura, the incarnation of the deified ancestor appeared to the people before ascending to join other gods at Orun, the abode of the gods.

The day was come for the Babura. The compound of Oba Igodo started to fill as soon as the sun was high in the sky and people stood on their shadows. No one in Igodomigodo was allowed to work that day, except the palm wine tappers whose palm wines were for the entertainment of the people at the Babura.

The night before, the best cooks selected from the wives of the men of Igodomigodo had stayed up preparing the meats brought by the hunters. There had been a whole week of collective hunting in which all the hunters of Igodomigodo participated and the game was pooled for the Babura. Young maidens were recruited to fetch water from the purest stream in Igodomigodo, which was very far from the compound of Igodo. Young men accompanied the maidens, ostensibly to protect them, but really to find their way into the hearts of the maidens. Children hung about without parental scolding.

Meanwhile, Oba Igodo remained in his charm house where his spirit was being fortified. Not trusting solely in the power of his own charms, he had summoned the best of Babalawo from the remotest corner of the known lands. For almost two weeks, they laboured in fortifying him, rubbing and infusing him with different charms and adding layers upon layers of power on him.

At last Oba Igodo was satisfied with his powers.

Oba Igodo sent words to the elders that the new god was ready to be revealed to the people of Igodomigodo. The elders sent messengers to alert everyone who had a part to play in the unveiling of the new god. A moment later, the sound of flutes and drums blared in harmony, and the dancers broke the tension of waiting. The air was charged with anticipation, for though no one yet knew which ancestor was to be deified, everyone was eager for the unveiling of the new god.

Then Oba Igodo revealed himself, radiant and fearsome to behold. His face was fierce, his arms bulged and rippled, and his raiment glistened in the sun. On his neck were beads of power; across his shoulder, protective shells; girded on his hips were corals potent with charms. He carried no sword or spear, and yet as he stood before the people and fixed his blazing eyes on them, they had no more doubt that they stood in the presence of a god.

But the elders of Igodomigodo were uneasy. They knew many gods who had been men before, according to the lore of the land.

But none had heard tell of a god deified from among the living, for the privilege of deification was reserved only for the deceased who had passed into the land of the ancestors, and whose intercession in the affairs of the living had earned them the right to be elevated among the deities of the land. And least of all, none had heard of a man who had declared himself a god. It was the people who created their gods and destroyed their gods when they deemed fit. But how could it be with this self-created god?

The new god addressed the people of Igodomigodo, and his voice was loud in the silence of the gathering. He recounted to the people how the gods had forsaken them when they needed help, because the gods lounged in the distant Orun. But he, Oba Igodo, had been sent from the sky to be a god among them, to be at their beck, to listen to their supplications directly, unhindered by distance. Henceforth, he was no longer to be addressed as Oba but as Ogiso, ruler from the sky.

His voice ceased and he looked upon the people of Igodomigodo with challenge in his eyes, but every man his eyes came upon lowered his gaze. Deep silence fell on the people, and many longed to be away from the sight of their new god, for his eyes tormented them. Yet none dared to leave when the command had not been given, and all waited for release from the spell of his presence.

But in the midst of the quiet, there came a shuffling from the crowd and a smallish man in a tattered red garment approached the new god. All eyes were turned to the stranger, for his appearance would have induced laughter in a less solemn time. His steps were wobbly, like a man who had had his fill of palm wine.

Ogiso Igodo regarded the stranger with stern and astonished eyes, for the stranger had passed the bounds of his charms unharmed. The stranger stopped a few paces before Ogiso Igodo and began to laugh.

'Igodo, son of Ivbiotu,' the stranger said amidst laughter. 'I have come to participate in your godhood.'

The people of Igodomigodo looked with pity upon the stranger. It was clear to them that the stranger did not know whom he addressed. Ogiso Igodo had killed for far less insubordination when his power had not grown to its fullness.

'Who are you that seek death so willingly?' Igodo asked, his curiosity overtaking his annoyance.

'I am the air in fire. I am the water in coconut. I am the pepper in soup pot. I am the oil in eyeball. I am the stone cast in the day of peace for destruction in the day of war.'

'Tell me who you are, stranger; not the riddle of your land.'

'I am whom you know but cannot call. I am what you see but cannot know.'

'You are insolent of tongue, and yet you speak with assurance. Temerity such as yours could serve a god, but your dressing is most unbefitting.'

'If my dress is the hindrance, then I shall change into something more befitting.'

The stranger bowed and rose, and his attire was a replica of the Ogiso's. The crowd cried out in astonishment.

But Ogiso Igodo was furious that of all the dresses to imitate, the stranger had imitated his, for he had arrayed himself to be distinguished above all. Ogiso Igodo retired to his hall and clad himself in another raiment as magnificent as the former. But the stranger, sighting the Ogiso in his new raiment, bowed again and rose clad in the same raiment as the Ogiso. Infuriated, but still containing his anger, Ogiso Igodo retired again and returned with different raiment. The stranger again imitated the Ogiso's raiment.

Ogiso Igodo, unable to contain his fury anymore, decided to humiliate the stranger. He twisted his fingers and whispered words of summons into the air. There was a slight howling in the wind from the distance. But soon it drew nearer until a single point of wind leapt into the gathering and settled upon the stranger and shredded his raiment about him. The crowd cheered as the stranger struggled with the wind for the shreds of his raiment.

In a moment, however, the stranger was draped in the Ogiso's raiment while the Ogiso was in the shredded raiment of the stranger. The people of Igodomigodo turned their eyes away from the humiliation of their king, their god.

The Ogiso retired for the fourth time and clad himself in different raiment and returned before the people. But his eyes regarded the stranger warily, for he perceived a power in the stranger which he could not understand. Not desiring to humiliate himself any further, Ogiso Igodo summoned three of his guards and whispered in their ears to dispatch the stranger from the compound. But turning to the stranger, Ogiso Igodo said:

'They shall take you to your place of service.'

'I am grateful,' the stranger said, 'may your godship prosper.'

There was something familiar in the stranger's voice at his parting words and Ogiso Igodo thought of recalling his command. But just then, the stranger began to laugh loudly. This the Ogiso could not endure. He could endure the stranger's challenges, but not his contemptuous laughter. The Ogiso's wrath was kindled and he commanded the guards to dispatch the stranger from life as well. And then he turned to the people of Igodomigodo, as if nothing had disturbed his deification.

But no sooner had Ogiso Igodo regained the audience of the people than the stranger returned, leading three dogs on leashes. The Ogiso was astounded, not the least in his order not having been carried out, but in the stranger's bringing dogs before him. The stranger, laughing, unleashed the dogs at Ogiso Igodo. The dogs circled but did not attack the Ogiso.

Ogiso Igodo, more than insulted at the daring, shut his eyes and conjured his favourite form in its darkest nature. His nails grew to claws, his beards turned to mane, his bust enlarged and hair grew wild on his legs and hands. His figure began to stoop until he was fully transformed into a tiger. He released a mighty roar into the air. The dogs cringed and stepped back. The tiger lunged and caught one of them in the neck. The rest took to their heels.

The tiger tore the head off the dog and cast it at the stranger. The stranger kicked the head back to the Ogiso, and as the head fell before the Ogiso, it turned into a human head. It was one of the warriors which Ogiso Igodo had sent to dispatch the stranger.

'Eat your dog, Ogiso son of Ivbiotu,' the stranger said. 'Next time, send something worthier to annoy me.'

Ogiso Igodo stood hesitant as the anger in him boiled. Then he lunged at the stranger with his claws, his teeth bared. But the stranger was swifter and dodged the tiger and his laughter was louder than before and was full of mockery. And more fury went into the tiger's claws and muscles as it lunged again.

The stranger stood his ground, and before the tiger was upon him, he transformed into an elephant and the tiger hit against its bulk and fell hard on the ground. The elephant raised its leg to bear on the tiger, but the tiger wriggled out of its way and dug its claws into the elephant's foot. The elephant's trumpet shook the compound and it charged at the tiger and caught it in its trunk and lifted it high in the air. The tiger transformed back into Ogiso Igodo and wriggled out of the elephant's trunk and landed on the ground.

Ogiso Igodo ran into his armoury for his bow and quiver and his long sword which had lain idle since he left forest life for the tranquil life in Igodomigodo. The last he had used the sword was for the slaughter of an enchanted wolf conjured by the wizard of Idomina against Igodo. The wolf's blood had turned the sword black, and black it remained thereafter, for no amount of cleaning could remove the foul blood that the wolf had spilled on the blade. This sword Ogiso Igodo now hefted, and his hand recalled the familiar feel of its hilt.

Although this sword had cut into the thickest hides and bones, Ogiso Igodo did not feel confident in the ability of the sword to deal with the stranger unaided. So he went into his charm room and greased the edges of the sword and tips of his arrows with poison. Then he stepped out to confront the elephant.

The elephant's back was turned to him. He strung his bow and aimed his target shot. It was swift and landed at the elephant's armpit. The elephant gave a loud trumpet and stamped its hind legs on the earth. Ogiso Igodo shot more arrows at the elephant, targeting its joints.

The earth shook as the elephant foundered. Ogiso Igodo ran swiftly to the elephant's swaying trunk and in one clean cut, slashed it at the base. The elephant lifted its forelegs and swayed, then fell with a heavy thud. Ogiso Igodo plunged his sword into the elephant's neck. It dived deep into the elephant until its hilt touched the neck of the elephant. The elephant's struggle became weaker until it ceased. Ogiso Igodo pulled his sword from the elephant, but there was no blood on it.

He turned with triumph towards the people of Igodomigodo, expecting their cheering. But instead, it was the laughter of the stranger that came to him. He turned and saw that the elephant had transformed back into the stranger and his taunting laughter was louder than before. Ogiso Igodo stepped back and watched the stranger warily, for now he knew the stranger and his laughter were not ordinary.

Still, Ogiso Igodo was unwilling to admit the power of the stranger. He bided his time and watched the stranger until his back was turned. Then, in a motion as swift as lightning, Ogiso Igodo slashed at the stranger's neck. The sword bounced from his grip and fell to the earth. But the stranger only turned at Ogiso Igodo and laughed still in derision.

Ogiso Igodo was kindled to more wrath and he was now determined to eliminate the stranger. But he now knew that neither sword nor arrows had power over the stranger. He knew few men who had charms potent enough to stay swords, but no man he knew had the power to withstand fire. So Ogiso Igodo purposed to eliminate the stranger by fire, but fearing that the stranger would be difficult to subject to fire without adequate force, he conjured enchanted ropes to bind the stranger. The stranger did not resist the binding, as Ogiso Igodo had feared; but laughing, surrendered himself as the ropes curled around him until he was tightly bound.

Ogiso Igodo sent for fuel to be piled on the stranger, and when this was done, he ordered that oil be poured on the fuel. Then, deeming that ordinary flame might not prevail on the stranger, Ogiso Igodo invoked fire with his charm. The fire caught on the fuel and kindled into great flame whose smoke rose high into the cloud. Not a struggle was heard from the flame, or a shriek of pain; only the cracking of wood as the fire consumed it. The people cheered Ogiso Igodo for his triumph over the stranger. But Ogiso Igodo watched still, waiting to scatter the ashes of the stranger before he rejoiced over him.

At last the fire died down. Ogiso Igodo stirred the embers for the bones of the stranger, but there were none to see. And while the fire was still smouldering, there came laughter from the crowd and Ogiso Igodo turned to see the stranger emerging from the crowd, unscorched. The stranger once more approached Ogiso Igodo and stood as on invitation.

'Who are you?' Ogiso Igodo asked, taking care to show neither fear nor admiration in his voice.

'Have you not learnt, Igodo, son of Ivbiotu? Who I am is of no import to you. My mission is all you need to know.'

'And what is your mission, stranger?'

'My mission is to put your godhood to the test, or strip you of it.'

These words Ogiso Igodo would not hear and his determination to eliminate the stranger grew stronger. But seeing as he could not accomplish this on his own, he retired to consult his divination calabash. The answer took a while in coming, but it was simple when it came: the stranger could only be decapitated with a blade of grass. Ogiso Igodo was surprised, yet he dared not question his calabash, for it had never uttered a word that did not come to pass.

Ogiso Igodo had a blade of grass fetched for him. Concealing the grass behind him, he walked up to the stranger and while the laughter was in the stranger's mouth, Ogiso Igodo slashed the stranger's neck with the blade of grass. The grass cut through both flesh and bone to the other side. For a moment, it seemed as if Ogiso Igodo had merely cut the air. And then the stranger's head detached from his neck and fell. The Ogiso held out his hands impulsively and caught the head and clutched it to his bosom before he was aware of his action. He then tried to throw the head away, but the head would not go. He prised it with both hands; still the head would not go. The stranger's head taunted and laughed at the Ogiso. And fear came into Ogiso Igodo for the first time; erstwhile, he had only wondered at the power of the stranger.

Seeing that his hands could not prise the head off, he tried his charms, but the head remained fixed to his bosom, ever laughing at him. At last he despaired of his own efforts and summoned his Babalawo to his aid. They arrived disembodied and took their forms before the Ogiso.

As soon as the first Babalawo took his form and approached Ogiso Igodo with his charm bag and his invocation staff, the stranger's head laughed and called out to the Babalawo.

'Obite, son of Obuta from the land of Ipetu, you are come in an auspicious time. But do you think your charms from Ikiru River will avail you before me?'

The charm maker was astonished at being identified without revealing himself, and still more by the talking decapitated head of the stranger. Still, the Babalawo cast his spell and commanded the decapitated head to release itself from the bosom of Ogiso Igodo. His efforts were in vain, and he got only laughter from the stranger's head. He tried to use his hands to disengage the head, but as his hands came upon the head, his hands withered and

flapped down against his rib cage like shrivelled flax. The Babalawo departed in sorrow and humiliation.

Ogiso Igodo summoned another Babalawo. At his materialisa-
tion, the head began to laugh and address the Babalawo.

'Dabo, son of Ekusi. Are you come from the land of Eduri to
try me with your charms from the forest of Udonri?'

The Babalawo ignored the taunt and proceeded with his mission. But he too got no better result than the laughter from the
stranger's head. Still, his fate was better, for he was prudent and
refused to touch the stranger's head when bid to use his whole resources to free the Ogiso from the stranger's head. The Babalawo
left with only the humiliation of failure.

Ogiso Igodo summoned still more Babalawo. But none proved
to be of any help. The head had grown more daring and taunted
not only Ogiso Igodo but also his Babalawo and their powers.
Ogiso Igodo bore the insults but his desperation increased.

The day had grown thin and had the Babura gone as expected,
Ogiso Igodo should now be a god and the people of Igodomigodo
would be carousing to his godhood. Now they watched his humiliation in silence. But Ogiso Igodo was no longer bothered by
what the people of Igodomigodo thought of him. He was more
concerned with the hunger which had now added to his woes.

He called for food and it was swiftly set before him. But as he
took a morsel and tried to put it in his mouth, the head snatched
the food and swallowed it. Ogiso Igodo tried another morsel
and the head wrenched and swallowed it as well. Morsel after
morsel the head swallowed, and kept growing bigger. Ogiso Igodo saw the extent of his peril, for not only could the head not
allow him to eat, but as it fed, it grew and increased his burden.

Ogiso Igodo was at last compelled to summon Baluwa of Iwo
land, the most revered of Babalawo, but also the most difficult
to summon. Many a time Igodo had summoned him, but his
spirit refused to answer to Igodo's summons. Today, the spirit
of Baluwa refused to answer to Igodo's summons until he learnt

fully of the Ogiso's plight. He answered the summons not for love of the Ogiso, but to demonstrate his power where others had failed. He appeared from the air in the most gorgeous panoply of charms. Every part of his body bore an item of charm and they jangled as his feet touched the earth.

The head did not laugh at Baluwa as it was wont, but it called out to him and named the order of his charms. Baluwa, looking upon the stranger's head, prostrated to the earth and began to sing fervently.

> *Esu,*
> *Esu Odara,*
> *Esu lan lu ogiri oko.*
> *Okunrin ori ita,*
> *A jo langa langa lalu.*
> *A rin lanja lanja lalu.*
> *Ode ibi ija de mole.*
> *Ijani otaru ba d'ele ife.*
> *To fi de omo won.*
> *Oro Esu to to to akoni.*
> *Ao fi ida re lale.*
> *Esu ma se mi o.*
> *Esu ma se mi o.*
> *Esu ma se mi o.*
> *Omo elomiran ni ko lo se.*
> *Pa ado asubi da.*
> *No ado asure si wa.*
> *Ase.*

> *[Eshu Elegbara,*
> *Divine Messenger of Transformation,*
> *Speak with power*
> *Man of the crossroads*
> *Dance to the drum.*

Tickle the toe of the drum.
Move beyond strife.
Strife is contrary to the spirit of Orun.
Unite the unsteady feet of weaning children.
The word of the Divine Messenger is always respected.
I shall use your sword to touch the Earth.
Divine Messenger, do not confuse me.
Divine Messenger, do not confuse me.
Divine Messenger, do not confuse me.
Confuse someone else.
Turn my suffering around;
Give me the blessing of the calabash.
May it be so.]

Baluwa rose from the ground and approached the head with suppliant palms.

'I bow before you, Eshu Elegbara. One who finds a mansion too small to sleep in, yet sleeps in comfort inside a coconut shell. One who throws a stone today and kills a bird yesterday. One who turns right into wrong and wrong into right. Pardon my intrusion; I have not come to annoy you. But one who is summoned is duty bound to answer, though he may refuse the reason of his summons. I have come to behold you, not to command you.'

The stranger's head smiled and when it spoke again, its voice was transcendent and held no mockery.

'Rise, Baluwa, son of Obatokun. Respect does not depart from the house of the man whose mouth is full of respect. It is with soft tongue that the snail rides on thorns and blade points. The eye which sees far is not for the restive head. The water does not run deep which chooses a path in the mountain. Baluwa, son of Obatokun: because you have seen where your peers have failed to see, and spoken with tongue of wisdom, I shall crown your mission with success.'

So saying, the stranger's head disengaged itself from the bosom

of Ogiso Igodo and joined its body, and the stranger once more
stood before the Ogiso. But the stranger was now taller and was
clad with red raiment of royal design. He turned his face at Ogiso
Igodo and it no longer held laughter but rebuke and Ogiso Igodo
trembled.

'Igodo, son of Ivbiotu, know me and know wisdom,' the
stranger's voice boomed, and Ogiso Igodo recognised it as the
voice which had spoken to him in the secret of the night, urging
him to godhood. 'I am Eshu Elegbara, maker of gods. In me is the
godhood which you seek, and yet you treated me with disdain.
For that, you shall never be granted the powers of a god.'

So saying, the stranger turned his face away from Ogiso Igodo
and held out his palm to the sky. He called out to the cloud, and
his voice echoed. Three times he invoked the cloud; three times
his voice released ripples of power into the air, and terror crept
into the bones of the people of Igodomigodo.

Suddenly the cloud rumbled overhead and a blast came from
it like a thunder attempting human speech. The response of the
cloud was brief, but it seemed to have answered the stranger's
purpose, for his laughter once again pealed in the air.

The cloud directly overhead the compound roiled and swirled
in rapid commotion towards the earth, until it stood above the
stranger's head as if it would engulf him. But instead, streaks of
flame began to form from the cloud. The flame enlarged and took
the shape of a throne. And the throne descended until it hung
suspended beside the stranger. The stranger climbed the flaming
throne and from the midst of the flame, his voice thundered.

'Igodo, son of Ivbiotu; wretched shall be the rest of your days
and no son of yours shall sit on the throne which you have glutted
upon.'

Then the fiery throne was subsumed in the cloud as the cloud
returned to the sky.

Ogiso Igodo returned to his hall and was never seen again in
the land of Igodomigodo.

But it was rumoured by the wise of Igodomigodo that Ogiso Igodo did not die, but bearing hard the humiliation of Elegbara, he had gone into Igbo Eda, the sacred forest of Olodumare wherein the powers of the earth were buried. It was said that as he could not be admitted into the abode of the gods, he besought Olodumare for the power of dominion over the earth. But Olodumare, mistaking his request, turned Ogiso Igodo into a tree whose root went deep into the earth's core. Nurtured by the earth's magma, the tree bore no fruits, and its leaves were red like flame, and bitter and poisonous, like the soul of Ogiso Igodo.

And to this day, men who seek the powers of the earth bow to the tree and tap from its pitch and drain the bitterness of Igodo into their soul, and the powers they wield are cruel and merciless.

MAMI WATAWORKS

by Russell Nichols

Nobody cried as little Pedro burned.

The villagers of 19:28 shed no tears, not now, not ever—a mandate straight from the cupbearer's mouth: "Keep your tears to yourself," she told the people. "You can't spare the fluids." Under the cloudless, dusky sky, fiery tentacles seized Pedro's frail body as the villagers, with open palms rising and falling, sang the send-off hymn:

> *Till the thief comes in the thunderous night*
> *From the plains to the sky*
> *As you reign from on high*
> *May we bathe in your wondrous light*

There, in the fairgrounds, Amaya stood with them but didn't sing. She leaned against her walking stick, scowling at the crowd. They didn't care about Pedro. The boy was only twelve. Same capacity for thirst as anybody. But they acted like he wasn't there every day outside the well house, eyes brimming with life, russet-brown hands asking for water.

Whenever he saw Amaya, he signed: "A beber y a tragar . . ."

And she signed right back: ". . . for the world is going to end."

Pedro was her friend. These villagers ignored him, assuming his being born deaf was proof of his mother's iniquity, that she was stricken by the Filth. But Ms. Rivera treated Amaya like a daughter. She was no transgressor—despite her current outpouring of lamentation: a screaming that tore at the parched air like fingernails in a coffin.

Up on stage beside the fire, the cupbearer glared at her, wary of fugitive tears. The cupbearer was a compact woman, bejeweled, in a blue tunic with a halo of cobalt hair, stiff and upright on the cyberlegs Amaya made for her mother to walk without a hitch.

"Attention, all!"

A voice boomed. The villagers turned around at once. On a raised platform in front of the giant Sky Tower stood Mr. Constance: an unusually pale man in a white poncho, who, as the local forecaster, was the de facto leader of 19:28.

"Villagers! Let us not be consumed by grief, for this boy was a siphonist."

"What about us?" a man shouted out.

"¿Dónde está la lluvia?" yelled another.

"Hark!" Mr. Constance waved a white cloth. "From on high, I have observed nimbus clouds in the distance. Very soon, the Great Rain will come and the days of drought will come to an end." Everybody applauded. Except Amaya, who moved her dreadlocks out of her face and shifted her body weight against the stick. "However . . ." Mr. Constance continued, "as we prepare for the Great Rain, it is imperative that we continue to conserve. Thus, for a limited time, we will reduce our water intake to one bucket per day, per household—"

As objections erupted, he pointed to the stage.

"Cupbearer," he called out, "is that clear?"

She nodded.

Again, Mr. Constance waved the cloth. "Now, I know these tidings sound less than ideal, but we are survivors, are we not?"

"¡Sí!" came the collective response.

"Have we not weathered every storm?"

"¡Sí!"

"Decades after the Filth seized this perfect world, segregating its citizens into these quarantine outposts, we are still here! And soon we, too, will thirst no more!!"

Amid spouts of praise, Amaya kept her eyes on the fire and vowed to bring change by way of science to this strange land of dearth and ash and dust.

It was dusk when Amaya finally returned to her hut.

Seated by the firepit, her mother was heating flatbread on a skillet, the crackling blaze tracing her face, which remained away from Amaya.

"I told you to come straight home, did I not?" said the cupbearer.

Amaya propped her stick against the wall, then eased her way to the ground. "I needed to stop to rest a few times."

After hours on her feet, her calf muscles had gnarled up like rope knots. What she neglected to add was how she stayed at the fairgrounds after the send-off, to say goodbye to Pedro in her own space and time. All he wanted was something to drink, but the boy had gotten caught roaming after dark.

The cupbearer flipped the bread. "Do you want to get torched?"

All villagers needed to be inside by sundown. Violators of any age would be accused of trying to steal water, branded a siphonist, and burned in public.

"No, ma'am," said Amaya.

"Come help me get my legs off," said the cupbearer.

Amaya scooted over, raised her mother's tunic to detach the cyberlegs. She pulled a quilt across exposed circuitry, loose wires crawling from stubs. Then put the legs in the lunar-powered receptacle for recharging. Outside, lanterns flickered in other huts. Amaya wished hers wasn't so cold. Beyond the crude shelters, the Sky Tower stretched high into the starry night.

Then, without thinking, Amaya muttered: "The forecaster is a liar."

The cupbearer laughed, shaking her head. "I'll pretend that is grief talking," she said and put a plate of flatbread and vegetables on the floor beside a tin cup of water. "Come take supper so you can rest up."

Amaya held her ground.

"Child," said the cupbearer, "I will not say this again."

Using the wall for support, Amaya walked past her mother, to the other side of the hut. By her pallet was her makeshift lab, where she kept all the metal and old parts she found.

"Ma, you and I both know these families won't survive on a bucket a day. And this village will end up deserted like 51:43. But not if we use this . . ."

From the scraps, Amaya pulled out two alloy tubes, a large bulb, a strap and other pieces. The cupbearer's face held firm. Amaya assembled the device, inspired by stories the cupbearer told her of African water spirits like Mami Wata and real-life angels like her mother's mother. Amaya never met Great-Grandma Jenkins but knew she was a spacewoman a long time ago. This intrigued Amaya, who wasn't allowed to roam after dark, let alone fly into the cosmos.

One thing Amaya never forgot was how astronauts in those days drank water. They used a recycling system, the cupbearer explained, which distilled urine, mixed it with other wastewater like shower water and sweat, then filtered out the solids like hair and lint. The fluid went through multifiltration beds, which removed contaminants by absorbing them or swapping ions. Any impurities that didn't get absorbed went into a reactor to be broken down into carbon dioxide, water and ions. After hearing this, Amaya lay on her pallet, gazing at the stars through the window and wondering: *If they could convert pee, what else could be converted?*

Once finished with the assembly, Amaya held it up for her mother to see: It looked like a modified bag valve mask.

The cupbearer said nothing.

"I know what you're thinking," said Amaya, "but this converter can save us."

"I recall hearing those very words when they made those artificial recycler machines."

"Ma, the recyclers worked—if it wasn't for the freshwater war, they'd still be working and we wouldn't be in this drought."

"We tried to play God and the Filth is divine retribution."

"God didn't create the Filth," said Amaya. "We did."

"Were you there?"

"I remember you said—"

"Were you there?"

The fire popped and Amaya lowered her head. "No, ma'am."

"You were not," said the cupbearer. "You didn't see all those fallen bodies, all those sickly people trying to scream and vomit at the same time with bloody diarrhea running down their legs. So I would advise you not to talk about things you know nothing about."

Amaya turned away, so her mother wouldn't see tears welling. "You are the cupbearer." Her voice wobbled. "I want . . . I need you to back me up."

The cupbearer stared at Amaya a long while.

Finally, she reached out her hand. "Let me see that."

Amaya's eyes lit up and she handed over the device. As the cupbearer examined it, Amaya explained: "You strap it to your face and it connects to your tear ducts, then converts tears into purified, drinkable water!"

The cupbearer said nothing.

Amaya went on: "But this is just the beginning. If it works, I want to build a park in the fairgrounds with way bigger versions of this—cry stations that many people can use at one time. And it will be called Mami Wataworks!"

The cupbearer said nothing.

Then put the device in the fire.

"Ma!"

Amaya reached out to retrieve it, but the cupbearer grabbed her arm.

"We have come too far to fall again, child," said the cupbearer. "You waste your time building contraptions when you could build new legs to make yourself useful."

Her mother's words scalded hotter than any flame, boiling Amaya's blood instantly.

"I don't want to be like you," said Amaya. "I don't want fake legs. I built you those only because you asked me to, but I'm not changing who I am to fit in. I'm not broken; this system is. The world is in pain and I'm trying to do something about it—"

"You think you know pain?" The cupbearer cackled. "Your little legs may get a little sore now, but the MD will only get worse. Wait until those joints stiffen up, wait till you feel those contractures." The cupbearer pressed her palm over Amaya's body. "In your heels, your neck, all down your back. Suddenly, your stick is not enough and you're scared of stairs and you can't eat or excrete without help. And every morning, you use every ounce of strength to get up off that pallet." The cupbearer let go of Amaya and poked the melting thing deeper into the pit. "See how it feels when you can't even hold a cup of water without thinking you might spill it."

Amaya kept her eyes on the fire and reminded herself, as the device deformed, that she had another converter, a backup in the stash.

"All I'm trying to do is protect you, child, till the Great Rain cometh," said the cupbearer. "You do not have to suffer. I overcame my limitations, and you can be something too once you lose that rebellious attitude of yours." She grunted. "Look how that worked out for your father."

"And you watched Pa burn. Just like you watched Pedro burn."

Amaya heard the words shoot out, cold and callous, and she couldn't take them back.

The cupbearer smiled, but her eyes didn't. She put Amaya's food and water away.

"Go to bed, Amaya. We have busy days ahead at the well house, so I need you up bright and early, is that clear?"

Amaya nodded and crawled onto her pallet and dreamed that the Great Rain actually did come and it short-circuited the cupbearer's legs—and she fell in front of everybody.

For the next seven days, the cupbearer woke Amaya before sunup. Amaya helped her mother get her legs on. They ate hominy grits and drank agua de Jamaica in silence, then made their way to the well house.

The well house was on the east side, opposite the Sky Tower, near the edge of the village. Fragments of granite columns rose from dead grass around what looked like a decrepit outhouse. The cupbearer said it was built on the remains of an old church. Through the narrow door, a stone staircase descended to the small crypt. The well itself was a cylinder made of chunks of limestone, which went down about forty meters.

The cupbearer came here every day. First, she said a silent prayer, then lit ceremonial candles for each year of the drought. After that, she was ready to draw water for the villagers. This was her primary role. She handled the task alone, usually. But in weeks like this one, heavy with traffic, she brought Amaya along to help direct the people, a thankless job.

The villagers lined up early, looking to beat the midday heat. Only one member of the household needed to be present to request a re-fill. But whole families showed up—kids, parents, grandparents—hoping the sight of their entire unit might sway sympathies.

Down in the crypt, in the glow of candlelight, the cupbearer used her clay cup to scoop fresh water from the well into each wooden bucket. Ms. Rivera, bleary-eyed from her recent loss, stood before her now.

"May your heart flow with living water . . ." said the cupbearer as she poured.

". . . and never thirst," Ms. Rivera responded.

But as Ms. Rivera turned, she stumbled and she fell, dropping her bucket. Water gushed everywhere. Frantic, scrambling, on her knees, she tried to contain the spillage, making a circle with her arms. But it was no use.

"O cupbearer," she pleaded, "have mercy!"

The cupbearer lowered her head. "You may ask your fellow villagers for a hand, but I cannot refill your bucket until morning. Lo siento."

"What is happening?" a man shouted down from the stairway.

Tears tugged at Ms. Rivera's eyelids. "Por favor . . ."

"Do not cry, dear," said the cupbearer. "You can't spare the fluids."

Was it seeing Ms. Rivera, soaked and sobbing, on the floor? Or knowing that not a soul would lend a hand? Or hearing her mother's depressing mantra? Amaya couldn't say, but she refused to hold back any longer.

Pedro appeared in the puddle, signing: "A beber y a tragar . . ."

Amaya signed right back: ". . . for the world is going to end."

Then she grabbed her stick and satchel and she left.

It took Amaya nearly an hour to get from the well house to the Sky Tower. Multiple times she stopped to rest. Once she reached the fairgrounds, Amaya could barely see, slathered in sweat and dehydrated. At the tower entrance, a foot soldier blocked her path.

"Daughter of the cupbearer, I'm afraid I cannot permit you to pass—"

"Please—" She didn't even recognize her raspy voice. "This is a Code 20-2. There's trouble at the well house. I need to speak to the forecaster!"

A slight exaggeration. But the code gave her immediate access. Without another word, he stepped aside. Amaya went into the tower. That was the easy part. Next, she had to scale a spiral stair-case. All three hundred steps. Her mother told her she had been up there before, at her swearing in. Amaya had never been to the top, but had no plans to turn back. So with her stick tapping on the metal, she climbed.

Tap. Left foot, right foot. Tap. Left foot, right foot. Tap. Each step harder than the last.

She climbed and she climbed.

And her left foot started dragging, her sandal bumping against the stairs.

Tap. Left foot, right foot. Tap. Each step higher than the last.

She climbed.

And feeling wobbly, she used her hands to lift her legs.

Tap. Left hand, left foot, right hand, right foot. Tap. Left hand, left . . . stop.

She had to stop. Looking up, she realized she was only halfway there.

Amaya hollered: "Forecaster!"

There was no answer. She rested. Let her breath catch up. Then continued. Climbing.

Finally she reached the top: a circular room full of devices she'd never seen before and a 360-degree window that showed endless desert in all directions beyond the village.

"Daughter of the cupbearer," said Mr. Constance, emerging from a bedroom. "I received word of a Code 20–2. How is it possible we are out of water?"

Amaya never saw Mr. Constance without his poncho. He wore a white robe and some kind of blanket wrapped around his head. The air felt cool, but he seemed to be sweating.

"Forecaster, forgive me for this intrusion, but I . . ." Amaya paused to catch her breath. "I would like to propose a shift."

"If there is no Code 20–2, you are in deep trouble, young lady."

Amaya was ready to pull the second converter from her satchel.

But after her mother burned the first one, Amaya couldn't be careless. "Just hear me out."

"All requests for a shift must be made with two or more—"

"I have a solution to our water problem!"

Mr. Constance cocked his head, then went to a bucket to fill a goblet with water. "Daughter of the cupbearer, we do not have a water problem. What we have is a temporary shortage. But soon, beloved, the Great Rain will come and we will be like a watered garden."

"I don't believe that."

Mr. Constance laughed and walked to her. "Well, you are entitled to your beliefs, but from where I stand, I can tell you: Every nation, all across this world, is having to cope with this dis-ease. And the moment some agitator starts spouting ideas about alternative solutions, do you know what happens? Because I do. Chaos, pandemonium, tohubohu. And we can't have that, now can we?" He held the goblet to her lips for her to drink. "Order must be maintained at all costs. Because nothing spreads farther and kills faster than faith misplaced."

Amaya nearly choked. She wanted to spit in his face. But she was thirsty.

With his robe, he leaned in to dab at her mouth. "Beautiful daughter of the cupbearer, I trust your intentions are noble, and you may think this way of life to be primitive. But it is my belief that if we, as a people, stand a chance of surviving, we must hold fast to fundamentals or we will surely fall once again."

"Show me the clouds."

"I'm sorry?"

"You said you saw nimbus clouds on the horizon." Amaya spun around the room, seeing nothing but clear skies. "That's how you know the Great Rain is coming, right? So show me. Show me or I'll tell everybody you're a liar!"

Mr. Constance smirked. "Yes, of course you will," he said, using his robe to polish the rim of his goblet, "and the cupbearer will be torched for giving birth to a blasphemer."

Amaya didn't know what to say.

Back in the hut, her mother remained silent after she returned from the well house. She didn't look at Amaya. She refused to eat supper. When Amaya tried to help her get her legs off, the cupbearer shooed her away.

After sundown, Amaya pretended to be asleep and waited for her mother to drift off. Then she snuck out of the hut with her stick and satchel. Covering her face against the night air, she became one with the darkness. Slowly. She crawled past five huts and stopped at the one with the yellow paper lantern out front.

"Amaya?"

Ms. Rivera's voice startled her. But before Amaya could explain herself, Ms. Rivera yanked her inside the hut and shut the door.

"I'd offer you something to drink . . ." said Ms. Rivera, indicating her empty bucket.

The hut had the same layout as Amaya's. But the space felt different: warmer, less empty. Smelled like gardenias. On a pallet by the wall were Pedro's clothes, laid out for him to wear.

"You can get yourself killed." Ms. Rivera patted a cushion for Amaya to sit beside her. "Dime, por favor: Why do you roam after sundown?"

Amaya took a breath. This felt right. She needed someone to back her up and she trusted Ms. Rivera, so she opened her satchel to show her the device.

Ms. Rivera squinted in the subdued light. "¿Qué es eso?"

"Un convertidor."

Amaya explained how it worked.

Ms. Rivera looked confused at first, but agreed to try. Amaya helped her put it on.

"And now you cry," said Amaya.

"¿Ahora?" Ms. Rivera hesitated, the cupbearer's warning, no doubt, echoing in her ear. But she turned to the pallet, where Pedro's plaid shirt with a green patch on the chest and brown pants with the cuffs rolled up lay splayed like a sand angel. She sniffed. Tears brimmed. Suddenly, the bulb reservoir began to fill, and she gasped at the sight of the clear liquid.

"¡Dios mío!" said Ms. Rivera.

"This is a prototype, and I know it's not much, but my plan is to build—"

Ms. Rivera grabbed Amaya to hug her and Amaya hugged her back, to console Ms. Rivera for her loss and console herself, too. Ever since the torching of Amaya's father, the cupbearer didn't care for hugs. Amaya stepped back. The bulb was half-full. She unscrewed the reservoir and held it up.

"Bébete," said Amaya.

Ms. Rivera took a sip, nibbled, then gulped it all down. Her eyes lit up. "¿Más?"

Amaya nodded and screwed the bulb back on. Ms. Rivera kneeled before Pedro's pallet and let the converter work its magic. As she did this, Amaya snuck out, back the way she came.

She crawled and crawled.

But as she crawled, the emergency alarm blared out.

Amaya spent the whole next day on her feet, detained in the wooden prison-house. She wasn't allowed to sit or talk or eat. At dusk, the prison door opened. The foot soldier blindfolded her with the forecaster's white cloth and ushered Amaya to the stage for her torching.

"Attention, all!" came the familiar booming voice. "Villagers of 19:28, in these last days of drought, acts of siphon shall not, under any circumstances, be tolerated. Thus, it is with great regret that we have gathered here today for the trial of the daughter of our cupbearer."

"Torch her!" somebody yelled.

Followed by a chorus of men: "Torch her! Torch her! Torch her!"

The blindfold was snatched off. In the field below, the villagers glowered at Amaya, condemning her. The cupbearer was nowhere to be seen.

"I don't want to steal water," said Amaya. "I want to make water."

"Make water?" said Mr. Constance. "What heresy is this?"

Ms. Rivera stepped forward and raised the converter. "I see it with my eyes."

Mr. Constance cocked his head. He motioned for his foot soldier to retrieve the device. On stage, he examined it. "So this . . . machine makes water, does it?" He held it out for Amaya with a smirk. "Show me."

Amaya moved her dreadlocks out of her face and stared at the crowd. Amaya had no stick, no leverage, and her legs trembled from standing all day. No matter what she did on that stage, she would be in trouble: either burned a siphonist or burned a witch. She didn't even know how to cry on command, especially with all eyes on her.

Mr. Constance put his hand on her shoulder. "Show me."

He pressed down harder. The weight made Amaya fall to her knees. A shock ripped up her spine. Amaya tried to stand. She held out her arms for balance. Left foot. Right foot. Hold it. But she couldn't hold it. Her right knee buckled. It felt like both legs got snatched from under her, and she fell again. Down there, as she faced the fake wooden planks, a tin cup appeared.

"May your heart flow with living water . . ."

Amaya looked up, and there was the cupbearer, holding out water to drink.

". . . and never thirst," Amaya responded, and drank from her cup.

Commotion rippled across the congregation.

"Hark! Hark, I say!" said Mr. Constance. "Cupbearer, you are out of line!"

The cupbearer paused.

She climbed onto the stage and helped Amaya to her feet, then lifted her arms to the crowd. "I am the cupbearer, but I stand before you now as a mother. My daughter, Amaya, has invented something she says could change the world. And I will admit, when she first came to me with this, I was scared she would end up right where she is now. But now that she's here, I'm not afraid anymore—"

"Villagers!" said Mr. Constance. "This is clearly a desperate plea from a—"

"Let her speak!" Ms. Rivera called out.

"Let the cupbearer speak!" yelled another.

And as others joined in, Mr. Constance backed down.

The cupbearer continued: "When I was sworn in as cupbearer, I was taken to the top of the Sky Tower, and there, looking out above the infinite sands, I took an oath to proclaim that the Great Rain would one day come . . . I lied to you all. The truth is, I do not know. Nobody knows."

The people grew more unsettled. Amaya couldn't believe her ears.

The cupbearer continued: "I do not know if one day nimbus clouds will seize the sky and burst over our heads and wash away the Filth. But with this converter . . ." She nudged Amaya and Amaya lifted the device. "This could save us all!"

Amaya fastened it over her mother's face.

The cupbearer leaned to Amaya. "What happens now?"

"And now you cry," said Amaya.

The cupbearer frowned. "I cry?" The cupbearer lowered her head. "I can cry."

Amaya watched her mother's face shift, its steely veneer melting away. What was she drawing from? Could it be Pa? Or Great-Grandma Jenkins? Or the current state of the world? Amaya couldn't say, but she felt a rock in her throat as tears welled in her mother's eyes.

"Cupbearer, you can't spare the fluids," came a crack from the crowd.

Some laughed, but most just watched with wonder.

Amaya unscrewed the bulb reservoir once it was filled with purified water.

The cupbearer drank.

"Yes, she can," said Amaya.

The cupbearer wrapped her arm through her daughter's. "We can," she said. "All of us. Together. This could be our Great Rain!"

And as Amaya stood on that stage, held by her mother, she couldn't predict what would become of them—whether they would both get torched or whether the people would accept this new creation—but standing there Amaya could feel in the air something was bound to change.

REAR MIRROR

by Nuzo Onoh

Vincent took his place on his white plastic chair and stared at the five men huddled around the large table. The table was round, just like everything in their business. Squares and rectangles didn't work well for the living whose business was with the dead. Those shapes mimicked too closely the graves and coffins they dealt with on a daily basis. Circles were safe, sanctified and holy, just like the blessed rosaries.

There used to be seven men in their group, but after the tragedy, there were just the five men left, together with Vincent. On the wall, the round wall-clock chimed the time, 6:00 A.M., the dawn of a new day.

Vincent stood up and the other men followed his lead.

'Let us pray,' Vincent said, weaving the sign of the cross across his shoulders. 'God of Abraham, Isaac and Jacob, we call on you at this holy hour, when your archangels are at their most powerful and witches, wizards and ghosts are at their weakest. Please oversee these proceedings and keep the souls that have returned to you chained to their posts in heaven, this we ask in the name of your son, Jesus Christ, Amen.'

'Amen!' chorused the men. They sat down and Vincent took a deep breath, crossed himself again and cleared his throat.

'Soul-warriors, before we go any further, is there anyone amongst you who wishes to end their time with us after what happened last month? I'll understand perfectly and won't hold you to your contracts.' He looked around the table. Four of the men shook their heads violently, their faces lit up with Christian fervour. But one man, the youngest in the group, barely out of his teens, glanced uncertainly at his companions, his eyes revealing the terror that still haunted his sleep.

'I'm sorry, *Oga,* master, but I don't think I'm cut out for this work,' he mumbled, unable to meet Vincent's calm and steady gaze. 'My clansmen have instructed me to withdraw from this employment with immediate effect. After what happened, they're afraid I might bring the curse of the dead into the homestead and have threatened to ostracise me from the clan should I continue.'

'Brother Gabriel, say no more. I understand.' Vincent smiled, a weary smile. 'Ours is an experiment in the new Christian cremation process. The people are suspicious of it and one can't blame them. After centuries of burying their dead in the customary manner, they're naturally suspicious of our new methods. We have been unlucky that our very first funeral went so disastrously bad, but I believe that once we all complete our training, there'll be no repeat of what happened last month.'

'*Oga,* I don't think any amount of training could've prevented what happened that accursed day,' Gabriel said, his voice pitched in terror. 'I was in that car with the coffin and it's only by the intervention of my ancestors that I'm here with you today in the flesh. I . . .'

'Brother Gabriel, give thanks to our Lord Jesus and not your ancestors,' Vincent cut in. 'We're all Christians now, and we have renounced our pagan ways and practices. I appreciate your point; of course, I do. But, do you think what happened would've occurred if Brother James had followed the instructions I gave at our initial funeral training session?'

Gabriel started to speak but Vincent raised his hand. 'Hear me out, Brother Gabriel. It's my firm belief that Brother James would be with us in the flesh today had he followed the training you all received before we embarked on our first job. Perhaps I was in too much of a hurry to bring our business to this town and rushed your training. Who knows? But, after what happened, I'd like us to start afresh with our cremation funeral training before taking on any more sleepers. But for the fact that we have some Christian converts in the city, who still trust us to send their departed back to heaven in the new way, we would've been out of business after the mess with Brother James. So, Brother Gabriel, I'll be grateful if you would recount again exactly what happened on that terrible day. You were too ill and frightened when I spoke with you after the tragedy, but I'm hoping that you're in a better place now to give us your account, so that all gathered here can learn from it. Afterwards, feel free to leave us and go with our blessings.'

All eyes turned to Gabriel, faces animated, eager to finally get the story firsthand from the only survivor of the infamous hearse crash. Gabriel lowered his head till his chin almost touched his chest. The silence in the dome-shaped room was complete, almost alive in its solidity. After what seemed like several moon cycles, Gabriel finally spoke.

'Soul-warriors, I know that we're all Christians, taught to abhor pagan superstitions and practices, trusting only in the words of our Lord Jesus Christ. When I became born again and was baptised in the Holy Spirit, I renounced everything pagan and put my faith in our Lord Jesus Christ. So, when *Oga* Vincent arrived at our town and set up his Christian funeral parlour, I was one of the first to apply for work. I was eager to learn a new skill and be trained as a funeral assistant, as there's a lot of money to be made in the new cremation business. It was the same with all of you, wasn't it?' Gabriel looked around the table and the men nodded, some mumbling their agreement. 'We all had the same training and were given the same rules of Christian funerals. I still recall . . .'

'Brother Gabriel, forgive me for interrupting,' said Vincent. 'But, if you don't mind, would you recount the seven tenets of

Christian funerals that you learnt in our training? Just that I need to know you were in full knowledge of your duties on the day of the accident.'

'As you wish, sir,' said Gabriel. 'Tenet one: repeat the sign of the cross three times and say the Lord's Prayer before touching, washing or dressing a sleeper for their burial.'

'Good, good; go on.' Vincent nodded his smiling approval.

'Tenet two: never use the word "corpse" when speaking of a sleeper to their hearing.'

'Why?' asked Vincent.

'To ensure their shocked ghosts do not arise and strike you dead for calling them a corpse. This is very important, especially when dealing with young corpses or those that died suddenly. These types of corpses do not always realise that they're dead and so, if you make the error of calling them a corpse, their shock and anger might make them harm you. So, we must always address them by their birth names, together with a Christian name of our choice if they have a savage name, to ensure their souls are allowed entry into heaven.'

'Excellent, Brother Gabriel. Please continue.' Vincent beamed.

'Tenet three: ensure you have an item of Christianity in your possession at all times, be it a small Bible, a cross, a rosary, holy water or blessed candle. This will protect you from harm should the sleeper be a secret wizard or witch in their lifetime.'

'Good point, Brother Gabriel. We all know that a lot of these villagers are rooted in wizardry and evil juju. Their Christian relatives might request a Christian funeral for them without revealing their juju affiliations, thereby placing us in mortal danger. So, we must always arm ourselves with the holy weapons of our saviour, Jesus Christ. Continue, Brother Gabriel,' Vincent said, his voice solemn.

'Tenet four: ensure that there are lots of circular and round objects in the funeral parlour at all times, from round tables to round clocks, coins, bowls, rings, rosaries, eggs, everything circular that can counteract the rectangular shape of the coffin and the grave, thereby distracting the sleepers, in case some of them are frightened of the grave and resist our efforts to send them home. The objects must all be consecrated with holy water and holy oil.'

'Excellent! Excellent!' Vincent rubbed his hands in approval.

'Tenet five: ensure that there are no mirrors in the rooms where the sleepers reside before their burial and that every reflective item and photograph is covered, including any glass windows, which must be smeared with ash. It is vital the rearview mirror in the hearse transporting them to their final resting place, our crematorium, is turned away from the driver, so he can't view the coffin at the rear of the vehicle. A blessed rosary must hang on the rear mirror at all times to protect it from the spirit of the departed.'

'Excellent, Brother Gabriel. Well said.' Vincent smiled. 'We shall return to this very important lesson when you're done. Go on, please.'

'Tenet six: when transporting a sleeper to the crematorium, always ensure that you carry the coffin with their feet facing the door, so that their spirit can have an easy exit to the other world. Do not walk a straight path but follow a zigzag walk while bearing the coffin, to ensure the departed is confused should they decide to flee and return to their homes when they discover they'll be cremated.

'Tenet seven. Finally, the most important lesson. Ensure that after the sleeper is cremated, the shoes worn by the soul-warriors to transport the coffin to the crematorium are consecrated with holy water to prevent the departed spirit following them home. These are the seven tenets of the Christian funeral.' Gabriel looked around the table, seeking confirmation and approval from his fellow soul-warriors.

'Well done, Brother Gabriel! Brilliant!' Vincent beamed, rising from his chair to embrace Gabriel. 'This clearly demonstrates why you were the only one to survive the disaster while your two companions perished. If all of you can recall most of what Brother Gabriel just recounted in the course of your work, then I'll know that I've trained you well. Being a soul-warrior is not something to be taken lightly, as you all know. Those who flout the rules pay with their lives. Listen carefully and learn.' He returned to his chair and nodded at Gabriel. 'Ok, Brother Gabriel, we are now ready to hear what happened on that terrible day. You may begin.'

Gabriel nodded and clasped his hands tightly between his thighs. After several tense seconds, he heaved a deep sigh and began to speak.

'As you know, the sleeper we were transporting on that day was a woman called Mgboye, wife of our Christian brother Ezekiel. Mgboye was a young mother who had died while giving birth to her first child, a daughter, who survived the birth. As you all recall, Brother Ezekiel had informed us that in her lifetime, his wife, Mgboye, had resisted the church with the determination of a ram to the butcher's knife. We all know that fact.' Gabriel turned to Vincent. '*Oga* Vincent, you may not know this since you're a stranger to our town, but Mgboye never once attended church service or prayer meetings in our church. She was a headstrong woman, being the only girl in a family of ten brothers, all older than her. We all know that her brothers used to regularly harass Brother Ezekiel every time their little sister complained to them about some minor marriage tiff.'

Gabriel paused as the men sniggered. Vincent nodded, his face stern. 'Go on,' he instructed. Gabriel cleared his throat and continued.

'Anyway, while Mgboye lived, Brother Ezekiel was powerless to convert her to the living religion. But when she died in childbirth, there was nothing her brothers could do because a married woman's corpse belongs to the husband. So, Brother Ezekiel asked us to give her a Christian cremation funeral, despite the furious objections of the brothers. In hindsight, we should've known that this funeral would not go well because we were dealing with a reluctant dead, a pagan woman who died very young and heartily loathed our faith in her lifetime.'

'We are aware of that fact, Brother Gabriel.' Vincent's voice was hard. He didn't want Gabriel to discourage his remaining soul-warriors. 'That's why you all went through the rigorous training I offered, to ensure you are all equipped to deal with the reluctant dead.'

Gabriel shrugged, his face showing the scepticism in his heart. 'Anyway, from the minute we brought her body into the funeral parlour from the hospital, strange things started to happen. As you all recall, it took almost six of us to bring in that body, something that is usually done by just two soul-warriors. Mgboye's corpse turned into slabs of concrete, a tree trunk that was impossible to lift. Try as we may, the corpse refused to be brought into the parlour. When eventually we succeeded, the body-table collapsed and crushed Brother Peter's foot. You were all there. You saw it happen.'

The men nodded, including Brother Peter, who still nursed a walking stick for his broken ankle. 'If you recall, whenever we called her by the Christian name, Mary, we started to sneeze uncontrollably. The violent sneezes would only cease when we apologised to her corpse and addressed her as Mgboye. That woman was a headstrong woman in her lifetime and an equally cantankerous one in death. I think the minute she discovered that her husband planned to cremate her, she decided to fight it with every spiritual power in her arsenal, no doubt worried that she might not be able to haunt her husband's next wife should the poor man ever remarry.'

'We know all that, Brother Gabriel. Just tell us what happened from the time you and the other soul-warriors drove out of the compound with the sleeper, en route to our cremation site.' Vincent sounded impatient. He could read the fear on the faces of his soul-warriors at the recollection of the terrifying events they had almost forgotten.

'We put Mgboye's coffin into the back of the hearse and sprinkled it with holy water as per normal practice. Brother James was driving, and Brother Paul and I shared the front seat of the hearse. We figured the three of us were enough to bear her coffin, since she had stopped giving us problems and her coffin had weighed as light as a newborn's when we put her into the hearse. I suspect it was because her ten brothers were there with us, begging her to go willingly into the hearse and promising her that they would deal with her husband later. I believe that without their presence that day, it would've been impossible to get her coffin into the hearse, recalling the earlier troubles we had with her.'

Gabriel paused, looking at the other soul-warriors for confirmation. They all nodded their heads vigorously, deep frowns ridging their foreheads. Each of them had witnessed the deadly antics of that reluctant dead, Mgboye. 'Anyway, once we were inside the vehicle, we turned away the rearview mirror as we were taught, till it almost faced the roof of the car. Her brothers and husband followed us in the cars behind as we headed to the church for the service before the cremation.' Gabriel paused, a faraway look in his dark eyes as he recalled the events of that fateful day. Vincent nodded with an encouraging smile, his eyes kind, Jesus-infused. Gabriel's shoulders lifted again in a slight shrug before he continued his tale.

'Halfway into our journey, Brother James noticed thick smoke coming from the bonnet. We pulled up at the side of the road and thankfully, the car engine didn't catch fire. One of Mgboye's brothers gave us water from his bottle, which cooled the engine. It was tough to get the ignition to work again and at a point, we considered transferring the coffin into a hired minibus. But, Brother James sprinkled some holy water on the engine and it finally started. But even after we resumed our journey, we noticed that the car kept jerking, refusing to pick up speed. It was as if a heavy weight was dragging it down. We began to beg Mgboye to let us continue our journey. Brother Paul and I called her every sweet name in the world, but Brother James was angry with her and started to shout at her, telling her to behave, otherwise he would dump her body on the roadside for the vultures to feed on. We tried to hush him, but he would not listen. Heaven forbid I speak ill of the dead, but you all know how stubborn Brother James can be. Finally, he said he was tired of Mgboye's tantrums and was going to stop the hearse and get her brothers to come and beg her to behave.

'So, we pulled over at the side of the road and called her brothers over. We explained what was going on to them and that made them very angry. They said their sister never wanted our stupid Christian funeral and that her husband was going against her wishes, aided by us. They said that cremation was an abomination, an evil that stopped a person from reincarnating back into the family. They started shouting at the husband, threatening to beat him up as they used to do while their sister lived. Fortunately, Brother Ezekiel's sisters, you remember the four fat women that wore the tall head-scarves; well, they were in the funeral convoy and defended him with robust vigour, punching several brothers on their delicate places and shrieking lunacy into the ears of the rest. I tell you, the fight that broke out in the middle of the road that day was like something you see in a Nollywood film. People stopped to intervene, some cursing us for what we were doing while others supported the husband. At that point, even Brother Paul got very angry and began screaming at Mgboye; and we all know how placid a temperament our beloved Brother Paul had. Yet, that wicked corpse riled him so much that he finally lost it too with her. He screamed at Mgboye that he would show her that our Lord is more powerful than her angry and disruptive spirit. He started to pour more holy water on her coffin and tried to prise open the coffin to douse her corpse with the water, but I held him back. I knew her furious brothers would lynch us if they saw us insulting their sister's corpse with holy water even though that woman was one person that needed holy water more than any other person in the world, living or dead.'

Gabriel paused, jumping from his chair to pace nervously around the table. Sweat poured from his brows and his eyes had a manic glint. The other men watched him, their faces reflecting the sympathy they all felt for the youngest member of their group. After a while, Gabriel returned to his chair and started talking again, his voice low, dull.

'The fighting eventually subsided after some passing policemen intervened and threatened to arrest everyone, funeral or not. Nobody wanted to pay the hefty bail-bribe money the police would demand, so they all swallowed their anger and returned to their cars and we resumed our journey. We hadn't driven half a mile when Brother James said that a thick fog was clouding his sight. Brother Paul also complained of the fog. I couldn't see anything, and the road was clear. Suddenly, we heard a car horn behind us. In fact, it sounded like ten car horns in a simultaneous deafening assault. That was when Brother James did the unthinkable and pulled the rearview mirror to look. His scream almost deafened me. He was like a man possessed, his arms flailing, screaming that Mgboye was sitting behind the car with a knife. Brother Paul turned to look and somehow, the coffin lid had come loose, maybe from all the potholes on the road; I don't know. All I know was that Brother James was ducking, trying to avoid the knife stabs coming from Mgboye's ghost even as he fought to control the car. Brother Paul was holding his neck, choking, saying Mgboye was strangling him. I remember reaching for the door handle and jumping out of the weaving car. I must have hit something hard because I lost consciousness. The next time I woke up was in hospital. *Oga* Vincent, you were the one who told me that both Brother Paul and Brother James had died in the fatal car crash and that Mgboye's brothers had taken her coffin with them from the roadside and buried her in their family home with the heathen rites she'd wanted.'

Gabriel turned to Vincent, his body trembling like leaves under an African thunderstorm. For a long time, he stared at Vincent with haunted eyes before finally shrugging his shoulders in a defeated motion. When next he spoke, his voice was as dead as the customers they serviced.

'That is all I know, brothers. I think I survived that crash because I never said a bad word to Mgboye and I was a young person like her, so she spared my life. I may not be that lucky again. I don't want to take the risk of battling another reluctant and angry dead. My clansmen have insisted I leave this job and learn a different trade and I agree with them. One thing that baffles me till today is the matter of the car horns that caused Brother James to look in that rear mirror. All the drivers in the convoy were adamant that they never blew their horns. In fact, no one else heard the horns except we three in that hearse. I'll leave you to make up your minds about what happened that terrible day.' Gabriel stood up and dusted his trousers, as if dusting off the invisible spirits of their sleepers. 'Brothers, I want to thank you all for the support you've all shown me throughout this ordeal and wish you our Lord's protection in your dealings with your future sleepers. God bless you all. Goodbye.'

As Gabriel turned to leave, the other men in the room got up from their chairs.

'Brothers, soul-warriors, what's the matter? Where you all going?' Vincent looked perplexed, even annoyed.

'*Oga*, we think we will follow Gabriel and leave too,' one of the men said, not meeting Vincent's eyes.

'What do you mean? Have you no faith in our Lord's powers? Don't you want to be part of something great, innovative, and something that will benefit you and your families someday when you call on our services for free?' Vincent was almost apoplectic.

The men shuffled their feet and looked furtive. They looked to Gabriel for help but he shrugged and looked away. Finally, the man that spoke earlier decided to brave the ire of their leader.

'*Oga* Vincent, it's not that we're not grateful for the opportunity you gave us, or that we don't think that what you're doing is good for our people. But you heard what Gabriel said. Even without the antics of that wicked woman, Mgboye, we think that this cremation business is not one that our ancestors welcome. It leaves them no bodies to reincarnate back again, and no graves as a portal to visit their loved ones. So we think that the ghosts will continue to fight us if we keep trying to cremate them. And as Gabriel said, he was very lucky this time. We may not be as lucky as him next time a raging ghost decides to wreak their fury on us. So, if it's okay with you, we'll take our leave now, and wish you success in the business. Please forgive us, Brother Vincent, but we do this not just for ourselves, but for the sake of our families. God bless you and keep you safe, Brother.'

The men trooped out of the room in a single file, leaving Vincent with the white relics of his doomed business.

DOOR CRASHERS

by Franka Zeph

"Are you absolutely sure you want to pursue this?"

"Yes."

Commander Mallard poured himself a single malt. "Drink?"

"No, sir."

"One should never drink on the job. It impairs judgement, among other things." Mallard sipped the eighty-year-old Japanese Scotch. His tanned face was threaded with ruptured blood vessels. He was an avid drinker but far from foolish.

"I understand the Gravenhurst mission was unpleasant but you got the job done. The work we do is of utmost importance to national security." Mallard eyed Yaro piercingly. His crew cut radiated from his head like bristles on a brush. "Your talent is a vital asset to our operations. Quite frankly, we don't fully comprehend how you do what you do. I have a theory that it's a genetic faculty, passed down by one of those Indian ancestors of yours—"

Arawak, you patronizing prick.

"—coupled with the tracking instincts of your Kalahari bushman predecessors. Lucky for us, you all didn't go completely extinct." He swirled the drink in his glass. "Getting back to the point, your abilities are uniquely suited for the Data Retrieval Unit. In my view, a transfer to Interspatial Surveillance is a step down the ladder. You get above-average compensation including evac to an off-world colony when Earth goes to hell in a handbasket. What's the problem?"

"Kraken, sir. His unpredictability poses a serious risk to the team."

"Oh, him!" Mallard chuckled, as if only becoming recently aware of this issue. Blood rushed to Yaro's ears but he kept his anger in check. The Commander leaned forward confidentially. "Now I know he's what you'd call a 'wild one,' but mark my words, he's critical to the success of our operation."

"Do you think employing a psychopath is wise?"

"Let's get one thing straight," Mallard replied testily. "I know how you and the rest feel about working with that son of a gun. We all know that Kraken is damaged—"

Beyond damaged. Dangerous.

"—goods but he can disrupt the electromagnetic field like no-one else we know of can. Your job is the abstraction of intel during the breach that our enemies would otherwise keep hidden from us. The operation cannot function effectively without the two of you. Therefore, I'm going to deny your request for a transfer."

They'll never let me go unless I quit. And that won't be easy.

"What about a replacement for Eckles, sir?"

"Eckles, that poor fellow. Post-traumatic stress disorder got the better of him. The assault on Van der Rees proved overwhelming, despite the fact it occurred in a shell dimensional construct. She'll experience recurring nightmares for some time; nothing that a good psychiatrist can't fix. And she won't know what took place."

Yaro cringed at the thought of Kraken's psychic imprint becoming a Sandman that would stalk Van der Rees' dreams.

"We should have the replacement ready for your next assignment. Anything else?"

"That's it."

"You're dismissed." Mallard sipped the Scotch, his muscle-bound bulk neatly contained within his medal-laden uniform. As Yaro walked down the corridor, he recalled the haunted look in Eckles' eyes.

"I can't do this anymore. Not after what that lunatic did to her face." Eckles' hand shook when he put the vintage Cuban cigar to his lips. "I don't care that it happened in an alternate reality; it's real enough for me."

"I know how you feel. I'm sorry to see you go."

"How can you stand it?"

By the grace of my ancestors, that's how.

"It's my responsibility to keep the team together." A horrific image of Van der Rees appeared in his mindspace. He banished it immediately. If he allowed it to dominate, he too would end up like Eckles.

"He's a monster. The Committee ought to retire him but they won't." He shook Yaro's hand. "Ciao, partner. I hope it works out for you. I really do."

Two weeks later, Yaro reclined on the Masai therapeutic gel chair at his penthouse suite in Las Vegas. The teletransmitter peddled its daily stream of state-sponsored propaganda; baby panda naming contest, volcanic eruptions on Io, unrest in Bucharest. The United Intelligence Committee's efforts were a last-ditch attempt to shore up this dying world of 2067. Civilians remained blissfully unaware, engaged in mindless consumption amid the chaos, confident they would continue indefinitely in this finite world.

It was all rather pointless really. But the Committee paid him well. He thought about life on Eclipto, an exoplanet two light-years away from Sirius; of its semitropical climate and endless crystal-blue seas. He could spend the rest of his life surfing and swimming in that idyllic paradise. There was no war, famine or pestilence. And the women with calf-length hair were apparently quite stunning, though their violaceous hue took some getting used to.

Then he reminisced about his childhood in Tabaquite, Trinidad. He was a skinny boy, or what Trinidadians commonly referred to as "maga," raised by his parents in a two-bedroom shack with no electricity or running water. All his clothes were hand-me-downs and he'd been plagued with running sores. But he was unusually bright, placing first in his class every term for three consecutive years. His parents quickly realized their son had great potential. So did his grandmother, Ma Rose; an Afro-Arawakan healer from Guyana. She'd doctored his sores with bush medicine and they dried rapidly. She taught him how to "see" and trained him in the spiritual arts of his African and Arawakan forbears. At fourteen, his parents sent him to live with his uncle in Vermont, thinking America would provide better opportunities for their only child. He excelled in high school and won a full scholarship to university. Through a referral from his physics professor, he secured an entry-level position at the United Intelligence Committee and quickly scaled the ranks to his current position.

Working for the UIC was prestigious yet isolating. At thirty-three, he had no wife or girlfriend to speak of. He could never disclose his occupation to anyone. He didn't know the true names of his team members, as they had all been assigned aliases. Yaro suited him perfectly. It was a West African moniker that, loosely translated, meant "humble dream warrior." It was also related to the Arawakan word for fish, which referenced his psychic abilities. His alias had multiple meanings like the alternate realities he hacked for a living. The UIC often referred to him as "the Retriever."

As for Kraken, aka the Disruptor, if the team weren't careful, one day he might take them down in his tentacled clutches like a hapless fishing vessel.

In hindsight, Eckles was the lucky one. He received a generous payout and first-class medical attention. He would also remain under surveillance for the rest of his life to ensure he didn't blab about the Committee. Motivated by money, Faika and Molotov would carry on. The Committee would not allow him, knowing what he knew, to resign in peace. He might as well jump from his thirty-sixth-floor balcony.

That was not an option he was prepared to consider.

Yaro turned off the teletransmitter. He should go relieve his frustration at the playgrounds in Nevada's notorious pleasure district. Make good use of his time off before commencing orientation with Eckles' replacement next week. Instead, he lit a ceremonial candle and connected with his spirit guides. He asked them for strength and continued protection for the thankless job of protecting a degenerate nation. He expressed gratitude for his privileged position. Prayed for the less fortunate. And requested a safe exit from this steel trap which had ensnared him with above-average compensation.

"I love the color of your skin!" Lark gushed effusively. She caressed his arms. "It's so coppery! What's your background?"

"Mexican." He could pass for one with his slight build and wavy jet-black hair. The pleasure mate planted fleeting kisses on his neck and chest. She wasn't bad; she had a good body and pleasant smile. He couldn't smell any trace of disease and her energy field was free of violent criminal tendencies. A lemony-green haze of dishonesty lingered on her fingers. Earlier on, he took special care to conceal the gold bangle his grandmother had given him.

"Yarro," she purred, trilling the *r*. A signal sparked within his brain that had nothing to do with pleasure.

Report to your domicile immediately. Transport will arrive at 01:15 hours.

"Sorry, I have to go."

"Why?" The pleasure mate pouted. "We were just getting started!"

"It's my stomach." He grimaced and gripped his belly. "Must have been the shellfish. We'll catch up some other time." Lark eyed him suspiciously. He got dressed and grabbed his jacket from the closet. "They serve a great continental breakfast here. You've got the best view in Vegas for the night. Enjoy it."

Half an hour later, Yaro boarded the chopper on the roof of his condo and departed. The city lights twinkled below in a gaudy display of wanton commercialism. He was disappointed that his recreation had been interrupted. It had been three weeks since his last mission; he had spent one week training the replacement. He hoped the new guy was up to the task.

"ETA zero one forty-five hours," the autopilot announced. "Have a safe flight."

At a secure underground facility in the New Mexico desert, the team met with Mallard for a debriefing.

"Interspatial Surveillance has detected an anomaly emanating from Canton, Boston. For this mission, we'll employ a different tactic with the King's Door. Instead of creating a shell dimensional construct in our present timeline, we'll be sending you to June nineteenth, 1999."

"Did I hear you right?" said Molotov. "You're sending us to the year 1999?"

"Correct."

The team were stunned.

"We've had simulated time travel drills, but I presume this will be a first for everyone?" Yaro looked to his team for confirmation. They nodded. "Are you sure the Door can get us there safely?"

"You know that nothing is one hundred percent safe," Mallard fired back. "We are testing the full spectrum of what the Door can do."

"What if something goes wrong?"

"Don't worry, we've got you covered." The Commander grinned reassuringly.

All you have covered is your ornery ass. We're the guinea pigs getting pushed through the grinder. Silus, the new replacement, looked visibly nervous. Kraken's expression was inscrutable. Yaro could never penetrate his mindspace. He always encountered an obstacle, like a tar-encrusted firewall that prevented him from going further.

"What sort of safety measures will you be taking?" inquired Faika.

"We'll monitor your thermal signatures, but that's the most we can do. If things get hairy, use your icons. Today, we'll be treading new ground with the Dalet. Experiments with inanimate objects suggest time travel is one of them. Let's move!"

Inanimate objects? We're human beings. But you don't give a damn.

Wired on microdoses of coca leaf extract, the team approached the Door. They wore Era Appropriate Wardrobe suits equipped with sensors that would generate the correct attire when they reached their destination. Yaro gazed in awe at the Dalet-en-Ijkmytiel that resembled a prismatic revolving door nestled within a reactive platinum sphere. Hieroglyphs were etched around the solid-gold fascia beneath its canopy. Fat cables snaked out of copper sockets that rigged it to an enormous motherboard. Constructed of polished quartz crystal panels, electrum, gold and unidentified elements, it had been found behind a false door in Pharaoh Sekhemes' tomb seven months ago and acquired by the UIC in a secret bidding war. They discovered it provided a more stable lattice for alternate-reality constructs than traditional methods. This allowed for more effective thought projections within "shells" that withstood scrutiny by targets. Engineers bustled in the control room, ensuring all checkpoints were fulfilled.

"Prepare to initiate entry," a technician announced over the PA, "in ten . . . nine . . . eight . . ."

O Mighty Corico, Awa, Niwi, protect me with your divine grace as I enter the unknown. The Door's motor hummed. Its crystal wings turned, slowly at first, then at a moderate speed. Yaro sensed the presence of his guardian, an ancient Malian warrior, looming tall and fierce over him.

"Grandson, you are protected."

First went Molotov, followed by Kraken, Faika and Silus. Yaro placed his hand on the crystal wing and let its motion carry him forward. The Door emitted a high-pitched musical tone that reminded him of a tuning fork. His skin tingled as though he had walked through a wall of feathers and he went out into whatever awaited him in Canton, Boston.

Yaro stepped from behind an evergreen tree and onto a grassy field. Incredibly loud repetitive music blasted his ears. He felt as though the ground was spinning beneath his feet and took a moment to orient himself. The EAW had kitted him out in a track top, relaxed-fit cargo pants and leather sneakers. A large wooden beaded choker looped around his neck. Molotov was likewise attired in an outlandish getup. Stylized leopard spots adorned his spiked blonde hair. Silus wore a fuzzy cap emblazoned with a kangaroo logo and Kraken sported a green hooded sweater with black bell bottoms. Thousands of people danced in the late-afternoon sun on an abandoned airfield, twirling glow sticks and streamers.

"Anybody know what this is?" he shouted at the team.

"It's a rave," replied Silus. "Very popular in the 1990s. Quite loud too."

"You're telling me!" yelled Faika, who was dressed in an oversized pink sweater and flared jeans. "They're having such a good time with this awful music!"

Silus grinned sheepishly, proud to be proving his mettle so early. "They don't look like a threat to national security," he said.

"I feel like an idiot in these clothes!" Molotov threw his hands up with exasperation. Kraken brushed his hands against his pants, fascinated by the fuzzy texture. An infant pacifier dangled from around his neck. Yaro gritted his teeth. Mallard had said there were no specs for this location, but nothing could have prepared them for this absurdity.

"High five?" A youth held his hand up to Kraken, who regarded him coldly. The youth promptly departed.

"Don't engage," Yaro cautioned the team. "Faika, check the perimeter for a suitable exit point." He patted the revolver in his holster. All of them were armed and instructed not to retaliate unless necessary. Faika slinked away, her black hair gathered in a glitter-gelled bun.

"I'd love to turn her crank," Molotov said aside to Yaro.

"She likes women."

"I'd love to give her one anyhow." Yaro thought his lecherous smirk looked incongruous with his juvenile wardrobe.

"Keep an eye out for security."

"Right." Molotov left. Yaro was deeply concerned about visibility. Their missions were usually conducted in clandestine fashion with few to no witnesses. Something was not right here.

"What would you like me to do?" asked Silus.

"Nothing for now." His main concern was Kraken. Mallard had advised him against excessive violence since the Gravenhurst fallout, but that was all hot air. His psychopathic traits combined with his vibratory signature were key elements in creating breaches. The UIC cared only about results. No-one could predict what Kraken would do next and that made Yaro uneasy.

After several minutes, Faika returned. "Exit point confirmed; south side of stage three. I relayed that to Molotov. He said event security are very relaxed. Good for us."

Kraken surveyed the festivities, fists jammed into his pockets, then strolled to the north end of the field. Yaro and the others followed. The crowd had thinned out significantly here.

"Stay close," Yaro whispered to Silus. "Stick to the plan, no matter what."

Kraken halted three meters away from a wild tangle of brush

that marked the boundary between the airfield and woodland. Yaro observed his aura begin to blacken.

What's he going to do now?

A baby rabbit emerged from the brush. It nibbled on the grass near the periphery and hopped onto the airfield. Kraken pulled out his pistol and fired. The rabbit bounded off into the small gathering of terrified ravers. He pursued the animal, his shots plowing the ground, sending dirt clods flying in random directions.

"STOP!" Yaro shouted. Kraken had discharged eight rounds but the rabbit had escaped.

The air rippled, like waves on a pond, indicating the breach had been initiated. Amid the fluctuating auras of fleeing guests, Yaro spotted a Melanoid female standing next to a cotton candy booth. A cloud of tangerine-pink particles vibrated around her elaborately braided hairstyle. Black darts of scrambled data pulsed within the volatile corona.

"That Melanoid woman over there!" he directed Silus. "Get her!" The woman's eyes, dark brown and alert with intelligence, met his. She dropped the cotton candy and fled, with Silus and Faika in hot pursuit. He radioed Molotov. "Northeast corner at two o'clock now!" Yaro caught up to Kraken and shoved him in the chest.

"What the hell were you thinking!"

"Reluctance is counterproductive to clear and decisive action," he replied, grinning broadly, pistol in hand.

"I don't have time for your psychoanalytic crap! Let's go!" Security guards sprinted towards them. Yaro ditched his earpiece and Kraken pushed people out of the way as they fled. They wouldn't make it to the King's Door without being seen. He considered activating the icon when a guard tackled him from behind. His head smashed against the ground and he tasted blood. He saw two of them bring Kraken down before everything faded and he knew no more.

"For the last time: who are you?"

An austere-looking woman sat behind the desk in front of Yaro. His body ached in a dozen places from the takedown at the airfield. He estimated her to be a fifty-five-year-old Native American, judging from her turquoise studs, cinnamon-brown skin and dual braids that rested on the torso of her black two-piece suit.

"I'm Russ Iverton from Long Island. I came to Boston with Earl," he nodded at Kraken, who sat in the chair beside him, "for the Happy Dazed Festival."

"Russ Iverton is not listed as a Long Island resident in our records. The police recovered weapons. And this." She placed the icons—metallic devices that resembled tiny hang drums—on the table. "Do you mind telling me what these are?"

"Party favors."

"I don't think you understand the predicament you're in. I'm the Director of Optics. I was contacted by the local precinct who remanded you in our custody. These objects aren't toys, my friend. They are time-travel devices."

There goes our cover.

"My people found similar artifacts in Four Corners when visitors from other worlds came long ago. You ain't from the stars. You violate the laws of space-time, which could have unforeseen effects." She interlaced her long fingers. "In my world, that's a crime punishable by death. No trial for the likes of you. We have enough on our hands with the Y2K crisis as is. We don't need you futuristic hotshots poking your noses around here."

"The Y2K crisis was a fallacy, madam," Kraken volunteered. "For your information, the world didn't fall apart and all networks ran virtually glitch-free."

"If I want your opinion I'll ask for it!" she snapped. "You don't get it, do you? My present and your future don't necessarily overlap. Are you working for the FBI? The Russians?"

"I work at my uncle's ice-cream parlor in Long Island."

"Obviously I'm not going to get straight answers from either of you. But my agents will when they work you over. Tell me one thing: do they still make ice cream where you come from?"

"Ice cream is a centuries-old favorite, loved by everyone from Roman emperors to grandmothers," Kraken replied with characteristic savoir faire.

The Director's pager went off.

"I'll be back. Don't do anything stupid while I'm gone." She left them in the claustrophobic silence. Yaro's head throbbed. He suspected he might have a concussion. Even worse, the mission had been compromised.

Corico, Awa, Niwi, I beseech you, reveal to me the enemy.

He closed his eyes and concentrated on the yellow dots forming behind his eyelids. They coalesced to form a large iguana, over four feet long, clasping the branch of a plum tree. It was Inyahé, one of his spirit guides. Images were projected onto its scaly body. From the shadows, a pair of dark hands pushed a briefcase across the table. Big white hands opened the little case filled with gold bars. He focused on piercing the obscure figure to see who the dark hands belonged to, but his headache made concentration difficult. The image faded. Inyahé's dewlap pulsed with ultraviolet light.

"Beware the crocodile," the iguana transmitted. *"And arrows from hunter in shadow."* Then, it was gone.

Yaro opened his eyes. Was it Molotov? Silus? Had Mallard sold them out? He surveyed Kraken, whose cuffed hands rested on his lap. An embroidered crocodile snapped from the corner of his hooded sweatshirt.

"Why did you do it?"

Kraken remained silent.

"I'm talking to you! Why you betrayed us? Answer me!"

"You think you're superior to me, don't you?"

"What are you talking about?"

"They never should have made you Team Lead. I suppose they had to fulfill their diversity quota by hiring a less-qualified Melanoid for the job."

"You're way out of line, Kraken. I'll have you written up for—"

"You're not writing me or anyone else up ever again." Kraken's blue eyes shot Yaro with a look that could freeze molten lava. "People like you should never be in charge of anything!" Hatred distorted his reddened face. "For months I've had to endure your belligerent backstabbing. You never could appreciate the finer aspects of my capabilities. Hardly surprising, given that you lack intellectual refinement."

"That's enough!"

"Soon you'll be tortured and executed. I can't wait to hear you scream."

With lightning swiftness, Yaro butted Kraken. A tiny trickle of crimson liquid seeped from the Disruptor's forehead. His eyes widened with almost comical surprise before he whipped his hands up and struck Yaro in the face, knocking him to the ground.

"You want to fight?" He jeered and spat on the floor. "Come on!"

"Who are you working for?" Yaro slowly got up, ears ringing, nose leaking blood. It had been a very long time since he'd felt this degree of pain. Kraken was six feet tall and weighed almost two hundred pounds. Yaro was no match for his size. Soon, the guards would be here. Or maybe, they'd leave him to die.

He ran towards Kraken then tripped and fell onto the desk. The Disruptor charged. Yaro pushed him away with his feet and he tumbled over, taking both chairs down with him. Bellowing with rage, he stood up. His thundercloud aura bristled with violet flashes of lightning. Before Yaro could clear the desk, Kraken was on him, his hands wrapped around his neck, squeezing. Yaro wheezed as the beaded necklace pressed against his throat, cutting off his circulation. His fingers curled in a desperate bid to hold on to his prize though he was losing consciousness. He heard shouts as the guards burst into the room.

"Playtime's over!" One of them restrained Kraken. The other seized Yaro and locked him in his cell. After the guard left, he opened his hands. The icons gleamed in the weak light of his prison cube. He placed Kraken's in his cargo flap pocket. That bastard would never return to 2067. But what if he had an alternative escape route in place, courtesy of his secondary employer?

Beware arrows from hunter in shadow, Inyahé had said. Was it the Director who was an obvious agent of a shadow security organization? Maybe she had orchestrated this interrogation to deflect suspicion from her informant. Who Kraken was working for raised more troubling questions than heads on a hydra. Yaro depressed the inner concentric circle on his icon and hoped that it still functioned.

"Who sent you?" Molotov demanded of the Melanoid woman bound in the chair. Faika and Silus stood on the sidelines, looking glum. He'd been grilling her for half an hour and still, nothing; not even after the anti-obfuscation serum had been administered. DNA analysis did not return any records of her existence. She was neither armed nor bugged. Molotov was irritable. He had not slept in twenty-four hours. Yaro could have provided deeper insight but he was missing and most likely dead. The UIC had lost track of his thermal signature shortly after the team had returned.

"I answer only to my Lord." She possessed a luminous quality that he found unsettling. He couldn't tell whether she was a terrorist or a religious fanatic.

"Answer this." He pointed his revolver at her. "Who do you work for—Palestine? Nigeria?"

"Stop!" Faika admonished. "This isn't working!"

"You have a better suggestion?" he retorted.

"Let me try." Molotov glared at her then relented. Silus continued to monitor the captive's physiological responses for telltale fluctuations. Faika pulled up a chair and sat opposite her. "Let's talk, woman to woman. You've got yourself in a bad situation. You may never return to your timeline and you'll be imprisoned here indefinitely unless you tell us who you're working for. If you cooperate, maybe we can cut a deal. Give us names and we'll arrange witness relocation for your protection."

The Melanoid stared impassively at the Pakistani female, her dark eyes reflecting the room's artificial lighting. She was of athletic build and exquisitely beautiful, with high cheekbones and preternaturally smooth skin. Her form-fitting bodysuit matched her sienna skin tone. It was embroidered with raised turquoise ribbing in geometric designs.

"We both know there will be no witness relocation. I came to do the work of my Lord."

The Melanoid smiled, revealing perfectly aligned teeth. Sparks flew from her eyes and mouth. Faika jumped up from the chair.

"Get back!" Molotov exploded. "Everyone hit the floor!"

Las Vegas continued its relentless march of the mundane. Traffic stalled, hustlers worked the crowded streets and the casinos blinked, oblivious to it all. A man approached a vandalized public phone booth; the last of its kind in the city. He was bruised, dirty and dressed like a vagabond. People crossed the street to avoid him. The graffiti-tagged booth reeked of urine. Discarded cups and filthy paper crowded the floor around his feet. He entered a code on the keypad that would route his call and bypass the geolocator. The phone rang several times on the other end. He was about to disconnect and try again when someone picked up but didn't answer.

"Winnows wile winsome ways on borrowed time."

"Where are you?"

"Kraken set us up. I confiscated his icon and he might never come back."

"Shit! Are you okay?"

"Have you got the target?"

"She's here. Or more accurately, she *was*."

"Was? Did she escape?"

"She imploded. She's an automaton. A type we haven't seen before. Molotov's analyzing her circuitry. She bypassed all our scans. Looked perfectly human, right down to her fingernails."

"What have you got so far?"

"Nothing. She kept insisting she only answered to her Lord. Silus just had the model plate translated. It's covered in some kind of obtuse archaic script. The English translation is Sentient Humanoid Auxiliary Bio-dimensional Telepathic Intelligence."

Whoever's behind this is big. It was all arranged, right down to that rabbit in the field. A shell dimensional construct that works in time-travel locality? Just wait 'til the Committee finds out about this!

"Anything else?"

"She's gorgeous. I'm almost sad that she expired."

"I mean clues. As in clothing, accessories?"

"Her bodysuit reminds me of our EAW except that it hasn't changed in our timeline. It's covered in turquoise color patterns."

"What kind of patterns?"

"Hang on, I'll take a look."

Sweat dripped down Yaro's face. He wished he were a carefree civilian. Perhaps he should have stayed in his tiny village of Tabaquite and lived a simple life.

"Mostly chevrons. Like arrows, stacked inside one another."

"Beware arrows of hunter in shadow . . ."

"Get out of there now!"

"What's wrong?"

"It's a trap! Get out now, all of you!"

Faika shouted at Molotov and Silus. A deafening roar boomed

above Yaro's head. He looked up and saw that the roof had disappeared. The sky blazed open in a fiery burst of crimson-orange to reveal three falcon-shaped drones flying over the desert. Pulses of light emanated from them and terrific explosions followed. He saw the King's Door shatter in a brilliant eruption of flame and shrapnel, killing several technicians in the control room. The line went dead. Yaro dropped the receiver and sank to the ground.

"I answer only to my Lord."

The automaton was a servant acting on behalf of Pharaoh Sekhemes. What else had it offered Kraken in exchange for the Dalet's location? Yaro's elimination, in all likelihood. It boggled his mind to know what Sekhemes was capable of. The UIC had triggered this backlash with their misuse of stolen technology. This was a minor setback for them. They would recover. His colleagues were gone.

He could not say that with certainty about Kraken.

Yaro considered his options. He could aim for exile to Eclipto or he could relocate to another country under an assumed identity. He raised himself off the ground and pushed the door open. The city roared like a ravening ocean. Today he could pretend to be a carefree civilian. Tomorrow would be the rest of his life.

THE SOUL WOULD HAVE NO RAINBOW

by Yvette Lisa Ndlovu

A rainbow arches in the sky during my grandmother's funeral. My tears must be the rain that invited the rainbow here. I tell it to go away; its beauty is vulgar on such a terrible day as this. Gogo is buried next to Sekuru, who died five years ago from complications from his injuries during the liberation war. It is a dignified funeral with no fuss. Gogo never liked fuss. After the funeral we go back to Gogo's house. I pass the basement door, my eyes lingering on the locked door that Gogo never allowed me to enter. Whatever secrets the basement holds, Gogo took them with her to the grave. I lock myself in the guest bedroom and take out Gogo's cookbook from the shoebox I hid it in.

The cookbook is the last piece of my grandmother that I have. I hold it tightly to my chest, imagining Gogo's toasty hugs and trying to will her laugh back into my ears. Tears stain the cookbook; I know I'm slowly forgetting the sound of her laugh.

Gogo's cooking was unmatched; she even bragged that she once cooked for a British prime minister but Gogo was always prone to exaggeration. Sekuru never denied her outlandish claims; the corners of his mouth would turn upwards into a little smile like the two of them knew something I didn't. I swallow nervously. I don't know why opening her cookbook feels like I'm walking in on her in the bathroom, like I'm about to see something not meant for my eyes. A photograph falls out from the first page. It's in black-and-white of Gogo and Sekuru smiling; they are a young Black couple in colonial Southern Rhodesia.

Last week, Gogo's belongings were divided amongst her relatives at the gova ceremony. People are greedy, always eyeing what they can take even before the deceased dies. I'd heard stories of widows who were kicked out of their houses by relatives who'd claimed possession of the dead husband's house. My relatives had acted no different when Sekuru died, fighting over his tiny house and even tinier car. Vultures, Gogo had called them. She fought to keep the house, angering my uncles, who called her a list of things ranging from "hure" to "muroyi." While my relatives were fighting over Gogo's property, no one paid attention to her musty cookbook sitting on the kitchen counter so I'd taken it for myself.

The cookbook smells like its age, earthy and comforting. My skin tingles a bit from having it in my hands. More tears stream down my face. On the first page is a note signed by my grandmother.

The soul would have no rainbow if the eyes didn't have tears, Langa. If you're reading this my mzukulu, it looks like my cookbook has called to you which means I have passed on. Wipe your tears before reading on, I don't want you staining the pages.

Gogo M.M.W.

Instantly I rub my tears from my face with my sleeve, laughing at Gogo's cheekiness. I frown. How did she know that I would take her cookbook? I turn the page expectantly, hoping to find a food prep method or one of Gogo's delicious recipes but I am met with the words NOMKHUBULWANE: GOGO MAGERA written in all caps at the top of the page. Below the words is a rough sketch of a praying mantis. The word "Nomkhubulwane" is unfamiliar to me but I know what Gogo Magera is. Why would Gogo have a drawing of a creature from inganekwane in her cookbook?

The mantis has prominent front legs, bent and held together at an angle that makes it look like it is praying. The compound eyes on its triangular head look so lifelike that I can imagine it blinking. I trace the drawing with my index finger thinking of the bedtime story Gogo used to tell me about the elusive creature Gogo Magera. It was when I'd lost my tooth and she told me to keep it under my pillow for the tooth fairy to visit.

"Better the tooth fairy than Gogo Magera," Gogo had said darkly.

"Gogo Magera? As in Granny Snip Snip?" I'd asked. "Is that another tooth fairy?"

Gogo laughed sharply. When she spoke her voice was a whisper: "The tooth fairy takes and gives you something in return. Gogo Magera, on the other hand, takes and never gives."

I already didn't like the sound of this Gogo Magera creature as I slowly drifted to sleep.

"Gogo Magera is a praying mantis," Gogo said. "Have you noticed that a praying mantis's legs look like shears?"

"I thought they looked like prayer hands!" I said.

"No, no, they look like shears," Gogo insisted. "Gogo Magera comes while you are sleeping and cuts off a strand of your hair or both your eyebrows with her shears and disappears into the night with your hair!"

I'd bolted up in bed, instinctively touching my face in horror, imagining what I would look like without eyebrows.

"That's why you must sleep with a doek covering your hair," Gogo had said, gently pushing me back down onto the bed and tucking me in. "Gogo Magera only cuts people who don't wrap their hair at night."

Gogo patted the bonnet on my head proudly. I breathed a sigh of relief, grateful that the tooth fairy was coming and that I was protected against Gogo Magera.

Looking at the sketch of the praying mantis now, my hands go to my locs and I chuckle. Gogo Magera is just another cautionary tale grannies tell their granddaughters. I wrap my hair every night so that it's not a tangled mess in the morning, not because of some mythical praying mantis. I wonder why Gogo would have a sketch of Granny Snip Snip in her recipe book?

I turn another page in the cookbook and a booklet, the size of a passport, falls out. I know immediately what it is.

"I can't believe Gogo kept this all these years," I say, leafing through the booklet.

The year is 1955 and Gogo is not yet Langa's gogo. She is twenty-five . . . in mortal years anyways. She is much, much older than that, older than this patch of sand they call a country. But she can't look down on the humans; after all she chose to become one.

As a human woman, she works as a cook in the white suburbs. Every day she makes the journey from the slums to the suburbs. She has to walk half the way and then take three buses. The bus always screeches to a halt when they reach the roadblock right before town. Rhodesian police officers order everyone to get off the bus, crinkling their noses at the sea of Black faces. Every Rhodesian is taught that the Natives smell. Even Native shit smells more than white shit, pure Rhodesian shit. The officers would never call themselves white-Africans. They are too pure-blooded for such a hyphen. Rhodesian sounds like the name of a conqueror anyways.

"Passes!" a Rhodesian screams, his spittle kissing the Black face nearest to him.

Gogo takes out her booklet. Everything of hers is in order. It has her ID, her job title, and the travel permit to the suburbs.

The two men in front of Gogo in the line are taken into the police van. Their pass booklets deemed unfit for them to proceed on to the white side of town.

"Purpose of travel?" the Rhodesian barks at her as he flips through her pass booklet, almost ripping apart the pages.

"I am a house girl at Governor Moffat's," Gogo says.

The Rhodesian frowns down at her booklet.

"They are expecting me soon so that I can cook lunch for their esteemed guest," Gogo adds. "The British prime minister."

The prime minister is doing a tour of the colonies to make sure that the Crown's territories are still in order. The name-dropping works. The Rhodesian throws the pass booklet back at her. He can't inconvenience his fellow good Rhodesians and the PM by delaying the arrival of the help.

Gogo goes back onto the bus. This is how every morning in the mortal world starts.

Most people from my grandmother's generation burned their pass booklets after Zimbabwe's independence. The painful memories and humiliation of being stopped constantly by Rhodesian policemen were greater than the need to preserve such a historic document. In my hands, the pass booklet looks innocent enough. If you didn't examine it closely, it looks like any other passport. The tiny thing feels heavy in my hands as if it can explode in my face if I hold on to it any longer. Such a small, small thing to have such weight. I carefully place it back between the pages of the cookbook.

"Langa, come eat!" Mama calls out from the kitchen.

I bury the cookbook under the pillows and plushies populating the bed and head to the kitchen. Mama is still wearing all black, her hair hidden under an austere doek. We eat in silence; Mama has been stripped of all joy and rarely says a word these days.

I try to distract her from the pain chewing away at both of us by complaining about my journey back to Zimbabwe from the US. Talking about the humiliation of air travel is an easier thing to do than facing that my grandmother is gone, disappeared forever under the soil with only a slab of stone above her grave to remind us of who she'd been.

"Can you believe that they took one look at my African passport and dragged me to a back room," I say, shoving a ball of sadza into my mouth. "They interrogated me for an hour about drugs."

Whenever I recount my airport horror story I try to brush the indignation off my tongue so that it comes out more like an anecdote than the humiliation it was. When I was dragged away from the line, the good white travelers sporting shiny blue passports had stared at me as if I were a criminal. I was detained in a cold, dark room when all I could think about was getting back home in time to grieve. An interrogation turned into a strip search. Naked and trembling in an unventilated room, I yearned to jump out of my own skin. If I wasn't me, I wouldn't be treated this way.

It was only when I showed them my documents proclaiming that I was a student at an Ivy League that they let me go without an apology. My heart races when I think of how I will have to go through all this again on my return trip. I wish I could take buses across the sea, anything to avoid being made to feel like a criminal.

Mama sucks in her teeth. "They come to our countries like we are a blair toilet but harass us when we go to theirs."

"I'm just glad I got here in time for the . . ." I trail off, unable to say "funeral" just yet because saying the word will make it real. I quickly change the subject. "I remember whenever we visited, Gogo used to tell me bedtime stories about Gogo Magera then she would spend hours in the basement."

Mama stops chewing for a moment, her body tense.

"Did she ever tell you what she was doing down there all the time?" I ask.

"Who knows," Mama says.

"Do you know what a Nomkhubulwane is?" I press. "Is it another name for Gogo Magera?"

Mama chokes on a chicken bone. Her coughs make her heave so much that I think something is going to burst out of her chest. She reaches for the nearest glass of water, her hands shaking.

"Why are you suddenly interested in this?" Mama says. Her words sound like an accusation.

"I'm just curious, that's all," I say.

"Gogo Magera is just a children's story, Langa," my mother says. "Nothing more."

I haven't heard my name ever since moving to the States. Everyone at school calls me Lana, Langa twists their tongues into too many knots for them to bother to learn it. I know Gogo would have been disappointed in me had she known I'd bastardized my name. Gogo named me for sunshine.

"I'm Lady Rainbow," Gogo always used to say. "And you are sunshine."

Mama stands up abruptly, clearing her plates.

"No more talk of Gogo Magera and Nomkhubulwane in this house, do you hear me?" Mama says. "Those stories died with Gogo."

How to Make a Rhodesian

Blue eyes
Water from a spring in the forest. Blueberries and
yoghurt blended together to make a smoothie. The
eyebrows of a Scandinavian toddler.

British accent
Yorkshire pudding, a biscuit, the beard of a gentleman
fresh off the boat from London.

White skin
Spoiled whole milk.

Cruelty
Vermillion. A pebble from a cold land. A piece of wood
from a ship. A thorn stolen from a black rose.

The prime minister and Governor Moffat enjoy afternoon tea in
the garden. The prime minister is visiting the colonies to show his
full support behind keeping the colonies in check. He has brought
with him weapons to be used to squash the little flames of rebellion
amongst the Natives.

"I dare say, Moffat, these scones are delicious," the prime minis-
ter says. The prime minister rubs his sweaty forehead with a nap-
kin, not quite used to the African heat.

"The natives are quite excellent at making our food," Governor
Moffat says. "I'm tempted to take my cook with me when I go back
to England."

As the prime minister gorges on the scones, a praying mantis
hops onto the back of his breeches and makes it all the way up to his
neck. The prime minister is none the wiser when the praying man-
tis nicks off a lock of his hair with its scissors-like legs. The praying
mantis jumps away, hopping back into the grass and darting across
the backyard into the kitchen. When the praying mantis is in the
kitchen it morphs into a human woman wearing a cook's uniform.
She seals the prime minister's hair away in a mason jar.

When I open another page in Gogo's cookbook, a key falls out.
The keychain has the word BASEMENT on it. The basement has
always been off-limits to me; walking down the creaky wooden
stairs feels like I'm sneaking into the kitchen to steal Gogo's
Choice biscuits. I pause before the grey door, a place that was
unknowable all these years but seems to be the last piece of the
puzzle that was my Gogo. I'm too scared to open it. I've always

wondered what was behind the door, yet here was the chance to know and I was shaking all over unable to will my limbs to open it. With a deep breath and hands trembling, I slide the key into the keyhole and the door clinks to unlock.

The basement looks like an abandoned pantry with mason jars lining the shelves.

Gogo heads to a funeral wake at a neighbor's house where the freedom fighters gather at night, the Rhodesians none the wiser. Gogo runs her finger over the red ribbon tied at the gate. Comrade No Rest Muhondo ushers her to the back of the yard, where all the comrades are gathered around a fire.

Gogo is a small woman but she casts a long shadow in front of the sea of hardened faces. They are silent as they watch her dark skin crack like broken glass, an unsettling paleness emerging from beneath. Her short legs elongated, honey-brown hair spinning across her feet like weeds, a moustache stretches above her lips and her voice deepens to a British accent. Within moments, the British prime minister is standing before them where Gogo once stood.

"We didn't have enough weapons to fight the British," Gogo says in her new voice. "But now we do. I walked right into their garrison and walked out with all their weapons in the image of their beloved prime minister."

The freedom fighters erupt into cheers and whistles as they distribute the firearms.

Dear Langa,
You have found the key to the basement at last; you're probably curious about the mason jars lining the shelves. Let me start at the beginning, my sunshine.

I am a goddess. Well, not quite anymore. I chose to be human, you see. I will get to the reason why later. You know me as Gogo Mbaba Mwana Waresa but before I was your gogo, I was Lady Rainbow, the rain goddess. Why would a goddess choose to be human, you may wonder? In the heavens all the gods were arrogant bastards. An eternity is so long. It yields no surprises, no joy, no flavor. I watched the humans and I wanted to know what it meant to live and to treasure existence because it can end.

So I went down to Earth and it so happened that I fell in love with a human man, your sekuru. He was a freedom fighter, passionate. All he wanted was to see his people free.

My father, the sky god, Umvelingangi, said I would regret my choice. He told me humans were violent, fickle creations. Still, I would not return to the heavens.

I was stripped of my immortality, stripped of my powers. When I set foot on the earth, I was born anew, as an African woman in a settler colony on the verge of revolution. I could never make rain again but look, I made your mother who is a storm and she in turn made you, sunshine.

I'm my father's favorite, he has a soft spot for me, so he left me with one power. Nomkhubulwane. She who chooses the state of an animal. The power of shapeshifting. That is why I told you the story of Gogo Magera, the praying mantis who steals hair from those who sleep without doeks at night. The hair I stole as a praying mantis (what does the science you learn at the school in America call it, DNA?) are the ingredients I used to make recipes that would turn me into anyone I desired to become. I used the recipes to win the liberation war for our people and never touched them again, locking them up in this basement. If you could have the power to become anyone you choose, would you stay yourself? This is your inheritance. I leave the recipes to you, my sunshine, all the ingredients pickled into mason jars.

A DREAM OF ELECTRIC MOTHERS

by Wole Talabi

Two hours into the third session of our fourth cabinet meeting on the border dispute with the co-operative kingdom of Dahomey, my colleagues finally agree that we need to seek the dream-counsel of our electric mother.

The dream-counsel consultation ceremony was usually a somewhat elaborate half-day affair, with a Chief Babaláwo being called in from the Ile-Ifẹ Technology Center of Excellence a day before to run diagnostics, read the Odù, dine with the Ọyọ Mesi and remind us of our history and culture before we link our brains with that of our electric mother. Officially, the ceremony is performed to maintain transparency, to formally ensure that the public knows when this collective resource is being used. But everyone knows that the primary reason the ceremony was devised and is still performed is to maintain a sense of continuity of tradition because some of our people still believe that any contact with the ancestors should be mediated by a Babaláwo. Even though they know that the electric mother isn't really the essence of our ancestors in the classical sense of the term, and that nothing more than an encrypted lifedock connection to the secure national memory data server and induced REM sleep are necessary to establish contact. Today though, we vote to forgo the ceremony and perform the consultation immediately due to the urgency of the situation. An efficient measure which I proposed, and which was thankfully agreed to by a majority vote without much objection. No need for all the bureaucratic *jagbajantis* that the government has developed a reputation for. We can make a full report after it is done. Besides, I have been waiting over a decade for an opportunity like this and I don't want to wait another day if I can help it.

"Are you okay?" I ask my colleague, the honorable minister of information and culture, who is fiddling with his bronze-framed spectacles nervously as we exit the white-walled womb of the secure ministerial conference room. He was one of only two dissenting votes in the cabinet and the only cabinet member I have ever engaged with more than a professional politeness since I was appointed by the Alaafin three months ago. This is the first consultation I will be a part of, but the records show that he voted against the previous four as well. I have come to like him, but I find his apparent resistance to the consultation curious, especially since he is the one that will be responsible for the report and official broadcast once we are done.

Jibola Adegbite shakes his head, the sound of his shoes a metronome against the marble floor. "No. I'm not. And maintain my objection. I really don't think this is necessary at all. At least not yet. It is a border dispute, not some brand-new crisis. We can figure this out ourselves." He pauses. And then he says, "Besides, these consultations always leave me feeling somehow."

"How somehow?" I ask.

"Like it never really leaves my head, you know? Even after. The voice, or something. It is still there. Do you know what I mean?"

"No, I don't actually," I lie.

I have read classified reports of others who made similar claims, who thought they heard the voice in their heads or relived experiences from the consultation long after they were disengaged from the server. I don't say anything to Jibola about the others because I know it's not possible. Not really. Whatever they think they heard or perceived were probably just electric echoes in their brains. Like visual afterimages that persist in our vision after overexposure to the original image. An adaption of the brain to external neural overstimulation. At least that's what the military intelligence experts that reviewed the reports concluded, a conclusion which I completely agree with. Maybe he just hasn't come to terms with that yet. I don't have fond memories of my time at the Ogun School of Military Engineering, or with the Army Corps, but I have found that a background in engineering gives perspective on these types of things.

Jibola turns his head and looks at me like he is trying to scan my brain and then he says, "Well I just hope it doesn't happen to you too," before turning away and walking a few steps ahead of me.

He is short, he'd stand shorter than I do if he didn't have his aṣọ-oke fabric cap on, with large sensitive eyes and an incipient potbelly that is starting to swell below his tailored white agbada. In a way, he reminds me of my father. At least the version of him that existed before the lunar spacelift accident. Not the broken, bloody version that spent his final seventy-five hours in and out of surgery as an army of Babaláwos tried to save his life while my mother and I watched and prayed and cried to all the Òrìṣà to save him. That's what broke her in the end, I think. Not just the unexpectedness of the accident but the brief period of hope we held on to before they came out of the operating theatre and told us he was dead. In some ways, the accident killed both my parents.

Jibola and I are the last ones to reach the elevator. Once we step in, a red light appears, and a door materializes from nothing as its constituent molecules are telecargoed into place. It almost makes me jump back with surprise, but I don't let it show. I don't think I will ever completely get used to building sections being beamed into or out of place on demand.

"I meant what I said," Jibola says as we descend quietly under the carefully calibrated control of the building AI, almost mumbling to himself. "We can figure this out ourselves. We should. We have been navigating issues along that border with Dahomey off and on for centuries."

I lean in and whisper, "Maybe that's why we need help, so that we don't have to keep negotiating with them for centuries more."

"Funny." He snorts, waving his hand at me like he is swatting away invisible flies. "But I don't think you see the point I am making. We keep returning to the electric mother instead of fully considering and debating our points to consensus whenever there is a threat to the peace."

He seems a bit more agitated than usual. Perhaps the stress of the issue with Dahomey is getting to him, even though I am the one that will have to send troops into battle if the situation really deteriorates and we get to worse-case scenario. I'm the young, newly appointed minister of defense, only the second woman in the history of the republic to hold the position, and I may have to a manage a war already. Besides, I've never done this before. If anyone should be stressed, it's me. And yet, I am not. I have other things on my mind.

"That may be true, but does it really matter?" I ask. "We will get the best possible advice in the shortest amount of time this way. With the least amount of acrimony."

"Maybe you need a little bit of acrimony to be sure you are running a republic properly, especially when lives are at stake."

That comment, uttered a bit too loudly, draws looks from the other ministers of the Ọyọ Mesi. I cannot tell if he is serious or not, so I stay silent, straighten my back and stare ahead at the plain white door while we continue to descend two thousand meters below ground level towards the subterranean cavern protecting the data server that has hosted the collective digital memory of the Odua republic since the 9878th year of the Kọ́jọ́dá.

We first began the mass archiving of memrionic copies of our citizens during the reign of Oba Abiodun III, when the great

Iyaláwo Olusola Ajimobi first observed that if two digitized memrionic copies of human minds were synchronized and uploaded to the same operating environment, they would temporarily merge to form a new entity with its own unique, emergent identity. This entity could easily be deconstructed back to the individual memrionics using memory pulse stimulation with no apparent loss of fidelity. She called it a *digital emulsion*. Free of the artificial borders of tissue and silicon between minds, thought patterns of sentient individuals, when allowed to mix and interact, seemed to seamlessly flow into and merge with each other like rivers, completely miscible and yet still separable, with the right perturbation. It was she who first proposed the application of this observation to the creation of the national memory data server. A server that could be used to create a unique national computational consciousness based on the recorded thought patterns of every previous citizen of the republic whose neural scans could be obtained before they died. She referred to it as an artificial memrionic *supercitizen*. An entity made up of the minds of citizens past that could process billions of input parameters, thoughts, opinions, experiences and feelings in an instant and give advice on matters of national interest. An encoded and accessible electric voice of the ancestors. The Alaafin could not resist. Neither could the Ọyọ Mesi. They approved her plans, gave her all the funding she needed, and she became the first director of the NMDS. In school, when they first taught me about the creation of our electric mother, I spent a lot of time wondering about Ìyá Ajimobi herself. I wondered why she had never taken a husband despite her reputation as a gentleman's woman. I wondered if she had intended for the new supercitizen to exclusively speak with what sounds like a chorus of female voices to everyone who makes a connection to their thoughtspace or if it had chosen (I suppose that technically, it continuously chooses) that voice on its own because of the magnitude of her influence on it. I never met her and yet her story has had such an influence on me and my life that I'd like to believe the latter. Perhaps our ancestral women are just more opinionated in liberated digital thoughtspace than their male counterparts or perhaps she is still driving its identity from the inside. She is, after all, one of the ancestors now. But mostly, I wondered why hardly anyone in my family ever spoke about her, considering the fact that she was my great-grandaunt before she became a component of her own electric dream.

My ears are about to pop when the elevator finally slows to a stop and the door dematerializes. A blast of cold air hits us as we step out and into the expansive grey space of the NMDS center. An array of thick, black cables cut into and run across the high, hyperbolic ceiling. That's the first thing I notice—almost everything in the center is geometrically precise. Circles, rectangles, ellipses, parabolas, hyperbolas, triangles and more. Shapes permute and combine in three dimensions all along the windowless, red walls which bear large abstract symbols drawn in harsh white, like academic graffiti.

In the middle of this expansive space sits the home of our electric mother. A large transparent cube housing an array of solid black cylindrical quantum-processing nodes. Six programmable nanomaterial chairs sit on either side of it, facing away, with an assortment of cables and jacks and connection ports sticking into and out of them, some of which are connected to the cube, like an extended nervous system. The surfaces of the chairs ripple and pulse like lovely dark skin to a lover's touch as the nanoparticles they are made of continuously adjust to micro changes in the environment. An array of holographic projections with information about the state of the server is constantly streaming around the glass in bright orange ajami calligraphy. I recognize some of the projected readings from the technical description and reports: temperature, humidity, memrionic integration coefficients, airflow vector fields. But many of them I don't recognize. I don't think I'm supposed to anyway. I may have studied engineering, but I'm not a Babaláwo.

"Welcome, ministers," a man in a white shirt, embroidered with red at the collar and sleeves, says as he steps into place beside us. He seems to be the on-duty Babaláwo, but I hadn't even noticed him standing there until he spoke. His willowy body is stick-straight, crowned with a halo of perfectly combed salt-and-pepper hair. His eyes are bright and focused, set into a wrinkled face like jewels set in dark oak. "My name is Yemi Fasogbon. I believe all of you have participated in dream-counsel consultations before, is that correct?"

There is a chorus of discordant "yes," with only one exception—me.

"This is my first time," I say.

"Ah." Baba Yemi focuses on me. "You have read the standard briefing notes?"

"Yes." I respond. *Intimately. And I have read reports from previous consultations too. Even the classified ones.* But I don't tell him that.

"Very good. Then there is nothing to worry about. You already know everything you really need to know." He smiles, and kind lines crease his face. "Just relax. I will initiate the encrypted neural connection to your lifedock ports. Once the connection is made, a signal will be sent to your hypothalamus. You shouldn't feel anything unusual, it's just like falling asleep. I will monitor your brainwaves and once you are in REM sleep, I will connect your brain to the great memrionic supercitizen, allowing information exchange. Most of this will occur via auditory stimulation but some of it might be visual or tactile."

He pauses, looking right at me. I wonder if he has any suspicions about what I am thinking of doing once I am connected. What I have been thinking since the day I found out that my mother had starved herself to death in the home our family had owned for almost three hundred years. She'd retired from her teaching position a few weeks after my father's death, sold the house they had bought together, the house I grew up in, and left Ibadan. She spent her final months desiccating in the family red-brick villa in Ijebu-ode, ignoring most of my calls and sending the occasional cryptic message with apologies and encouragements and brief but false assurances that she was fine. I should have asked for compassionate leave from the battalion commander, but I was on the fast track to a promotion, and I felt I couldn't lose momentum. Not when she had always told me I had to be tough, to push through adversity and show them I could be every bit a soldier and military strategist as the men that made up most of my cohort. I thought the few messages and our quiet but constant love for each other would be enough to get us both through our grief but in the end it wasn't. They found her sitting in my father's favorite leather chair, thin and depleted like all the life had been slowly leached out of her. The coroner told me that she hadn't eaten in fifty-three days. She didn't leave any final message. I never even got a chance to say goodbye. I want to change that. I need to change that.

Baba Yemi continues, "We are using the diminished external stimulation and increased brain activity of your minds in REM sleep to enable a direct connection to the complex digital system of the memrionic supercitizen. This is useful, but it also means that the connection can sometimes take on the inconsistent and unstructured qualities of a dream. Some of you may have experienced illusions before. It can seem unusual and perhaps even frightening sometimes, I know, but do not panic, no matter what happens. Just ask your questions and receive your answers. Open your mind to the ancestors and they will guide you. That's it."

I nod my understanding at him. I know all this. I just haven't experienced it yet.

"How long will this session take?" the energy minister asks.

They are the oldest serving member of the Ọyọ Mesi and often concerned with time, so I am not surprised.

"You will all enter REM sleep at different rates depending on your unique brain chemistry and response to the direct neural sleep stimulation, but we hardly see any consultations taking longer than five minutes," Baba Yemi replies. "Once you are in REM sleep, the consultation itself should not take more than a few seconds. However, I will use a neuromodulation protocol to try to synchronize your emergence as a group."

"Thank you," they say.

Baba Yemi holds up his finger and flicks it once like it is a lever. "One final thing. Don't worry too much about the details of your consultation. All of you will receive the same answers regardless of how you ask the question, as long as it is indeed the same question. In fact, we count on it. It's a good control procedure, to see if there is any alternative or minority report of the consultation conclusion. I will manage the debriefing session once you are all done. Does anyone else have more queries?" he asks.

I look around and catch an earnest look in Jibola's eyes like he is about to ask a question of his own, perhaps something that could delay or derail this consultation session, but then he changes his mind and looks away.

"Great. If there are no more questions, please follow me. I will make the connection." Baba Yemi bows gently.

Jibola takes what I imagine is a resigned step forward. I exhale with relief as we all march to the chairs surrounding the glass cube and take our places. Out of what I think is sympathy, I take the one beside him. I think it would be nice if he sees the face of a friend when he emerges from thoughtspace. Or maybe I'm lying to myself and I'm scared that I am the one who will need the comfort of a friendly face when I am done with what I plan to do. The moment is so close at hand, I am starting to feel nervous.

Baba Yemi makes the rounds: adjusting cables, pressing keys

and checking displays while we sit there quietly, the hum of the servers constant and almost soothing, like waves on a beach.

When he comes to me, he smiles his open and kindly smile and asks, "Are you ready?" as he fiddles with the cables behind me, twisting and turning them without looking.

I think open my lifedock port and tell him, "I am." *I have been waiting for so long.*

"Good," he says, straightening up. "We will begin in a few minutes." And then he moves away.

I stare ahead at the symbols on the walls. I know that they represent something, something about the unclear nature of our connection to the ancestors, but I cannot place what it is exactly. I read about it when I was researching Ìyá Ajimobi's work on modern Ifá theory. I'm still trying to remember when something slides into the open lifedock port at the base of my neck, sending what feels like a pulse of pure ice through my spine. My vision goes blurry, my body limp as the progmat chair adjusts to cradle me like a child falling asleep in its mother's arms. My consciousness starts to fade. The last signal I am sure my brain receives from realspace is Baba Yemi's voice repeatedly chanting in calm, confident Yoruba, "Relax and open your minds to the ancestors. Relax and open . . ."

Darkness.

Suddenly, I am somewhere. Thoughtspace. Stark and white. There are no corners or seams or edges or signs or horizons or anything to help me orient myself. I bring my hands up to my face to see what form I have taken but I see nothing. Am I just a mass of information floating around without a body? A disembodied consciousness? Or perhaps I am transparent, and I just see right through myself. I don't know. The sensation of being myself here is so different from realspace that I have no real frame of reference for comparison. It's a bit like floating in perfectly clear, colorless water. But also, not. I just feel . . . strange.

"Hello." I speak into the emptiness.

There is no response and so I try to clear my mind and repeat myself.

"Hello."

"Our daughter, welcome," a voice choruses.

It sounds like it is coming from everywhere and nowhere at once. In it I hear millions of women speaking in unison—mothers, daughters, aunts, sisters, friends, lovers from generations gone by. But Ìyá Ajimobi's voice, which I heard so much of in the archives during my research, still stands out, like it is both the first and the last one to be added to this superposition of sounds entering my consciousness.

"Thank you," I respond.

"I am all. I am complete. What do you seek?"

The white of thoughtspace suddenly turns into a pale blue. Then cycles back to white. It keeps alternating, mesmerizing me. I don't know how long I have been silent when I finally remember both my duty and my real reason for coming here. I decide to start with duty by asking the question which every other member of the Ọyọ Mesi will also ask.

"As you must already know from the data feed, we are in dispute with Dahomey again. They have violated the Treaty of Allada by sending their representatives to the Ajashe region, claiming that the population voted to be part of their kingdom in the last referendum."

"This is true. We have validated the data."

I'd read it in some of the reports, but I am still surprised that the electric mother converses more like an AI than an actual person. I suppose I have been anthropomorphizing her for so long that I started to expect a more conversational human response. It's easy to trick your mind into things.

I continue, "They claim they want to renegotiate the treaty and so far, there has been no violence, but this is clearly a threat to us. We cannot allow them to just take away our control of the region, it is a part of the republic."

"This is true. Territorial integrity must be maintained."

"We need to take it back. But if we send in troops, we risk another war."

"This is also true. The probability of war exceeds current national security thresholds for conflict prevention."

A bit tired of the constant agreement, I ask finally, "We ... I mean, I ... have come to seek your guidance. What should we do?"

Thoughtspace adds a new color to its cycle, a deep, dark green, like moss. The cycle continues.

White. Blue. Green.

White. Blue. Green.

White. Blue. Green.

"Military confrontation with Dahomey is inevitable. Projections indicate that the probability of war increases with time. Projections also indicate that the probability of a successful invasion will also decrease with time. The best course of action is to invade now and take control while our chance of success is highest."

I am more shocked than I expected to be. The reports indicated that the electric mother typically highlights considerations that have been overlooked and points out trends in data that have not been cross-referenced and as a result, does not usually provide simplistic answers. This, a basic analysis with a simple conclusion, is not what I expected to hear. A straightforward push to war. I don't want to believe that this is the best advice we can receive. I wonder if the other ministers are hearing this and thinking the same thing I am.

"But to initiate a war would go against the Alaafin's policy of continental integration and cooperation. Besides, it will violate the will of the people in the territory and cost many of our people's lives."

"This is true."

More agreement. Another color joins the cycle. *Red.*

"Surely there must be better options?"

"This is not true. All considerations have been included in the evaluation of this situation. An extended negotiation will only delay war. Invasion is the best course of action. It will maximize the probability of the republic's life quality index remaining above eighty-three percent over the next one thousand years of the Kójódá. There are no better options for the overall good of the republic."

This feels wrong. I don't know why exactly; it just feels wrong. Like a badly constructed response based on fear, not logic, despite its scaffolding of data and numbers. But I don't know what else to say and I have done my duty, so I decide to finally attempt the thing that has been increasingly stepping out of the corners of my mind since my mother died, since I researched the archives, since I proposed this consultation.

"Ìyá Ajimobi, are you . . . in there?"

I have always wondered if she could distinguish herself from the supercitizen, even briefly, if she could float to the surface of this churning ocean of data and memories and instincts and thoughts and feelings. Her research notes indicated that she thought it was possible, that one or more memrionic records could sometimes "take over" the digital supercitizen for brief moments.

"I am all."

Apparently not.

I'm disappointed. If any mind could do it with any measure of control, surely it would be hers.

"Ìyá Ajimobi, can I talk to you? Just you?"

"I am all."

I have never been the type to give up easily and I am not about to start now. Not when I have been waiting for so long. Not when I am so close. Not when there is even a sliver of hope.

"Ìyá Ajimobi, please. If you can hear me. I need to talk to you," I say, not willing to lose this chance to get answers and say goodbye the way I should have. "It's your great-grandniece, Brigadier-General Dolapo Balogun. Please. I need your help." And then I break into

rapid Yoruba, using her oríkì, her traditional praise greeting, which
I have been practicing, to remind her of who she is and who I am.

> *Olusola Ajimobi, daughter of the great warrior clan*
> *The one who gathered the threads of her people's minds*
> *And wove a new Òrìṣà of them*
> *Olusola Ajimobi, daughter of the moon and the sun*
> *The one whose eyes deciphered the secrets of Ifá theory*
> *And wrote the name of her family in the heavens*

"Please, answer me," I plead.
There is a deep, overwhelming silence. Then, "I am . . ."
A pause.
The cycles of color seem to speed up.
White. Blue. Green. Red.
White. Blue. Green. Red.
White. Blue. Green. Red.
And then . . .
Red.
Red.
Red.
I can sense an abstract pressure on my consciousness like some-
thing is struggling to manifest itself in my mind but can't. The
pressure grows and grows until it becomes something like pain. It
is overwhelming, like I'm diving deep underwater without equal-
izing. I begin to see the symbols from the wall of the server room
scroll past my vision like falling rain, but I still don't remember
what they mean. A rattling sound like an opele being thrown ac-
companies the falling symbols, and the cycling colors seem to be
coming closer, approaching me somehow. I am trying not to panic
but it's hard to keep my composure without my body, without being able to apply all the techniques they taught me in the Army
Corps—closed eyes, steady breaths, stillness, mental focus. Here
my mind is skinless and exposed, with all of these sensations and

stimulations flowing in unrestrained. It all becomes too much and I am about to let out something like a scream when finally, it stops. All of it. The cycling colors, the lights, the sound of the opele. All of it stops. Thoughtspace is white again and there is now a giant head in front of me, projected vividly like it has been sculpted from solid blue light. I recognize the wrinkled oval face: sharp-chinned, wide-nosed and wise-eyed, with a crown of plaited grey hair.

"My daughter," the head says to me in a voice that is not a chorus but is hers. Just hers.

"Ìyá Ajimobi!" I cannot contain my excitement.

"Brigadier-General Dolapo Abimbola Titilope Balogun. I have heard you. You are one of my brothers' great-grandchildren. I have tracked you in the datastream. Your ori has guided you well. You have done the family proud."

I feel myself fill up with emotion and I am still struggling for words to use in response when she continues, "Child. We must either be all or none. There is now a steep memrionic gradient. I cannot maintain this unstable state of the digital emulsion for long. How can I help you?"

It is strange not being able to exhale and relieve what I still sense as pressure in my chest. There are so many questions I want to ask, so many things I want to know, but I know I don't have much time, so I tell her the true reason I have come. "My mother, I need to talk to her. I just . . . I need to ask her why. And maybe say goodbye."

Her face seems to flicker, like the light it is projected from just experienced a power surge. "My daughter, even if I can do what you assume I can, surely you must know that it is not truly your mother here with us? None of her essence, her ori, is here, only her memories and her knowledge and a record of the neurochemical pathways that primarily drove her emotions."

It's even stranger, the sense that I am holding back tears when I am disembodied. "I know, ma, but you came to me. You came." I am pleading again. "If there is enough of you here to answer the call of your kin then I believe there is enough of her. I know she had her last memrionic scan appointment three weeks before she moved back to Ijebu-ode. Please. This is the only way I can speak to her now. I have to hope it is enough."

She flickers once more, this face that I have studied so much since I was a little girl, at first solely because I wanted to be like her: brilliant, full of life, independent, strong. And later, because I wanted to find something in her notes, something that maybe would lead me to this—my last chance to speak to my mother.

"I know you designed the architecture of thoughtspace. I know you can help me," I add.

Please help me.

The light flickers again and her face fades.

"I will attempt to retrieve her records and establish a direct connection only to you, but I don't know what form her isolated memrionic packet will take or how long it will remain stable."

"Thank you!" I think I am shouting, but I am not sure.

"Thank you for thanking me," she says with a smile. And with that, she is gone. Thoughtspace suddenly seems to gain dimensions, directions, a sense of solidity. It's only when I notice that I am falling that I realize that I have also gained a body. What seems like a vast wall of nothingness sweeps past me. I am falling, falling. Falling into an endless void. I can see my legs tumbling around and I try stabilizing myself by spreading my arms and puffing out my chest, facing the oncoming emptiness. It is just starting to work when I see it appear—a square of green and red in the middle of the nothing ocean. I close my eyes and brace myself.

My landing is hard, but silent and painless even though it throws up a mass of compact red soil and displaced elephant grass. I stand up quickly, brushing the dust off my body, and see a small redbrick hut with a thatch roof ahead of me. I can smell efirin-and-honey tea, her favorite, and I know where I am.

I am standing outside the hut that sits at the center of our village villa, the one that my great-great-great-grandfather, Oluseyi

Balogun, had built with his own hands when he first migrated to Ijebu-ode at the end of the Second Akebu-lan War. The hut that had spawned what would become the family compound. The hut where I used to play games with my cousins every year during the Olojo Festival. The hut where she had finally gone to die.

I cannot linger. I don't have time.

I sprint to the thick wood door and knock, remembering that she hated it whenever my father or I came in without knocking. The door swings open on its rusty hinges before I finish knocking and so I enter. The hut is mustier than I remember but everything is where I expect it to be. Except . . . The sight of her sitting in my father's favorite chair and staring at me with a steady smile stuns me to sessility.

"Mummy" is all I can manage to say. Her large brown mahogany eyes, lustrous hair and full cheeks are the same as they were when I saw her last: two weeks after my father's funeral, the day I went back to base.

She rises and I step forward to engulf her in an embrace. Her warmth suffuses me, and I allow myself to steep in it. The smell of her hair, the softness of her neck, the thinness of her arms.

"Dolly Dolapo. My darling. How are you?" she asks, when she finally pulls away.

She walks to a table made of iroko wood where a pot of efirin-and-honey tea is brewing, turns over an old mug and starts to pour. It doesn't feel like this is thoughtspace or even a dream anymore. This feels . . . real.

"I'm fine," I say out of habit before catching myself. "Actually . . . I'm not fine."

She hands me the mug with a querying look, and I take a sip. Sweet and bitter dance on my tongue. I realize that my sense of urgency is gone. I've almost forgotten that this place is unstable, that Ìyá Ajimobi is giving me every precious second with my mother and I can't waste any of it.

"I . . . I need to know why. Why did you leave me?" I feel the tears that have escaped my eyes roll down my cheeks as the emotions start to overwhelm me. It feels good to be able to feel things in this place. "I know you were heartbroken when Daddy died but why didn't you stay . . . for me?"

"Leave you? I didn't . . . it is hard to explain, Dolly," she says mildly, picking up the mug. "Your father and I, we'd known each other since we were children, we went to the same school, the same university, we planned our lives together and we planned for you, together. When we lost him, like that . . ." She pauses and looks up at me. "I knew what the right thing to do was. I knew that I should have focused on you, but I couldn't. I couldn't imagine a world without him because I never had. I was overwhelmed with grief. With a sense of hopelessness. That filled me with fear. It clouded everything."

I turn away from her and take a long sip of the tea. "It clouded your love for me?"

"No! I never stopped loving you, but I knew that you were okay," she responds, dropping her mug and taking my hand. "We'd raised you to be self-sufficient. To be able to take on the world by yourself. You were our strong Dolly," she says, her voice soft. "I knew you were strong enough even if I wasn't."

"I was strong because I had you and Daddy! Without you I have been . . ."

My voice catches as a memory rushes to mind: my father walking me up to the neighbor's dog, a fearsome-looking Azawakh named Rover, when I was no older than six. My mother stood back, framed in the doorway of our Ibadan house. She kept calling out words of encouragement. *Don't be afraid. The dog won't bite. Not every animal that has sharp teeth is dangerous.*

"I wanted to be there for you, but I couldn't sleep. I couldn't eat. I didn't want to burden you. I know you would have thrown away your entire career just to come and try to care for me, and if that happened, I would have only hated myself."

I remember wondering why she wasn't coming with us to play

with the neighbor's dog, why she was trembling, shaking visibly. I'd put my hand on the dog's neck and he barked. But my father held my hand in place, telling me to be gentle but firm. *Don't act out of fear. Not every animal that has sharp teeth is dangerous.* So, I held, and Rover eventually warmed to me. When I turned around to show my mother my new animal friend, she'd shut the door and continued to watch from the kitchen window. In my entire life I never saw my mother around any dogs or any animals, definitely none that had teeth.

"I just couldn't go on, Dolapo. But I knew you could. Please understand."

I think I am starting to understand. She'd raised me to be the woman she'd always wished she was. The image she idolized but never became. Strong, fearless, confident, independent. She was none of those things. Not like the great Olusola Ajimobi. On some level, I think I understand now, the depth and complexity of the emotions that drove her to do what she did. In the end she couldn't fight her own emotions.

"Mummy, I just miss you so much."

"I love you, Dolapo. I have since the moment I first felt you inside me. You are a better woman than I was. I hope you know that. Because it's all I ever wanted for you."

I let the tears fall as we fall into each other again and hold on tightly. I don't care about the border with Dahomey. I don't care about the cabinet meetings. I don't care if this is thoughtspace or a dream or an illusion or whatever. This is all I have left of my mother, imperfections, complexities and all, and I want to hold on to her with every fiber of my being.

My head still nestled in her shoulder, I open my eyes and notice that the chair, the mug and the assorted items of furniture around us are starting to elevate off the ground, floating like we are entering a low-gravity environment.

The warmth of her body suddenly turns cold.

No.

I disengage and look into her eyes. She is perfectly still. There is an emotion frozen in place like sadness set in amber. Her lips start to move but it's Ìyá Ajimobi's voice that comes to me now. It's straining, stretching like it's being pulled.

"We have reached a critical memrionic gradient. I can no longer maintain this unstable state." I know this is the end. "I hope you heard what you needed to hear."

This is as much as I am going to get and for it, I am grateful. "Yes. Thank you. For everything."

"Thank you for thanking me." My mother's lips move with the voice of Ìyá Ajimobi and somehow it seems . . . right. "You know, that dog, Rover, it bit your mother when it was still a puppy."

I'm taken aback by the fact that she could sense my thoughts but then I realize I should not be; my mind is completely porous and open to her here in thoughtspace. Still, I wonder, "But . . . Then why did she lie?"

"She didn't want you to be afraid just because she was."

Of course. "I think I understand."

"Good. Don't hide from your fears or doubts. Embrace them. I hope you heard exactly what you needed to hear."

Before I can reply, the digital version of my family hut is gone, like it has been painted out of my vision in one broad brushstroke. I am plunged back into the absolute, directionless whiteness of empty thoughtspace. Disembodied and alone. The rattling sound like an opele returns and gets louder and louder until I feel something yank on my consciousness violently.

The last thing I hear in thoughtspace is her voice, once again accompanied by the chorus of memrionics, exploding into my consciousness like a bomb.

Exactly what you needed to hear.

I shoot out of thoughtspace like a mind missile, and my eyes fly open in realspace. I immediately collapse to the floor, vomiting all the moin-moin I ate for breakfast and retching violently, until I am so weak and empty that I feel separate from my body.

I am not sure if the feeling is real, an illusion carried over from memory or just an electronic echo. I can feel Baba Yemi's hands on my neck, trying to hold up my head, to get me some air, and close my lifedock, but I cannot see his face. I remember that nausea and dizziness are uncommon but documented side effects of the dream-counsel consultation, but I didn't expect to feel this way. The edges of my vision are dark and wooly, and I know I am probably going to pass out.

Darkness.

When I come to, I am sitting, staring up at the white ceiling of a conference room. I almost panic, thinking I have somehow been reconnected to thoughtspace, but then I see the corners, the edges, and I look down to see my fellow ministers seated around a long table with lightscreen voting panels in front of us, Baba Yemi at the head.

They are all staring at me, a few of them furrowing their brows, chattering to each other or shaking their heads.

"Welcome back," Jibola says, when our eyes meet.

I smile. It *is* good to see a friendly face after all that.

"It seems Minister Balogun has recovered and is with us again," Baba Yemi says, staring at me. "How are you feeling?"

I tell him, "Great actually," because it's true.

"Good. You worried us for a bit, but all your neural scan readings are normal. Let's call it first-time thoughtspace-sickness." He smiles. "We can begin the debrief session now. It should not take long."

He rises and speaks to the group of us as a hologram of yellow light appears at the center of the table and begins to display information about the consultation. "Total consultation time was six minutes and three seconds. Stability of the digital memrionic emulsion was maintained throughout the session."

I start to raise my finger but hold it up to my lips instead, hesitant. Surely, there must be some kind of record of what I did. Some kind of anomaly in the readings?

"No local discontinuities or neural interface breakdowns were observed. Minister Balogun may have had a rough exit but nothing some of you haven't seen or experienced before." Baba Yemi waits for these facts to sink in as the information displays in front of us. "I believe you should all have received the same answers to your queries. Accordingly, I open the floor for a motion, after which you may vote."

I look around and that is when I notice it. They are all hesitant too. They must have all gotten the same advice—go to war. No one wants to disbelieve the advice of our electric mother, but given the consequences of such dire action, and the resistance from the Alaafin that would be sure to follow, no one wants to admit what they must know we all know.

The silence grows sharp and piercing. I think of my mother, sitting in our ancient family hut, unchanged after hundreds of years, contemplating a life without my father, a life she couldn't even imagine. Can I imagine a world where we don't honor the dream-counsel of our electric mother?

Exactly what you needed to hear.

The voice in my head is clear as a talking drum. An electric echo? Or my own memories of that encounter just being replayed? What difference does it make? Perhaps Jibola was right all along. I look to him and he meets my gaze.

As a flood of emotions begin to blanket my mind, I think of my mother standing in the doorway of our Ibadan house. She told me Rover wouldn't bite even though he'd bit her in the past. I start to wonder what it means to help someone you love, to give them good advice, to help them become the best version of themselves that they could be, perhaps even better than you. Perhaps sometimes a useful lie is the best way to point someone in the direction they need to go.

My finger goes up, confidently this time.

"I propose that we put this consultation on hold and reconvene our original cabinet session. We can continue our deliberations until we reach a consensus."

I can almost feel the eyes of the ministers on me, focused like lasers, but I keep my focus on Jibola, whose face breaks out into a broad smile now. I think he understands, just as I did, why the electric mother told us to go to war. I expect an uproar, objections, voices raised in protest for wasting our time, but there is nothing. The silence reestablishes itself.

I scan the room quickly and take in an assortment of expressions, but the only one I cannot read is Baba Yemi's. The only thing I am sure of is that he does not seem surprised at all even though I don't remember reading any other consultation reports which were frozen at the debrief stage. When he finally speaks and breaks the silence again, his words are clear and deliberate. "The motion is moved. I put it to you now, ministers of the Ọyọ Mesi, do you wish to put this consultation on hold? Your voting panels are before you. Yes or no."

I watch as the votes are entered, a lightstream of encrypted data beamed into the central hologram, and as I do, I start to wonder if I ever actually reached Ìyá Ajimobi and my mother at all, or if the digital supercitizen, our collective electric ancestor, simply showed me and told me exactly what I needed to hear.

The lights continue to weave themselves together. I enter my vote and when the weaving stops, the light in the center displays a unanimous *Yes* in bright yellow ajami calligraphy.

SIMBI

by Sandra Jackson-Opoku

A family trudged homeward in the setting sun, bundles of cassava piled atop their heads. Raiders intercepted them on the village path, a group that was small but well armed. The farmers dropped their harvest and scattered in all directions. Some would be captured, not all.

As one of them ran for the river, a voice boomed at his back. "Come back, slave! I will punish you."

Kasese was not a slave, nor was any member of his family. Even if they had been, none would have belonged to any marauder with rifle. Kasese darted down a bush path and reached the water. He searched for his father's fishing boat but couldn't find it. The Kongo was wide at this bend, crocodile infested and unswimmable. Kasese dropped to his knees, calling on his closest ancestor. "O my mother, I am doomed."

At the river's bottom a gorgeous woman lay sleeping, heavily pregnant and wrapped in blue raiment. She is known by many names: Mami Wata, Mistress Fish, Mamba Muntu, mermaid. Her rightful name is Simbi.

Noise from a plunge, the ripples made by a plummeting body roused her from rest. Simbi clicked her teeth in irritation yet took pity on the boy. Grasping him around the upper body, she swam to the surface and pulled him onto the riverbank.

Kasese blinked, stunned to find himself back on land, his lungs clear and clothing dry. The slaver waiting there yanked him to his feet and tied his hands behind him. "Do not waste yourself on drowning. Strong boy like you will fetch a good price."

"My mother," Kasese moaned as he was dragged away.

"I am here," Simbi whispered. She reached into the water, drew out a serpent, flung it around her neck and followed.

Simbi was troubled as the slave ship crested the waves. It was not just from the abject suffering onboard, the rape and casual murder, seasickness and suicide. She was a freshwater deity and the salt spray stung her skin. Simbi found the sea airs suffocating as she writhed in labor.

A delegation climbed aboard, spirits and sodden ancestors: Yemaya, Olokun, Agwé, Sedna, all demanding a sacrifice. They returned to frigid waters carrying Simbi's stillborn child.

Finally there came an island where freshwater abounded, surrounded though it was by sea.

"Hey, Kasey," a rusty voice squawked on the phone. "That you, boy?"

"Yes, Mr. Cherry. I can hear you fine."

Kasey wasn't bothered by the shouting, the old man's stubborn pronunciation of his name. Everyone back home called him Kaysay. If Jameson Cherry's call was from Cymbee Island, it must be about Granny. Any long-distance news about his ninety-eight-year-old grandmother was unlikely to be good.

"Dem gubmint buckra, Kay-say." Selima Drayton selected a plug of tobacco and bit into it. "They 'bout to brick up the spring. You know Cymbee ain't like nobody messing with her water."

"Don't worry, Granny." Kasey knew better than to challenge her favorite superstition. "I'll take care of it."

They weren't "government White folk" after all. The Cymbee

Island Management Association were a group of wealthy land-owners. They'd been fretting over seasonal floods that inundated a golf course abutting the old Drayton Plantation. Kasey made phone calls and filed an emergency injunction, though he wasn't licensed to practice law in South Carolina.

Five months later, Irma hit. They even felt the tailwinds in Atlanta, three hundred miles inland. Granny called from a shelter in Columbia, claiming it was Cymbee's vengeance.

"Granny, I'm glad to know you're safe. This storm is reeling up and down the coast. But nobody bothered your spring."

"Child, dem buckra weren't studying you." Granny Drayton pronounced the word "wore-rent." "Soon as you left, they went and plugged it up."

When the hurricane retreated, thirty acres lay flooded: the Drayton property and Granny's trailer, a high-end housing development under construction, and the Cymbee Island Greenway. After Kasey got his grandmother into assisted living, he put in a call to North Carolina, where a law school classmate headed the Land Loss Prevention Project.

Granny gradually adjusted to her new surroundings. Kasey married Orin, his longtime companion. Low Country Land Trust bought the family acreage and renamed it the Selima Drayton Wetlands.

Visitors over the years would swear they saw a Black woman dressed in blue wandering the preserve with a snake around her neck. Guidebooks attribute it to sightings of the great blue heron. Yet the story was so tenacious that it began to be included in guided tours.

"Here there be monsters," old sailing maps warn. Yet many of us abide here in the deep. God's gonna trouble the waters, it is true. We trouble them too.

HOUSEWARMING FOR A LION GODDESS

by Aline-Mwezi Niyonsenga

The new apartment smells like wood polish. I roll out my Persian rug and lie in its scarlet centre. Gold edges contain the red, deep like a lion's maw.

Jean-Fi helps me dust the windows. By the time our sneezing competition ends, the crown moulding no longer suffers a hairy coat. I win the sneezing contest because mine overpower his, like roars.

Deliverymen ease my new couch onto the rug, a suede finish with fuzzy throw pillows that feel vaguely like a traditional warrior's headdress, the kind my late husband wore. Plopping onto the couch, I let my fingers run through the pillows' white hairs, wondering why I bought such obvious substitutes.

Jean-Fi lounges next to me and lays his head on my lap. I slip my fingers through his tight curls. He's growing them out, lubricating them with oil and water so they stay curly.

"I looked up your name," he says.

I laugh. "Why?"

"To find out its origin." He turns his head. "Who knew you were named after a fierce lion goddess?"

I let my fingers hover above his skull, contemplating how fast I can arch them over his throat, should his next words prove disastrous.

"It's a shame she killed her husband," he says. "If she'd only trusted him more, I know he would've kept her lion form a secret."

I bite off my first thought and settle on the second. "It wasn't worth the risk. He could have done more harm than good, knowing her secret."

Jean-Fi arches an eyebrow. The movement contorts his forehead into waves. "You think so?"

I smile, kissing those lines away. "I know so."

After assembling my dining table, Jean-Fi and I play igisoro. I pick up seeds from their pit and plop them into the next, hand sweeping across the board. I end my turn by taking most of Jean-Fi's seeds. He smiles and says I'm cheating.

I faux gasp. "When did I cheat?"

"When indeed?" He winks. "Don't worry. I'll let you win."

It's true I'm keeping an extra seed in my palm. It's moments like these I wish fending off conquerors could be as easy as playing igisoro. Maybe I'd have won against the great Ruganzu. I didn't stay long enough to face him.

The translucent drapes I installed shift in the spring breeze, absorbing the balcony's sun. Jean-Fi's curls leap gold, his smile as white as a warrior's headdress. I almost call him by my husband's name. Maybe they have the same charm.

"Are you sure you don't want me to help with your house-warming?" he asks.

I shake my head, taking a moment to swallow guilt. "Yes, I'm sure. It's been a while since I've cooked for a crowd. It's time I showed them what this lioness is made of."

I bite my tongue, only relaxing when Jean-Fi laughs. "Okay, oh wise protector," he says. "I'll leave it to you."

I throw the extra seed at him.

———

Amandazi, ibitoki and umutsima. Those are the three dishes I want to make for my housewarming.

I sink into my couch, wondering what to make first. Burrowing into Jean-Fi's hot-pink hoodie, I settle on amandazi. Its scent still lingers on the hoodie, evoking the memory of a hot summer day, oil popping while the soft dough cooked into sweet gold. Jean-Fi loves making amandazi. After I taught him how, it's all he wants to make when he comes over. He frequently brings bowls full of his many attempts at getting the perfect texture.

"Crispy on the outside and soft as cream on the inside," he once told me, holding up one of his nebulous creations.

"But then it's not really amandazi anymore, is it?" I told him mid-chew. "It's okay if it's harder to chew. That doesn't make it less sweet. And it shouldn't be sticky sweet. The sweetness should be subtle, balanced."

He considered this and decided to burrow his nose in the crook of my neck. I laughed because it tickled. My fingers reached for his curls, impossibly moist ringlets in my fingers, soft like the throw pillows on this couch.

I twirl my fingers around the furry felt of the pillows, trying to remember Jean-Fi's hair in my hands. I remember instead a warrior's headdress, the kind my late husband wore generations ago. Why did I buy something so reminiscent of times past? Jean-Fi isn't my husband. He wouldn't betray me.

There are many ways to make amandazi. Mine requires all the process of dough-making.

Add yeast to a mixture that is half dough, half wet pancake batter. Let it rise like my thoughts about Jean-Fi and then knead them into submission. Our relationship is the longest time I've let a man stay in my life. He is like the dash of orange juice in the mixture: sweet overpowering the sour.

"I'm not who you think I am," I once told him.

"Okay." He chuckled. "I'm not who you think I am."

I watched him watch me. Showing up to my traditional dance classes because he's "always wanted to learn." Challenging me to countless games of igisoro. Blending into the batter of my life, he became an essential addition. Amandazi is never complete without that dash of orange juice.

Let the oil chatter around a small dollop of the mixture. Wait till the dollop browns before starting for real. Scoop a round ball and place it in the oil's leaping arms. Taste the first creation: mildly sweet, doughy in the middle. When amandazi hovers between just right and undercooked, admit that Jean-Fi might stay in my life for longer than I planned.

In my dreams, my fingers stroke the white hairs of my late husband's headdress. The earth smells like my balcony after rain. I sit on a rock that the great Ruganzu didn't kick a footprint into. I'm protecting it from him. My husband sits at the foot of the rock, letting me stroke his headdress as if it is his hair. I'm protecting him from Ruganzu. He doesn't know I can. My power is this secret.

I hear a growl. Inkuba, mighty thunder itself, roars in warning. A spear whistles towards us. I crush the shaft between my teeth.

Reaching for the splinters in my jaws, I realise that my hands are paws. My husband yelps. His miniature form scrambles away from me, dragging his butt through the dirt. I cast a wide shadow over his stricken face, only it isn't his face. It's Jean-Fi's, from the mole next to his trembling mouth to the small eyes and angular cheeks.

I raise my claws and strike.

To make spicy ibitoki, slip knife under green banana peel. Slice like water through hair. When Jean-Fi washed my hair, his fingers were gentle against my scalp.

"This is so embarrassing." I covered my face with my hands.

"Why?" he chuckled.

"Normal people wash their own hair."

"Normal people go to the salon."

"You're not a salon!"

"You're right. I'm better."

Place the shaved banana in a solution of water and vinegar and move on to the next, fingers becoming sticky with starch while the air tastes of salt. Jean-Fi glued his arms around me as I cried. I don't remember what the trigger was, but my guilt was the same. I left, when I should've stayed to protect.

While the bananas soak, heat water in a kettle and pour it on a bowl of tomatoes. Pour the rest in a pot for quicker boiling.

How quickly I said I'd leave him in the end.

"Okay," he replied.

"Okay? This is the part where you get angry and leave."

"Do you want me to leave?"

"No," I sniffed.

"Then why are you being silly?"

Slice the bananas in threes and gently slip them into the water. Dash olive oil and onion in a separate pan. Dump a variety of curry spices, as if they'll burn away his sweetness.

Take the soaked tomatoes and gently peel off the skin. This is the way Jean-Fi disarms me. He showers me with the same boiling warmth and peels back the armour. At first it was confronting, this friend of a friend who actively sought me at parties and get-togethers.

"What do you do for fun?" he asked.

I thought about sunbathing, yawning into my paw, the valley leaping gold.

"There's a game called igisoro," I said. "It's fun for two, but no one wants to play it with me."

"I know that game." He beamed.

I pulled out the set. He gleefully mirrored my actions, putting the exact number of seeds in each pod. Then he lifted his head and said, "Now what?"

"I thought you knew it!"

"My parents never taught me." He laughed.

Other partygoers clamoured for a demonstration, so I taught him. His questions irritated me like the onions sizzling in the pan. Then the striking heat dissipated and his voice soothed me.

Cut the peeled tomatoes into cubes and dump them into the saucepan. Last are the chili peppers. Jean-Fi loves spice. I eat spice to forget. The itchy taste is so persistent that I can almost pretend Jean-Fi didn't look up my name.

Once the ibitoki are soft, add them to the sauce. Mix until even sweetness surrenders to spice.

I cough at the vapour. Jean-Fi looked up my name. Clouds compress into grey outside the kitchen window, dulling the richness of the sauce. I sway on my feet and lean a hand on the counter. My throat feels scratchy.

Rain rattles my windows like a desperate neighbour calling for help. I shiver in my bed, a feverish mess caught between now and ancient storms.

Is it Inkuba that roars at me or simply thunder? Does Inkuba blame me for leaving? Like those old times, I roar back, and hear Ruganzu's pointed laugh at the gesture. "You left and I came!" Him and his spreading footprints.

Tonight he looks a bit like Jean-Fi. Strange. I growl as he presses a damp cloth on my head, and warn him to leave his symbols elsewhere.

In the flashes I see whizzing spears and thumping drums. Each rope of lightning is a warrior's headdress flicking through the bush. I groan, thrash, spitting a spoon thrust in my mouth, thinking it's a poisoned spear tip.

"Please, eat," Ruganzu says. Or is it Jean-Fi?

Later, the storm calms to mist. Warriors dance in the fog, boasting of their achievements. Just like my husband. He would have been great, just like Ruganzu. As a lion I could have been his lucky charm, the mysterious element to his success. Even if he took all my doings as his own, I would have loved to see him speak of it. He was elegant when he danced.

I sob quietly. "I didn't mean to kill him," I sniff. "I had to. I didn't know if he'd . . ."

"Hush, it's okay," Jean-Fi says. Was he here the whole time? Am I awake or sleeping? "It's over now," he says, squeezing my hand.

When I open my eyes again, I realise it's my paw Jean-Fi squeezed.

Spinning into sleep, I dream of Ruganzu, strangely enough. That conqueror king claimed swathes of land with the talent and charisma of a hero. His footprints mark all his conquests. I protected my home against many like him. In my dream, he sits across from me, stroking his chin as he ponders his next move across the igisoro board between us.

"Do you regret it?" he asks. He finally moves a few seeds without claiming any of mine.

"Killing my husband?" I pick up some seeds and take some from him. "No."

He raises his head. His face looks exactly like Jean-Fi's. "No, I mean abandoning your home. Failing to stay and protect it. Do you regret it?" He picks up some seeds and steals nearly all of mine.

"I . . ." I wasn't there when Ruganzu came.

My throat closes up. Like the igisoro seeds left on my board, I'm trapped. I can't move without at least two seeds in a pit. I've lost.

He can't know, I mutter sleepily.

There are no more dancing warriors outside my window, only grey. A glass of water rings in the silence. I drink it and remember hunger. My apartment smells like burnt igikoma, earthy sweet. In the kitchen, I scoop some of the sorghum porridge into a bowl. There is a hot-pink sticky note on the fridge. I rinse my plate, wash my face and scratch grocery items onto a notepad.

My housewarming is two days from now. I think about postponing, but the event is a good distraction from the sticky note on the fridge.

When I come back with groceries later, I turn to the fridge. The sticky note says there's soup and hardboiled eggs. I relax a little.

For the final dish, fill a pan a quarter of the way with water, a bit of oil. Wait till it boils and add sorghum flour. This isn't ubugari, but umutsima. At first, it's an even mixture. Add more flour until I'm flipping an ocean with a wooden spoon. Grit my teeth in frustration. Frustration at moving. From an unruly share house, from the airport, from the last war. Blink against steam. Grip the spoon with the strength I should have used to protect others. Grip the fact that I ran. Wipe my eyes with a forearm and pant at the finished product, a glutinous mass swirling into itself.

Smell my hands, sour, like the earth beneath my paws.

Admit it. After I killed my husband, through all these years, I chose to protect myself.

Candles waver on the table I assembled with Jean-Fi. Friends laugh and cheer over plates full of my cooked assortments—umutsima, ibitoki, amandazi—along with extra dishes that I meant to cook but never got around to: isombe, sambusa. I bite into a triangle of sambusa, eternally grateful for the friends I have.

For the fifth time, I check my phone and glance out the balcony windows, where rain streaks the bobbing city lights. Rain is supposed to be a blessing on special occasions. My new dwelling is blessed, but Jean-Fi's absence is a dry patch in my throat, unsatisfied by the sips of water I take between gulps of wine.

Sitting at a table like this reminds me of another dream I've had recently. In the dream I sat next to Ruganzu at the King's banquet. He turned to me quite often, whispering about how hungry he was, when the food was coming, asking if I was hungry too. I staunchly ignored him until he turned to the assembled party and announced that I was his wife!

"How fortunate are we that my wife protects the kingdom!" he exclaimed. His hand pressed on my shoulder, pinning me to my seat. I stared at him, long enough to recognise my husband's hunger in his smile.

The King sat back, frowning. "How has she accomplished such a feat?" Even he looked at me like an offering. I was the main course.

Before Ruganzu could open his mouth to answer, I unsheathed my claws and woke up.

The last guest's footsteps echo from the stairwell. Rain chatters on, heavy with the promise of thunder. Inkuba warned me.

A knock reverberates through my apartment. It's Jean-Fi. Water rolls down his face as he stutters nonsense. I give him towels and the extra clothes he keeps here. The shower wails while I slip into his hot-pink hoodie and inhale the amandazi scent. The kettle grumbles to a crescendo. When Jean-Fi comes out, I have tea ready. He asks if he can hold my hands, if he can talk to me about something.

Understand my distress.

My late husband was a warrior. When the war started, he tasked me with protecting our home. To me that was a house. The entire kingdom was my home. And he was its hero. He could have been as great as Ruganzu.

I waited for him to leave and told one of the servants not to disturb me while I prayed to Imana. Sneaking around the compound, I morphed into my lion self and bounded to the war zone.

The battle was gruesome. I found my husband tripping over a body while another warrior crept behind him. My husband couldn't die. He was supposed to be the hero.

Leaping between them, I caught a spear in my flank. That didn't stop me from mauling its owner. Once the enemy limped north, I padded back to our house. Blood trailed behind me. I was dizzy and careless.

My tea scalds my tongue. I don't notice through the shivering. My elbow supports itself on the other arm of my couch, far from where Jean-Fi sits. He sets down his cup and offers to take mine. I trade it for my throw pillow, which I rip to bits while he fiddles with his thumbs, telling me excuses about his crazy day and anyway he's been thinking about me, about us. My fingers pause. He takes it as a cue to lay his head on my lap, giving me his beautiful, damp hair for my fingers to stroke. I do so tenderly, carefully avoiding his eyes. Some of the lamplight hits them, revealing churning embers in the deep brown.

"Nyavirezi, I love you," he says.

How dare he make this harder than it has to be?

"I see a future with you," he continues. "I would accept any part of you—*every* part of you if it means spending the rest of my life with you." He raises a hand to my face. "All I'm asking is for you to trust me."

I was entrusted. From my family to my husband, important chief to mighty warrior. For both our families to be strong, I became my husband's. We lived together in his family home, our house at the centre of the clan's compound. Trust was a roof over my head. Trust was working in his shadow to ensure his success.

In Jean-Fi's case, trust is a hand on my cheek and a steady, unassuming gaze that asks a simple question. Don't I know him by now? The "Fi" in Jean-Fi stands for Fidel. Loyal. There is no doubt he will be, yet my claws still arch over his face.

"You *know*, don't you?"

When I woke, my husband stared back with a look of fear and awe.

"We must tell the King," he said. "He will be overjoyed to hear the lioness who saved us is so close at hand."

I shook my head, throat parched. My mouth tried to form the words for water, but my husband wrapped himself in plans to tell the King, of our future now, what this would mean for his clan. He was already so far away. He stared at me the way he gazed at a new spear.

"We'll be known as heroes," he said, lashes quivering.

"No," I coughed. I'd be known as his tool. How long before he ordered me to kill for him?

When I woke again, it was evening. The smell of meat bathed the air. I asked a servant what the occasion was. She said my husband had killed two cows, in preparation to receive an envoy of the King.

Breathing hard, I let Jean-Fi draw circles on my trembling paws. Jean-Fi who still looks at me steadily and asks, "Do you trust me?"

"You can't *know*," I sob.

"Do you trust me?"

"Don't make me do this."

The circles go round, slow and steady. In my head they form the enclosure around my husband's compound. But this is Jean-Fi, and he's only giving me a pattern to focus on, to breathe, to say I'm safe with him. Was I safe with my husband?

I shake my head. Why did I assume human form? After all these years, why did I do it again, if it only leads back to this?

Jean-Fi continues to trace circles, round and again, until his hand slows and stops.

After the fact, they said a lion tore through the warrior's compound, and the King lost all trust in that clan.

I lost all trust.

It's hours before I finally doze. I dream of Jean-Fi kneeling on a cloud of sticky ubugari. His hair is all fluff. I pluck out the lint in it while he fishes through his pocket and pulls out a scintillating ring.

"Let me see if it fits," he says.

I hold out my paw. The ring slides snugly onto one of my claws. Jean-Fi beams while my mouth swells with pride.

I wake up sobbing. No matter how you look at it, the ring doesn't fit.

Jean-Fi's hoodie is the last of the items I have to return, but I can't take it off. The tote bag I'm supposed to put it in sways on the doorframe, tied to the handle for the past week. My phone's been buzzing for the past hour.

I burrow into the hoodie's embrace. The smell of amandazi hasn't faded. I fancy myself snug in the donut's doughy centre, while the rest of me fries in heartache.

The swaying bag bangs against the door, pushed by the wind from outside. The balcony doors are wide open, their mosquito mesh creating crisscross shadows across my hand, like a net.

I meant to be free from my husband. That meant keeping my secret safe. Jean-Fi promised he will, but his arms felt like binds. I told him to let go.

Digging my fingers into the mesh, I smell the freshness beyond the rain damp. Beneath a foamy sky, engines drift past, muffled voices squeal and feet clomp through the stairwell. Sounds of moving on. My phone buzzes again.

"Jean-Fidel," I breathe.

Squeezing my throw pillow, I wonder if I'll ever call him back.

A KNIGHT IN TUNISIA

by Alex Jennings

John had spent enough time with children his own age to know he should hate this place. He hated his need to be here, but the way the sunlight fell like rain stole his heart. When he ducked to let himself out onto his bedroom balcony and the flat bright light dazzled his eyes, he felt like a traveler on the farthest shore, on the far side of a starry ocean—scarred, wounded, alive. For a moment, he'd forgotten what drove him out here: another report of a Paranorm teenager detonating like a bomb. This time, a twelve-year-old girl had violently manifested in Trieste, Italy, burning so bright that her parents' shadows had been scorched into the walls of her bedroom. She'd fled into the forest and was still out there while the Italian military decided how to respond.

It wasn't a common occurrence by any stretch, but by John's rough count, this was the third such incident in the past year, and as his Ghost Corps CO used to say, *Three make a pattern, dunnit, lah?*

He lit a cigarette for a slow drag. The constant fuzzy pain in his head receded a bit. Sooner or later, he'd have to quit these things, but nearly everyone at the clinic smoked, so kicking the habit would have to wait. Just the other day, he'd seen a brown-skinned boy standing on the street, smoking with casual familiarity. The kid had reminded John of himself at that age. Well. This kid, at least, had been born planetside instead of finding himself stranded here with Mr.—

"John?"

Behind him.

"Dad." On the knife-edge of motion, John stopped himself reacting. That was something, at least. Deliberately, he turned.

"Sorry." Like John, his father was freakishly tall—almost seven feet—with broad shoulders, light brown skin, and kinky copper hair clinging close to his scalp in waves.

"Don't worry about it."

"I didn't mean to startle you."

Even through the brain fog that ruined his telepathy, John understood layer upon layer of meaning beneath his father's apology. *You didn't sense me. You're sicker than we thought. My broken son. My amputee—*

"I'll be ready in five. I don't have to be there for another hour."

John's father wavered inside the room. He started to speak, stopped.

"What?"

"It's Thursday," he said. "You have Group in twenty minutes."

John frowned.

"What is it?"

"I don't . . . How long is that? Twenty minutes?"

"Oh. Ah. Minor-fraction, third watch."

John had been back on Earth for years. He'd followed a class schedule at school. It should have been easy to understand local time—after all, he spoke the language, passed for native. . . . No. Not passed. He *was* native.

Still, nothing made sense about the way time was reckoned here—the minutes, the hours, the seconds—all were fractions of one another, and the intervals were surprisingly regular, but John had never gotten the hang. He understood days and weeks, but months gave him trouble, as well. He knew they were more or less thirty days long, but the "more-or-less" was quite a snag. Since his . . . *illness* began, he'd lost the ability to pretend.

Like the villa, the clinic was all whitewashed concrete with blue doors and grills, and marble floors everywhere. The grass here was unlike that back in Maryland—harder, scrubbier, almost as if it had something to prove. To the north, Sidi Bou Said was mostly white and blue, but this neighborhood was greener. Here and there trees John couldn't identify boasted rioting red leaves.

He'd gone missing for a while, but Errand Boy—Jawal—was back in place at the foot of the clinic's front stairs. He was a pubescent Tunisian boy who would complete little tasks for the inmates—for the *patients,* John corrected himself—in exchange for loose bills and change. Something about the nickname bothered John. He didn't like the idea of calling the kid by a vigilante-style codename, so he'd made sure to ask for the real one.

John stopped and drew out his wallet, then stopped short. "Jesus. You okay?" he asked in French.

"Sure, why not?" Jawal said.

"Those circles under your eyes," John said. "You look like you haven't slept in a week, buddy."

"You would too if you had a faceless monster chasing you every night."

"Who says I don't?"

Jawal laughed a little. "You *do* look like I feel." He gestured at John's wallet with his chin. "Need something?"

"Ham and cheese—not from the one shop, from the next one down. Capers, no lemon, clear?"

"You think I don't remember your order?" Jawal said. "You're the only American bothered to learn my name."

"Your name's *not* Errand Boy?" John fished out a twenty and handed it over. "No change."

"Thank you, thank you," Jawal said absently in Arabic. "Can I ask you something?"

"What?"

"How is your French so good? Your father's American, too, no?"

John didn't bother thinking up a lie. "Telepathy," he said.

Jawal made a rude noise. "Funny guy," he said. "Funny, funny guy."

"Get yourself a sandwich, too," John said. "If I come out here and see you only have one for me, I'll take back all my change, understand?"

"Roger, baby, over and out!" the boy said in English.

As he ascended the long, steep stairway to the clinic's east terrace, John was surprised to find Sarge sitting at the near end of a stone bench, puffing on a Gitane. Dark-skinned and raw-boned, Sarge was the closest thing John had to a friend among the clinic's patients. He appeared no older than thirty, but during Group he'd spoken of fighting at Dunkirk, in the Boer Wars, and the Haitian Revolution. Today, he wore crisp khakis and a black-and-white camp shirt open to reveal an A-line tank top. He kept his kinky hair shaved into a high-top fade, but something in his bearing made even that hairstyle seem timeless.

Sarge's shoulder twitched, and John could tell the other man had almost saluted, then caught himself and turned the gesture into a wave. John took a seat beside him, and they sat in silence for a while.

"Almost done here," Sarge said.

John laughed softly. "Maybe you are. I'm still shit-house crazy."

Sarge didn't answer right away. "Not why you're here."

John didn't take the bait. He just shrugged.

"Ready?" Sarge asked.

"No," John said. "Nothing I say will make sense to the group."

"Might surprise you."

"People don't know," Rhetta said softly. "The littles aren't just robots. They're—They were my babies."

Usually, her face was carved into a vacant stare, but now Rhetta was present. She was a dark-skinned Black woman with red-brown hair gathered into poufs. Broad-shouldered and big-breasted, she would never have appeared on magazine covers and billboards if she hadn't begun her career battling Doktor Impostor over Norfolk, Virginia.

"The scientists say I made them up—I guess that's true, but they're *alive*. I feel it when they get hurt. He—Boss—was the first person to—to—to—*kill* one. And back then, I didn't know how to bring them back." Tears welled in her eyes and rolled down her hard high cheeks.

The room was overlarge for group therapy—it doubled as the clinic's cafeteria, serving the in-patient guests three times daily. The ceiling was high—fifteen feet, at least, and large intricately designed carpets lay on the marble floor to dampen the echoes. John imagined the room's size was a tool meant to help group members face their fear of openness literally as well as metaphorically. He sat beside Sarge in a blue wingback chair, positioned directly across from Rhetta in the circle. To his right stood a tinted glass wall with doors opening on the terrace that overlooked the lower quarter of Byrsa Hill.

He fought to pay attention—named Transistor Bettye by the press, Rhetta had been one of his childhood heroes. She'd come long after the first generation of Accidentals, but she was one of the first John had seen on TV battling Klansmen or underwater warlords along the coast.

A flutter in John's chest stole his concentration. At first, he couldn't identify the sensation, but the more he examined it, the clearer it became. It was fear—not hot or electric, like the terror that froze his heart back in his infantry days—but a quieter, sadder cousin to the same. What if he opened his mouth to speak and found he'd forgotten his English? That he knew no Earth

languages? He'd stutter and stammer to make himself understood, and the group would stare at him, hard-eyed, knowing he
wasn't one of theirs.

". . . look at me like that?" Rhetta said.

John blinked. "What?"

"Why do you look at me like that when I talk?"

"Like what?"

"Like you're *scanning*."

John shook his head. "I'm not. Couldn't if I wanted to."

Rhetta sucked her teeth, unconvinced.

Dr. Hatira let the room settle, then smiled at John. He was a fat,
barrel-chested man in his early forties, and there was something
about him John had liked the moment they met—even before he
learned the man's history as Bin Shadaad, hero of the Maghreb.
"Do you realize, John, that this is the first time you've spoken
during a group session?"

John flashed a tight smile and tried to ignore the discomfort he
felt with all eyes on him. "Ah. No. Uh. Hello."

"Please. Introduce yourself?"

"I'm John. John Kingston. I was—I was off-world a long time,
but I been back a few years now. I'm not adjusting so well, I guess.
Things are . . ." He trailed off.

He suppressed a flinch as Sarge's hand fell on his shoulder. "It's
all right."

"What was your name?" Rhetta asked. "What did they call
you?"

John swallowed. "Nuh—They didn't call me anything. I wasn't
in that life." This wasn't strictly true. During his first stint in the
mercenary army, he'd picked up the nickname Earth Boy because
he kept asking everyone about the out-of-the-way planet.

"Then why are you here?" Rhetta asked. She turned to the doctor. "Why is he here?"

"There was nowhere else," John said. Something threatened to
uncoil inside him. He pushed ahead, trying to finish speaking

before he had to withdraw into himself for safety. "I wasn't a hero; I was a soldier. I killed people. Lots of them. Probably why it's so hard to cope these days, yeah?"

Nobody laughed.

"Clinic Taofiq is not only for vigilantes," Hatira said. "We offer a refuge where Paranorms can seek healing."

"That's nice," John said. "But there's no healing from some things. Rhetta's right: I don't belong here."

Hatira's office wasn't as open as the therapy room, but it boasted its own glass wall that looked out on the Punic Ports. Every time he saw it, John thought of Hannibal routing the Romans with his imported elephants and felt a twinge of fierce and deadly joy. Hatira sat in a sunken carpeted area, waiting as John took his seat.

"Well," John said, finally.

"Would you like to talk about Group today?"

"Not at all," John said. "But fear means I'm moving in the right direction."

"That sounds very military."

"Does it?" John asked. "You never dove into a burning building to rescue people?"

"You mentioned you've taken lives. 'A lot,' you said."

"Be careful what you get good at, right?"

"You sound bitter."

"Maybe I am," John said. "But I've been dangerous a long time. A couple joggers found me in the woods near my parents' house the morning after I manifested. I guess I got out of bed and wandered out there in a haze of psionic madness. My folks wanted to keep me at home, to care for me themselves, but getting near me caused headaches, nosebleeds. My mom gutted it out and held me anyway, but nobody else could stand to get close."

"How old were you?"

"Ten."

"And when were you . . . taken?"

"A couple months after they put me in Druid Hill," John said. "I . . . broke out, I guess. Or I was in the act."

"With your telekinesis?"

"Yes. But no. Something . . . something else was happening."

"Beyond your psionics?" Hatira asked. "What was it?"

"What was your thing? What did you do?"

"The basics," Hatira said. "Speed, strength, invulnerability, flight."

"What about your prayers?"

A caught look appeared on the doctor's kindly face. "You've read about me."

"Why wouldn't I?" John asked. When interviewed by the Egyptian scientist Al Zayat, Hatira had explained that sometimes, when his powers were not enough, he was able to pray for a "miracle." That way, he could boost his strength, alter the laws of physics—he had once grown fifty feet tall to battle an ifrit outside of Douz. "A lot of us have elements of our manifestation that don't fit with our power set as we understand it. Things we shouldn't be able to do if our powers work the way we think. I can summon the Night into my hands. I never figured out a way to use it, so I would just show it off once in a while to my friends."

John's memory removed him from himself, took him to the graduation party at Pat Stegall's house. He remembered Pat steering him by his elbow into a corner of his parents' living room to stand before two girls from another school. One had olive skin and freckles, while the other had dark brown skin with a red undertone and hair that had been twisted into a braid that crowned her skull.

"Yo, show them," Pat said. "Show them the Thing."

"I don't know," John said, but he held out his left hand, palm up, and let a blot of darkness coalesce in his palm.

"Whoa!" the light-skinned girl said. "What is that?"

"It's the Night," John said. He tried to sound like a circus fortune-teller, but to his own ears he sounded more like Vincent Price in *House of Wax*. "It knows me and responds to my will." He juggled the ball of darkness from his left hand to his right and back again. "It takes no special talent. Just a willingness to . . . *listen*."

He held out both palms. This was when the splashes of darkness should have sublimed into the air. Instead, they clung to him. John frowned, shook his right hand, then his left. The Night in his right palm winked out of sight, but the patch in his left remained. He was covering well, and he knew that to his audience, he still appeared fully in control.

The Night in his left hand had begun to chill his fingers. If he couldn't get rid of it, he might have to—Acting on instinct, John brought his left hand to his face and inhaled through his nose and mouth.

A sensation of rapidly popping bubbles effervesced inside his skull. The feeling grew until it felt like light bulbs gasping, popping, against concrete.

John! John-boy. Hey! Johnny, hey! John! Hey, clownjohn! Heya! Johnnnnnnnnyyyy!

The sharp blue scent of wandfire scything through tall red grass. John sidestepped, snarled, half-turned. Patrol. This was patrol. Recon? No. He had to get his bearings, but where was that wandfire coming from? An orange-skinned native blinked up at him from the doorway to its hut. John grabbed it, one-handed, by the neck. "Where the *fuck* did that come from?"

"What?"

"Who's in the brush, motherfuck? Who's wanding at us?"

He grabbed the native's chin with his left hand, pulled it up to bare its throat. John pressed the fingers of his right hand into a fleshy knife and held it there. "Play dumb and play dead, clear?" he said. "You hostile? Think you can thwart the Empire?"

"JesusGodholyshit!"

John blinked. "Pat?"

"Please, *please* fucking let me go, John. I didn't do nothing, okay?"

The native was Pat? John blinked again, shook his head. He withdrew his hand from his friend's throat. When he let go Pat's shoulders, instead of standing, the boy dropped to his knees, breathing hard.

The music was still playing, but all eyes were trained on John. Shock stood stark on every face, on the faces of the girls he had tried to impress. He felt like a villain on *Scooby Doo*, freshly unmasked. He realized now that he hadn't spoken English when he'd threatened Patrick: he'd said everything in Vell.

"Fuck," he said. "Fuck me! I've got to . . . I've got to *go*. I'm sorry!"

He could have ducked into the kitchen and called his father, but the more distance he could put between himself and these . . . these kids, the better.

Dr. Langford, a friend of John's father, said that it had been a seizure. The morning after the party, the three of them sat on the screened-in porch drinking a pitcher of dega made from the fruit John had smuggled back to Earth.

"It's the stress," Langford said. "The breakup, the graduation, the prospect of schooling another four years at Yale. He's fine. You're fine, Youth."

John's father frowned, looked at John sidelong. "War catching up with you? Crowding your head?"

John glared. "I'm *not* fine," he said. "I could have killed my friend. I could have leveled that place. I'm coming apart, and I'm *fucking lethal*!"

"Listen," Langford said. "We infantry, we jump-men, carry war in the belly. We—"

"I wasn't Jump," John said quietly. Now the two other men watched him closely. "I was Corps."

"Fucking hell," John's father said.

Langford's bushy eyebrows rose. "Maybe you *are* dangerous."

"Ghost Corps," John's father said. "Like your uncle James." He shook his head sadly.

"There's a clinic in Tunisia," Langford said. "Paranorm only. They treat post-traumatic stress."

"The kind you get from fighting as a child in a thousand-year galactic war?" John sneered.

"Hear him out," his father said. "Let's hear him out. This might help."

"The kind from warring on crime," Langford said. "On other Paranorms."

John's head felt soft and ruined like a rotting peach. He wanted to flip the whitewashed iron table, to scream with his mind. He wondered how long he'd been coasting along the edge of his endurance. Instead of cracking the earth like an eggshell, he hung his head.

"Okay," he said. "I'll try anything."

After the session, instead of calling his father to pick him up, John caught a cab back to the villa. The driver was a neat little man with skin as dark as John's own and a fez cocked jauntily on his head. John couldn't help grinning at the cabbie, but as the scenery of Carthage scrolled by out his window—all those white, cream, and beige walls—he felt a pressure inside his skull. Was it a memory from the night he broke down, or a sensation of the present, his mind ready to hatch?

Back at the villa, John didn't feel like counting money for the fare and handed over far too many dinar. He felt wrapped in a cocoon of—sadness? Anxiety? He wasn't sure. Familiar voices drifted to him from the kitchen as John let himself inside the front door. His scalp tightened.

In the kitchen, John's father stood with his back to the bisected sink, pouring from a bottle of his prized Novan theed.

On the other side of the island, Zanne Caughlin half-stood-half-sat with one asscheek on a heavy metal stool. She wore a blue-and-white tie-dye dress that contrasted well with the brown of her skin and the crimson highlights in her box-braided hair.

"I thought you'd call," John's father said. "Wouldn't want to surprise you like this."

John grunted softly and sought a glass from the cabinet. He took the bottle from his father and poured himself a couple fingers of the hard sweet wine. He sipped without speaking or looking Zanne's way.

"Hello," she said.

John sucked his teeth.

"If you're looking for a response, 'hello' is very good," Zanne said. The tenderness in her voice made John feel like a monster.

"Hello."

He drained his glass with one swallow and blew the fumes out his nose. Then he turned on his heel and left.

Before his manifestation, before his abduction, before the war, John and Zanne had met as children. Fighting for his life on alien streets and far-flung rocks, he'd never forgotten: He'd been five and she was six, and her parents had hosted an old-fashioned garden party at their Maryland home. He'd worn his Easter clothes.

The party must have been catered—the Quinlys were well-off, but not so wealthy they could permanently employ servants. Now he thought of it, his father must have brought tech to Earth when he fled the galactic interior with his brother, sold it, the same as John had. He must be a very wealthy man.

Jamaris Howard had called John "Big Dumb," mocked his slow

deep voice, so John had called himself storming out of the party. Instead of leaving the property, he had skirted the house and found Zanne covered in mud, holding bunches of ruined flowers in both fists. Even then, her skin had a sheen to it—a red undertone that answered when the sunlight kissed it. One look at her told John everything he needed to know: She was the most beautiful person he'd ever seen, and whatever she was up to was *not* allowed.

Zanne opened her mouth and imitated John's wondering expression, but instead of shaming him, it made him picture what he must look like and laugh out loud. "Mom says stay out of the flowerbeds. . . ."

Zanne shrugged expansively and said, "I'm a farmer, though. I'm planting the corn."

"Can I help?"

Zanne nodded, suddenly deadly serious. "Gotta get this sumbitch done before the drought wipes us out," she drawled. "Get the hose!"

Three years later, as John stood with his mother beside Zanne's open casket, he watched her silent face and thought of that meeting. It was obvious to him that the puffy, shut-eyed body before him wasn't his friend. Someone had taken her away and left this waxen decoy in her place.

Every so often, John would climb onto the balcony's stone rail and stand there, deciding whether to step off. The fall wasn't far enough to be dangerous, but there was a chance that his mind would instantly summon a platform of extraphysical force to support him, and then he'd know for sure he wasn't in remission. He stood there, pretending to weigh the question, as Zanne knocked, impatient, on his bedroom door.

After a beat, she opened it without an answer and crossed out to the balcony. She looked pointedly at John's wrought-iron chair.

"Should hold you," he said reflexively. He didn't see a reason to make this easier for her.

Zanne acknowledged the gesture with a soft sniff of thanks. She sat, set the theed bottle on the table before her.

She was thickly built, but not thickly enough to betray her weight of five hundred pounds. It seemed absurd, but she was more beautiful than ever. "I'm not here to spar," she said, "but I won't be ignored."

"Sparring," John said. "Is that what it was?"

"If you didn't want me to come, you'd have left word with my mother."

John dropped silently onto the balcony floor. "Didn't think I had to," he said. "You left me."

"We're not children," she said. When they arrived on Earth in the summer of 1985, they'd been shocked to find only five years had passed since John's abduction. Time was reckoned differently in the Interior, and it seemed it must pass faster there, as well. John guessed he and Zanne were in their early twenties.

"Might as well be," John said. "We have as much to learn about life here as teenagers do. Is it anything like you remember? Because it's not like *I* remember."

She shrugged. "Not my memories. I'm a clone."

John sighed. "Slavers don't clone, Zanne. They wanted your cancer. You remember the beam. You remember being lifted to the ship." He knew enough by now not to ask her what difference it would make.

"I said I'm not here to fight," Zanne said. "It's not—I know you love me. I love you, too, but I just wasn't . . . I'm not sure who I am."

"Neither am I," John said. "Now."

"What happened?"

John explained.

"A seizure? Are you sure?"

John hated the question. Hated how many times he'd asked it

himself. "No," he said. "Telepaths usually die before adulthood, and more often than not, it's the seizures that do it."

"But."

"But what I remember most is how *exposed* I felt," he said. "Like someone turned a spotlight on me."

"Well, it's not the Empire," Zanne said. "They can't spare the resources to hunt us down. I ran into a couple of Sweepers in Singapore. They said there's been a ceasefire. Both the Empire and the Yolei have declared victory and withdrawn all forward forces."

John had to lean back against the balcony to keep from falling. Relief was a curtain that descended on him to make his blood sing. For a moment, he tried to estimate how many lives—No. It didn't bear thinking about.

"Which means," Zanne said, "that our little clique ended a timeless war."

John just looked at her. Her rounded chin, her broad nose and sharp cheeks, the clean careful lines of her clavicles.

She poured them each two fingers of theed and waited until John realized what was happening and picked his up. "Shah'leeh," she said.

"Hail," he said.

They drank.

"You know what this means?"

"What?" The more he looked at her, the less able he was to keep from grinning. Was he drunk? A little tipsy, maybe. No more.

When she looked up at him, there was no pretense in her expression. She made no effort to keep from glaring like a tiger. "We're not enemies anymore, we two."

Afterwards, John and Zanne lay together, hip to hip in his king-sized bed. Zanne didn't need sleep, but she enjoyed it. She slid effortlessly into unconsciousness, and John watched her for a little while, feeling a soft dark pull on his own mind. He considered resisting—this didn't feel like a normal urge to sleep, tired as he was, but in the end, he let go his body to descend a winding stone staircase cut into the earth. Normally, when he left his body this way, he felt his power in a cloud around him. Now, he just felt nude, but the feeling was not upsetting.

At the base of the stairs, he found a café like one in the suq— low stone benches hugged the walls and the aromas of chichia smoke and cut fruit melded into a pleasant red-brown blur. He found Errand Boy sitting at a back table, gazing into a small glass cup at the coffee residue collected in the bottom. John sat with him.

Jawal didn't look up at him. Instead, his body tensed as if he expected a blow.

Hey, John said. *It's all right.*

"It's not," Jawal said.

Whatever's after you, I'll deal with it. You're under my protection.

"Under—!" Jawal sneered, and stopped short as he got a good look at his companion. "Oh," he said. "You're one of them."

Yeah, John said. *I don't—I'm not sure my powers are working, but they're not all I have. I'm a soldier. And there are others at the clinic whose powers work just fine.*

"Are they scary like you?"

Scary?

"Your skin is pale and your face is a skull," Jawal said. "And your eyes . . ."

John cast his vision from his astral body and turned to look at himself. The boy had told the truth. His face was unnaturally pale, gaunt, and his eyes burned bright. The thing that surprised him was the halo. It bloomed in a dark nimbus around his head, afire with negative light.

With Night.

John returned to himself. *Where are you right now? Are you sleeping?*

"There's an abandoned house in La Soukra. I used the money you gave me to take a taxi here."

The thing stalking you—can you feel where it is?

"It's in Carthage, at the Tophet. I snuck in there and slept one night, and that's always where it starts looking."

The Tophet was an ancient burial ground full of infant remains. It wasn't the sort of place anyone should spend the night, but everywhere in Tunisia, the ground was full of human remains and ancient treasures.

Do you know what it wants?

"It wants to—It's trying to make me one of you."

Stay where you are unless it gets within one hundred meters. If it does, run. Help is on the way.

John sat up in bed to find Zanne pulling on a pair of tights. "Well?" she said. "Let's go."

"You know what's happening?"

"You told me before you woke," she said. "Let's get your friend."

Rain fell like a cascade of marbles, and cloud-to-cloud lightning intermittently fractured the darkened sky. John gripped the wheel of the battered Peugeot 505 his father had bought when they arrived in Tunis, pushing the engine hard as they raced down the X-2. He realized now that he didn't know what Sarge's manifestation was—whether he was up to a fight like the one in store. Of course, he'd never seen Sarge in news footage or heard of any Paranorms who fit his profile, but if his war stories were to be believed, he should do just fine.

John parked at the foot of the clinic steps and took them two at a time as Zanne blurred past. At the top of the stairs lay a circular courtyard framed by benches. At its center stood a statue of Atum, first of the current generation of superhumans.

Just as John realized he had no idea which room in the complex belonged to Sarge, he saw the man step out of a door twenty yards down the central hallway that radiated like a spoke from the courtyard. John wasn't sure why it surprised him, but Sarge wore street clothes tonight—a short-sleeved forest-green African suit and a pair of BK diamonds.

I need your help.

"Yes," Sarge said. "But there is something we must first discuss."

"You mean the fact that you're not a patient here?"

Sarge reached John and smiled. "You figured it out. Who's your friend?"

Zanne drew two fingers past her face and tapped her temple in a Yol salute. "Zanne," she said.

"You're very dense," he said. "Strength. Speed? Flight?"

"No flight," Zanne said. "But I can jump like a motherfuck."

"Beams?"

Zanne shook her head.

"And you," he said, looking back to John. "I see your psionics are working nicely."

John realized that no rain had touched him since he left the car. Without meaning to, he had teked himself a shield against it.

"I suppose they are."

"Does that disappoint you?"

"I don't have time to be disappointed," John said. "Something is hunting Jawal, trying to manifest him."

"Do you know who I am?"

"Hannibal," John said. "Hannibal Baraq."

"Yes," Sarge said. "I've known countless wars. Some were recognized by mankind, some were not. And I am here to tell you that we are entering a war unlike any you've seen. I know you're tired. Frightened. Confused by what is happening to you. But lives hang in the balance. I will fight alongside you, but you must *fight.*"

"I am," John said. "I will."

"We'll take the car," Sarge said.

"What—? How will I . . . ?"

"Fly."

John swallowed. He could levitate with the best of them, but he'd never flown unassisted. To learn hands-on—it worried him that he wasn't afraid. That he was excited.

"Go," Sarge said. "We'll communicate telepathically."

Pure Night gathered into a clot at the center of John's chest. It burned cold there, and its power was unmistakable. John seized on it with his mind, pushed it into his belly. He exploded into the air.

The power was overwhelming. John had suppressed it for so long that it rioted inside him, threatened to take over. He saw the TGM station below with its stubby segmented trains and realized he was going the wrong way. He banked right, found the N-10, and flew northwest along it, scanning for any sort of psionic disturbance. The houses below lay clustered like white and beige bricks, an array of confections meant for giant mouths. He found the disturbance near the house where Jawal had holed-up—too near.

I told you to run.

Run where? Jawal's mind was bright with terror.

Away, John thought. *Run away!*

The creature had been human, once. It had taken the body of an elderly man, returned his vitality, and pushed him beyond mortal limits. Its mind was a quiet roil, but its thoughts flowed like a river in one direction. Its focus was on Jawal, who burned like a small flame. The creature flew low above the road, which was good—if it had arced up and across the way John had, it would have reached the boy much sooner.

John turned his mind toward Zanne and Sarge in his father's car. *Contact. Humanoid, but very much empowered. You're still a mile out, so I'll engage, see if I can distract it.*

Pull it off the road, Sarge thought. *We don't want wrecks.*

Clear, John thought.

John, Zanne thought. *Be . . . be careful, okay?*

I'll do my best.

John aimed his body toward the being, and once he came close enough to see it, it appeared as a Body wrapped in a cloud of distorting energy. His mouth was open in a silent scream. John touched down lightly on the road a few yards in front of it.

"Stop," he said. "I can't let you go any further."

The creature stopped, cocked its head, sizing John up with borrowed eyes. From this close, John could smell it—the clean-laundry smell of ozone and something . . . something else. Something familiar. He felt a burning cold resistance building in his forearms. It fizzed within him the way the Night had effervesced against his skull.

"Naar?" it said.

The Arabic word for "fire."

"No," John said. "No fire."

The creature seemed to decide that this distraction was not worth its while. It took a step in John's direction. John brought his arms up in front of him and let the resistance boil over in his hands, explode in a burst of darkness.

The rain had tapered to a drizzle, but the noise of thunder was deafening. John started to look round to see where the lightning had hit, but there had been no lightning. The cold, dark energy that he'd thrown at the creature had sliced through the air, and its path had filled in with a clap.

The creature lay on its back five yards from where it had stood. A column of black smoke rose from a smoldering wound in its chest. It looked like a burn, but a cold one. Now John slipped into the dreamlike clarity he had experienced only briefly since returning to Earth. Time distorted in a sort of telescoping effect, and John felt as if he stood on both ends of a continuum, now and also-now.

When the creature sat up, a flash of recognition lit up John's mind. It didn't look like his uncle James—and it wasn't his uncle—not exactly, but it seemed to be a piece of him, of his consciousness and essence. That moment of recognition stole John's balance, and the thing caught him flat-footed, slammed him into the road with one blurred fist.

John's sternum cracked. His organs tried to flee the pain of the impact, but instantly, the Night that was all around rushed into him, healed him and more than healed. It lit him from the inside with power, with negative light. John reached through the creature's energy field to grab it by the throat. The more power the creature used, the faster its stolen body dissolved, and John knew that when it was completely gone, the creature would be powerless without a host.

So all they had to do was wear it down.

"Here!" Zanne shouted aloud.

"Engage!" John yelled back.

She grabbed the thing in a bear hug, one arm over its shoulder, the other coming up from its waist so that her hands met in a clasp. She squeezed it like a giant tube of toothpaste. The creature screamed its alarm and pain, and Zanne changed her grip. She palmed the back of its head like a basketball and drove it face-first into the asphalt.

Away from the road! Sarge reminded them. Zanne grabbed the creature by one ankle and turned like an Olympic shot-putter, hurled it westward into a vacant field. She glanced back at John, the wildness of the fight shining in her dark eyes.

Sarge drew the Peugeot to a stop in front of them and leaped from the driver's side. Zanne looked at John again, questioning with something less than a thought.

He gave the barest shrug, and Zanne rushed to the car, rolled it onto her back, then leaped hard and high.

"Sitrep," Sarge said aloud.

"It's running out of juice. We exhaust it, we win."

"Could you tell anything of its origin?"

John wasn't sure how to answer. "Maybe."

The blunt sound of crumpling metal rang out in the distance. "I cut, you blast," Sarge said. "Clear?"

"Clear."

John rocketed up from the road again, following Zanne's trajectory. By now, after crushing the creature with the car, she had seized it again, dragged it to the ground. She cradled it between her legs and with her left arm, driving her right fist into its chest over and over. She rolled out from under it as Sarge streaked toward them. Now he held a shining curved sword that he must have summoned into being. The rainy air reacted with it, as if the blade were so sharp that it sliced through the barest atoms of the atmosphere. He drove it through the creature's chest, and the body within all but dissolved.

John readied a bolt. This time instead of throwing it, he would pour it into the creature's blurred body, upping the intensity until it was all over. "Come on, motherfuck," he whispered in Vell.

"Jack-jack?" the creature said sleepily. "Zzat you . . . ?"

"Hit it!" Sarge shouted. *"Now!"*

"What's . . . Jack-jack, you wake me . . . ?"

"Fuck," John spat.

"Jack . . . nnnh—*NAAR!*"

John threw the Night-bolt, but the creature had pushed itself off Sarge's blade to stand upright. It gestured, and John sensed, rather than saw, a flash, about a mile away. "Fuck!" he shouted. "I'm sorry! He did it! I gotta get Errand Boy!"

"If you leave us to finish it, we *will* finish," Sarge called.

"Clear," John said. "Wipe it out."

He had only seconds now—minutes if he was lucky, and he knew in his bones that he wasn't. Even at a distance of several thousand feet, he could feel the change in Jawal's consciousness. Where before, he had felt tired and panicked, now his senses began to unravel. The boy had collapsed outside the mossy wall of a villa with a swimming pool. For a split second, John thought to teke him into the pool to smother the oncoming explosion, but he knew that was no good. Three sleeping minds lay inside the home, and if this explosion was anything like the ones on the news, nothing short of the sea would mitigate it.

He touched down by Jawal and gathered the boy into his arms. A sizzling sound rose from the boy's sandy skin, and his body was so hot to the touch that if John had not been powered-up, the action would have killed him. He had a dim idea that the Mediterranean lay behind him and to the left, so that was the way he headed when they left the ground.

I've got you. You're okay. You're going to be okay. You're alive and I will shield you.

A quick sharp memory of his uncle James before his death rose unbidden into John's mind. It had been some time since he considered how like the man John had grown to look. The high cheeks, the coppery-brown complexion, the heavy straight hair with the family colors—red, yellow, deep green, plaited into a long braid.

He realized now that not just his uncle, but his father, as well, were like him—Paranorms. They must be. He should have talked to his father about it directly, but now it was too late. Now he was about to die in a holocaust of a manifestation.

I don't want to—! The people! Jawal's thoughts wailed through John's mind.

We're out to sea! John called. *I think we're—Let go! You can let go now!*

Whaaaaaat about youuuuuuu!

Don't worry about me. I'll funnel the energy into the upper atmosphere.

No, Jawal thought. *No, I w—!*

John worried for a moment that his teke might have been lost as his manifestation changed. He let go of Jawal, thinking he'd need to levitate him in the air, but Jawal seemed to be doing that on his own with what must be an emerging flight power.

John thought of his old *Green Lantern* comics and whispered the Oath like a prayer. He erected a closed-bottomed cylinder of telekinetic force around the boy just as the detonation began. A spray of blood leaped from John's nostrils as his teke strained to the limit. He closed his eyes, threw back his head, and thrust his palms toward the boy. He wasn't dead yet—*!*

A pillar of pure plasma erupted into the sky, boiling the clouds away. John didn't know how he was still airborne. The thought rang over and over in his mind: *Somebody's got to do something. Somebody's got to do something. Somebody's got to do—Somebody is!*

Something dark spread from the back of John's mind. It was almost a voice. He could almost make out its—

I am Night. You are my knight and my clown. Midnight Paladin. Ask the power to survive. Claim the power of the darkest hours.

John thought of Zanne, of Sarge, of his parents and sister. Of his uncle somehow partially awakened from death. Sarge was right. This was war, and there was nothing John did better than make war. There was no choice.

Yes! Give it to me! Please!

He felt the cold dark flow through him. The moon's far side. The vastness of space. The wine-dark quiet of his father's home planet. Holding Jawal became as nothing, as holding aloft a glass of theed and letting the dark shine slant through it. John blinked, and now he sat again in a café—but this one was more Parisian than a product of the suq.

"What—? What the fuck?"

Gently, John's uncle took the glass from him and set it on the table.

"Oh, shit," John said. "I'm dead."

You aren't. You have left your body behind and crossed into Spirit.

"If you're here—that means *you're* dead after all?"

Uncle James half-shrugged. *Life and death are not as firmly divided as you might think. Not in our tradition.*

"If you were Ghost Corps, you were a Paranorm. Had to be."

Yes. Do you remember Armistice? Of the Allies?

A chill passed through John, almost as if he were on a starship again. "That was you. *You* were Armistice?"

Yes. And now you have inherited my power.

John shuddered. "Your Peace Light?"

James shook his head. *Not that. My mantle as the Warrior Priest of Osa, Qing of Night and Games.*

John shook his head, slowly, then faster. "I don't—I can't. I'm not The Guy. I'm not even a believer. The prime commandment of the Osan religion is First, Do No Harm. I've harmed so, so many. I've killed."

Osa will scour the sin from your heart. They will elevate you toward your destiny. Besides, it's too late to deny them. You've already accepted.

From here, John could see back across his entire life—even to the periods he could not remember. Cradling his prized doll, Mr. Clown, like a football as he foraged for anything edible under binary suns. Dodging wandfire and magisters on Dega City, and realizing that the Imperial Hatch was his only way out. Retired from the army and living at the theedery on Nova. Discovering that he was the spaceman son of another spaceman. That the Earth he remembered was more than a fable.

"Just tell me one thing," John said. "If I accept this, will it—will it end the pain? Will it give me control to keep from hurting anyone else?"

Yes, James said. *After a fashion. Your scars and injuries will be wiped away. But John—*

"Yeah?"

James concentrated, to make his mouth move as he spoke. "Other wounds and burdens will replace them. Osa recognized the mistake they made with me. They—You'll be immortal. Immortal in a way that I was not."

"And what's the alternative?"

As I've said: There is none left.

John shut his eyes, let the sunlight show red through his lids. He still felt the Night coiled inside him, dormant for the time being. He felt the present around him like a soap bubble, and he understood that if he chose, he could push through it in any direction, perceive any of a myriad of futures, to his past and the past before him.

He opened his eyes again to his uncle's sad and watchful gaze. "All right," he said. "Tell me about your life. Tell me everything."

THE DEVIL IS US

by Mirette Bahgat

In the 1980s, Abu-Ammar was a laborer in the Ministry of Antiquities, a digger who would take orders from his superior on where to dig and how deep, without knowing what he was digging for. Little by little, he discovered that the whole village of Ein-Saba was built over the ruins of an ancient Egyptian city; that thousands of artifacts worth billions of Egyptian pounds were buried under shabby old houses. He dreamt of becoming a digger of a different kind; the kind who would locate the digging sites, hire men to do the dirty job, build connections with the foreign antiquities collectors, and seal the deal. In a few years, his dream came true. He relied on the valuable maps he stole from the ministry's office that located potential excavation sites in the village. He was skilled in networking and securing allies in the Egyptian Ministry of Antiquities and the Tourism and Antiquities Police in return for them getting a piece of the pie. He made friends with the British and German collectors, but his most important alliance was with Sheikha Afrah. Without her, his business wouldn't have flourished the way it did; he wouldn't have been able to buy his mansion by the Nile, and the vast stretches of land, and cattle, and horses, and a deal with Satan himself.

It is believed that good jinns follow the orders of Allah, and bad jinns follow the orders of Satan. To be a masterful sorceress, one had to befriend the good jinns and appease the bad ones. Sheikha Afrah knew that only the bad jinns would take part in her affairs built on deceit and greed. Born to a single mother and an unknown father, she was thought to be the daughter of a jinn herself. Her mother was a sorceress, never been married, never seen courting a man, and never showed any signs of pregnancy, until one day she woke up with a growing belly and a sharp pain, and within a few hours she gave birth to a four-kilogram baby girl with long black hair. She called her Afrah. Sheikha Afrah had the curves of a woman, and a deep raspy voice that was thought to be of the jinn possessing her. She learnt the secrets of the craft from her mother—summoning jinns and exorcising them; preparing amulets to protect from evil spirits, and talismans to impose harm on others; reading the past, present, and future through palms, seashells, and coffee cups.

Sheikha Afrah hosted a weekly Zār ceremony in the family house she inherited from her mother in the outskirts of the village, surrounded by palm trees and corn fields. Every Friday at noon, when men went to the mosque for Friday prayers, their wives would come to Sheikha Afrah, carrying chicken, rabbits, incense, fruits, rose water, and small cloth pouches filled with strands of hair, nails, and whatnot.

Sheikha Afrah's helper would lead the women to a dimly lit big room on the ground floor. The room had a high ceiling, smelled of frankincense, and a portrait of Afrah's mother hung up on one of the pale green walls. Not long after the women got into the room, Sheikha Afrah would follow along with her disciples—a band of six women and men dressed in white *galabeyas* and carrying daf and drums. The women would sit in a circle on the floor, with the band in the middle, and as soon as Sheikha Afrah lit the incense on the far corner of the room, the drumming would begin. She would instantly identify the women in the crowd who were possessed by a jinn, approach them and ask them to rise on their feet, get into the middle of the circle, and start spinning, following the beats of the drums, and the singing of Sheikha Afrah and the band praising the Prophet and Sayedna El-Hussein and asking for their protection.

Spinning and spinning into a trance until they lose their balance and fall on the ground, pulled to their feet again, asked to step over the burning incense, while Sheikha Afrah's helper slit the throat of a pigeon and marked the foreheads and palms of possessed women with the warm blood to appease the jinns. Slowly, the drumming would fade into silence, the ecstatic women come back to their senses, feeling at peace with their jinns, and ready to go back home to their husbands.

Abu-Ammar was introduced to Sheikha Afrah by one of his helpers, a man named Ouf. He used to go to her place every week, and she would read his coffee cup and foretell what the future held for him. At the end of his visit, she would give him sacred incense, holy water, and advice on what actions to take and what to avoid during the week based on her divination.

During one of his visits, he shared some of the challenges to his business with her.

"Ya Sheikha, guide me. I've been digging for months in Al-Zaidan and Al-Barakat's land, and I couldn't locate the artifacts. Based on the maps I have, this is where the ancient cemeteries are located, but I couldn't find them, and the landowners are running out of patience, and will soon ask me to stop digging. What should I do?"

"My brother," Sheikha Afrah said, "the only ones who could help you are the jinns. They see things we don't and their knowledge is all-encompassing."

"I seek refuge in Allah from Satan the accursed. No, I never dealt with the jinns before and never will. No one is safe from their tricks."

"My brother, only the jinns could grant you the power you

desire. As long as you appease them and keep them happy, you're safe. Trust me."

"And how could I make them happy?"

"Only one thing pleases the jinns: power over the human flesh."

Just like humans, jinns ate, slept, and made love. Made out of fire and air, they could make humans soar towards the seven heavens, or burn them to ashes. They lived in an alternative realm, but if they wished to interact with humans, they manifested in different shapes and forms—sometimes an animal, sometimes a man on a stallion. When humans were touched by a jinn, their bodies weren't theirs anymore; they turned into *majnun,* with a foot in heaven, a foot in hell; one body occupied by two spirits.

Humans got possessed in two ways—they would either ask for it, to mate with the jinns, to share their superpowers and dual dimensions; or jinns forced themselves in, upon mediation of a sorcerer.

Jinns, too, desired the closeness and warmth of human flesh. Penetrating a human body put out the fire in their bellies and cooled them off. Some jinns believed that God chose to leave the heavens and made flesh in the womb of a woman because he craved the feeling of it; to be confined to a warm body with skin and blood instead of an impersonal omnipresence. As much as humans desired the infinite skies, jinns longed for the groundedness of earth.

Ikbal was a villager from Ein-Saba. Ever since she was a child, she was obsessed with stories about the prophets. She waited impatiently for the religion class at her school to hear a new story from Ms. Iman, her teacher. All the stories her teacher told were about male prophets. *Why can't I be a prophet too?* Ikbal thought. *I'd rather speak to Allah and roam from village to village preaching*

than spending my time cooking or taking care of my younger broth-
ers. The only problem is that girls can't be prophets, only men.

One day, after Ms. Iman told the story of Yacoub and his brother Esau to the class, Ikbal started having a recurring dream every night. She would dream of herself sitting on a rock under the stars, and above her, a ladder stretched from earth to heaven, and the angels of Allah were ascending and descending on it. Soon, the angels would morph into fire-like creatures that Ikbal believed to be the jinns.

When Ikbal came of age, she married Zain from the house of Al-Zaidan in Ein-Saba village. On her wedding night, after losing her virginity to Zain, she fell into a deep sleep. The dream changed that night. Only one jinn descended the ladder and sat next to Ikbal on the rock under the stars. *You've always wanted to be a prophet, Ikbal,* he told her. *Even if you were denied that right. I will give you a daughter and both of you will become prophets.*

"One of Abu-Ammar's assistants visited me today at the warehouse," Zain told Ikbal while they were having dinner.

"What for?" she asked.

"They want to dig around our house. He said there is some sort of ancient cemetery with invaluable artifacts underground."

"Well, if that's the case, why don't we find the artifacts ourselves and sell them?"

"Are you insane, woman? Do you think Abu-Ammar would let us do so? You know he's the one controlling the artifacts business in the village, besides he's a dangerous man. We're still going to get a good sum of money if they find the cemetery, and we don't have to do a thing."

"You're going to let complete strangers onto our land to dig Allah knows for how long for a few thousands of pounds? What if the police find out? We'll be in trouble."

"Look, Ikbal. The whole village knows that Abu-Ammar has the police in his pocket, they get their share of the deal as well. There is nothing to worry about. We need this money, at least to pay for the doctor's fees to get you pregnant. Isn't that what you wished for day and night for the last thirteen years, to have a baby?"

Ikbal was promised a baby, but never had one. Her recurring dream of the jinn stopped; she stopped dreaming altogether for a while. Until that night when Zain told her of Abu-Ammar's offer, the dream came back to her; this time the jinn descended the ladder with a baby girl in his hands and asked Ikbal to breastfeed her.

The next morning Ikbal woke up feeling exhilarated. She told Zain that she's ok with Abu-Ammar's request, that they should start the excavation right away.

Every night, once the village was asleep, Ouf would come with other men to Zain's house. The plan was to dig a narrow, deep trench and then expand. They couldn't use loud motor equipment, to avoid getting anyone's attention, and used shovels and hoes instead.

Four months into the excavation, nothing was found. The men were getting tired.

We have to resort to the other plan, Ouf thought to himself.

The next morning, Ouf showed up at Zain's house.

"Ikbal, good morning," Ouf said as Ikbal opened the door.

"Ouf? What brings you here at this time of the day? You usually come at night. Zain is at work."

"I know, Ikbal. I came to see you. We need you to find the artifacts. Only you could help us."

"Me? How?"

Ouf told Ikbal of Sheikha Afrah. "She's the only one who has the keys to the world of jinns in this village."

"Jinn," Ikbal said. "No way!"

"The jinns are the only ones who could help you. Sheikha Afrah is their strongest ally in the village. They will help us find our way to the artifacts. She told me that they will even help you conceive and have a baby. She knows how bad you wanted a baby. She knows everything."

"I'm scared, Ouf. Only Allah knows how much I want a baby. I've done everything I could, and I would do more, but—"

"No buts, Ikbal. Consider this an answer to your prayer. Allah must love you that much to not only grant you a baby but to give you the riches beyond your dreams. Trust me, Ikbal, there is no need to worry. I'll be with you all the way."

"I will go with you on one condition: swear on your mother's grave that if I feel scared while I'm there and ask you to leave, you will obey right away."

"Deal, Ikbal. On my mother's grave, I swear."

Ouf agreed with Ikbal to meet her at the outskirts of the village on Friday once Zain left for Friday prayers. Together, they drove to Sheikha Afrah's house. Two guards greeted them at the front gate and escorted them inside. A bulky woman in a black dress welcomed them in and offered them sweet tea.

Ikbal sat next to Ouf, clutching her purse close to her chest. She had a pouch inside with what Ouf asked her to bring: a snip of clothing from her husband's undergarments; a strand of her hair; and five hundred pounds. They also brought a cage with four pairs of male and female pigeons. After a long half hour, the woman in black invited them to follow her across a long path into a dimmed side room.

"Long time, Ouf," Sheikha Afrah said as she stepped into the room.

"Marhaba, Sheikha Afrah," Ouf said as he shook Afrah's hand. "This is Ikbal, Zain's wife from Al-Zaidan house."

"Marhaba, Sheikha Afrah," Ikbal said as she approached Afrah. Her body was stiff and cold, her face pale.

"Marhaba, sister. Ouf told me everything. Jinns are our allies, as long as we keep them happy. And I happen to know from Maalouf that you two have a special connection."

"Maalouf? I don't know anyone with that name."

Sheikha Afrah grinned. She asked Ikbal to sit next to her on a majlis red sofa facing a round copper tray table with a large incense burner. She asked Ouf to go to the kitchen and slaughter the pigeons. She took the pouch from Ikbal, opened it, and took out the strand of hair and snip of undergarment and tossed them in the incense burner while reciting prayers to summon the jinn. Sheikha Afrah placed both her hands on Ikbal's head and called the name Maalouf three times. Ikbal felt the air getting heavier and thicker with the smell of the incense. She felt her head spinning and she heard murmurs and chatters as if coming from a faraway place. She was sweating heavily and felt short of breath before she passed out.

"What happened?" Ouf asked as Ikbal slowly recovered from a short loss of consciousness. Afrah sat in the far corner of the room sipping tea.

"All I could remember was that I was having sex with an invisible creature. I couldn't see him, but I could feel his heavy breath next to me. He took my hand and led me to the digging site outside of my house back at Ein-Saba. He showed me where the cemetery lay, four hundred meters deep next to the tilted palm tree."

Maalouf was a Si'lat dwarf jinn with a dick half his size. Si'lat jinns were the smartest and most malicious breed of jinns who took different forms and shapes, usually mimicking a beautiful young woman or a good-looking man to lure humans. They lived in deserts and the belly of earth, and were made of fire, yet were able to shift to physical forms to interact with the human world.

Maalouf enjoyed controlling people's lives, giving them false hope before taking it back.

Maalouf enjoyed being with Ikbal, smelling her young skin, feeling the moistness of her insides, laughing at her shy moans when they slept together. He believed that as long as she was under the illusion that he would impregnate her, she would remain under his control. *Foolish humans and their obsessions,* he thought to himself. *Some selling their souls to have children or reconnect with the dead; others fighting over money and power or giving up everything to win the heart of those they love. If only humans knew that the devil would have no business on earth if it wasn't for their obsessions.*

"Abu-Ammar," Sheikha Afrah said, "the prince of the Si'lat jinns of the Upper Egyptian Desert visited me in my dreams last night. He requested that you pay him twenty percent of any earnings you make from selling the artifacts from now on. You can bring the money next week when you visit me."

"Do I look like a fool, Sheikha Afrah? Is it the jinns or you who want the money? I'm already paying enough, all those gifts and offerings I send you every week. What would a jinn do with all that money anyway, do they use it in the world of spirits?"

"Watch your words, Abu-Ammar. You can't play with fire without getting burned. You're the one who summoned the jinns, and now you have to pay the price."

"Over my dead body. I'm the one who summoned the jinns, and I'll be the one to expel them. I don't need them anymore." Abu-Ammar stormed out of Sheikha Afrah's house.

In the deepest hour of a long winter night, a hasty small flame rolled out of the office room where Abu-Ammar kept the ancient maps and scrolls, before it got out of control and turned into a big fire that engulfed the whole house in a few minutes. By the time the fire engines arrived, the whole mansion was in ashes, including Abu-Ammar's body.

Over the next fourteen days, thirty-three houses caught fire, all in which excavations took place. The special investigation unit couldn't find the cause of the fire. In each of the thirty-three houses, only those who mated with the jinns survived, while the bodies of their spouses and children were consumed in flames.

Ein-Saba village became known as the village of the thirty-three widows and widowers, who, with the help of the jinns, burned their families down to ashes.

After the fire, all the villagers ran away in fear for their lives, turning the once bustling village into rubble.

The fire unearthed thousands of artifacts and ancient cemeteries that lay underneath the burnt houses. Every night, at the fall of the sun, looming at a distance, were the haunting shadows of thirty-three widows and widowers dressed in black, roaming the village, one house to the next, accompanied by an army of jinns, collecting artifacts, placing them in big straw baskets on top of their heads, and heading back to Sheikha Afrah's house.

CLOUD MINE

by Timi Odueso

His dreams are filled with the smell of rain, an alluring redolence that painfully tickles his throat. The smell teases his thirst and his mind wanders to droplets sliding off smooth petals, his mind conjures the delicious aroma of petrichor, of wet earth, a forest brimming with so much green, it would take years before they could mine out all the juices from the soil. He dreams of humidity, his kaftan sticking maliciously to his skin, the air pregnant with moisture that makes his hair slick and shiny.

When the muezzin's call rings out, he wakes abruptly to find that his singlet is not even drenched in sweat. He tries to remember the smell from his dreams, he tries to remember the abundance of water he had seen, but all his mind can reel out is an image of the wells in Da'if, large crevices with raised brick borders, filled only with the echoes of dried-up rivers.

He hears a knock on the windowsill and he is thrown out of his trance. The rapping sound comes thrice, an orotund sharpness that contrasts the muezzin's silky voice.

"Dan Allah," he replies. "I'm coming, Hyelni. If you keep making that noise, the guards will hear you and then they won't let me go out."

His brown kaftan slides over his body in a quick swoop and he slides the bottle of water left at his door into his pocket; for a short moment, he considers leaving his *dadduma* behind. When the second call comes, slinking behind the first, he decides against it and picks up the prayer mat, a special one his uncle had had woven with vivid purple and grey fabrics from Kano; *Nothing but the best for you,* the Sarkin had said.

He opens the door very slowly and finds the guard gone, the passageway empty but for the candelabra dangling from the high ceiling. He turns left and moves as fast as his ten-year-old legs can carry him, turning back to check behind him every now and then. When he reaches the gate, he finds it empty too. The sky is painted a light hue of violet, its edges rimmed by a deep orange that will bloom into yellow to illuminate the world. He turns to the head of the gate and finds the image of the jar that has been molded into the wall with crisscross lines of varying shades breaching the rim. The thought excites him and he stares at the image, imagining what the full jar means for all of them, enough money to afford one for the whole town. He shudders at the thought—their town drunk on joy and water; Da'if where the sands are wet with moisture, where ablutions are performed with cool liquid running down their arms, where he can drink as much as he likes without Hyelni's scornful eyes jealously glaring at his throat as he swallows. He thinks of his uncle who has been gone for two weeks, on a trip to find a rainmaker to bring back to Da'if, and he thinks of what life will be like when the man returns with the rainmaker in tow.

Fingers wrap themselves around his mouth and he is startled back into reality by fear. He almost screams but the dainty fingers stained with swirls of henna close his throat up.

Hyelni's brittle voice fills the air around him. "Salim, were you scared?"

Salim swivels to face her, a pixie-ish girl with a heart-shaped face, kohl lining her almond eyes, her dark brown hair tied up with wool. She stands a few inches shorter than he is, but her shoulders are hoisted by a confidence he has just begun to build.

"You shouldn't be sneaking up on me like that. What if I screamed *fa*?"

"Then they'll catch us, my mother will scold me and the whole village will report to your uncle that you've been sneaking off to the mines at dawn. With a girl," she answers with her left hand askew as he quickly casts his eyes on the floor, his lips struggling from curling into a smile. In her right hands, Hyelni holds a device with a sharp-ended metal prong on one end and an open-ended horn at the other, all connected to a rectangular body with buttons on one side. White flecks of paint dot the body of the portable Cloud Mine with brown-gray of rust peeking from beneath.

He ignores her taunt and gestures that they should leave. "Why did you bring the mat?" she asks. "You know we can't go to the mosque, if they see us we won't be able to explore today."

She points in the direction of the mosque, the only place in the town with electricity other than the mines.

"I don't want my kaftan stained. All my trousers are stained with dust and I don't want washers to notice. We can sit on it while we search," he replies.

They walk past the houses in a quick haze, slowing down only when they reach the edge of town where the interlocked tracks lead to the old water mines. They walk till the tiny town of Da'if appears like a blimp in the horizon, a tiny splatter on the desert's large easel. They stop two miles from Da'if, when they reach the mine where the baobab plant they found days ago lies, where a large Cloud Mine has sunk into the sandy ground beside a large black empty water tank. They should be done with *asl*, he thinks. The guards will have returned from prayer to find the Sarkin's nephew gone, again; their eyes spending the next hours darting around the town.

He finds the empty white jerry-can where they left it, and spreads the mat down a few metres from the plant. He beckons to Hyelni and takes the portable mine from her, pushing the metal prong into the soil beside the plant, leaning hard till the whole length of the prong sinks deep in the soil. Hyelni picks up the jerry-can and places the mouth beneath the horn, before thumbing the button on the mine. The floor is illuminated in a bright red light as the horn flares up with a whirring sound that makes the ground around them vibrate.

"You never wait," Salim starts. "We should always wait till it turns blue. What's the point of putting the jerry-can there when it hasn't even found water?"

Hyelni ignores him as he collapses on the *dadduma*, stretching his legs far out so his calves sink into the sand. She looks up at the sky which has now turned a watery orange and says, "What if we doze off and water starts rushing, ehn, it'll just waste away. You're only talking like that because you rich people don't have to worry about water. That's why you can drink as many cups as you like."

Salim smiles sheepishly as she settles in beside him. "Don't worry," he says. "It's just until my uncle returns with a rainmaker. Then, everyone will have enough."

She grunts, her eyes trained on the vibrant redness of the mine. "What if he can't find one? Mallam Shafi'i says they're as rare as they're expensive," she says.

"Well, we have the money. Everyone has given enough; we've been saving up all these years, didn't you see the community jar, how full it is, Allah will reward our hard work. And it's my uncle we're talking about, the Sarkin never fails."

"What if it's not a powerful one, like the one they have in Kajuru?"

He remembers tales they've heard of the rainmaker in Kajuru, how only short drizzles that dampen the atmosphere drop from the sky, how long it takes for the rainmaker to recuperate. "Even then, it will be a blessing. Drizzle or storm, as long as it's rain, Da'if will be better for it. And my uncle went to Abeokuta for it, that's where the best rainmakers are made."

"Well, what if—"

His fingers grasp hers as he stops her. "Nothing will happen, Hyelni. The rainmaker will come and she'll bring more water than the wells of Da'if can hold."

For a short while, as their fingers are intertwined, he wonders if her chest burns too when their skin touches, he wonders if her heart vibrates like the mine.

"*It*," she replies with brows furrowed.

"What?"

"You called it *she* again. The rainmaker is an it, you must remember what Mallam Shafi'i said. We mustn't think of it as a person, it will feed off our emotions. If we give too much, it will drown us in an instant. Remember what happened to Funtua? They gave too much and it—"

"I don't think that's true, Hyelni," Salim interrupts. "How can being kind bring destruction? I think Mallam Shafi'i was just trying to scare us. The same way he scares us when he shows us that picture book of how Southern cities make their rainmakers work so well."

"He's not lying. You know Mallam Shafi'i grew up in Eko, and people say that's the biggest, most beautiful place in the world. And it's all because they treat their rainmaker the right way."

His fingers release hers and he ignores her words, thinking that perhaps there are things Mallam Shafi'i can be wrong about. He cannot imagine anyone wasting water on drowning people when they can simply wait for them to shrivel to death from thirst. He knows what his people think of rainmakers, but he finds the only difference is that rainmakers don't have to use Cloud Mines to get water since their prayers reach the heavens faster. He thinks everyone should be grateful, happy even, for a person that prayerful, a person who has direct contact with the heavens.

It is why he has taken time to clear the room adjacent to his, where he will convince his uncle to let her stay. He imagines sitting with her, what she will be like. He imagines what to teach her, if she would like to learn Hausa, if she'd explore the wells with him and Hyelni, if she'd follow him to Mallam Shafi'i's house to learn history, to learn about times when Da'if was called Zaria. His thoughts lead him down a road that steals his consciousness and he dreams that he is in one of the wells, now filled with water, swimming with Hyelni and a faceless girl as they swirl in the pool of water and laugh the aridity away.

Hyelni watches the Cloud Mine, waiting for its color to change. She imagines what shade of blue the light on the Cloud Mine will be when it finds water, a wispy light one like the sky, or a deep one, like the hues of faded henna on yellow skins? They'd been at it for almost two weeks, since the Sarkin left for Abeokuta, running off at sunrise to search for pockets of water for her family, and in all that time, the machine remained the same color. She wonders if she should ask Salim, this was his idea after all, but one look at him, eyes closed with a smile on his face, and she decides against it; she lets him stay that way, asleep, till the sun is directly overhead, biting hard. She prods him awake and he opens his eyes to find that the horn is the same shade of maroon. "We have to go," she announces. "It's past noon and I have chores before I can come to the Islammiyya. I almost got in trouble last time we stayed late."

"We'll try again tomorrow," he says, digging out the mine. "There's a plant here so there's surely water somewhere close by."

They walk back in silence till Da'if looms in the distance, knowing that speaking will permit the sun to lap up what little saliva their tongue creates. The image hits them before they realize what it means for their thirst. They had read of clouds in Mallam Shafi'i's books; they had seen illustrations on Cloud Mines, ashen silhouettes that looked like misshapen balls of *gullisuwa*. They'd even seen clouds once or twice, the light fluffs floating lazily across the sky as people trooped out of their houses to watch traffickers siphon away what little water was stored inside. They had never seen anything like this though, the clouds they'd seen were white, almost diaphanous, and his uncle always said they were weak clouds: "Those ones can't fill a single jerry-can even." The ones over Da'if, now, crackle with energy, lightning bolts zipping in between the swirls as if in a race. They are the color of henna, the color of his own skin, a deep blue black that excites and scares them.

Salim breaks into a sprint towards the violent dark clouds that now settle over Da'if.

"Your uncle must be back with it," comes Hyelni, who follows in the rapid dents his feet make in the sand. He doesn't reply, he can only imagine the town, the people drawing out several containers in anticipation of the rain; black drums that haven't seen water in years, clay pots molded by old hands, jerry-cans with their mouths wide open. He imagines the happiness on their faces, he imagines the rainmaker too, watching them happily as her prayers call thunder and lightning to suck clouds down onto the earth. They reach the edge the same moment the rumbling begins, the sky making sounds like a large man with indigestion, the air filled with shouts of the people as they wait in anticipation. They find no one in their homes and their feet trail the roads to the mosque where the people have gathered in a circle, eyes wide opened, mouths chattering at the promise of rain. Everything is as he thought it would be. He hears Hyelni calling his name as they breach the crowd but his excitement sidelines his loyalty. He pushes through the people who are tightly packed in the circle, dodging swaying hips and diving to avoid swinging arms. He hears ululations, *Alhamdullilahi*s and *Masha Allah*s ringing out from space he manages to squeeze into. This is perfect, he thinks. Da'if will finally be a perfect town: prayerful people, a booming trade and now, modifiable weather, all with his uncle leading them.

His imagination is broken when he reaches the middle. The rainmaker's skin is an ashy teak with lines mapped across her skin the shapes of swirls and waves; her hair is electric, a light blue that gleams with the sharpness reserved for whetted blades. His eyes find hers, upturned holes with irises matching the clouds above them, eyes that hold more water in them than he has ever seen, eyes that burn the rest of his happiness away and bury fear into him. Whips bite into the rainmaker's skin and the chains wrapped tightly around her jingle in symphony with her cries. The music she makes—the jangling of her chains, the thunderous blaring of her cries—are smothered by the people's excitement.

Salim turns away and finds the Sarkin beside him. His uncle wears a yellow babanriga, the rims of its edges embroidered in white. "Where were you?" the man shouts with a smile. "We've been back awhile. The guards tell me you've been frolicking around with some girl, eh?"

Salim watches his uncle's gleaming eyes, the curve around the edges of his lips, his nose twitching with amusement at his nephew's escapades. The boy points to the rainmaker, shuddering from the fear welling up inside. "Why?" he asks.

"What?!" his uncle yells.

"Why?!" he repeats as loudly as he can. The crowd still roars around them and the jangling melody of the chains lends an air of festivity to the event.

The Sarkin takes Salim's hands in his and leads him out. The people part like sand flecks being washed away by a pulse of water. The two walk till the sounds are dim, till he hears the jangles no more, till the shouts are like murmurs from an angry people.

"But Mallam Shafi'i should have taught you this. You know rainmakers, they're like flames, Salim," the Sarkin says. "You feed them only what they need to survive or they'll burn everything to the ground."

"But you're not feeding her anything. You're whipping her as if she's one of the cows. How will she give us water now when you're being wicked to her?"

His uncle laughs and squeezes his hands tight. "There are ways of making people do whatever you want them to do. And for rainmakers, it really isn't a choice, they have to let it all out or it'll drown them from within. It looks like we're being cruel to her, I know, but we're really helping her."

"But—"

"Aren't you happy for us?" his uncle says with a darker tone. "Do you think that Eko got to where it is by feeding its rainmaker milk and honey, ehn? Do you know how much more successful Kajuru can be if they flicked their whips at that sorry excuse once in a while? I've been to Eko, Salim. I've seen just how prosperous our people can be. We can be bigger than Kajuru, we can be the Eko of the North. Don't you want that for us? Don't you want to see your people smile?"

Salim keeps mute as his uncle takes a different route. "This is good for you too, you know. Just imagine how big the herd will grow when the harvest starts to flourish. Your friend, Hyelni, will stop fighting you because she'll have water to drink. I'll also be able to take you on my trips since we'll have enough water to last us the journey. I can buy you anything you want from Kajuru, or Eko. And when people start coming to trade with us instead of going to Kajuru, we may even find something very special you'll like."

Salim watches his uncle's eyes, the humourous gleam replaced with furrowed brows, the curves at the edges of his lips now turned downward. "Don't worry," his uncle says. "I'll tell Mallam Shafi'i to revisit lessons on the rainmakers. Now that we have a live one, he can even give you examples. He's the most experienced with rainmakers so he'll be leading its training. I'll make sure he lets you participate so you can learn firsthand."

That night, Da'if rejoices as the darkened sky releases a torrent of tears. When the muezzin calls for prayers, they do not perform tayammum, they opt for wudu instead. For the first time, everyone ablutes with water, discarding their limestone sponges and cleansing their arms, their faces, their ankles with water as they troop into the mosques. The people fill their tubs with water and soak in them, the children dance in the rain and stomp into puddles. Everyone is brightened by the lightning zipping across the sky but Salim's fear is fed by the colors of uncertainty that raindrops paint on his face. In his dreams, later, he is in the well with the rainmaker again; Hyelni is gone, and so is laughter. He can see her face now, her dark blue eyes, her sky-blue hair, the tattoos dancing across her skin like birds in the sky. They swirl in the pool, round and round in a tiny circle till the waves push him downwards, till all he sees are the rainmaker's eyes looking down on him as he sinks to the bottom.

RULER OF THE REAR GUARD

by Maurice Broaddus

The cold stone of what remained of the ledge of a window of a slave dungeon chilled Sylvonne Butcher. The previous night she'd had a nightmare, having fallen asleep in the same clothes she'd traveled from the United States in and collapsed on the bed as soon as her host family showed her where it was. Only snippets of images from her nightmare remained. The leering faces. The claustrophobic swell of bodies pressing in on her, lost in a forest whose trees moved to block her way. By the morning, the only thing left behind was the lingering fear. Which she thought she had left behind in America.

The world of Ghana, however, was a dream. Endless skies dotted with patches of clouds stretched above her. A series of drones flew by in a patrol. One hovered overhead. She held up two fingers in a V to bid it "Deuces" and it departed. Sipping lamugin, the bite of lemony ginger soothed her while she listened to the birds. The breeze was a velvet finger caressing her face, though she was happy not to have to wear a rebreather mask like she did in Indianapolis. The oxygenators covered her entire face and she resented how it clutched to her mouth even though she needed its protection against the hazy quality of her hometown's air. Environmental collapse had taken a toll in a lot of western countries, but not here.

The Castelo de São Jorge da Mina was originally constructed in 1481 and later rechristened Elmina Castle. There was a heavy spirit about the place. A powerful presence, the call of many souls crying out for home. Lost and searching. The sensation dogged her steps as she walked back to the house of the Pan-African Co-ordination Committee host family who sponsored her. The whole family had awoken to greet her when she first stirred from her rest before they scurried off to work, leaving her in the hands of the oldest son.

"Good morning." Kobla Annan bowed, the sleeves of his white tunic stamped with indigo Adinkra symbols. Taking her glass from her, he offered her a bowl of Hausa kooko, a spicy millet porridge, and maasa, a pile of maize fritters. The family shared what they had with enthusiasm, rising to attend to her before she even knew what to ask for. "We're honored to have a student from the Thmei Academy with us."

"The honor is all mine, believe me. Thank you for hosting me. It's very generous of you." She waved him off. The idea of people going so far out of their way for her put her on edge. She couldn't help but feel like she was imposing.

"Aren't you hungry? If it's the food you don't like, we have a Burger King in the city." Though she also detected a mirthful sarcasm to his tone, he smiled enthusiastically, trying to be helpful. "And a KFC! To comfort a delicate palate that's attempting to ac-climate."

The words still had a bit of a sting to them. Sylvonne turned off her reflex to not be her full self. That ingrained way of cutting off part of who she was to make another culture comfortable. Too often that wasn't reciprocated, with that culture never giving two thoughts about her comfort. Here, she was a repatriate, returning to her ancestral home, moving forward through—not just away from—her problems.

Relenting to his overwhelming hospitality, she scooted her chair to the table. She blew on the first bite of the porridge, an excuse to bring the food closer to her nose, before chancing a bit of it. She canted her head in approval. "You seem awfully young to be part of the PACC."

"Father always says, 'If you're old enough to form a sentence, you're old enough to speak out.'" Kobla straddled the chair across from her. "Besides, you're not much older."

"A few years makes all the difference at our age." She waved a fritter about, using it as a pointer between bites. "Your English is . . . elegant."

"We haven't employed our systems AI as universal translators. We're still, how do you say, old school in that way. In Wagadu, we speak English as a courtesy. I also speak Akan, Yoruba, and am working on Wolof." Kobla's generation kept referring to Ghana as Wagadu. "My father speaks Ewe, Swahili, and enough Kikongo to do business. What about you?"

"I speak American." Sylvonne tapped her chin in consideration. "And hood."

Kobla threw his head back in laughter. "So, Miss Sylvonne Butcher, I know you have only been here a day, but I was curious: What gift do you have to offer the community?"

"That's not exactly a small-talk question," Sylvonne said over a mouthful of fritter.

"I leave small talk for small people. I'm interested in you." Kobla leaned forward like a proctor taking keen interest in his test questions. "What brings you to us? What are your talents and passions?"

"I don't know." Wondering if the PACC onboarding family thought the screening interview might go easier with someone closer to her age, Sylvonne started to form a better follow-up response. Something along the lines of wanting to live a life in service to a cause, to make the world a better place, but all of that felt pat and almost being disingenuous. Taking stock of herself, she couldn't list any discernable talent or skill. She only knew that she would suffocate in America, literally and figuratively. But also that something called her here. None of which meant she necessarily had anything to offer. All she knew was that she needed time to figure out what she wanted to do and who she wanted to be. "There's a greater conversation going on between Alkebulan and the Diaspora and I'm trying to find my place in it. I guess all I have to offer is just me. Is that okay?"

"That's a great answer." Kobla directed the kitchen bots to clear the dishes.

"I need to get to my orientation." Sylvonne dabbed her mouth with her napkin, tossing it in the empty bowl before a bot skittered away with it. "Maybe I'll have a better answer later."

Kobla bit into the last fritter. "Maybe tomorrow."

Jammed full of people, the tro tro was a brightly colored maglev train which snaked its way from Elmina to Accra. Not too long ago, she'd have ridden in a rust bucket on wheels that had no business running, a minibus taxi that rattled to a halt at each bus stop along its route. Though even as it sped along, it wasn't like there were scheduled arrival and departure times, so Sylvonne was quickly adapting to no longer being married to her clock. As people held on to straps or overhead bars, the mate wove about and under musty armpits collecting fares. Sylvonne let him know she was heading to the Marcus Garvey Guest House. Glancing her up and down, he already understood her story and smiled.

The trip would take a half hour, but a vague unease filled her at the thought of nodding off to pass the time. Sylvonne's mother was born in Jamaica. Watching the scenery roll by, the winding trip of the tro tro reminded her of her mother's stories of the bus rides through their hills. Whipping through traffic and pedestrians, skirting the cliffs' edge, moving at breakneck speeds. Her mother also told tales of the fierce Maroon tribe who fought off the British and kept their cities out of the hands of colonizers. Theirs was a storied history, a proud past. Meeting the man who would become her father, her mom left her home for love. Sylvonne fled hers for freedom.

The tro tro crawled into its station. Hawkers passed by with water and juice for sale, the exchanges happening through the open window. The mate called out, "W.E.B. DuBois Memorial Centre for Pan African Culture."

"Bus stop!" Sylvonne yelled in response. She was picking up the customs quickly.

Accra was different than she imagined. She tired of the constant stress of LWB in America. Living While Black. The threat— that horror of existential ache—of the endless monochromatic aggression. So she set out to find something new. Stalls filled the open-air market, with red, yellow, or green disks spinning above each one, both fan and canopy. The smells of cooked meat or grilled vegetables caused her belly to rumble despite her breakfast. Musicians played while spontaneous dancing broke out if the spirit moved the people. The crowd pressed in all about her without them producing the sense of dread which had been coloring her feelings lately. Sylvonne loved seeing the black people on billboards, families, couples, just vibing and being. The smiling faces of random people passing her. In her mind, any place in the continent meant safaris, beaches, and potbellied children. All tribal clothes and no modern buildings. No air conditioning, just endless hot. She'd been made to think, conditioned to be ashamed of the African part of her.

Even as she walked about, her hair was done in a twist out with a flat twist in the front, yet no one wanted her to straighten it, make it more professional, or tried to touch it. A gold disc with a matching hoop drop dangled from her ear. Sunglasses covered most of her face, the tint filtering the world through her already unrealistic lens. She was surrounded by people who looked like her. Who didn't want her to become part of their assimilation construct. Who could provide her with a sense of authentic, black belonging.

As she milled about the market, she had a feeling she was being followed. Ghana wasn't perfect. Among the milling folks were Sons of Br'er Nansi, ready to "chop your money" and separate wallets from tourists. But she wasn't a tourist. She was a student of the Thmei Academy on a pilgrimage. She activated her wristband to display her orientation message; the letters scrolled by, a reassurance to occupy her as she walked.

PACC Wants You!

- *In 2019, Ghana called for the return of the African Diaspora.*
- *The year marked the 400th anniversary of the Dutch ship White Lion arriving in Jamestown in what would become Virginia.*
- *The beginning of the holocaust known as the Maafa.*
- *The delegates from the Pan-African Coordination Committee (PACC) have called to continue that homecoming conversation.*
- *PACC wants further collaboration between the countries on the African continent as well as the communities of the Diaspora.*

PACC rolled out a pathway to citizenship and a "Right to Abode Law" which allowed the Diaspora to settle, all towards building a strong, unified Alkebulan. What the brochures never explained was how the political winds fomented by the militias of ARM, the American Renaissance Movement—which sprang up like weeds in the United States—complicated such journeys. Listening to their rhetoric, they said the wrong parts out loud: They didn't want black people, but they didn't want to lose them either. Their compromise was to make it harder and harder for them to leave. However, Sylvonne was determined to claim her birthright, her heritage.

The W.E.B. DuBois Memorial Centre for Pan African Culture consisted of four buildings: his home, an administrative building, the Marcus Garvey Guest House, and his tomb. Hard light constructs allowed her to interact with him, like a movie projection she could walk into. Snippets of him and Marcus Garvey, AI re-creating them as holograms. She stopped at the statue, a bust the size of W. E. B. DuBois.

"Pan-Africanism equals community. A shared story against the negativity of racial caste supremacy. We were once fierce and noble warriors. Now too many don't like to rock the boat. Too many stand ready to run home and hide in a cupboard rather than fight for their rights." Wrapped in black-and-gold kente cloth—with a matching stole—a tall man whose belly jiggled as he moved sidled up to her. He had the regal waft of privilege about him. A carefully trimmed close beard—his edges were clean and tight—though his face had the doughy quality of having been pampered for decades. "I'm Safo Atakora Asantehene, a board chief of the Bureau of State Acquisitions."

"I'm Sylvonne Butcher." She hated her name, finding the portmanteau of Sylvia and Yvonne—her grandmothers—more than a little cheesy. She also loved her name, with it being both unique and tying her to the family she knew. "I'm a black woman on sabbatical."

"There are no black people here." His lips peeled back to reveal rows of bleached white teeth, an affectation of his wealth. "We know who we are. Igbo. Akan. Ewe. And so on."

"If I'm not black, what am I?" She bristled. Too often she ran into those who questioned her blackness, her commitment to The Cause, because she didn't talk, act, or dress the way others defined blackness.

"You have had a lifetime being taught the illogic of race. You may spend a lifetime unlearning it. There was no such thing as Africa until Europeans showed up, either. Just imperial powers using the cover of wars for their land grabs, assuming control of Alkebulan history."

"Yes." Sylvonne stopped him before he asked. She was equally used to these kinds of insulting "black quizzes" to prove she was authentic. "What we named our continent. 'The Mother of Mankind.'"

"Exactly. Those powers not only changed our names, but they carved up the motherland according to a geography which matched their interests. Whenever they need to rebuild their economy, they do what they have always done: turn to us. Our mineral and agricultural wealth. Removing our chieftains and kings in favor of more . . . progressive forms of government under their control."

"Seriously, y'all need to work on your small talk. Maybe ease a sister into this." She took a step back in case he erupted in a case of full-blown Hotep. Or whatever the Alkebulan equivalent was.

"We don't have time to ease. We dare to dream. Big. If we are to forge a new African community, a United Empires of Africa—if we want to build a new world—we have to have a new way of doing things. We need to promote unity, cooperation, and action. Getting people to want to do what must be done. We must be prepared to defend ourselves because imperialism always finds its way to us."

"What would you have me do?"

"Relationships and time are critical to the work moving forward. It's important to know yourself. It's important to know your identity." A masked woman appeared, her robes fluttering with each step. Her wood headdress was carved into the image of a face, the nostrils pierced for her to see out of, though the nose shadowed her eyes. Bird's wings—an African gray parrot—formed the superstructure of the mask rising across either side of it to create a perch for the bowl cradled in it. Her hair a crown of long, gray braids. "Quit bending the poor child's ear, Safo."

"I was just making, uh, small talk until you arrived." Safo bowed, a stiff, awkward thing, stepping away from Sylvonne in the same movement. "How went your survey of the United States, Elder of the Night?"

"As always, the West views us with a mix of horror and disdain," she sniffed.

"And sympathy. Never forget they are always sympathetic."

"It's easier to do that than wrestle with this being a problem they are responsible for. Allow me to introduce myself to the girl." The mask turned away from him.

Dismissed, Safo scuttled toward the administrative building without another word.

"Men. Always so transactional. They see everyone as opportunities for weapons or wealth. The ways of our oppressors so deeply ingrained in them." The woman extended her hand. "You must forgive our security chief."

Sylvonne hesitated, but accepted her proffered hand. "Who are you?"

"That is the question you are asking yourself."

The woman brought her hands together. The dangling sleeves of her robe formed a curtain when they met. "I am the Ban mu Kyidomhene."

"That sounds more like a title than a name."

"It means 'Ruler of the Rear Guard.' It has become my name. The name I have chosen."

"What's with the mask?"

"We all wear masks. At least mine is visible."

"Are you my mentor?"

"That is the question before us both. I answered your call. Come, walk with me." Her arm swept in a direction for Sylvonne to lead.

The maze-like structure reminded her of a labyrinth. A winding path through a garden gilded with bright flowers; their placement had the intentionality of design behind it, a sculpture of petals. As they strolled, they passed through several gates. A calm settled into her, pieces of her slipping into place, but she still knew that something was missing. A fragment that her mind, her body, her soul, whatever that part of her was, didn't have the tools to recognize what was absent. Her mother often regaled her—mostly unwanted intrusions on early Saturday mornings as Sylvonne was trying to sleep—with stories of rising before sunrise to walk to the caves a few miles from her house to collect the water they would need for the day. She hung clothes on the line to dry long after the family could afford a washer and dryer simply because those were the old ways her mother knew. Sylvonne didn't know why that memory sprang so fully to mind right then.

"Where are we going?" Sylvonne slowed to make sure her pace matched the woman's.

"You can't know until you get there."

"*It's not where you're from, it's where you're at.*"

"What?" The Ban mu Kyidomhene faced her.

"I was quoting Eric B. and Rakim. It sounded just as vaguely deep without meaning anything. I figured that was what we were doing."

"You're so . . . American." She said the word without heat of insult.

The path forked. The Ban mu Kyidomhene paused, waiting for Sylvonne to choose the direction. She went left. Loud birds chirred from the bushes. Sylvonne felt it again: the palpable sensation of authentic, black belonging. She didn't know how else to describe it. Give her that feeling that she was important. That she mattered. This was how it felt to be among her own people. Welcomed. She had come home. She knew it in her bones, the deep ancestral call in her soul. It hadn't always been this way. Her people fought and survived for her to return here. She wanted to keep it safe.

"Safo called you an Elder of the Night. That have anything to do with the mask?"

"I am of the order of the Iyami Aje. Both are titles of respect for a woman considered to be Aje, one who wields the power of womanhood. The Gelede mask symbolizes our society. Some even hold festivals to honor us, thankful for our protection and support."

"What power of womanhood?"

"To understand that you have to know our story. It is old, starting with Odu, the creator of the Universe and all that thrives in it. The only female among the three other male divinities. The other gods tried to create the world but failed. Only when they included her could the world be formed, since creation, child-birth, and protection was mostly the domain of women. From her, the womb of all origins, the life force breathed into all things and with a single oracular utterance—'Ase' the power to command, 'So be it'—created existence. 'Aje' became the word for us. A feared and revered term which our oppressors translated as 'witch' to demonize us. We are the creators and sustainers of life. Sometimes the destroyers."

"Destruction sounds like people ought to be scared of you."

"Destruction isn't always bad. Some things must be destroyed to be birthed on higher ground. That said, a mother is the guardian and protector of earth."

"So you have real . . ." Sylvonne's voice trailed off as her mind scrambled for the right word.

". . . magic?"

"No." She settled on a different one. "Power."

"Power is easy." The Ban mu Kyidomhene unclasped her hands. She waggled her fingers in a complex pattern. Light without heat trailed her fingers in a rainbow afterimage. When she closed her fingers into a fist, the light became a ball. She shoved it into the air. It dissipated in the sunlight above them. "I draw my power from the spirit of Nehanda, a mhondoro. A powerful and revered ancestral spirit. Her name means 'The beautiful one has arrived.' Mhondoro are particularly revered because they help people interpret the wishes and desire of our creator."

"What was that, a hologram? Activated by gestures, like keying in a program using sign language?"

"Our technology has come far. However, science is but diluted magic."

"Magic, huh?" Sylvonne rolled her eyes.

"You cannot give what you do not have. You cannot speak on what you do not know and have never been taught. According to our elders, the Iyami are neutral forces. They can work for the positive or the negative."

"Is this what I'm to become? Is there some sort of initiation?"

"No, my little, lost tourist."

"I'm not a tourist." Sylvonne spat the words out like a curse. "It's just . . ."

". . . a story."

"What?"

"Tell me the story. Of what made you uproot your life and come halfway across the planet in search of . . ."

"Home." Sylvonne slowed down. "My father born and raised on the east side of Indianapolis, where not even an ARM militia member was bold enough to set foot. But gentrification is the new colonization. ARM-backed politicians talked about his neighborhood like it was some savage wasteland, the streets turned over to animals. Neglecting the part of the story about the local government allowing the militia to cordon it off, set up checkpoints to detain citizens. It was easier to call us lazy and declare 'This is bad neighborhood.'"

The Ban mu Kyidomhene swayed back and forth, a reed caught up in an unfelt breeze. Though she produced no sound, Sylvonne had the distinct impression that she was humming. Or perhaps chanting.

"One day the sun set earlier than I expected. It was sometimes hard to tell what was encroaching night and what was pollution choking out light. These days we treated every town like it was a sundown town. Despite the empty storefronts, residents who took flight to suburbs, and the businesses who followed them and police and militia left behind them, everyone sang the same song. Spreading the myth of how well everyone got along. But we knew. We understood that we could pass through the streets by day—work and shop, certainly hand them our dollars—but had to be off them by nightfall. Otherwise, we risked being detained, arrested, beat, or . . . worse."

The Ban mu Kyidomhene wriggled her fingers. The surrounding

bushes faded to black. Sylvonne was no longer sure she was on the path, but she kept walking, taking each step in faith.

"They caught me slipping. Only a few blocks from my house, my porch literally in sight, an ARM militia rolled up on me without warning. The men hopped down from their truck. An American flag, frayed from how it whipped about in the wind when they drove, dangled from the back. The men surrounded me."

With a fluid movement, the Ban mu Kyidomhene gestured. The drape of her sleeves a curtain drawing back. Sylvonne found herself surrounded by the men of ARM. A man in a baseball cap whose message she couldn't make out extinguished a cigarette under his heel before approaching her. His eyes full of anger and resentment.

"Their leader asked me if I was lost. When I told him 'no,' he demanded my identification, proof that I belonged there. They closed in on me, their bodies pressing so close I could smell the beer on their breath, the aroma of cigarette smoke bleaching their clothing. And the rush of authority they were drunk on. All eyes leering at me. No safety in any of them to ask for help. To trust that they had my best interest in mind, if I was a person in their minds at all. They could stop me on a whim. Corrupt police, judge, and law could remove me from my family. Their leader snapped my wallet shut and handed it back to me. Letting me know that they knew where I lived and I'd best make my way there directly if I knew what was good for me. That I'd do well to remember my place."

The Ban mu Kyidomhene raised her arm and lowered it again. When her improvised curtain fell, Sylvonne as a little girl stood there. Alone. Scared. Clutching a blanket desperately wrapped about her like a totemic shield against the harsh cold of night. Lost, unable to find her father. Unable to hear the stories of her mother. Untethered in the world.

"And I broke. I was tired of my body being weaponized against me. I didn't want my children to have to worry about looking over their shoulder worrying about the police or militias. I never wanted to be powerless again. So I quit."

The Ban mu Kyidomhene dropped her arms. Daylight chased away the darkness. "Your job?"

"No, the US."

"You quit the country? Can you do that?"

"I'm not sure. But I did."

"If you do not listen, you will feel! If you don't listen, life will teach you." The Ban mu Kyidomhene laughed, a sad, rueful thing. But she had stopped walking. Sylvonne studied the surrounding topiary. They were at the center of the labyrinth. A stone waterfall bubbled at the crossroads of several paths. "What would you do, what would you have done, if you'd had the power?"

"I would keep them from us." Sylvonne tapped her chin. "I don't know, been a shield somehow. Keeping them away from our neighborhood. Us."

"They are always coming after us."

"That's why I left."

"What makes you think coming here will help?"

"They can't reach me here."

"Really? How did you and your people get 'there' in the first place? They'll always come for us. The question is what are you going to do about it?"

"I need to . . ."

The Ban mu Kyidomhene held up her hand to stop her. "There's the flaw in your strategy already."

Sylvonne reflected on her choice of the words. "We?"

The Ban mu Kyidomhene nodded.

"*We* need to become strong."

"*We* cannot compete with the West on their terms. They have a devouring serpent at their hands. A long, writhing army with nuclear missiles for fangs. So how do we do that?"

"I don't know." In her heart, Sylvonne just wanted to be able to laugh, dap folks up, and simply . . . exist. Without being seen as a threat. It was why she wished to return to where her people originated. "It's just, it's important to know where we came from. Find our roots. Find our history. Gain the sense of confidence that comes from being with those who share your story. That's what I want to join in on."

"Iyami choose who they want."

The Ban mu Kyidomhene filled a pot with water from the fountain creche. "Not all women are prepared for such a journey. Few have the discipline or moral aptitude to walk the path. We Iyami Aje each have our own approach. These healing waters symbolize the primordial waters that protected every child in the womb. A mother is the first teacher. The first person you look upon when you are born." The Ban mu Kyidomhene poured a bowlful of water over Sylvonne. As the girl shivered, the Ban mu Kyidomhene refilled the bowl again, reciting words like an oath. "A mother experienced pain and a near-death experience in order to give us life. This is your inheritance. You are worth everything. Take the first step into being your full self."

A subtle agitation fluttered in Sylvonne's spirit. She felt whole, herself for the first time in a long time. "I need here. And here needs me."

"You have spoken a deeper truth. You have earned my face." With that, the Ban mu Kyidomhene lifted her mask. The woman's high cheekbones and wide nose gave her a regal bearing. Markings had been painted under her eye, almost like it could see into many realms and hearts. "One of the first things those on such a path often do is choose a new name for yourself. It is a promise you make to the creator, the story of yourself you present to the world."

Stories began, but they never truly ended. They simply went on, passed down from one generation to the next. Sometimes they wound back to their beginnings. Sylvonne studied the sky. The bright sun removed the chill from her bones. "Maybe tomorrow."

PEELING TIME (DELUXE EDITION)

by Tlotlo Tsamaase

[Intro: Anonymous Girl]
♪♫ **"My Religion" (Ft. GBV)** ♪♫

Ay-ay, yo.
Yeah, yeah, yeah.
The corpse of her voice hangs from the murdered legacy tree exhumed from the placenta of her being. *I am a proper woman,* she sings. The burning tree blazes in the dark, the floor made of dark, the ceiling made of dark, the air—there is no air.

Severed organs and limbs crawl from various distances to join her abdomen. No jury. Court in the bundus. Seven men in the audience. It's a tie-reduction function, *we so fitted.* Spotlight on this—*hashtag* me, brah—campaign. Runway show. *Girl, slay, slay, slay*—off-screen voices chant.

Kwaito rises from the grave; the killer's marionette, a woman, devoid of color, hobbles forward; her dismembered limbs attached by invisible senseless tendons are tugged as she bends and sways—*we good, my ho's got some sick moves*—and when she dips forward for the vosho dance her head rolls to the ground—*woo, woo, bag her, gonna bag her.*

A choir of women march behind her, toyi-toying, as the dead body dances, becomes a viral dance challenge, sparking further outrage. A judge comes in doing the kwassa kwassa, gavel in hand, moonwalks by the choir of women. Taps one, announces, "Twenty-year-old girl. Only worth two years in prison. Going once, going twice—gone to the killer brother in the back." *This how we do it, teach 'em a lesson. Girl slay, slay, slay.* The killer brother stalks her with a machete, drags the twenty-year-old off-screen, her screams a good five-octave—

[GBV]

Abide. Shut up. Fuck off. Bitch. Stop overreacting. Shut up, woo! The dead victim watches, unperturbed by the Klaxon of her voice flickering, spitting ash, burning, singing as it burns:

I am a proper woman.
I am proper Black.
I am proper African.
This is my religion, he is my sermon: the brother, the son, the father, the grandfather. My roots tethered, burned for their lungs. I am a proper woman. My voice is my only freedom, bleached, burned, stomped, slaughtered, hacked by the day, the week, the century—

A horrifying sweetness. A chyron ends the night.

And the scene freezes, splices itself, extrudes itself from inside a cranium, outside the galloping brown eyes of a woman, as we dolly-zoom from her face to the outside harrowing dimensions of the four boundary walls of a twenty-seven-inch screen.

Across from it, a twenty-seven-year-old man, Motsumi, slouches in his ergonomic chair, finishes editing the last frame of the dream-song to upload later and send to his associates; the fiery hands of the voice, trying to strangle him, are a neon-saturated flare on his monitor, trapped. Before, ten hours of work in a day produced only one minute of animation. But it's now only taken five hours to produce 50 percent of the film. He re-plays the song. Again. Again. *The judge carries a newborn into the same grave, takes the time from her body, gives it to a sixty-year-old man, then his gavel knocks the nail into the coffin of her torso.* Motsumi stares at the screen. He needs more women. More . . .

BEFORE
[Pre-chorus: Motsumi]
♪♫"Broke-Ass N*gga" ♪♫

The stress was homicidal. Critic reviews murdered his film direction/rapping career: the plot watery, the narrative nonsensically violent, the subpar acting drowned by a poor story line. His fussy girlfriend, emotions exploding all over the fucking place, wailed that he stole her abuse story, splashed it on the screen in such a shitty impersonal way. Not that anyone would fucking know it was her. Girl, trippin'. Mxm, bitch getting *too* comfortable. Some bite, some banter. She'll be back.

He's hit rock bottom, the nadir of his career, a suicidal seesaw. Two options: kill himself or ask the devil for help.

So he bought the muthi-tech in the township of Old Naledi—so proximal to Gaborone's purity—in an unusual way: He had to spit in an obscure half-cut plastic bottle, which was swirled with some chibuki-like liquid. The other men spat in it, holding on to it with grimy fingers, then disappeared into a shack, returned with the liquid, now thick with red clots of something he didn't want to compute. Next, they proceeded to a surgical routine of removing his foreskin, dear God, casually in a banter of tsotsitaal jokes. The blood from his manhood, which formed part of this concoction, was important for his astral travels and the initiation of being a spiritual husband and nightmare-sex, if you believe in such things.

Muthi-tech wasn't actually a device, it was part-hardware part-virus that transmuted a typical laptop's software to edit abstract things that stood outside reality's frames once you poured something—*anything* into it. It arose because some men in the city were fed up of not getting away with the shit they used to get away with. There's always a solution for a problem, for a rapist, a murderer, a dead career, addiction et al. And Motsumi found one.

He returned to his home in Oodi, hid the container from his girlfriend, drank the mixture that night when she fell asleep. Toward midnight, sweat-sheathed, he writhes in bed from a cataclysmic pain. He tries to piss, shit, vomit—nothing comes out. Except, standing under the wan light of a moon, his trauma desiccates itself from his form. "Well, let's go murder us some," it says.

His trauma, shadow-embossed, is a dark abyss of what could only be evil. He needs it, what it can do for him. The last days have already cleaved him from reality, and this makes more sense.

But when he looks back, his body's snuggled in the folded duvets of his bed, spooning his girlfriend. His gossamer form and his trauma climb the back of night and, firefly-lit, travel in its medium, thick with ectoplasm, to various homes, hunting, hungry. It's hours of traveling the span of villages, the midst of bundus through Gweta, Letlhakane, Mmadinare, Shakawe, Tutume, until a sticky innocence caws through the gable roof of a building apartment, on the fifth floor of a two-bedroomed unit.

They slip in through the wooden window—no DNA left behind, no signs of forced entry—and see a sleeping woman, a slight snore. Following the didactic actions of his trauma, he nests on her chest, crows their lust. Their tongues wind their way deep into her ear, wetting themselves with the last sounds she heard: a South African soap opera, the microwave pinging, the voice of her mother on a call—then finally their tongues stride along her ears' canals, float into her mind-tide and swim with the velocity of her dreams . . .

Hours later, intoxicated with the dream syrup, Motsumi and his trauma escape into the thickness of night, returning to the house exhausted. He finds his body, no longer full and bone-shaped, but fabric-wise. There it is, the chrysalis of his skin, waiting, beady with crystals, as if decaying into some jewel. Drowsy, he slips into it, cocoons himself in his skin, digesting himself into the larva of the sleeper's dream and him, fusing them into one being.

The next morning, he wakes, fresh, awash with vitality. Prepares eggs benedict, chakalaka and butter-furred bread, drizzles them with the homemade hollandaise sauce. His girlfriend returns from a steaming shower, dressed, surprised at the preparation. No apology, but all's forgiven. He kisses her as she sits down across from him at the kitchen island.

"What are your plans today?" she asks, chewing.

"Well, I'm thinking of animating this idea—"

She quips. "See? I told you an idea would come through."

He laughs. "Had a dream last night, and I want to get it whilst it's still fresh."

"You know, I've read some books and watched some movies that originated from a dream. It's crazy what an imagination can develop from a tiny scene of a dream, huh." She realizes his pause, his fear. Reaches for his hand. "Hey, it's all right to be scared, but I believe in you. This time it'll really work out."

"You think so?"

She smiles sweetly. "I believe so."

He wishes her a good day at work. She walks into the garage smiling, thinking, *He's back. The sweet guy I fell in love with is back.*

When her car exits the entry gates, and the trail of its dust disappears, Motsumi slides the curtain back into place, walks into the basement, a bomb-shelter design constructed to contain screams. He sits at his workstation, spits out an insult at the self-defilement of connecting himself to this muthi-tech, a fusion of muthi and technology formed from the hardware of bones, peeled skin, eyes of a particular ethnicity, and the typical cliché of men's desires hunting albinos, virgins and the Sān. Of course all this hardwired into the motherboard. It doesn't run on electricity, rather the bio-energy of the culprit, a devil-wannabe—plugged into the orifices of man, hence why it's unpopular. Now, Motsumi pulls his pants down to slip the tentacle of this thing inside himself . . .

[Verse 1: Anonymous Girl]
♪♫"P***y Love (interlude)" ♪♫

I wake from the assault, in darkness, then neon lights, bling flowing, pussy dripping money. I sit up, my knees lead, my legs lead, my ass drops, splits into twelve of me, twelve mannequins dancing. Dressed in skin, no bone, flexible. Into black, into fog, and I float in that vapor until the next play. My screams heighten the tempo of this song, this song my prison . . .

[Verse 2: Motsumi]
♪♫"Another One" ♪♫

Stylus in hand, dream-famished now, face lit by his glowing monitor, he realizes something strange: The woman from last night is trapped in the retina of his screen.

He uploads the dream sequence from his first video, "P***y Love (interlude)," onto his social media pages, a mini-trailer of his upcoming work. It's beyond what he expected, comments flowing in. The imagery, the narrative, the process—his trauma nears him, leers as Motsumi gets to work on the next one, "My Religion," after getting his laitie GBV to ad lib some sick rhymes. He stops, the flow no longer there. He needs another woman for this one. Or rather a couple more women. This video is more complex, so best he works on it after he's collected more women for the other videos. He schedules "My Religion" to be his fifth video that he'll share with the world.

"I don't understand what's going on," Motsumi says. "This is impossible. Before, to produce one minute of animation run time, it'd take me ten hours. Today it took those hours to produce a half-length film, running time forty-one minutes."

His trauma smiles, a hoarse voice, a nothing voice. "Conjuring an image in your mind costs nothing and is time-quick. Requires no special effects, no production sets, no labor hires of production assistants, directors, producers, DOP, actors, dancers, set locations and all that fucking money-leeching cohort. The universe that can be conjured in a mind requires no budget—you could be riding a bike in fucking space. We won't even need a green screen and those gimmicks—it'll all be simulated by the imaginations and fears."

Dazed, Motsumi splays back into his chair. "Jesus."

"Exactly."

"You know what I can do with this?"

"Exactly."

"Where the fuck were you this whole time when I really needed you?"

"You're welcome," his trauma says, sardonic. "This will not only garner us wealth, we'll be powerful. Untouchable."

"But the women—"

"Comatose," it says, "no one will ever find out. Trust me, no one will touch us. Anyway, once these women end up in hospital, their families will probably kill their life support after some time. *They* always run out of money to sustain them." It leans in. "Now let's go fuck up more shit. Here's what happens next . . ."

♪♫"P***y Love (extended version)"♪♫

He stayed in a sleepless state to pour things out from his dreams onto the floor of his basement until he was dream-famished, rapping all the while, writing down lyrics, editing the mix. Tonal darks. The aesthetics of the human body splayed on his screen. Then as soon as his girlfriend fell asleep he began his nocturnal travels.

The next one, he entered a woman's sleep cycle and speared through the tunnel of her uterus, where unbeknownst to women, hauntings were seeded and as much as men released sperm into that uterine realm, they cleansed their energies by purging their darkness into them, and sapped what they could from the woman. In this woman's dream where she lacked control, he trickled his cum-poison that would tie her to him. He was giving her p***y love.

During the origami process of bending and folding music, Motsumi's fingers, nimble meticulous creatures, work with the sharp metallic jutting of the sonic electronic music from the wire framing that imprisons the sculptures of women who stand six feet tall. Motsumi's got her voice, and it takes on a white-orchard shade, as he tries to fill the negative spaces with a softer piece of her sexuality. He sits in the sternum, calibrates the subconscious, tweaks the actions, the thoughts. Waits for the waking hour. She's tweaked slowly until she can't tell she's drowning. He continues, working, bending kidnapped women into rap songs . . .

[Verse 3: Motsumi]
♪♫ "Spiritual Bastard I" ♪♫

He woke to the treatment and visuals completed for two songs, "P***y Love" and "Embryo," the notable chorus of the fucking century of his career. His fans were loving it all.

Thirty kilometers north of Gabs, a low-key gathering in Ruretse, straddled with five-hectare farmlands. Some elites of the creative industry: investors, producers, directors, singers, actors et al. His trauma points him to the ones he can trust, who are in the business of making money. He'll snatch their voice and their faculties if they screw him over. Finds two potential investors, Fenyang and Joalane, gritty with deception, and he begins, "Conjuring an image in your mind costs nothing . . ."

"Listen to this crazy asshole," Fenyang says.

Joalane adds, "Listen, we already have a team. We're due for filming in a week. Everything's down on paper."

"You won't need them," Motsumi says. "Fire everyone."

"You're sucking the wrong dick," Fenyang says. "Run along. Desperation doesn't look good on a man, and you're starting to piss me off."

Motsumi raises his hands. "Fine, fine, give me another artist's concept to develop. Like that newcomer reality star chick, Sewela. You could gamble with her . . . I could do something cinematic and dystopic and ethereal for that song of hers, 'Embryo' . . . I mean, how much did her last one, 'Skin's Prison,' cost?"

"About six million," responds Joalane.

"What were the sales, revenue, rates—"

"Didn't break even."

Motsumi adds, "For a higher quality than that, I'll charge you a mil—"

"Nah, you've dunked all your projects," Fenyang says. "We'll put you on trial. Show us what you got first, then we'll talk."

"Sho, sho skeem," he says. "I'll have it to you within five days."

They laugh. "Mfetu, what you smoking? You keen on burying your career further, huh?"

"Five. Days," Motsumi says.

"A'ight, we'll give your 'ad hoc idea' the green light. See you in five days."

After talking to the investors, they put him on a trial. He knows they're trying to cheat him. If he produces something good, they'll run away with it and screw him over. But if it's so good, to maintain working with him, they'll hire him for other projects.

He ends the night by flirting with a writer, more open and

flexible than the others. Tenth girl this month. They're sitting in some gazebo, getting high, snorting stuff, laughing over their munchies.

Forgetting he's in reality and not the other realm, he leans over, whispers wetly into her ear, "My emotions are narcotics. I don't know if you can sniff this well, that you can roll it well. I don't think you can handle it, but you sure you wanna try?"

Gone, gone, he's gone into another world. This body too tight to breathe in, emotions hotboxing inside his body.

"Shit, brah, you good?" she asks.

"The dark, gonna let the devil out," he whispers.

Smoke pillows out from her lips. "Hee banna. You got there faster than me," she says. "Don't leave me; shit, lemme catch up, give me something to chase this down."

"Shit, shouldn't have mixed it," he says. "Time ain't clocking in right. Where the sun at? Where my head at?" His head, it's going up the stairs, where they drag themselves into one of the rooms.

He doesn't get horny anymore, and this is not a typical sexual act.

As they kiss in bed, she reaches for a condom in her handbag, gives it to him. He unwraps it, and she lays back waiting, at peace. He scoffs, thinks, *Women, so fucking trustworthy. Just 'cause I'm well-known she thinks I won't do anything reckless.* Then, listening to his trauma, Motsumi pretends to put the condom on, but throws it aside and enters her, contaminates her with his sperm, unlike that of usual men: He disposes something, not wholly semen. Seven days later she loses her job, her car dies in mid-afternoon traffic, her uninsured house burns down, and two years down the line, she'll find something in her womb killing her babies. The other women, the more viable ones, they'll find new partners, get married or pregnant out of wedlock, matters none. When they give birth, it'll be his being inside their baby, another him, another him, another him—"Me, me, me, fucking me," he croons—a certain immortality, living simultaneous lives . . .

[Chorus: Motsumi's Doppelgängers]
♪♫"Embryo"♪♫

The only place I am my own is the planetary region of the womb, before any of us are disposed of our identity, of place, of sex. This is where he put me and this is where I wait for the other sperm to join me before we fuse with her egg. To be born. To replicate him. To immortalize him. To live in parallel of each other, building the brand, becoming the workforce of our empire. The sole reason behind the hubris of a man with talent and fame is not his vices, his crimes, his inhibitions—it's the people who see, who encounter, who collate evidence in their interaction with him to strip him, to see him put away for his crimes. These people are generally employees, his social circle, his colleagues. If he eliminates the workforce that sees too much, then no one will see the workings in his studio. If he multiplies himself to be his own workforce, that way, no one will know; twenty people can keep a secret if they are the same person multiplied in one reality, the same time, the same context. Sure, when we're born, we'll be a tad diluted, but purity's useless when it ain't used.

Contraceptive agents can't begin to eradicate us. We wait, in many wombs, where he put us. So far, twenty-three wombs and counting . . .

CGI-taut and noir-classic tinged lights fill the soundscape as she rises in the dark-fog center. She wonders who she is, how she got here and why her thighs hurt. A mirror looks upon her, but her reflection bears no skin or hair. If her identity is stripped and she can't tell who she is, then who will? "Hello," she tries to say, but a hurt throbs in her voice box like an open wound. It hurts to attempt speaking. Screaming will stretch the wound wider. A sonata voice drips through, light but hazy as drowning rain, and she realizes it's her voice pit-pattering around her . . .

[Verse 4: Motsumi]
♪♫"Spiritual Bastard II"♪♫

He sent in the draft music video at 02:00, the call comes in at 02:02, way before the music video is over. He answers, groggily.

The voice that comes at the end of the call is alert: "A car will fetch you at six, contracts will be prepared and we'll be convening with the artist and her management team to prepare on developing Sewela's music video 'Phallic Gun.'" A pause. "If you continue being this good, fuck, we'll hire you for our dossier of clients . . . we have another one, 'Whores and Nuns,' if you can do that in one week, we'll pay triple."

He yawns, smiles. "Ayoba, let's get it."

[Verse 5: Sewela]
♪♫"Skin's Prison" ♪♫

Sewela Gauta. Motswana. Twenty-six. Actress, singer, filmmaker. A triple threat. A quadruple threat if you add the bitch part, but whatever. She's prepping dance moves for her gqom track, "Skin's Prison," at her rustic residence in Ruretse village. Sewela and her choreographer, Leungo, have been watching music videos, analyzing dances moves to assist with her routine that she wants to discuss with her new team who'll be producing her music video for "Whores & Nuns."

They've spent hours doing variations of the vosho dance and the gwarra gwarra, with some fast footwork in her living room, donned like a dance floor with strobe lights. The first hit she takes, at this equivocal terrain, time is unpeeled, past and present stirred with a dash of the future. It's February. The sky is scant grey and creased with sunset as they're scattered on the dance floor; the swaying gravity and air's tessitura climaxes to a high as they drag another round of powdered white into their bodies, time slips into their nostrils like molten lava. Oxygen shouldn't burn like this—took too much.

On a teaspoon, they've burned the molten form of morality, God and the devil into a liquid drug. "Take this," Leungo says, "gonna make the vibes grand." He leans back, watching a song play out on her Plasma. "I swear Michael Jackson was a pantsula, I mean look at those dance moves, brah, shayamagetdown." And he's elevated; he hops up, drops low, screaming, "Woza, woza! Hae-haebo!" as Sewela laughs.

She does this a lot. Hasn't killed her yet, instead catapults her career. Allows her to straddle realms. It's all good for her creativity, narcotics that is, which she started sipping from her ex's lung, except the breakup didn't wean her off them. On the last round, when the strobe lights knife the room in sharp bursts, her inner being pulsates outside the boundaries of her skin; its viscous form spreads out to the edges of the room, expanding her silhouette. If she hangs on to this dizzying moment, not giving in to slumber or purging, it'll shuttle her into that utopic zone burning with a delicious death-taste.

So she sniffs in more, punches her veins with needles.

Inside her body, everything is a beautiful mess, a tornado of thoughts, anger and hatred spinning to a climactic explosion catapulting her to the stratosphere of her being. Her eyes are quickly blind to the reality outside her body. She's never felt this sin-struck, the culmination of her ideas. Her viscous soul-matter repeatedly blasts against the cavernous boundaries of her skin, can barely perforate the fucking epidermal prison—finally she breaks through the empyrean of her consciousness where anything is possible. Her body spews her soul-matter out, a spluttering potent creative juice, sprawled on the dance floor. It sits there, a glob of an entirely different universe as it watches the physical body it's been ejected from: Her body, life-wan, falls to the floor, a loose fabric of skin and bones. This time her mother's bewitching words may come true, that her addiction will kill her, that this time she's gone too far, that what kind of woman is she living like this, dancing like a whore on stages, twerking her voice as an insult to their culture, telling her: *Black woman sit the fuck down, shut the fuck up, abide, respect him, respect your culture.*

Initially domiciled in domesticity, she's exiled herself. Name any artists this devout to their craft, willing to sacrifice all for its evolution. She's not hurting anyone, just herself. Slippery on this weird terrain, she tries to rise on her soul-feet, but she's sucked back into her cranial vault, wreaking havoc with the meteoric crashes of her thoughts—she gonna die, she gonna fucking die this time! Darkness ensnares.

Sewela wakes to the results of last night's escapades. A tome of written-down lyrics, snippets of singing in the booth, additional tracks for her deluxe album, *Peeling Time.* Leungo video-recorded what they got up to, some of which she barely remembers. In one of the videos, she stands on her balcony's balustrade, singeing her voice with high notes. No wonder why it's hoarse this morning. Now, time for the detox. If she's experienced her death like this, a creative magic, what would the outcome be if she murdered and experienced someone else's death? No. She's not that far gone. She will be the only victim to her villainous actions.

[Verse 6: Motsumi]
♪♫"Kill Me Saintly" (Ft. Sewela) ♪♫

Boss up.

Motsumi and his trauma watch the hit-maker bitch he's supposed to work with. *I'll be gentle, baby.* Sewela's mind slips, trips into an EDM-tranced coma that hustles her into REM sleep. Her electrifying meridian lines are probed by a horny bastard. In bed, hands touch her. Move her. Hogtie her voice. She watches her voice, black-slicked, crippled and tied under the blinking eye of the moon. She knows she'll be dead before death's even bled into her. They shush each other, the things in her room. She prays that no man rapes her. Her thoughts scream: *At least kill me saintly. Kill me saintly and quietly so I go quick.* She tries to scream again, kick again. But they clip her voice with some utensil, gleaming in the light. When she looks back, her body still remains in bed. Peaceful. Comatose, as these monsters take her . . .

[Verse 7: Sewela]
♪♫ "Placenta of Evil" ♪♫

There's a hammering in her head. Her brain is a quarry; a migraine blast makes the splintering daylight unknown, the location unknown, her body unknown. The room is opium, muffled in moth-smoked perfume. It's too husky to define. She is half elsewhere, half here. Here? Suddenly the present time billows into her sight the daylight and morning traffic, the white curtains undulated by a morning breeze into her bedroom. Then she's spat back into that other realm: It's a song, a music video, and in it her searing fear colors a sculpture with a sharp taste of red.

Present day pools around her. Sick groans in her gut. She stands on weak legs, shaking, terror bleaching her brown skin—no, no, no, it's her sight, sapped of color. The labor pains of evil burn her thighs. She reaches the toilet, hangs her head in. Tremors spurt vomit into it. Not enough. She rises, sits, pushes, pushes, pushes, exorcising the haunting from her uterus. Then, a plop. Suddenly, relief, the peace, vitality. She wipes, turns around, inspects the thing: The placenta of last night's haunting is gaunt, fleshy and slick, cuddled in the toilet bowl like large dark clots. She knows with a keen sense someone tried bewitching her, didn't take all of her. She fetches the *thing* into a plastic bag, the key to trailing him. She reaches for the toilet handle, whispers, "Bastard, fucker, I *will* find you."

[Verse 8: Motsumi]
♪♫ "Monster" ♪♫

Motsumi, skin stammering crystals. He bends over the bathroom sink, splashes cold water onto his face. Fists his hands, punches the mirror. Shatter, blood.

"Bitch!" he spits.

His trauma, a flickering flame of shadow, watches from within the bathtub, with deep, dark sockets, and says, "Her blood was salty from a protection, from an elder who doctored traditional medicines. The times during the wars, when they'd raid this area."

It burned like acid, and almost dissolved him, almost killed him in the act. He returned home, half himself, because of her fucking spiritual warfare.

"I'll be careful next time," Motsumi says.

"You're getting greedy," it says, a venom of dark. "Such greed only leads to mistakes—"

A door, opening. "Babe?" His girlfriend peeks into the bathroom. "You all right?"

The thing in the bath, a venom of dark, spreads itself toward her. Motsumi grabs the door, pushes her back. *Does the bastard actually have a heart?* it wonders, no longer in him so unable to discern. It smiles: *No, he doesn't trust women now.*

"Listen," Motsumi says, "you're gonna have to sleep somewhere else tonight."

Her eyes, sadness. "What? Why?"

"Something's come up, I can't explain."

"You *never* can explain. Oh my God, is that blood? What happened?" Pushes herself in, and the thing inhales her, drinks her—*Don't get greedy,* it reminds itself. She shrinks back, instinct suddenly on alert, eyes scanning the room as if . . . *As if what?* she thinks. Something's amiss, she can't pinpoint it, but she's suddenly afraid. *Run,* her thoughts, a clamor. She swallows. Steps back. "All right," she whispers.

Feeling jeopardized, Motsumi assesses her as she backtracks. She's never seen him like this, menacing. "No," Motsumi's trauma says. "You can't leave a body behind, not in this reality. She's too close. You'll be the first person the authorities come for—it's too, too soon, the rest aren't even born yet. This will compromise everything we've done. She doesn't know anything. She's nothing. Get rid of her."

Motsumi's shoulders slack. "Get your shit and leave. It's over."

[Bridge]

Not a one-hit wonder. Twenty million followers on every social media account of the prolific animator and rapper, Motsumi.

In the visual album, twenty-eight-year-old Motsumi has been producing and creatively directing stellar hits for various popular artists. Fans are hungry for his latest work, which he gave a glimpse of on his social media pages. This industry juggernaut has released the name of his upcoming song, "Phallic Gun," featuring popular rappers like GBV-Son, Me2 Thug and Ami Next, slated to be the hottest tune this summer. Some reviewers were disturbed, declaring that the song glorifies violence. In the video, the male protagonist leers, says in his lilting voice, "The song is a satire, a metaphor on how media and society normalize violence against women for pleasure and profit, which is why we brought in Sewela, who's basically killing it in the industry. To get this support from a hitmaker like her really lends the music video a feminist twist as she becomes this empowering femme fatale freeing all these trapped women."

Fans have noted that Motsumi, the male protagonist, bears a striking resemblance to the *Peeling Time* singer's ex-fiancé, Atasaone Ewetse, the famous actor of *The Innocent Devil,* who's been in hot water for his unorthodox ways of attaining superstardom; his spokespeople declined to comment on this piece. The "Whores & Nuns" singer heavily made references to the dark side of his hedonistic lifestyle. Particularly intriguing to fans are Sewela's notable songs, "Motsumi's Doppelgängers" and "Placenta of Evil," which exemplify the singer's unresolved emotions. That, despite the bitter breakup, Sewela still feels contaminated and bewitched by Atasaone, possessed by him, something she can't exorcise given her self-destructive habits. Fans applauded the quality of makeup and wardrobe used in the visual album *Peeling Time*, but noted that if you really looked carefully at Motsumi's facial expression, it's actually Sewela, imprisoned within her ex-fiancé—*that's messed up, she's clearly not over him, nigga still has a hold over her, their on-and-off relationship is drowning her, sis needs help, someone save her.* Worried fans tweeted consoling words, praying the singer won't give in to her suicide attempts, given her myriad relapses and rehab trips . . .

[Verse 9: Anonymous Girls]
♪♫"Bars of this Song" ♪♫

A man twerks in the center. Strikes out his leg. Twirls. Spins. *Viral, now we viruses. They twisted my thoughts into the ligature of the chorus. Harness your thoughts.*

The structure of this song is phallic-tone. *We revolve behind the bars of this song, flames of lyrics tousling our hides.* The structure of this song is decibel-wide and tall, a synchro-cinema.

No matter where you hide, the barbed wires, the tall walls, the thick craniums, they will find you, get in. Her voice, a screaming saxophone turns to dusk, dissipates . . .

End credits, and the dancing women return to the quiet fold of the music. There was nowhere else to go, until the song was played again, as it'd charted number one for nine weeks. The streaming service didn't allow them to trespass into other song-boundaries, which offered far more freedom than this bullshit sexist song. They were fucking trapped. All they could do was sit in the gardens, waiting . . . wondering if they'd ever leave these song-boundaries.

The song below theirs sang of empowerment, had women naked, brazen by the force of their boobs, warriors of their sex. It was intoxicating.

"If we can't leave back into our physical bodies," says one woman covered in some milky liquid, "that's the island of song I want to flee to."

"What's the song-island called?" asks a bone-skinned woman.

"'Whores and Nuns'," replies one. "You can be a nun, a whore, it's all good. And that's what I want to be, a nun-whore. So tired of these straitjacket labels. It's liberating, and it belongs to that Motswana musician, Sewela, right?"

Cue in, Sewela. Knives for braids. Skin a smattering of brown. Hooves for feet. The women stare at her, astonished.

Sewela surveys this musical prison. "Why's she crying?"

A woman with gold-sequined skin whispers, "Oh, she found out that her family switched off her life support, it was getting too expensive for them. Now she has no body to return to, that's if we ever get out of this hellhole, oppressing rap song."

"Well, we're going to change that," Sewela says.

"Do you know who did this to us?" they ask, heads spinning.

Sewela shrugs. "I have something that belongs to them. They attacked me. They gonna come back for me."

"Shit," pipes one, "funny ain't it? We had to clean and cook and slave out there. Now we doing it again. We cooking bars, cleaning stripper poles with our bodies. Shit never changes. Culture still the same."

"What's that you got there?" A woman without eyes points at something in Sewela's hands.

Sewela stares at the plastic-covered item she's gripping. "Thought it'd be safer to analyze it here. The bastard's name is Motsumi." She crouches, exposes it on the gold floor. She has a bit of Motsumi's trauma, this placenta of evil. It looks like wet tar expelling smoke. She probes it, sticks her finger in it, to find the root of him, but it begins to burn her. Clearly it must burn Motsumi or he's that far gone to not realize how dangerous his trauma is to him even. But it can't kill her in here. Her eyes roll back as the trauma's essence travels into her being and her mind and the memory of its root cause plays out in her mind: *Motsumi's trauma didn't know what it was sometimes but a foggy agglomeration of all those bad times from Motsumi's childhood, sticky dark memories of the beatings, the starvation, the abuse he suffered that stuck into the core of who he became and what he believed in: that wrongdoing is normal, that killing or kidnapping is fine, that women are playthings for his picking. He was abused, now the habit is overkill, overflowing in his brain, his heart out into his actions to people who don't deserve his wrath and pain. His trauma looks on at Motsumi, pleased by this habitual feeding. The more crimes Motsumi commits, the more satiated it becomes. Motsumi is a sick motherfucker, but if he were to ever resolve his issues, to really heal, his trauma will die. And his trauma can't have that happening. No fucking way will it die. So the women must die.*

"Not in this story. Not on my watch," Sewela whispers with the fervor of anger, and the women gather around her as she clenches her hands into fists and speaks: "No woman dies. No more. His trauma does not justify getting away with murdering our women. If it's death he wants, it's his death that he'll get. *He* must die."

"I'mma dagger them with that stripper pole," says one woman.

"It'll only kill their avatars. Not them," another responds.

"Then I'll kill myself."

Sewela says, "Violence and sex raises the ratings, so really your death will be ineffectual to yourself or the cause. They'll get another you, and another you. See that gold statue there?" She points to a fountain, goddess-like, stripped, spurting water. "Some chick thought death would revolutionize everything, free you guys. But, look what they did with her body, apparently that's a money-making shot. And the way she did it, now they hemming more of you in, hoping you get as creative as her to die." Sewela exhales smoked anger. "You know, it's really hard to be creative, that's a gift not everyone has, a gift some will pirate."

The sequined woman slumps forward. "Bliksem. Fuck. How you gonna start a revolution imprisoned in a song?" She kneels forward. "And I thought the real world out there was worse. 'Least you could wear what you want, have a sense of control in your own house, deal with shitty governmental laws once in a while. I had a home, you know. Built it with my savings. Sacrificed living to own something. Only lived in it for a few months before they took me. It's true what they say, I guess. Live, you never know when you're going to die. I never lived . . . at all. Lost it just like that." Snaps her fingers. "If I'd known. All that work . . . all that work . . ." She starts to cry, bleeding her pain into the chorus of the song . . .

[Verse 10: Sewela]
♪♫ "Armageddon" ♪♫

She woke up from the dream-song. Stood up. The news report on her Plasma caught her eyes: "In a span of five days, across Botswana, at least thirty-five women in Gaborone, Modipane, Palapye, Kanye, and other districts have been found comatose with no underlying symptoms. At least five subjects have been pulled off their machines. Given this rising phenomenon, doctors are studying the remaining subjects to halt this endemic. The subjects have no connecting features—ranging from young to old, various jobs, varying body sizes and ethnicities—except that they are all women. Gender-based-violence organizations claim women are being targeted, but toxicology reports, rape kits and forensic investigations indicate no foul play, signs of physical abuse nor drugs. The women simply go to bed and never wake up."

Sewela's jaw stretches into shock. One hundred and twenty-nine women in two months. Women trapped in songs.

She's been manicuring her fear. She's safe, she could pretend it's over. But another one like him will come again and it will be over then. How can she turn a blind eye to their suffering? Has to stop this. Braces herself. *I could die,* she thinks, realizes. *I could die saving them.* Weeps as if she's already at her funeral, one too many times. Her thoughts reckon: *What's the difference? We've been killed and killed over by this culture. Metaphorical, emotionally, infantilized—the genocide of our identity, our being for their ideals. We're already dead. We die here, we die there—the dichotomy, the difference is we die into a new birth of reorder. No one will come at us again. This is the only power. Dying is not an end. Life cannot be destroyed, it changes form—whether by death or transmutation—we transcend. This is our power.*

Okay. She steels herself. *I can do this.*

A clock ticks. She sits at her kitchen table. On a porcelain plate, the placenta of evil. She has to consume it. Taps her fingers, drums the courage. Shuts her eyes, throws the chunk into her mouth, pinches her nose, chews to not taste.

Reality subsides . . .

[Verse 11: Sewela]
♪♫"Whores & Nuns" (DJ Don remix) ♪♫

A gospel cry wakes her up on the floor of an anthem, a religious choir's fabled tones. Walls and ceilings peel back, folding around a hallway and its red-tinged yonic interior. Monochrome lights and diegetic sounds pulse in her ears as she walks about. One corner, a white woman wears a melanin coat, getting rates for it, certified gold—that appropriating song. She turns toward her. No. She stops herself. She's not here to remedy that. First, the women like her: dethroned, destroyed, cauterized, utilized by men for their silly hubris. Surveys the transparent doors. The hallway's flanked with various rooms of songs climbing the charts:

gqom, rock, kwaito, rap, RnB, kwassa kwassa—cadent beats at their doors.

A man in hot pants follows her, twerking. Then a door, the one she's here for. Behind it, Motsumi's baritone voice builds builds builds, dissipates into violin hands. Her fingers clasp around its doorknob. This is the one room that will lead to the music video he designed, where she'll kill him. The door creaks open, and through that slit, the devilish light of a song spears her chest. She falls backward, skewered in the chest by sexist stanzas—*this my bitch, this my pussy, pussy got money.* The rap, a martial beat, is delivered quickly to her face, jarring her vision, pounding her flesh. Sewela tries to stand, but she's weighed down by the human-sized cross of the stanza protruding from her chest. Her fingers grasp it, to pull it out, but it burns. *Don't be rude. Don't touch the cross.*

Motsumi slips through the door, squats, breath upon her face. "They used to make women better in the old days," he says. "They knew their place. What makes you so special to think you stand above the rest? The system? To be treated different?"

She's never had an answer for this before, but the anger, the injustice throttles through her mouth. "Because we're not in the old days, you fucking fossil." Her scream rises, hits five octaves. She rams her gun-heel into his mouth and pulls the trigger, exploding him with lyric and tune. The little shit hobbles away, slippery with blood, closing the door behind him.

Sewela lifts herself into a stand with this misogynistic stake, and moves around the realm with his phallic protrusion, stalking her predator. She coughs out blood as the mass of women parade in thongs and bras and wimples, shaking their booties, knees knocking out the gwarra gwarra moves. She's prepared herself well: her body the weapon, the gun shoes, the shooting boobs, the knife-braids ready to slay, the venom in her spit, her burning melanin, gathering smoke. Finally, Sewela bangs through the door, entering the room labeled:

[Verse 12: Sewela]
♪♫"Phallic Gun" (Remix Ft. GBV,
Me2 Thug & Ami Next) ♪♫

The architecture of this song is concrete-bound. The shriveled cries of women, a choir. The structure of this song is bone-made as they hum,

> *I tried to make my thighs bleed,*
> *squander myself on the floor with his demons.*
> *Tried to kill myself in this room.*
> *Only it wasn't any room: his voice was my jail cell.*
> *The rooms were skin-thin.*

The warehouse room, dark fog. Twenty monochrome women's silhouettes stand still as statues, each a slogan of sex and flapping wads of money, chloroformed by masculinity. They wear their skins like expensive fashion labels. Sewela pauses in the doorway, cranes her neck. Sees no one but the statues. *How'd he disappear so fast?* she thinks. Her mouth opens to whisper, "Hello," but she's seen enough horror movies to shut that up quickly. She can't be stupid at a time like this. She steps forward, her gun-feet clopping against the concrete floor. The women spin, triggered by her steps. In swift synchronized movements, they bend backward, arching their backs; fifty steel swords of dancing poles rise from the concrete ground, like jail-cell bars, spear through their spines to the ceiling. *Skrr-skrr-scream, more blood, more money, yeah, woo!*

She turns, shocked by the voice. Too late. The voice ties around her body, contorting her into dance moves. She tries to fight the strain in her muscles. Closes her eyes to pinpoint the voice, find the coward. Around her, the women's screams rise into a choir's siren. Dark electro smoke billows through the room, suffocating Sewela of her thoughts. Motsumi's baritone voice scrapes the gqom beat into hip-hop, stretching her body into gruesome gestures. Sewela didn't know she could dance on shoes made from guns. Here goes another bar, another round—*and we smoking it up*.

Motsumi appears. Confident now that she's hogtied by his voice. His fist punches the air as he continues rapping, walking with swagger toward her. She's split from herself before, she can do it again. The placenta of evil is just like any drug she's consumed. She must let it into her, overpower her. She seals her eyes shut again, pushes herself into the darkness within her and wades into the viscous waters of her inner being, which is turning hard, cold and sharp. She realizes she doesn't need to exist outside herself to be powerful. Her body *is* power. Inside her body, she jitters, a volcano ready to erupt. Her body, the thing she can't control, shakes under the conflicting forces of Sewela and Motsumi's voice. Finally, she catches on a tiny thread of power, pulls pulls pulls until it becomes a whole fabric of her body that he loses control of. The dancing pole—*boy you got me dancing, just for you, ooh*. She yanks the pole, spins it in her hands, throws it sharply as a javelin, a bull's-eye hit in Motsumi's forehead. He sprawls to the ground. Rebirths himself. Starts rapping: *Yeah, yeah, challenge accepted, woo! Skrr-skrr-scream! I'ma get her, I'ma get her— Armageddon (bitch)*.

He won't die. He won't die *easily*. He smirks. She circles him. Surrounding them, the women swing and pirouette around these steel blades, slicing their thighs, as his rapper swag maneuvers them. *More blood, more money, girl gotta respect*. He opens his mouth again, but Sewela quickly grabs his tongue, yanks his voice from his larynx with scraping nails and on this composed film score, Sewela rides his song, paces his low tessitura. Desperate and hobbling about, Motsumi whips out his phallic gun. The pistons of her breast glare at him, and her voice, a siren, screams shayamaGETDOWN. The women quickly fall and she lets the bullets rip through Motsumi's body. *His* body, life-wan, falls to the floor, a loose fabric of skin and bones. *Repeat. Repeat. Repeat,* the women chant, rising free from their concrete graves, recognizing this falling action from the song "Skin's Prison."

In the bleak dark of mind, Sewela rubs the texture of kwaito onto his last reggae heartbeats. She hacks at the limbs of generational trauma, gnaws it with her teeth, drinks the blood by the gallon, spews culture with her tongue. Deskins herself of law, lore, loin. She sits on the throne of his hide and bone without label, gender, premise. Peeling time, she's going forward and backward simultaneously whilst he groans, and the film slackens, a stasis. She strikes him again, unspools time from the recording reel, throwing him into the prison of his actions.

I am monster, unlawful, new territory, new kingdom, a disruption. A monster here, god elsewhere . . .

She wears his taxidermized masculinity as a crown, chugs his death to the outro of her visual album, sits on the throne made from his bones and the leather of his skin—this powerful shot graces the front cover of magazines. She's a powerhouse auteur of glitz, glam, gore for her studio album collection *Peeling Time*, seventeen songs long, featuring top hits "My Religion," "Another One," "P***y Love," "Whores & Nuns" et al. Gold microphones surround Sewela, interviewers inquiring on the concepts behind her visual album as it plays on all screens:

[Post-Chorus: Sewela]
♪♫"My Religion" (DJ Topo Club remix) ♪♫

The corpse of Motsumi's voice hangs from the murdered legacy tree exhumed from the placenta of his evil. He is a proper man. The burning tree blazes in the dark. Thirty women watch, getting loose on the dance floor to the Klaxon of his voice flickering, spitting ash, burning, dying . . .

THE SUGAR MILL

by Tobias S. Buckell

I can feel the sale I desperately need slipping away when the sugar hits the tea and the whiteness dissolves away. Before the ghost of sweetness gets whisked away by the trade winds that struggle their way up the hill in erratic blasts, the thin woman looks down at my carefully prepared tray to wrinkle her precise nose, a nose tipped with a messy thumb's width of frosted sunscreen.

The sugar is a miracle. Empires grew on sugar, fortunes rose, entire peoples kidnapped, shackled, and whipped across an entire ocean to an entirely different continent to make it, and she says, "I do my best to avoid sugar. It's unnatural. My friend Monica runs a juicing business: everything you need comes out of the fruit. All the sweetness you need."

I drink simple instant coffee. Hot water, some scoops, and go. But whenever I come out with a silver tray of teas and pour the hot water, they all but swoon.

There's a little plastic honey bear in the kitchen. I should have poured some into a small bowl and found a tiny little spoon.

I read an article once about how great real estate agents bake cookies in a house before they show it. Get that chocolate-chip cookie smell filling the house, and you get everyone thinking of home. "Find your own favorite childhood memory smell and fill the prospective home with it!"

Fry up some plantain and fill the grounds up with that? I didn't think it would translate for these prospective buyers. I was born here, ate like here, had a parent who grew up here, and one from abroad. I could shift into either parent's accent, and I looked white. So, people from the US mainland feel more comfortable with me as a real estate agent, though few would ever admit it.

The woman is Katelyn. The man is John. He doesn't want to talk too much about what he does, but it has something to do with derivatives. She runs "a studio." "I can just see starting up morning yoga down on the beach. Sunrise. The photos online will sell it."

They were impressed by the mountain goats and asked if there were tame ones that they could use for goat yoga.

"I can look into that for you," I tell them.

The wind whips at the tablecloth under the silver tray. I set up some lawn chairs on the grass because there wasn't much to see in the small cabin behind the tamarind tree. A kitchen, a common room, a bedroom nook. It was a caretaker's cabin, roughed up by many a hurricane, clinging to the top of this hill with weathered, gray concrete block and not a lick of paint to it.

I can't sell these two a concrete-block cabin. Katelyn of "the studio" wouldn't be caught dead in it. They're staying in an open-air eco-lodge with even fewer amenities than the cabin, a glorified tent on the beach.

But the land has a view of five nearby beaches that curl out onto the turquoise ocean. From our tea position, they can look down the hill. They can listen to the distant sound of Ms. Hennigan's rooster carrying on, the taxis blasting music as they move people around, and life on the island doing its thing.

Never mind the cabin, I needed them to see potential.

Because it had been three months since my last sale. I was out of savings. I was out of credit. Even Evan down at Happy Dogs wouldn't front me a drink at the bar anymore.

Any more of this, and I would be looking at a job delivering blended drinks to sun-blistered people sitting on the sand looking at the windsurfers and being oh-so-polite and smiling in hopes of a shitty tip.

"My friend Jason, from Australia, when he came to the US he said the bread here had so much sugar in it, he thought it was cake! Cake!"

I don't want to talk about bread, so I point at one of the boulders near the edge of the far point of the hill. "From that rock there, pirates would look out at the channel between the islands. They could see their prey approaching and would rush down the hill to row out and prepare to catch them."

The pirate shit always works. They rush over to examine the rock.

"Right over there in Baston Bay," I continue, "old man Baston heard a knock on his door, one day in 1873. Two raggedy old men at the door said they had been given a map by their grandfather to treasure right in Baston Bay. They promised to share it if he let them dig on his land. He refused, shut the door. And you know, a week later, old man Baston's walking his land, and he comes across a huge hole at the top of the beach. Inside is a single doubloon at the very bottom."

Katelyn and John are impressed.

It's the Caribbean. Steady winds, heat, beaches, and rum. They're here for their paradisiacal experience. The one they've felt they've deserved their whole life, so deep in their bones. And I'm trying to sell it to them as hard as I can because . . . I need that commission. So much of the island's been snapped up, carved up, developed, sold to outsiders. Most of the real estate agents on the island are from overseas now, so those parcels are just passed around by entities abroad, billionaires parking their wealth in the land and passing them around like trading cards. "My mega-marina is a rarer find than your gaudy hotel."

I need a first month's deposit and several months' buffer to get myself out of the tiny concrete-block cabin I've been squatting in anyway. I'm not supposed to be living on the property I'm selling, but the old owners want nothing to do with the old mill.

I need the money to move out because I'm tired of all the old ghosts wandering around the property.

When I get home I toss a heavy potato-and-chicken roti on the plywood table and unwrap the foil keeping it warm. I blow on my fingers, and then stop to toss several mangos into the corner of the dark room.

Sandy-gold and sunset-orange skin wobble across the cheap tile.

An offering, just as my mom taught.

"Please," I mutter. "Please leave me be."

"Hey child," one of the shadows in the corner of the concrete house says, voice scratchy like the dry brown leaves out in the bush.

I pick at the shiny bits of aluminum foil and stare at the heat rippling off the roti skin. Green flecks of ground-up peas and spices from inside the dhalpuri skin glisten in the light of the bulb over my head. Under the skin the wedged edges of potato push out, like a child's hand from within a mother's belly.

"Child."

Two shots of cheap Cruzan rum. A Heineken, the bottle as green as the fresh palm frond hat that shifts in the dark. The kind that tourists love to buy on the beach, take home and hang on the wall until it's brown and brittle.

"*Child.*"

"Damn it!" I slap the table. "I respectfully asked for you to leave."

"We respectfully cannot," they murmur.

"Why must you always be vexing me like this?"

Several pairs of glowing eyes regard me. "Vexing?"

Queen Atarah stands up from a tiny three-legged stool, her shaved head gleaming in the bulb light as she wobbles forward, the crutch in her right hand tap, tap, tapping against the floor. With disgust for me clear on her pinched face, she spits. "This isn't vexing. We asked you. We called you from through the veil, and then listen to you whine about it."

"Five figures," I snap wearily. "Five."

I hold up a hand, fingers spread out. Wiggle them.

"*Co-mission* . . ." Queen Atarah says. "We hear this over and over again. But what profit a man to gain the world and lose his soul?"

"That's the sort of shit broke-ass people have to believe," I say. "Or what hope do they have?"

"What have you done to earn all that anger, son?" Queen Atarah asks me. She gestures down at the stump of her leg. "When you can see us all before you?"

She eases herself down to sit across from me. Her tiny coral-flecked eyes glint. The others step out to her sides. Two shirtless men, scarred torsos, one missing his right arm, the other both his hands.

I lower my head.

The breath I let out is long and rich with rum and roti.

"Your veins, our blood." Queen Atarah taps the table.

I lay my sandy hands next to her deep brown. "But so little, Queen."

Queen Atarah laughed. "Knew a boy like you. Sister dark, brother pale, twins. Parents both brown as good earth. And they took him up into the main house. Favored him. Got him apprenticed and all of that. But they hung him just the same when that white woman up by Smith Bay said he touched her. When the knives come out they know who you are. Just as we know who you are. Can't run from it."

"I don't run from it," I said.

"And how your accent sounds when talking to buyers?"

I open my mouth, and then shake my head. "Five figures. So I can start my life. So I can be somebody."

"But you put on an accent for anybody, not just them. Hide your island self away for the sale."

"Guilty." I roll up the foil into a ball and shoot it right over Queen Atarah's head in an arc. It hits the trash can. Perfect shot.

"No one in this room blames you. Survival we understand."

"So leave me be, leave the land be."

Queen Atarah shook her head. "We can't. We're bound."

The first time I'd met her, she grabbed the ragged stump of a man's nearby hand and shook it. Food for the mill, she'd told me. The price we paid to squeeze the water and sugar from the cane. So many limbs eaten by the infernal machinery of profit and power.

All that blood, soaked into the dirt around the mill. It kept them here.

"The land seized us, then," Queen Atarah would say.

"Five figures, great-great-great-grandmama. Five figures. This land will be sold to do something else and everything that stood here will be forgotten so that we can all take the money and move on."

"Give us the address where the white man and woman are staying so we can haunt them," Queen Atarah says. "*Respectfully.*"

For Katelyn and John, the next step isn't just buying the land. No, nothing that simple. There's some kind of construction loan scheme going on, so today they're back with a bigger camera and an iPad.

"Visioning," John says.

There's someone from the bank and a surveyor coming by later as well.

John is using an app on his iPad to look at potential builds. "Buddy of mine did some mocks."

Over his shoulder I can see virtual architecture, colonial windows and shutters attaching to the mill.

"This would be the master bedroom," John says, looking over the iPad and back to reality. "Just right there."

I retire back to lean against a young mango tree in the shade as they meander about the property, looking at their computer-generated visions.

"The dining room table is right by the gears of the mill," Shadrak whispers into my ear. Shadrak is another haunter, but with baggy linen trousers and a tool belt slung over one shoulder like an old Western gunslinger. Less intense than Queen Atarah.

"The gears," everyone in the shadows whisper.

"I know," I reply. "I know. I know."

"But you're not saying anything."

"What do you want me to say that would make any difference?" I snap at the shadows cast by the searing sun. "They know what they're building on."

Once they build on this, I can imagine someone asking them where they lived. "Up by the old mill!" They'd say that proudly, wouldn't they.

"Do you know what will haunt you more than us if you let them do this?"

"What?" I ask sourly.

"That you just let it happen."

Katelyn takes a selfie, flashing a peace sign and gaping into the fish lens of her phone. She's standing in front of the mill's entrance. The dark maw to where the machine used to live. The machine that ate all the ghosts' limbs.

I can't see all of them. Queen Atarah has told me there are hundreds here, their bodies ill at ease, separated from being whole.

"Sometimes," she whispered once to me. "Sometimes they just ground it all up with the cane. Can't stop the process. Just pulp and mash to be dried with the rest of the plant squeezed for its sweetness. Then our blood was boiled with the juice, boiled until sweet crystals for their tongues in other countries."

Exported to those smacking lips, to be poured out of fine china, or ladled with silvered spoons into delicacies.

John shouts, and Katelyn yips. She picks her phone off the neatly cut, thick grass and runs inside.

"What?"

He leans against the bleached, gray wood of the doorjamb. "Thought I saw something," he said. "Just a mouse, I think."

"Or an iguana," I shout.

"It was Shuffling Peter," Queen Atarah corrects.

"Please, for me, move on," I beg. "Isn't there a light to go find?"

When this commission hits I'll have to be careful not to mention where I would be staying after this. I didn't need the mournful past clanking around an apartment.

Katelyn and John hop around to the back of the mill, looking for iguanas to feed with red hibiscus flowers.

"We're going to head back to the hotel," John says brightly after their small adventure ends fruitlessly. There are no iguanas up here; I won't tell them that though. They love iguanas, they haven't had to clean up after iguana shit everywhere, the hotel they're in does that quietly in the background so they can feed their mini-Godzillas. "We have a rum tasting scheduled, and some more consulting to do."

And then they leave, weaving around the wrong side of the road in their rental Jeep, hitting every pothole in the road with such jarring slaps I wince from up the road.

"Remember when they first reached out to you?" Queen Atarah asks.

In the middle of the hurricane. An email, right before the cell tower got ripped up by the winds and flung clear out over into Donaldson's backyard. Big news up in the US covered the destruction live. Property damage. Winds so powerful they compared the energy to nuclear bombs.

And after the bombing, real estate speculators came in to pick over the remains.

"We've always dreamed of moving to the Caribbean," John's email said. "And we're hearing about a lot of land coming up for sale."

Before I'd replied to the email, days later when we picked ourselves up, cut trees and pulled them off roads, pushed roofs off to the side, I promised I'd put a portion of the commission toward post-hurricane recovery.

Ms. Hennigan came by to help cast out the ghosts three weeks back, when I'd been working hard to clear out dead brush from the hurricane and try to make the mill as presentable as possible.

All the time the shadows spoke to me with the rustle of wind through skeletal, bleached branches stripped of their pre-hurricane green. I had stopped to stare at a single playing card, embedded deep in a tree's bark. Five of clubs.

An old man, sucking on a long piece of sugar cane, grinned toothlessly at me. "When mama mistress opened the door at night, and she hung the purple-windowed lantern, we'd line up in front of the house."

All that visible muscle, lean from too little food. Abs that John would die for.

Mama mistress would lick the sweat off their skin before she tied them down and bid the others to leave after she made her choice.

"Where do you think your uncle's light brown skin comes from?" the old man asked, laughing at my discomfort when he gave me the vision. "They bred us in shacks at the back of the property."

Ms. Hennigan made a lot of claims about her old ways, but in the end, all the smoke and chanting just left a sour smell in the air that the ghosts complained about.

"Who she think she is?"

"Get that from here."

The undead swirled about, furious at the interruption.

"Exorcism is a delicate thing," Ms. Hannigan had told me, her bird-thin wrists clacking with wooden beads. "Best to walk away and leave them to be."

I told her about the commission.

"Ay," she said. "I would take that money and run, you know?"

I did.

Hands. I think about all those hands and feet. Buried in the ground around the mill, and the rest, eaten by the massive stone that grabbed anything near its raggedy lips to chew.

Balled up, intertwined, undulating, writhing in pain.

I sit up in the humid night, gasping, grabbing for my chest where I'd sworn hands had reached out from under the bed to grab me.

They can't talk. They can't howl. They can't do anything other than skitter about the edges of my vision.

"Not just us ghosts here," Queen Atarah says.

I pour warm water from a sweaty glass pitcher. We sit and watch the moon over the bay out the door.

"I miss my house," I tell her.

Put everything I had into it, but the morning after the hurricane what did I have? Not a roof over my head. It blew off into the ocean. Nothing but the bathtub I'd cowered in as what sounded like a train thundered over my head.

The insurance company? Folded. Money sucked up into another shell company over that. All of it a game to extract money out of us.

Sell this mill, get into an apartment, see if I could start rebuilding.

Queen Atarah appeared that first night after the storm, as I hid here in this mill that I could never sell. She sucked her teeth in annoyance at my screaming and carrying on.

"Hold your head up like the king you are," she hissed at me. "My blood in your veins. You are royalty. Do not run from it."

I ran from it.

At first.

Now I'm sitting here chatting with the ghost of a woman whose father lost a war, was sold to Portuguese traders, and then packed into a hold off Sierra Leone. The daughter of the same man who sold Atarah into slavery was on the ship, and Atarah strangled her to death by the end of the week with the very chains that kept her shackled to a nearby post.

"I tried to kill the sailors," she said to me once. She showed me horrible marks on her arms. "But they shot the men, and punished the rest of us. You know, though, I made their voyage far less profitable. I'm proud of that, at least."

We watch TV together, the ghosts and me. They like shows with a diverse cast. But they don't want things too serious. Comedies get the best reactions. The laughter of shades slips around the walls and fades through the air, carried away whenever the salt breeze kicks up.

When I try to watch dramas, or history, I get vetoes that come with wailing and moaning.

Talent shows get turnout. The room, empty in one way, but packed full of the dead if you turn your eyes just so, erupts in excitement when an old gospel choir breaks out into joyful song.

I feel the brush of a clean, Sunday-best dress against my back as a young girl twirls and twirls to voices raised in harmony.

"What a thing to see," Queen Atarah says, her face twisting and faint in the blue glow. "What a thing."

They all groan and warble with anger when the judges vote against the choir continuing on.

"Are you going to haunt those people when they move here?" I ask.

"Haunt them? They don't have our blood. They won't see us. Maybe we could make them feel unease. That's it. You're the one we hope will stop them. They *see* you. They don't see us."

I look around at the half-seen presences. Just barely island enough they could haunt me. But not Katelyn and John.

"I'm tired, Queenie," I say, using the nickname the others use for her.

FEMA has a timeline for how people recover after disasters. Getting through the storm, that's adrenaline and dealing with the disaster. People even feel better than normal after. The community comes together. People share food about to go bad, help clear driveways, check in on each other.

But then, there is cleaning up, rebuilding, and the scale of the work sets in.

It's months after a disaster when the price starts getting paid.

I rub my face and turn off the TV to disappointed groans around me.

Bad enough on an island everyone knows you, and all your relatives are always up in your business. Now I have to negotiate with the distant ancestors complaining about what I watch as well.

"We're all tired," Queen Atarah says. "We're all surviving, best we can."

I feel ashamed, because I know my problems are inconsequential to her suffering. I pour rum so that this time I can sleep without hearing anything.

I meet them on the beach by the hotel, to sign the memorandum of understanding. Katelyn has an early-morning painkiller in a coconut, John wants a pure temple for a body, so he's drinking something green. Grass-clippings green.

Deep, deep breath.

"You said you felt unease, you had a nightmare the other night?" I ask.

They glance at each other. "Yes."

"I think . . ." I look off at the shimmering ocean and a medium-sized yacht bobbing by, someone on deck fumbling about, trying to get a sail up.

This bay used to be a quiet place when I was a kid. We'd come down and shatter the silence, scare off the seagulls and pelicans on the rocks with our wildness.

"You do know what the mill was?" I ask them gently.

"A sugar mill," John says brightly.

"And, how was sugar made in this mill?" My voice is blunt now, my face no longer scrunched up in cheery sales mode.

We're all tired.

"Is this about . . ." Katelyn starts off.

The way John lowers his voice, it sounds like we're about to conduct a drug deal. He glances around, as if worried about being busted. "*Those* times?"

"Yes. *Those* times." I lean forward. I can feel my stomach lurch.

"Will the locals try to stop us? Is there trouble?" Katelyn asks. She grips the table, eyes wide.

I set aside the way she says locals. I set aside the way it rankles me that they don't see me as one of the locals, merely because I look like her and John. I set everything aside and let go of my driving need to get something, anything so I can start building my own house again on the hurricane-scoured land.

"You want to build a home there," I say. "But the people enslaved and forced to work there, so many died there. So many lost limbs to the mill. Do you know what happened to a slave then, if they were injured at work?"

They didn't go on disability. There was no social security.

"Are people angry . . . with us?" Katelyn asks, her lip trembling.

"Your living room on those plans, it would be right over where the gears ripped limb from body. Your carpet will be tossed over the bloody floor. If you have dinner there, it would be like having tea in an abattoir."

Nibbling finger food where someone's fingers had been yanked free . . .

Katelyn pales. That's right. Animals. Of course animals would be the thing that shocks her most in that comparison.

Screw it. I'll lean into that. If it's animals that get her attention, I can work it. "How different would it be than eating dinner under swinging meat hooks, where cattle once screamed and panicked—"

"Stop." She looks sickened.

"You're building a house in a graveyard, and you're asking me if people will be upset. The question isn't will people be upset, the question is, why would you do this?"

I push my bike up the hill and pant. I lean it against the wall of the cabin and take my groceries inside. The bottle of champagne I take out with me to go sit on the "pirate" rock to watch the sun set.

"You're drunk already, why you need that?" Queen Atarah asks.

"Because I'm celebrating," I say.

They're all out in the shadows, watching me. I can feel them.

"Celebrating what?" Her eyes narrow.

"Losing the biggest commission of my life." I pop the cork and laugh as champagne mists the air around us all. I drink from the bottle. A rivulet of champagne misses my lips and trickles down the side of my neck.

"He's a fresh one," someone mutters from the hibiscus bush.

"Leave him be," another shade says.

"All that money," I say to Queen Atarah.

"For what?"

"I know. I know this place needs to be a museum. Or—"

"I meant, what would you do with that money?"

I stare out at the silvery waters of the bay. "Start my new house? Trip around the world? Fancy dinner? Maybe a boat? Just a small one."

My ancestor, the queen, looks around. "They were focused on that. Money. Sugar made this island one of the richest, most productive places in the world. And those men who took us, they were fueled by it. The sugar powered all that money. They were more drunk on it than you right now."

I don't feel I can argue that. But . . . "I'm going to be sleeping in a tent after all this, you know that, right?"

"But you're free," Queen Atarah says. "And your conscience is light. The world is yours. We are so excited for you. Can't you see that?"

I look over my shoulder. They're all just outside of my ability to easily look directly at them, yet I can hear the happiness in the hum of the bush all around me. A different tone.

"We survived so you can thrive, yes, but you can't look away or turn your back," Queen Atarah tells me. "We won't let you. Not for long."

"Maybe we can convince someone to turn this into a museum," I say. "A thoughtful, tasteful, but honest museum."

Because what else could a plantation be? Who would turn a forced labor camp into a restaurant, or a set of villas? Queen Atarah had been stolen from her own land, but bled and died here, and now she is a part of it.

I'd been so focused on money, and development, and my own misery, that I'd lost perspective.

"What do you think of that, Queenie?" I ask, finishing the champagne off in a final swallow.

But there is no one around me. Just the rustle of the trade winds, the bleached bush, and the shadows of the old mill.

THE CARVING OF WAR

by Somto Ihezue Onyedikachi

Odili cupped the scream falling from her lips. It had been twenty years since last she saw it. There it was, in her bedroom, coiled under her child's head. Walking, then running, then stumbling, she made for the kitchen. From behind the pot cabinet, she drew a cutlass, the one for splitting the coconuts. Darting back to the room, her breath steel in her chest, she inched towards her child's cot. She reached into it, her fingers clattering against each other, and picked him up in one swoop. Setting him in his chair, far at the end of the room, she took the cutlass and hacked everything to pieces. The cot, the mattress, her árùsí—familiar; bright gold pyramids trailing down its body, she hacked at it all, wood, foam and skin scattering across the room. She did not stop, until her child began to cry.

The rest of the night met Odili awake. She kept turning in bed every time the crickets buried in the walls broke into their high-chirped songs. Checking on him for the fourth time, she found her child silent with opened eyes. In his little face, Odili saw her grandmama. She lifted him, pressing his temple to her lips and pulling away when she felt warm liquid seeping into her clothes.

"Naughty, naughty boy," she sighed.

She nuzzled her nose on his and he smiled, his incisors, specks of white. Changing his urine-stained clothes and putting him back to sleep, she headed for the bathroom and met her mother at the door.

"Gods!" Odili cowered to the floor.

"Foolish child, what have you done?"

"Ma—Mama?"

Odili had not set eyes on her mother, not in years. With the markings of the old faith etched on her face, cowries from the Eke River clasped around her neck, her hair, silvered milk, her mother was starting to look very much like her grandmama.

"You took all I sowed in you, and you left it to the crows!"

On the floor, hands wrapped around her body, Odili sat noiseless. With her mother came the memories, the ones she locked behind walls. Now, the walls came tumbling down and the memories poured in, drowning her.

"Where is its body?" her mother asked, anger sewn into the wrinkles on her face.

Like a baby learning to walk, Odili drew herself off the floor, out the back door and into the bushes behind her house. Her mother followed, a shadow on an ill-lit street. Coming to a spot, Odili stepped aside and like an arrow, her mother's cry pierced the night. Odili had never heard a thing like it, it was anguish given voice.

"Mother of my mothers, gouge out my eyes for I have seen the unseen," she cried, collapsing to the ground, next to the lynched corpse of the familiar. Ash and dust was all that remained of it. "Insolent child!" She threw a glare at Odili and in her eyes, something built. "You will be the death of us."

Odili just stood there as her mother resumed her wailing. She had never seen her cry, not once, not even when her grandmama died.

"How did you find me?"

"You have always been a slow one." Her mother dried her eyes, turning to her. "Did you think you could just leave?" she continued, mockery stealing into her voice. "The path before you is set in stone."

"I didn't leave . . . I was taken. I thought you'd come for me."

"The way back was ahead of you, you just chose not to see it."

"I was a child. I was lost. I waited for you." Odili caught the tear making its way down her face. "You abandoned me!"

"And when you became a woman, what held you from returning to your duty, to your mother!"

"Mother? You are dead to me."

Her mother's slap fell like a gush of cold breeze on her cheek. It would have stung more if she had been there in flesh, not projecting her spirit.

"I want you to leave," Odili said, unfazed.

"You must come back to Obosi, you must atone for this atrocity."

"I'd rather die a thousand deaths."

"You think you have known suffering?" Her mother's eyes narrowed. "Something is coming, something unlike anything you have ever seen."

"Leave, please!"

In a blink, her mother vanished into the night.

Odili had been but a child when Nkeala, her grandmama, died. All she remembered of her were her braids, a tangle of clouds that reached for the floor. She remembered her eyes, how they swallowed her face. To look into them was to be lost in a vastness, it was to find eyes—owl eyes, bold eyes, brown eyes—staring back at you. Most of all, she remembered her kindness, an unending sea. Odili remembered everything.

Nkeala had been dìbìā—keeper, to Idemili; the roaring python, they who drowned oceans, mother of mothers. At the birth of time, Idemili, like beads dancing on a woman's waist, had wound herself around the clans of Obosi. Out of her mouth, the Eke River poured, its brooks and streamlets giving sustenance to the corn in the farmlands, the antelopes of the wild and the Irokos that split the sky. Odili's family was bound in perpetuity to Idemili.

With her grandmama's passing, the fanged staff fell to her mother, Adaugo. In the past, a few keepers had met their fate with defiance. Odili's great-great-grandfather, Agbadike, had refused the staff when it passed to him. Setting the shrine of Idemili ablaze, he invoked the ritual of blood in a bid to sever the bond that tethered his life to her. Three days after, a breadfruit fell from a tree and split his skull in half.

Like moth to fire, Adaugo embraced the mantle of keeper. Before her twelfth birthday, she could already perform the passage rites of ancestors. Beneath the glow of a horned moon, she'd slay a ram, its body thrashing beneath her knee. Immersed in its blood, she'd wade into the Eke, bridging the fold between the living and the dead. Ancestors past would come walking through her, blessing and cursing the ones they left behind. When she was heavy with Odili, Adaugo ventured into Idemili's mouth and emerged unscathed, spirit water coursing through her veins. One of the dwindling few, Adaugo knew the words to the eternal scripts and the anchors that held them. The clans of Obosi had revered Nkeala; Adaugo, they feared. She was power unbridled, her dedication to Idemili, undying. Like her mother and keepers before her, Adaugo stayed unwed.

"We are the rage of Idemili, unburdened by the constraints of love and companionship," she'd remind Odili. "We are fire and water, we are rain and lightning, our bodies are nothing but vessels."

Still, keepers were mandated to bear offspring, but only with those from the root of princes, thus, sustaining the purity of their line. Without a father, a mother who in all entirety was of another realm, Odili roamed the village unchecked, her python familiar slithering beside her. More than a companion, it had become a parent, regurgitating rabbits and bush rats for her to roast.

When the first missionaries came to their village, Odili was drawn in by their flaky bread and the trinkets that hung from their neck, how they shimmered in the light. At the rooster's crow, she'd run into the village, into the shack that doubled as a chapel, to watch the priests bless communion, to watch Edward. Edward was a mass server and Edward was beautiful. With her eyes, she'd follow him and when he caught her stare, she'd hold it till he flushed red and looked away. He intrigued her, the sapphire of his eyes, his hair; the burning of dawn, the way he said her name, like a song lived in the walls of his lips. When first he kissed her—a gentle kiss, his nose brushing against hers—he had closed his eyes. Odili kept hers a door, ajar.

When the priests baptized her in the Eke, Odili didn't feel new, born again, like Edward had said she would. And when she received communion, the blood of Christ sweet on her tongue, only then did her mother come raging like a flood, her screams, claps of thunder.

"I curse you, I curse you all!" Her outstretched finger trembled under her voice. "You touched a seed of Idemili, you defiled her waters." She paced around them, leopard to prey. "Come, come and see how you fall."

That night, the chapel burned to the ground and Edward with it. When the last of the missionaries left Obosi, they took Odili with them. She was sixteen. Her mother, far off in the spirit wilds, had not been there to stop them.

Odili held a heart in her hands, red ants crawling over it. She ate it whole. Out of the hollow in her chest, she took out a rock. She watched as cracks tore across its rough exterior, like they did on her bedroom walls. Breaking open, a python, fanged and rattled, lunged at her. Odili willed herself awake. She had not slept in days, not since her mother's visit. Even in the heat of daylight, she kept seeing things, the bread hawker with two heads, three men with bellies like drums swinging from a guava branch, her reflection missing in the mirror.

With her sheets, she dabbed the sweat the nightmare had brought with it, looked over into her child's new cot, and he wasn't there. Odili panicked, tearing through the baby blankets. She spun around, dread crawling onto her face. Thinking perhaps she had left him in the living room, even though she vividly remembered tucking him in, she made for the door. Hand on the knob, she stopped. She turned, towards a closed-off corner of the room, and found her child cradled in the hands of a darkness.

"He has our eyes," it said, the echo of its voice, the crackling of fire.

"Give him to me." The dread on Odili's face disappeared, and fury took its place. "Give him to me!" The walls shook as black veins zipped across her skin, her pupils eclipsing the white of her eyes.

The darkness faded, melting into the crevices on the floor, leaving the child behind.

"They came for our boy, they came for him!" Odili said, ushering Nnayeleugo into her house.

After the episode with the darkness, Odili had sent for him. They had met years ago when he ran with the ghost masquerades of Okija. When she had told him she was carrying their child and he asked her to marry him, she refused. Nnayeleugo was a river, forever on the run. He was everywhere and nowhere and Odili had no interest in being part of that. There was also the reminder at the back of her mind that she was promised to another, one clearly as testing as they were vicious. However, she and Nnayeleugo remained friends as well as parents to their child, with him swooping in from time to time, bringing wood carvings and sweets that tasted of ginger.

"Whatever it is, we must trap it and banish it," he said, scanning the house, hands akimbo.

"Banish it?"

"Yes, banish its connection to you."

Odili nodded. This was why she sent for him. She may have forsaken her belief in the old faith, Nnayeleugo had not. A boy, he had been an apprentice to a local blacksmith in a land whose name was not spoken. When stone morphed to gold in his hand, he spoke not a word of it, and when the flames from the hearth spoke to him, he spoke back.

"Bring my boy, let me hold him." Nnayeleugo laughed his coarse laugh as he returned to his jaunty self.

Come nightfall, he took strands of hair from Odili's head, bound it to a half moon and when the night started to speak, he summoned the darkness.

"Biá—come, biá rùsàlà ókú ògū—come wrestle fire," he chanted, dancing round the runes he had drawn on Odili's bedroom floor. Odili sat in the corner, their baby resting on her shoulder.

"Biá kene, biá fúrú ògū." Nnayeleugo's voice pulsated. "I fú, I gbá, I fú, I gbá—" He stopped in his tracks, his eyes darting around in their sockets. "It is here."

"Where?" Odili sprang up.

Nnayeleugo did not respond.

"Nnayeleugo?" Odili put the child down among his carvings. "Nna?"

He charged at her in scattered steps and pinned her to the wall. Drawing his dagger, he brought it to her throat. Odili, still reeling from the suddenness of it all, raised her face to his. In his face, she did not find him.

"It—something is—something—inside—me—" He strained, blood streaming down his ears. "Gba oso, run."

Crawling from under him, the blade grazing her skin, Odili picked up their child, but she did not run. She turned to Nnayeleugo and she saw it, shadowed claws gripping his neck from behind. From over his shoulder, an eye peeped at her, then a second, then a hundred, all shrouded in darkness.

"Let him go!"

Like a puppet, they strung Nnayeleugo forward, up to her. He let out a cry as the claws dug deeper into him.

"Please," she cried, falling to her knees.

One by one, they took their claws out of him as Nnayeleugo exhaled. And in all their voices, "Come drink with us," they said. Their claws to the front of his neck, they slashed his throat open, and like a black hole, vanished into themselves. Nnayeleugo's hands went to his neck as he reached for his voice and crashed to the ground. Odili ran to him, tying her baby to her back. Unsure, tears clouding her sight, she pressed her hands against the gash, blood spluttering all over.

"Help! Somebody help!" She stood in an attempt to find help and Nnayeleugo held her, his touch weak, cold. He did not say a word, he didn't need to. Odili sat with him, in his blood, in the pieces of her heart. She stayed till the light left his eyes.

Odili threw her things into a box, torched her house with Nnayeleugo's body in it, and she ran. Journeying for days, her child on her back, she made it to the bank of the Eke River. Regardless of the serpent horde weaving through its waters, the river was the fastest route into Obosi. Making the crossing on a crowded ferry and hoping no one recognized her, she got to her mother's hut. It was how she remembered it, a roof built out of palm fronds, an unkempt hibiscus hedge, and the constant bleating of goats. Her mother was bent over a mortar, pounding cocoyams when Odili walked in.

"I knew you'd come," she said. She didn't even look up at Odili. "Ngwanu, let us begin, for night gathers."

In the passing months, they performed the cleansing ritual of rebirth. Every third market day, Adaugo washed Odili in the Eke. Her body breaking the waters, it reminded her of her baptism, of Edward.

"*Mere mortals would be whipped through the village for this sacrilege, but you are my child, the blood in your veins, spirit water. Your shame is mine alone to bear."*

The nights when Adaugo flung open the ancestral gates, she'd balance a calabash of python eggs on Odili's head and have her walk naked into the wilds. Odili just prayed she didn't run into a night-wolf.

"Before the ones who came before us, be bare."

In between bathing in the Eke and running from wolves, Odili's days became cold and terrifying. Today, her mother nowhere in sight, she sat in the yard, in the gentle breeze, and watched her child build mud dunes.

"What is his name?" Adaugo sprung from behind her.

"Nkeala," Odili said, recovering from the fright. "I named him after Grandmama," she added as it dawned on her that her mother had never asked for her son's name.

Adaugo sat in the sand, next to her. She had not heard her mother's name in a while. "Like its bearers, it is beautiful," she said, her gaze on the boy. "He has her eyes."

"He has yours too."

They were looking at each other now. For the first time in a long time, Odili saw her mother. She placed her hand in hers and Adaugo squeezed it, a knowing squeeze. Hand in hand, they sat in silence.

For the final rites, the ashes of her familiar—Odili had brought it along in an old milo tin—were scattered into the Eke, a wake held in its honour.

"Weep, child, for we lay our mothers to rest."

And weep, Odili did. At the end of the rituals, a grave illness overtook her. On her mother's mat, sweat soaking into her clothes, her breathing was raspy, and her body felt paper thin. Wiping her with a cold towel, Adaugo chanted incantations under her breath, her head bobbing back and forth.

"What—what is happening to me?" Odili's speech was starting to leave her. "Did we do it wrong?"

"Be calm, the ritual is taking its toll," Adaugo hushed her. "Atonement is a long hard road and you have much to atone for," she continued. "Abandoning your sacred duty, murdering your familiar, then there's that peasant trickster you spawned a child with, good thing I got rid of him."

"You—you got rid of—of him?"

"Quiet now, you need rest."

Sitting up, Odili pushed her mother's hands away. She saw clearly now, for in Adaugo's caged eyes a darkness lingered, the darkness that had come for her child . . . the darkness that murdered Nnayeleugo.

"Gods, it—it was you." All the colour drained from Odili's face.

Adaugo straightened up from the mat, her face vacant, unapologetic.

"Why, Mama?"

"Idemili is merciful . . . it is my duty to be her vengeance."

Drawing strength from nowhere, Odili leaped at her. From the soil, Adaugo summoned taut roots that grasped her, binding her feet and wrists. Like threads, Odili tore through them and descended on her mother.

"Die!" she screamed, her hands wrapped around her throat. Adaugo flailed and clawed, spitting into Odili's eyes, striking her with blindness. Odili wiped off the curse like it was water.

"You are old and like you, your power wanes." Odili tightened her grip. "No one will mourn you."

As Adaugo gasped for her last breath, Odili shrieked, letting go of her. Something was wrong. She could feel her muscles tearing off her bones, the bones, breaking, crushing into each other, pain tearing through her.

"What have you done to me!" She glowered at her mother, her eyes, cut diamonds.

"To right this wrong, there must be a reckoning," Adaugo coughed, coming to her knees. "A strand of Idemili was torn and it must be replaced."

"What?"

"Doing this to you, it wounds me, but I am without a choice."

"No." Odili's legs had started to morph into one. "Mama, stop this, please!"

"Don't worry, I will raise my grandchild to be stronger."

Odili inside of herself, her heart racing faster than a hummingbird's wings, watched her body come undone. As the transformation edged towards her chest, Odili reached, grabbing her mother by the leg.

"This is not the last of me, Mother," she hissed, her tongue forked in two. "Brace yourself for I will be war, and I will come."

Letting go, of herself, of the fight in her, Odili fledged into a python the brown of bark and into dusk, she slithered.

GHOST SHIP

by Tananarive Due

2060

"One last thing," Nandi said in Zulu, not English, at the dock, so Florida knew she didn't want to be overheard by crewmen or waiting passengers. "I'll need you to carry this box to your cabin. Open it *promptly*. And carry it with *both* hands, please. I've paid for your rations on board, so no need for these."

Then Nandi had whisked the packs of cookies from Florida's hands—the sweets Florida had been collecting for weeks and had shepherded so carefully past security, tolerating insulting questions ("Don't you think you're big enough?")—and in their place given her a frightfully heavy box, at least seven or eight k, decorated with warning arrows and stickers, also in Zulu: *Carry Upright*. Who knew how long she would be stuck carrying it? Why couldn't Nandi have sent this to the cargo bay with the rest of Florida's deliveries like any other passenger?

Now Florida understood why she was being sent on her Pilgrimage by sea, a re-creation of her long-ago ancestors' Middle Passage, rather than a hyperflight that could have taken her to New York in only two hours. Even a sixteen-hour jitney plane would be so much faster than a ship, and the price would be less than Nandi's new ostrich feather hat. Ships could be beset by pirates and rough seas and seemed primitive even to Florida's unpampered sensibilities. The true advantage, for Nandi, was that

flight security was stricter. Why would anyone bother to blow up
a passenger ship?

Florida was now a smuggler, then. Diamonds or banned tech
or who knew what Nandi sent on the ships with her couriers when
she offered Pilgrimages: passage to the States for a year. Florida
had never imagined Nandi would choose her, the way she pro-
fessed she couldn't do without her; the passage alone was more
than a month each way. Florida was also surprised that Nandi
would risk her on a smuggling trip—the penalty for almost any
infraction on a US-bound ship was being cast overboard. Theft.
Assault. Even vandalism. The orientation had been very clear:
passengers had a 5 percent voyage fail rate! But here she was, and
Nandi had been brazen enough to set her package in Florida's
hands in front of witnesses, begging for inspection. (Though
Nandi had gotten it past security herself as far as the dock, at
least; wealth and standing had true advantages.)

"I don't see how you eat that poison," Nandi said, in English
this time. She slid Florida's cookies into her pocket. "It's just like
a USian to eat for pleasure. Don't get spoiled already."

Nandi did not say goodbye, never mind that she had raised
Florida since she was eight, in a way—if obtaining ownership of a
child through her dead mothers' labor contracts constituted rear-
ing. Nandi seemed to want to touch her, but she only gave Florida
a knowing smile, bowed her short-shaved silver head at her and
pivoted toward the shore to return to her domed palace. Florida
watched her feather hat floating away above the crowds.

For the first time in her life, Florida was among only strangers.
Wealthy strangers, based on their colorful coats. Wealthy *USian*
strangers. Florida's clothing was shades of dirty white: grays and
tans and browns. Worker fashion. Now she would have to put up
with stares from USians who were returning home after safari.
Florida had never seen so many USians collected in one place.
They were loud, shouting to be heard over each other. They wore
mountains of soft clothing. All were eager to go home, happy and

smiling, except when they saw her. Noticing brown or black skin was the favorite sport in the States, so most stared at her. Fine with her. Most of the Aggie campus in South Africa was made up of African-American expats, so this was the first time Florida had noticed her skin in as long as she could remember. She hadn't reached the States yet and she was *Black* again. And in a sea of whites.

Racism still thrived in other parts of South Africa, she had heard, but the New Azania Campus of Naidoo Industries, as it was called—made up of agricultural engineers and workers—was a world unto itself. Privilege and prospects had everything to do with contracts and little to do with skin color. Nandi herself was proof: darker than Florida by shades and too much wealthier to even compute. Nandi's father had built New Azania, buying up once-prized drought-ravaged lands near Cape Town to experiment with bioengineering. This rising need for workers and scientists in South Africa had coincided with the Purging in the States, with millions of nonwhites driven beyond the US borders to avoid prison or police executions in their homes.

But "freedom," Florida's mothers had learned, was only earned by release from service contracts. And the debts they had accrued over the years had not been nearly enough to repay Naidoo, so they had died penniless, much like the sharecroppers of their forebears. So many others in New Azania, like Florida, were trapped by the decisions of others, trying to save for liberation, or passage back to the States out of nostalgia for familiar accents and home soil—even if it was a land that did not want them, winnowing down the population to whites remaking the storied multicultural nation in their own pale image.

And here they were, sneering at her. The USians were returning to their world of dominion. They did not like Florida. And she did not like them.

"There's a story, ya know," Florida said in her best USian accent. "About a ghost ship. Bet they didn't tell you there's a ghost ship floating out at sea, full of the rotting bodies. Maybe we'll pass right by?" It was half a truth, but she felt like an actress. Such liberation! To speak whatever was in her mind, unafraid of docked rations. And it was so amusing the way their smiles faded. At least they stopped staring at her. And crowded her less. And let her pass.

But her improved mood didn't last long as she remembered the cookies Nandi had taken from her. She would not be free of Nandi even at sea. Nandi would control every bite she ate.

All Florida had wanted in exchange for forty days of boredom and peril on the ship was a sweet taste on her tongue every day, something to look forward to. Now she would not have that. All that waited ahead of her now was time. And risk.

Shovel it, then. She would not return to Africa. She had a year to either escape or plot a way to earn a living on the dying lands for which her mothers had named her. Her older mother had been a biologist, the younger an engineer, neither of them treated much better than slaves from the time they had set foot at the New Azania campus. Both dead of Red Lung by the age of forty. (Red Lung: as if chemical poisoning were a demonic dust.) No, that would not be Florida's fate. She had avoided Red Lung in Nandi's well-ventilated dome and labs, but she would wrest more from life than healthy lungs.

She had found a way to escape, her mothers' dream for her.

The mysterious delivery in her hands was her chance.

On the US-bound ship, a passenger cruiser called, predictably, *Whistling Dixie,* Florida learned the meaning of the orange tag she wore around her neck. The uniformed greeter at the portal was covered in facial hair except for sharp, watching eyes, even hairy across the bridge of the nose. Florida had never seen anyone so hairy.

"Huh—slow down, you!" Hairball said, and Florida thought

she would have her package confiscated. Instead, Hairball flicked at her tag. "Orange cabins are helpers' quarters. Not this way—*that* way."

The entrance forked. *This way* was gleaming and satiny, with conveyor seats and trays of water for the light-hearted crowds. *That way* was gloom and poor lighting, with no offerings except a long walk down a narrow corridor.

"But . . . I'm a passenger, not a worker," Florida said. "I have a private cabin."

Hairball sneered. "Yah—like anyone else would fit with you! Keep moving."

Of course. How could she have expected Nandi to pay for even second-class passage? She'd probably gladly acquiesced to the racial segregation that had become the norm in the United States again.

Florida tried to prepare herself, but the cabin that matched the color and number hanging from her neck still was worse than she'd imagined. She'd hoped for at least a sponge bed, picture window, a chair and desk where she might enjoy the solitude that had been impossible for her in New Azania. She'd rolled her eyes through most of the orientation, believing only the privileged were susceptible to anxiety caused by boredom. More than a month with no concerns but (mostly) her own? No constant summoning? But the cabin was hardly bigger than a closet, with a thin pallet that would barely contain her, a retracting sheet of metal as a "desk" and no window. *No window!* No way to see the ocean. It looked more like a prison cell. And she saw no comfortable space for the box. Florida let out a frustrated shriek. Her neighbor tapped the wall, complaining already.

Florida was about to pound back when her box . . . *thunked*. Something inside shifted, scrabbling. Florida remembered Nandi's last instructions: to open the box right away. Whatever was inside was either growing or . . .

"Oh, please don't let it be . . ."

Yes. It was *alive*. Florida knew that before she pressed her thumb to the lock pad Nandi had configured for her, but it was confirmed when she saw a spray of thin gray fur, a white belly, lashing tail, rounded ears, large eyes, sharp teeth. And claws. The creature slashed at her, raking Florida's right ear, drawing blood. Florida cried out as the creature leaped from the box and desperately sought to hide, wobbly from the trank Nandi must have given it. It fell to its side, disoriented, paws scratching the metallic floor.

"So, by now you've seen the favor I need from you."

Nandi's hologram appeared from a pinprick of projection light on the box, splayed so convincingly across the pallet in her purple robe that Florida wondered if it was a live feed. But no, the 3-D hologram was recorded—Nandi's eyes were looking in the wrong direction, toward the door.

"You kaffir," Florida said to Nandi's projection, wishing so badly that Nandi could hear the banned word from history that Nandi loathed. Florida touched her ear, felt the dampness of blood. Not too much, but still. It *stung*.

"Don't be angry. Anger is the meal of fools. Nelson Mandela said that."

"You liar. He never said that." Florida hated the way Nandi recited supposed quotations from Nelson Mandela, usually about industry and obedience. Florida had been twelve when she learned through research that Mandela had said *none* of the things Nandi claimed.

Cursing out the hologram was therapeutic, clearing her head. Anger melted, replaced by terror. Florida had smuggled a *live* creature aboard a USian ship! If she were found out, she would be expelled like a stowaway, thrown into the ocean. The orientation had been specific.

"The first thing you should know: it's mute. No voice box. So have no fear of discovery. If you are smart—and I've told you many times, Florida, you are *very* smart—you'll have no trouble keeping it hidden for the voyage. The tranquilizer is under the flap. You'll also find a sedative mist: it's safe for both of you . . . but *conserve* it, only at night. You have a long journey ahead. Keep that same box for storage and use it when you arrive."

The States, Florida reminded herself. This was all so she could go to the States to wade in the Atlantic off the shores of whatever areas had not flooded in the state of Florida, her namesake. USians avoided the sun most of the day because of UV, but there would be beaches.

"I paid for double rations. One is for you, the other for your charge. You must play with it several times a day—they grow aggressive when they're bored. Actually, so do you—you'll be good company for each other. The crystals beneath the flap will help disintegrate the waste for easy disposal. You'll receive delivery instructions when you land. You must deliver it personally. This breed is from Naidoo Labs, so it will be the first of its type in the States. You're a pioneer! Once you deliver it, I will deposit a full two percent of its price in your account."

A one-of-a-kind animal delivery would fetch a hot price. Two percent might be significant. Not worth dying over, but it might clear her debt. Was Nandi setting her free?

Nandi's voice turned hard. "Needless to say . . . if any harm should come to this animal, if it is injured in any way, you will be sent back to suffer severe consequences."

"I'm not an animal handler, you—you—stain on two continents."

What did she know about animals? Pets were rare in the Aggie districts because of lack of space and long working hours. Naidoo Life Systems specialized in biotech to help humans adapt to environmental shifts—and Nandi's personal hobby was the genetic manipulation of animals. One of her experiments apparently had gone right. But Florida was far from an expert.

The little creature was already on its feet, sniffing the door. Searching for an escape. They were alike after all.

"Is this a cat?" she asked the hologram, forgetting Nandi was not on the other end. She had read about cats, although this animal's face seemed too narrow, the ears too big.

"Be very careful, my little tsotsi. This is dangerous work. But you will be fine."

The hologram pixelated and vanished. One-time play.

Florida faced the creature, whose mouth was frantically miming a memory of speech. Florida saw the shaved neck, the fading scar, and realized Nandi had surgically removed the animal's voice box instead of finding the right stew of genetics to silence it. Had she done the cutting herself, too proud to consult anyone else for her plan? Florida rubbed her ear, wondering why Nandi hadn't removed its claws too.

Tentative, Florida reached her hand out. The creature's face crinkled to pure loathing, baring its sharp teeth. Was it trying to spit at her? *That* was unpleasant.

"You listen to me," Florida told the cat. "We're stuck together. You don't like me, I don't like you. But neither of us wants to get thrown overboard, so don't be afraid of me."

Already, secretly, she felt herself becoming glad. The cabin was disappointing, but now she would have amusement, or at least chores. What Mandela had said about industry was true—it sharpened the mind as well as passing the time. (He had not said it, but she had learned inspiration from the quote before she realized Nandi had made it up. Same difference.)

She lifted the flaps in the box and found the supplies, including a powder marked as food. Once Florida hydrated it, the powder turned a gray-white color, thickish liquid in texture. The creature made a silent motion with its mouth and ran for the dish, licking greedily.

Good. Feeding it was the first step. Keeping it alive.

Florida realized she needed to give the animal a name.

The name she chose was Burden.

The first few days were horrid.

Florida was so worried about discovery that she did not dare leave her cabin, more awful confinement. Sleep, too, was difficult, because each sound the creature made in its endless investigations of the cabin woke her. She used far too much of the sedative mist on both of them those first days, inhaling calm so she could stop their racing hearts.

"This is new for both of us," she told Burden in a gentle voice. Instinct told her to speak gently, since she preferred soft talk herself, and soon Burden was sleeping against her, a warm mound at the small of her back. She began to understand why someone would want a pet, even if she would *never* understand why any USian would want a pet transported from a lab.

When Florida was ready to explore the ship, she chose her destinations carefully according to the map she had memorized. Whenever she left her cabin, she made sure no one saw the tiny paw trying to force its way out, and that the door was securely closed, locked. The other travelers housed on her corridor were USians and held themselves above her although they were helpers too. They clung to imaginary distinctions on this floor where they all had nothing. In New Azania, at least, the distinctions were real and not imagined: you were either growing richer by controlling the bio systems, or you were hired labor. Little in-between. But fine. She would not make friends. Fewer people to explain herself to.

She heard the din of laughter and conversation before the elevator deposited her at the first observation deck. But a polite alarm sounded when she tried to pass through the door, and her badge flashed orange. Lower Observation was for black badges only, she remembered. A separate elevator took her to Upper Observation.

And there she sat, with nothing but the ocean all around her, the frivolous USians below. They had plush seating and silly gaming, but she had the most unhindered view of the sea and its white, undulating crests. She felt as if the watery void *hugged* her, somehow.

Florida tried to feel excitement for approaching the nation she had heard so much about but felt only growing dread: the US might mean discovery. The US meant uncertainty. Even if she weren't discovered, the US meant even worse discrimination. If only she could stay in this place, this one time, between destinations, with no responsibilities except the care of Burden. If she could perfect a constant state of leaving. Maybe that was what had happened with the Ghost Ship, she thought. Maybe the passengers and crew had chosen the journey over their destination.

Florida had learned about the Ghost Ship during her research when Nandi told her she was being sent out to sea. She'd seen reports that the official 5 percent passenger failure rate was a lie—the actual failure rate was much higher. Ships had vanished more than once, never heard from again. Florida scoured the blue-black waves around her for her ship's twin floating somewhere off-course, its comms disabled and useless. A passenger ship would have enough rations for years. What reward might she win for spotting the lost ship?

"Hey there!" a deep voice said behind her, terrifying her. The authoritarian ring made her assume it was a crew officer, perhaps one who had discovered Burden in her absence. But she turned and saw only another passenger, this one with thickly knotted black hair in braids, rocking slightly off-balance from what might be some form of intoxication. Or . . . happiness?

The hair-laden passenger grinned straight, lovely teeth at her. "My name's Lesedi. You look so grim. The trip just started."

Florida sneezed, standing up to exit the observation level. Her sinuses had been irritated since the trip began, and now she was allergic to company. Standing so quickly made her dizzy.

"I am . . . Florida." It was rare, so rare, to share a name with a stranger. Her full, proper name was Florida of Naidoo Life Systems, but Florida did not want to say so. That was not a proper name, anyway.

"I come here every day," Lesedi said. "This—" she said, signaling the ocean, "is what I asked to come for. Here I am. On a ship. It's worth putting up with my mistress."

"Your what?"

"My . . ." She paused, as if embarrassed. "The woman who hired me. From New York."

"You call her 'mistress'? And . . . do you also have a 'master'?"

"Only on this ship. It's a pretty easy job, since everything they need is here. I don't care what they want to be called." Florida must have looked appalled despite her efforts, so Lesedi said, "What do you call *your* employer?"

"To her face?" Florida said. They both laughed, which turned into a sneeze for Florida. She sneezed into her arm. "At first, before I knew better, I called her 'Mother.' She was 'raising' me, or at least training me at the Aggie camp. I was young. Now I call her Nandi."

"Well, you can't call an employer by their first name in the States," Lesedi scolded. "Don't let anyone hear you."

"You've been there?"

"I've heard stories from my cousin. She told me not to come, but . . ." Lesedi indicated the ocean again. "How could I miss this? Saltwater air. No noise. No trash."

Florida had seen a trash mountain through her binoculars, but she decided not to mention it. Trash was everywhere. "Will your employer send you back home?"

"No, I'm only a ship's valet. I'll have to work and save up. But I'm not worried. I'm a good worker. The States will suffocate you only if it's all you've ever known."

Florida wasn't sure about that.

"So . . . is it true . . . ?" Lesedi began.

"What?"

"That Aggies . . . the Blacks who came from the States to work . . . you're like slaves?"

"Who said that?"

"My mistress said I'm lucky I'm not a slave like the Aggies. With a long-term contract."

Florida felt more anger than she would have expected, but only because of the sting of truth. Her mothers had said the same thing before they died. "That's insulting."

"No offense meant, I just—"

Now Florida felt tears to accompany her anger. She turned her face away to hide them. "It was good to meet you, but I have a headache. I need to go."

Florida hurried away, sneezing again, but with every step she regretted her emotional response and hoped she would see Lesedi again. She already missed having a human to talk to.

As she left, she heard Lesedi sneeze behind her.

Florida would not see Lesedi before the power failure.

Just a blip, a flicker, a slight browning of the corridor lights, and then the reliable hum of the auxiliary rod and the ship's cabins were fully powered again.

The cabin's minor anomaly happened in the middle of Florida's sleep cycle—she'd been sleeping longer than usual because she hadn't felt well for a couple of days. The outage made little sound except ambient noises she had learned to sleep through. She did not wake to see her cabin's holo-clock flicker off and on, from blue to red and then back to blue, or hear her toilet automatically refresh, or hear her door hiss open the same way all of the C-wing cabin doors did at 01:18 A.M. Passenger 77-C, Florida of Naidoo Life Systems, heard none of this.

But Burden heard.

Burden stared with fascination as the lights floating on the wall flickered off, then on. Motion was rare in this lifeless cage. Burden was immediately upright, ready to spring!—when a *whishing* sound made his back arch.

No giant challenging predator: it was Door! Retreating!

Any mammal primarily derived from *Felis silvestris catus*, no matter the cosmetic genetic variations, would be drawn to the scent of newness in the open space that had once been Door. Burden crept from the pallet, senses alert, moving quietly so Big would not be disturbed. Burden could still smell the trap Big had hidden under the floor.

Burden had not been feeling well for a few days, but now the creature's limbs felt wild and strong. Burden stepped free just as Door *shooshed* closed again.

Florida's first waking instinct, always—*Where's Burden?* And for the first time the animal did not turn up on the pallet or in any of its favorite hiding places in nooks and shadows. She knew he was gone at a glance, her heart pounding, but she searched anyway. She scoured places that defied reason and logic, tears blinding her. (She would never learn of the power failure. She would convince herself she might have opened her door in her sleep because of the strength of her sleep supplements from Nandi.)

Soon—door securely locked behind her, just in case—she moved her search to the corridor. To the elevator. To the observation deck. She was noticed everywhere she went, but she could not afford to care about staring. However unlikely, in her mind she saw herself sweeping the animal under her clothes undetected, scurrying back to her room.

But she could not find Burden anywhere. *No, no, no, no, no.* The horror stayed glued to her thoughts. The impossibility of it alone! *Why?* Why, why, why?

She cursed herself when she remembered to check the supply/transport box Nandi had given her for a tracking device, and naturally she found one nestled beneath the waste crystals. Her hands shook as she powered it. So much time wasted!

The device displayed a three-dimensional rendering of the ship, but no signal from Burden's tracker. Had someone thrown him overboard? She backed the tracker's control several hours, to the point when Burden was still in her cabin. She found it, zoomed the image to isolate the Stacks. No movement of the white dot at first. Sleeping in her quarters.

Then—rapid motion down the corridor. Florida gasped. She slipped in her corneal lenses to view the tracker privately, then she followed the white dot that raced around the corner ahead of her. She chased it, as if Burden were still close enough to catch. Florida could not fit into the vent beside the tube, but she rode the elevator down another level to match the dot's motion.

But the elevator door would not open for her. Black card level only. Florida's heart raced as she watched the dot make its way in a corridor beyond the sealed entrance. What to do?

Then, abruptly, the dot stopped moving. Florida held her breath. The tracking dot stayed fixed for a time, then . . . it was inside one of the black-level cabins. It remained there one hour on the tracker's timer. Two hours. No motion. Then, the tracker's dot vanished. Gone.

Florida scurried out of the passageway when she heard approaching voices. She did not want to be seen where she did not belong if Burden had been discovered. Had a passenger or crew member found the animal right away and expelled it? But how? Not from the cabin, certainly. The tracker had not moved beyond the passenger floors. No—someone had found Burden and realized its value. *Someone had disabled the tracker.*

It was all clear to her. These were USians: they treasured pets. Of *course* someone would hide the unusual-looking cat. But had they scoured the chip for information about its owner? Did the tracker lead back to her cabin as surely as it led away? Had Nandi been so careless?

Back in her cabin, Florida wept until her face was burning and raw, until her eyelids were acid. She did not eat. She sat frozen on her pallet, waiting to be accused. Waiting to be stripped and thrown into the ocean to feed the sharks. She calculated scenarios again and again, and she came to the same answer: she would die. Any passenger might have smuggled the engineered cat on board, but any simple investigation would point toward Florida—the Aggie.

She longed to talk to Nandi, but even if Nandi were willing to pay the comms fee (Nandi could afford virtually anything she liked, but was famously stingy with expenses for Florida, as her cabin attested), Florida could not hope their communication would be private. Even if she were to risk it, what could Nandi advise her to do except get the animal back and to cease communications?

Her fear spurred a coughing fit. Florida coughed until she was doubled over. Until her lungs pinched and she could barely draw a breath.

Florida did not remember her mothers. Nandi had washed away their memory, claiming it was to erase the trauma (Florida had later found the record of her watching her mother claw her chest to breathe as she died), but in an odd way Nandi wanted to be the only mother she had known even if she did not mother her. Naidoo Life Systems had been Florida's home—she'd been trained in genetic food engineering since she was old enough to read.

Florida was convinced Nandi cared about her, or Nandi would have left her to sleep in the lab quarters with her cohort. Nandi was not cruel. Nandi had only developed a cool amorality that

Florida had decided might be necessary when the stakes were life and the future of the planet. Earth was sustaining its last generations, unless science engineered radical breakthroughs to fight the changing climate with its droughts, floods and food scarcity. But sometimes radical breakthroughs bore questionable methods. Nandi was not cruel at heart, but by trade.

But sending the animal with Florida had been cruel, even unintentionally. What Nandi believed was deep "trust" in Florida's wits was only her willingness to throw her away. It had also been hubris, which also meant that Nandi might have made other mistakes. Because Florida did not remember losing her mothers, this was the worst moment of her life. She could not confront the other passengers to claim ownership. She could not arrive in the States without the animal. And at any moment, because of another passenger's whim, carelessness or spite, she could be pulled from her cabin and expelled. She was helpless and silent.

After a good rest, her cough went away. She also realized she'd been tolerating a small, constant headache for days, but that, too, was gone. A week passed. No one questioned her about Burden. Perhaps the other passenger was as frightened of discovery as she was—that was best.

More than a week after Burden vanished, Florida ventured to the observation deck to try to find Lesedi, but she was not there. No one was in Upper Observation with her, and only two or three USians were in the vast space below, without abandon, games or laughter. Just sitting and staring out to sea, transfixed. One, she noticed, was quietly sobbing.

The sound of crying made Florida miss Burden. Florida had been learning to manage the fear and problems Burden had brought, and now she slept alone. A pet was a companion if you were lonely. She giggled, remembering how Burden had whipped and chased its tail. Then she sobbed too, her body unfamiliar with laughter. She studied the ocean again. Now, so much vastness did not feel like a hug, but more like a tomb. A place to get lost from memory. She searched, anxious for movement, for any sign of the Ghost Ship floating rudderless.

Was there a face staring from somewhere else, looking for her too?

Quick research told her where to find Lesedi's cabin. Florida had no Burden to rush back to now. They might be friends now. They might love each other now. They might be family now.

Florida knocked. Waited. Knocked again, more loudly. Waved to the door's camera.

Finally, Florida's video monitor flared on. Lesedi's hair was covered with a scarf of deep, dazzling red. So much brightness! Florida's face became a smile—

—and a sick knowing stole it from her. Lesedi was ill. Her eyes were bloodshot, her skin dry and flaking. She was lying down, had been ill for some time. For how long?

"Florida," Lesedi said with a smile in her voice, but not on her face. Her throat was parched. "I've wanted to reach you, but I can barely lift my head."

A horror was swallowing her. "What's happened?"

"I've caught something. A lot of us have. You should stay away. People are dying."

Florida almost, *almost,* remembered her mother's gasps.

"What do you mean? No one told me."

"It's disarray—I'm telling you, a *lot* of people are sick. On the crew too. It comes so fast. And they don't send medicine to our wing. But I hear it's not curing them. The only working elevator is to Observation. We're sealed off." She heaved for a breath, weary from the telling.

Florida had not tried to go anywhere except Observation since Burden left. Everything she needed was in her cabin, including enough flavorless food packets for a month.

"I was sick," Florida said. "I'm better now."

Lesedi took a long breath and shook her head. "Then you're the first I've heard. No one survives. The ship is—" She took a long breath. "—quarantined."

"What does that mean?"

"It means . . . we're infectious, so they isolate—"

"I know what 'quarantined' means. What does it mean for us on the ship?"

"Think and you already know," Lesedi said. "They leave us to die. Leave us *here*."

The passenger failure rate was a *ship* failure rate. Of course.

"But . . . the ship costs too much. The passengers, with so much money—"

"Tomorrow's problem," Lesedi said. "We all agreed to . . . the terms. They salvage the ships down the line. When they figure out what caused the . . . plague. It's happened before. My cousin warned me about getting sick on a ship."

A plague, and maybe not the first. So there *was* another ship floating on the route between Africa and the States. Perhaps more than one.

"I just hoped . . ." Lesedi said, and heaved to breathe. ". . . it wouldn't be mine. Yeah?"

"Yes," Florida said. "I hoped that too."

"I wanted to see New York."

Florida wanted to tell her everything: about how her employer had forced her to smuggle in Burden, and how Burden had scratched her, and how she had gotten sick. Since she was an Aggie, perhaps, her body had fought off the illness. But maybe Nandi had carelessly released a contagion with her smuggled goods: a living creature was never mere cargo. And maybe Florida had spread the illness. USians were not Aggies who had been raised on supplements their immune systems could not fight. All because Nandi thought she was so clever.

Florida wanted to tell it all, and not telling might have felt like dying if Lesedi had not been dying before her eyes.

"When I come back," Florida said, "get up and let me in."

Florida was healthy, so she had brought only a light health pack in addition to her supplements. The Mother's Cure Nandi had made up for her was meant as a general curative for infections or viruses specific to travel. Florida had been saving it for a serious illness, so she hadn't considered squandering it over a headache and fatigue. Once the overnight coughing passed, she'd been fine. (In fact, she'd attributed some of her illness to the stress of losing Burden. She'd finished off the sedative already.)

Now Florida took a dose of Mother's Cure to cleanse her blood of any remaining infection. With time, she could factor in whatever virus Burden had been carrying to perhaps create a better antidote, but Mother's Cure might save Lesedi. Might save any of the other survivors.

But Lesedi first.

Lesedi was so dehydrated, Florida was almost too late. For the first hour, Florida was convinced Lesedi would die in her arms, a new kind of void ready to swallow her. For the first time in memory, she prayed.

The days passed slowly, so slowly, and Lesedi did not improve. But she had lived longer than the rest, it seemed. No matter how much Florida made a racket with banging and screaming or endlessly tried to open comms from Lesedi's cabin, or her cabin, or a call box on the wall, no one answered.

Was it contempt? Or were they all gone? From time to time, she thought she saw sudden movement, or heard a clatter, and called out for Burden. But the cat never came. Nandi's failed lab experiment was probably long dead too.

With time, Florida overrode the codes to open C section so she could explore. She reached the black-level observation deck— empty, by now—the dining hall (the smell told her not to investigate), the rations stations (all, apparently, in good working order and well stocked). She brought food and water to Lesedi's cabin.

Florida hoped it was a sign of good things to come, but it was a ragged hope in a ship crammed with the dead. The smell was not too bad yet because the cabin doors were sealed, but she would have to start throwing the carcasses overboard, one at a time.

Florida cleaned Lesedi's waste as she had cleaned Burden's. She bathed Lesedi. She sang her the shards of long-ago songs, making up the words she had forgotten. Lesedi's needs were so great the Mother's Cure was quickly depleted, but she was smiling at Florida now. Lesedi seemed, maybe, to be getting better. At least then she would not be so alone on their ghost ship.

While Lesedi slept, Florida went to the observation deck—the luxurious one with comfortable seating and beverage dispensers that still worked, not the workers' deck where now-dead crewmen had tried to confine her.

She spent hours staring at the vast, empty sea, the captain of her own ghost ship.

LIQUID TWILIGHT

by Ytasha Womack

Souleymane said I wasn't wearing the right shoes for a rock beach. My gold bangled sandals with the clanking fringe ankle had the grip of a surfboard. The black boulders harkening from Dakar's volcanic past blanketed the deep sands that kissed the ocean. There certainly aren't any rock beaches on the harbors of B'More and I don't recall slipping across any during my childhood summer in Cape Verde. It was best to take them off, Souleymane said, and I obliged. He took my hand to ease the fall that seemed to await me. There was a symmetry in the rocks' dispersion and I achieved some elegance in my balancing act that didn't go unnoticed by a slim man in sky-dyed linen who seemed to be watching me from above. The Café Dakar was on the low cliff's edge and we had to climb low to go high to get there. We made it just in time to catch the wondrous reddened sunset splashed across the horizon.

The Atlantic has a majesty from Africa's coast that surpasses the view from the American shoreline. I had a great-grandfather who was a whaler, working on vessels that chased the mother of mammals from ocean to sea. That sense of adventure wasn't handed down my way. But I was gifted with the ability to press forward. My persistence came in handy when organizing to topple what others deemed time impossible. Dehumanizing systems were a whale of sorts. My protest efforts required the fortitude that I'm sure my ancestors' whale hunting mandated. But large mammals aren't oppression and dismantling otherism isn't exactly akin to harpooning from a rocky boat ride. Who knows what compromises came with the freedom of being a Black man sailing the seas? Speciesism is a problem. Lack of humanity is a problem. I stay on the ground, working from the root up, to keep underinvested people atop of their rights.

That said, the sea isn't my brand of tea. I crave serenity but I'm not adept at finding it. My rose-colored braids belie my pragmatism. Radicals are buoyed with messages of self-care but I ran myself into the ground many moons ago. I hexed the patriarchy a minute ago but don't have time to wait for the whole thing to topple. The ocean holds the promise of escape but the waves are no guarantee of a recharge. I'm charmed by the waves but deferential to the grandness. Was it awe or terror that had me in a trance? The vastness of the ocean was as intimidating as it was inviting. There was a whole world below and I'm not talking about sea creatures. The lost souls at sea, the ones chained and sold across; part of my soul was anchored in that ocean. These not so dark waters were a veil and I could only submit to a dance of enchantment.

"This view never gets old," Souleymane said. Souleymane was born and raised along Dakar's coast, so the wonder of the ocean view wasn't lost on him either. It's the reason he poured milk in the sea from time to time before he went body surfing most evenings. Transgressing this liquid body that romanced the shore was one that commanded respect. An homage to the sea's mothers whose protection was our shadow and the blessed shade.

Earlier today, Souleymane and I hung out on the Isle de Madeleine. An epic wonder of rock and baobab majesty, the island is a ten-minute boat ride from Dakar's coast. The story goes that a spirit lives on the island. You can visit, you can splash, but you can't stay after nightfall. The spirit doesn't want anyone to make the land their permanent habitat and all the aspiring colonists who hoped to call it home perished. There's at least one half-constructed brick home that remains after a man lost his wits. Maybe he thought building on high ground would make a difference. He was wrong. I'm not one to tango with spirits so I left change on the shallow hole of one of the baobabs.

Lunch was held just below the high cliffs where the island split in two. A clear, salty pool formed between the narrowed landings. Small groups of friends in swimwear brighter than the rainbow were chillin', blastin' their Afrobeat, and soaking in the joy on the shore's edge. If I'd thought about it, I'd have brought my speaker and played some B'More house. Good music, good company and good food atop ancient volcanic ash and rock beaches could be paradise.

Souleymane and I shared a sunshine-colored beach towel. My tan lines were becoming more defined, his were never evident. The umbrella shading us from the glints of sun that made it through the island splits. We were at the point in our friendship where our chatter had evolved into comfortable silences. When he stepped away to check on the fish, I tipped away to sit in the waters. The clear pool was speckled with turtle-sized black rocks, too. As I dipped lower, the wash of times unknown kissed me. The residue of volcanos long gone held me in their bosom. It caressed me, massaged me. I didn't want to leave. "What are you doing?" Souleymane asked me when he found me sitting with the water just below my nostrils in the sea. I lifted my chin to answer.

"This is everything," I said.

Souleymane and I weren't exactly lovers, but the time we were spending together was leaning in that direction. We'd met at a community-organizing training session two years ago in Chicago. He was focused on climate change and ocean health; I was preoccupied with defunding the police. His smile was easy, his wit was sharp and he was one of the few people I knew who didn't think of talking as arm wrestling or a death by fire sport. I welcomed the ease. We found ourselves relying on one another through WhatsApp calls over the torrential rain of pandemic horrors not so long ago. I yearned for a take on life that didn't require an offense and defense strategy. I found myself clinging to the beauty of a full breath or standing too long in hot showers. Sometimes I cupped my hands in the shower trying to see my reflection in the puddle. I was lost in palm lines, singing a song I was hesitant to read. Some days, my puddled hands held my own tears. I was up for any battle, but every warrior needs a break. A few weeks after my vaccination shot, I was on a plane crossing the Atlantic.

My mom is from Cape Verde, an island which is a paper plane toss away from Senegal. Souleymane's great-grandmother was African American, one of the few who'd returned to the continent after the Civil War. He was Lebou and sea inspired. I grew up around harbors and lakes. Our fathers were pilots, too. Mine always ranted about the wonders of African cultures; his dad relished in the intriguing ironies of Black American life. The longing prevailed on both sides. We found ourselves circling the diaspora with our conversations about freedom, culture and influence. Dakar is a city that relishes in the interweave. I'm not saying Souleymane and I had a future but we did have a woven past that made for hearty chats and excuses to get blacker on rock beaches.

After hanging out on the Isle for most of the day, we took a boat back to Dakar's coast to catch the sunset. The Café Dakar was an island bar that serenaded with its view and bohemianism. There weren't many people there, so we picked a table for two closest to the oceanside. "Is this your friend?" a man asked, handing us both oversized mojitos. The blue-clad man who hovered above earlier eying my tightrope walk on the shore was before us. His bluish-green print mask was slipping from his nose. He pulled it up as I noticed.

"Asha, meet Boubacar," Souleymane said. "Our mothers grew up together."

"Na nga def," I said.

"Maa ngi fi," he responded. Boubacar's smile glimmered beneath his woven fabric. His motions were all feline as he pulled up a grandiose wicker chair between us.

"I'd kiss your hand but I don't want to impose," he added as he repositioned himself in the chair.

"I heard you moved to Rabat," Souleymane said.

"I move where the waves take me," he said. "And I always wind up home."

Roamers fascinate me. My terrains were all too land-locked. The steps of my path were ordered in the terra. Keep your nose to the ground. The uplift is in the grassroots. I could never allow the lakes and streams to carry me without pinning it down for some questions first.

"Asha, have you been swallowed by the sea yet?" Boubacar asked. The question made me laugh.

"Not that I'm aware of," I said.

"You stare at it long enough, it becomes you. That's what happened to me. When you become like water your thirst is always quenched."

"This man and his stories," said Souleymane.

"Oh, come on, you know it's true. Mama spirits are all around us on this coast, why can't I have a father from the ocean?"

"Your father is not from the ocean," Souleymane said.

"Are you calling my mother a liar?" he asked.

"If I was, I wouldn't be the only one," Souleymane said. Souleymane was firing shots and I really didn't understand why.

"Asha, Souleymane and I have a friendly difference of opinion regarding my heritage," he said. "He thinks magic is dead. I think magic is life. You see, my father is a man of the sea," he said.

"All our fathers are men of the sea. We're from a land of fisherman and boaters," Souleymane said.

"Yes, but my father lives below sea level. Once a year he rises from the depths of the ocean and we have poisson et riz on Isle de Madeline at night."

"I swear the last time you told this tale you said it was at sunrise," said Souleymane.

"You're lost in the details, my friend."

"Your father lives in a submarine?" I asked. I didn't know about that side of marine life but I was up for learning more.

"He thinks his father's a Merman," Souleymane said.

"Merman is so très ordinaire," Boubacar said. "But he's not human, if that's what you mean. Or at least, he's not anymore."

"No one goes to Isle de Madeline at night," Souleymane said.

"My father has special privileges," he responded. "Clearly," he added as the waiter brought him a mojito of his own. Boubacar slipped the straw under his mask and took a hearty gulp. "I don't know what kinds of deals my papa makes on the ocean floor but the spirit of the Isle welcomes us both with open arms. Hassan, the fisherman, takes me there after nightfall and picks me up in the morn for our annual dinner date."

Souleymane shook his head in disbelief. Boubacar was apparently accustomed to people challenging his story and pressed on.

"My mom met him thirty years ago to the day right here on this beach at sunset."

"Really?" I asked. I was willing to suspend belief if the payoff was right.

"Please don't tell this story again," Souleymane said.

"What is life if we don't repeat our stories," said Boubacar.

"If it helps, Boubacar, I saw a ghost when I was twelve," I said. I swear I felt my grandmother's spirit in her rocking chair just days after she passed on. I woke up in the middle of the night and could smell the tobacco from her cigars. I tipped out and warned her that if I saw her, it would scare the crappola out of me. She didn't respond, I didn't look, and I ran past the den to the bathroom like a frightened cat.

"Ghosts, spirits, we're all surrounded," Boubacar said, nudging his elbows as if to get the invisible world off of him.

"One day my mother felt this cloud of sadness descend upon her," he said. "She had no reason to be sad. She had a good life, a loving family, an adoring husband. But she felt like she was living a life that didn't reflect back to her in the waters."

"What do you mean?" I asked.

"Every now and then you can see your reflection in the sea, but the woman my mother saw didn't resemble her at all. She surmised that she was living someone else's life and was never the same."

"She felt she wasn't living her purpose?" I asked. Everyone was talking about living life with intention these days.

"No, she felt she was living someone else's life."

"Whose life?" I asked.

"She didn't know so she yelled at the ocean and demanded answers. She took the water, cupped it in her hands and spat. That's when she saw him, my father, emerge from where the sea met the horizon."

"So her answer was a man. This is predictably sexist," said Souleymane. "Was he a serpent and your mother was Eve?" Souleymane's tone was unusually harsh. I wasn't sure if he was jealous or masking his frustration with a radical feminist pretense.

"So disrespectful you are," Boubacar said. His eyes twinkled with mischief. "It's okay, these tales aren't for everyone."

"What happened next?" I asked.

"Each night she escaped to be with him. She confessed her new love to her husband, arguing that she could be a good wife to both, just as her husband was to her and his second wife. Reluctantly, he agreed. And she married the man of the sea."

"Really?" I said. The idea of a woman leading a life of polygamy where she had several husbands had me intrigued.

"Asha," Souleymane said, touching my hand.

"Let the man tell his story," I said, pulling my hand away.

"For the first year or so, all was well. She was with her first husband on land, she was with the second husband at sea," said Boubacar. "One night, she went to the sea as always to meet my father and he wasn't there. She did the same the following night and then again and again, until one day he emerged chained in sea moss. My mom tried to swim towards him but he shouted for her to stay away. Just as he delivered that message, a wave descended over him and dragged him into the sea. She never saw him again. A few days later, she realized she was expecting with me," Boubacar said. The dimming rays flashed over his face.

"What happened to him?" I asked.

"People talk. Some say her first husband worked with a few fishermen who trapped him in a web. Others say the spirits of the water disapproved of his transgressions."

"What does your mom say?" I asked.

"She's not one to live in the past," he said. "We moved around a lot. But when I was a teen, she sent me back here to live with my grandmother. I'm sea-born, so it was important to her that I know those ways." Boubacar's saddened tone cornered for an uptick. "That's when my papa appeared to me and we've been meeting annually ever since." A woman in orange tapped Boubacar and he excused himself to greet her. When he was out of earshot, Souleymane leaned in.

"Asha, everyone knows that Boubacar's father was in the Tanzanian navy," he said. "They had some tour out here and left. That's how his mother met him. She was a married woman, it was a big scandal and the poor woman fled. I don't know why he keeps returning with this fairy tale."

"What difference does it make?" I asked. "Indulge him."

"I've been indulging him for years," he said.

Boubacar returned with fresh drinks for both of us. I saw no harm in playing along.

"Is your father coming back tonight?" I asked.

"Would you want to meet him if he was?" Boubacar asked, looking at me squarely. Boubacar's eyes were the depth of the ocean. A brisk breeze ran across my shoulders. I'd heard my host of game and bar tales but there was something different about this one. After a 2020 of emotional seesaws and upward spirals, my grip on reality's ground floor had loosened. I was poised to toss that real-world Frisbee to whatever rottweiler wanted a bite.

"What if I do want to meet him?" I asked. His fabric-covered Cheshire grin was magnanimous. I could feel Souleymane stiffen.

"I like her, Souleymane," he said. "Some of us still know magic when we see it." Souleymane sighed and took a few gulps of the bottomless mojito. "As for your question, Asha, no, he won't be here tonight. Tide's too high."

"So, you have to wait another year?"

"Don't encourage him," Souleymane said. His interruptions were annoying me.

"Oh, I don't need encouragement," Boubacar said, flicking his wrist as if he were shaking off water. His flick revealed a coral watch and beaded bracelets. "Some things, I have to keep to myself," he said. People were spilling in under the awning. A band was lugging their instruments in and setting up around a small stage.

"What's all this?" I asked.

"It's Kizomba night."

"Since when?" Souleymane asked. He couldn't hide his disgust. Souleymane knew I adored Kizomba dancing. It was the one dance he could not do. The ebbs and grooves took a near master of the dance to lead, and partner dancing wasn't Souleymane's forte.

Kizomba was in my blood. The Angolan-born movement was all the rage for Cape Verdeans. My mom brags that it was my dad's ability to catch on to the dance so quickly, one that aligned with his native Chicago stepping flow, that sealed their love. It was a dance of heart chakras' connection. I had a hard time teaching it although it was second nature, much like roller skating backwards or assembling a voter registration drive.

"We planned to go dancing tomorrow," I said.

"Looks like tomorrow is today," said Boubacar. "And who plans to go dancing?"

Souleymane's phone rang. The band was warming up and he excused himself to a quieter corner to answer.

"I have so many questions," I said to Boubacar. What was his mother doing now? What did he and his father talk about? Had Boubacar gone below the sea? How much of this tale had he thought through? How far was he willing to go with it?

"I'd rather talk about you," he said.

"I don't live at the bottom of the sea," I said.

"No, you fight tidal waves and swim upstream in the name of justice."

"Are you questioning my approach?" I asked. I don't know how Boubacar knew about my work, but if he was gonna say I wasn't in the flow and blame the state of human affairs on a faulty meditation practice, I'd likely walk away. I didn't want this trip to unravel into a heady debate on social justice tactics by a novice observer all because he'd run out of yarn to spin.

"Oceans run deep and you're riding the surface," he said. "Every fight needs ample positioning. If you're on land, you take the high ground. If you're a bee, you role-play in the hive. But what do you do at sea, Asha? What is power when you're on the ocean floor?"

"Like I said, I don't live at the bottom of the ocean, so I don't know," I said.

"But you'd like to, for a few days anyway," he said, removing his mask. "Don't you want to go to the bottom of the sea?"

"Is that an invitation?" I challenged. A war of puns was better than an argumentative sparring match. But any theory should be applied. Putting me under a microscope wasn't going to make his tale any truer.

The band had passed their warm-up phase and the guitar phrasing was serenading us all. The drums tickled my hips. I welcomed the musical ease in tension. Boubacar seemed to be thinking something over. Honestly, I just wanted to dance. I took in the sights, sinking into the sweetened melodies. When I looked back to my storytelling friend, his hand was extended.

"We only have so much time," he said. I looked about for Souleymane but he was nowhere in sight. I needed to dance some things off and I wasn't looking for permission to do so. I placed my hand in Boubacar's and he ushered me to the floor before the stage. The measured beats were steady. His right hand slid to the small of my back. I pressed closer to feel which direction he was likely to move in. I feared I'd have a rough start. But it all slipped away when I felt his heartbeat. He waited for mine to sync with his. When the rhythm was one, we began.

Kizomba is a dance of feel. As sexy as it looks, love is not top of mind when synchronicity is the mission. If you're in your head, as most are, it will never work. My heart work was all head in the organizing world. Leading from the heart made me feel wounded. Was I wounded?

"It's easier when your eyes are closed," he said, feeling my anxiousness.

I didn't want to close my eyes. My offense/defense strategies were waning. Had I fallen numb to the beat? Why was I fighting myself? I shut my eyes. Our motions were close knit at first, midsized rotations that opened in brief shifts. The drum beat knocking on the door of my soul, our rotations were tighter, the undulations controlled. We pressed closer, much closer. The strumming guitar collapsed into the soft simmer of the waves. I felt like I was floating. His skin was the ocean surface. His bleeding heart the pungent coral. His brain, a distant whale. I opened my eyes to recover, but Boubacar and I were floating above the ocean's floor. I was tranquility.

An octopus lurked, but he wasn't a danger. My chilled response was a liquid dream. Souleymane dug his fist into the sandy bottom, digging both hands rapidly as if he were digging a sandcastle. He pulled out a rusted chain which he handed to me. As if on cue, I yanked as hard as I could. It didn't budge. I yanked again and an explosion unfurled. My soul unraveled. I was shot back and then sucked in and tossed to a coral reef. No pain came over me. Speed had no measure. I was a bubble. A school of tiny fish circled me. As a single unit, they squeezed me like I was in an octopus's grasp and released. I spotted Boubacar, flecked in gold and shaved lava rocks, floating. He spun, storming the waters. I was swirling in the fever. As the speed slowed down, I was tranquility once again. Serenity was pumping through my veins. I placed my hands before me and saw nothing. I was like water. I shut my eyes.

"Stay if you like. Leave when you want," he said.

I was rising to the surface. As I neared the top, a woman with a red-and-yellow headwrap came into view. She cupped me. I was droplets in her palm and she spit on me. I spat back, my saliva shot up like a geyser, and the woman went soaring towards the full moon above. I was formless. I was form. I wiped my eyes and Boubacar was staring down on me. For a moment, he appeared to be in a naval uniform but it dissipated. We were back in Café Dakar. Boubacar had me dipped, my braids draping the floor, and the audience applause cascaded over us.

"Beautiful," he said, and whipped me back up. We were the only two still on the floor. I was dizzy, whirling in two spaces at once. Boubacar escorted me back to the table.

I looked to where the setting sun should be and saw the last sliver of orange submerge below the water.

"Just in time," Boubacar said.

Souleymane returned and I nearly jumped. I know I looked dragged, sea-drugged and out of it. But I felt revitalized. I was tossed about but the underwater serenity had become me. I'd released something. Was it stress? Trauma? Anger? An old me? Souleymane noticed none of it. Did he notice anything?

"Asha, a giant snake worked its way into my mother's house. The dog's going crazy. I'm going to help her get rid of it. Her assistant's not available and my brother's out of town and . . ."

"I can take her back," Boubacar offered.

"Or I'll take a cab," I added.

Souleymane kissed me on the cheek and ran off.

"You're a lovely dancer," Boubacar said.

"And you're like water," I replied.

"As are you," he said. "Shall we?" he asked. I looked to the dance floor and off to the ocean.

"Yes," I said. I knew what I was agreeing to, but the moon and the hypnotic trumpet were our sonic red carpet to the ocean shore. Hand in hand, we walked until the ocean waves covered us.

"Take me back to the ocean floor," I said. "That's where I do my best grounding." Boubacar spun me deeper into the sea.

Some lies have a liquid truth worth uncovering. When I surfaced this time, my admiral from afar awaited.

ONCE UPON A TIME IN 1967

by Oyedotun Damilola Muees

The year was 1967. The atmosphere had sensed it all: the hatred dispersed all around like agbalumo seeds spat out and kicked on the hot ground by little children. What was supposed to usher us into a new era of dispensation became a breeding ground for a looming war. Mama warned about my contact with humans. I get that she didn't want me in between crossfire when the humans go at loggerheads.

I like my job as a sale assistant in Madam Aina's shop. Some of the clan members persuaded Mama to let me. Besides, my presence there brought boon to the clan. I fed them information about what humans talked about. The market is a place where the unleashed breeze carries every iota of information.

Rumours have it that the Easterners are planning a secession. That will be an effrontery on the part of their leader. He knows better than to split from a state that is indivisible according to the constitution.

And so the rumours turned out to be a truth. On 30 May, 1967, the Easterners through their military commander made the declaration that they now ceased to be a region of a budding Nigeria. Then came the retaliation from the Nigerian government. All efforts to return sanity to the tension erupting in the state became futile.

The markets were no longer safe. The Easterners stocked up their armories, getting ready for what comes next. A pogrom ensued. An inevitable clash would be witnessed by the ground. Blood, cries, sweat, death and its cohort will soon spread its arms on us.

Mama refrained me from going to the human settlement. Family is everything, she said. We too, geared up for the unknown—our settlement will soon be a target.

Jinadu gave the signal when the tang of humans interloped into our territory. Those fucking bipeds who think the world belongs to them. Insatiable ingrates who hunt us down at every chance they get. From our hideout we fixed a surreptitious stare, waiting for the signal to leap a ferocious assault on them. By my calculation they were three hunters. Sunken eyes, gaunt neck and head, dirty clothes. Except one of them who had a paunch belly—he would fill our tummies well. It wasn't an arduous task. The intruders eventually dropped dead. Tolu paid the price when she got shot in the head.

I watched the clan tear at their flesh after our leader took his share, slurping sound everywhere. Limbs torn apart. Blood smeared on their lips. Mama saved me a chunk of meat, dropping it at my feet. She noticed a morose look draped over my face.

"For how long will you starve yourself?" Mama said in a soft tone. "You are like the rest of your family members. Careless humans are the easiest to come by these days. It is a suicide mission leaving our territory, searching for other kind of meal."

I processed her words for a while, allowing them to anchor at the base of my thoughts.

"Mama, I agree, I am like the rest of the clan. But I am also werefox. I desire the taste of roasted fish and other kills. Not some flesh-bloody—"

She raised her left paw, tutting. Umpteen times she had warned me about the words I use. Some members of the clan still see me as an outsider, scanning my every move, scared that I would one day give them up to humans. Once, we had gone hunting when we hid at the sight of humans. A man and woman were taking pictures of birds roosting on tree branches. Jinadu gave the order for the attack. I pushed Bala to the ground when he clenched at the woman's feet. She made a run for it, but her strength didn't take her far. The boys snarled at me, planned to beat me up, save for Jinadu. I took the items from the dead tourists, stuff the clan considered a deadwood.

The lifeless meat gaped at me, waiting for me to munch it. Obstinate flies perched on it, nibbling out their share. I put my nose on the meat, sniffing. The jungle is no place for a weak animal or werefox. Fires could no longer be made. It will give our locations to humans, coyotes and wolves.

"The child is scared to eat a kill," someone said from the clan.

A bout of guffaw laughter resounded about, quaking the swaying leaves. I had to prove a point, telling them I am no frail fox. Silence hung thick in the air, all eyes on me. I let out a deep sigh, resting my gaze on the imperious boys who use invectives on me. They came closer, cheering at me for my bravery.

That night when I returned to my human form, basking in the beautiful pictures from the camera I took from the dead tourists, my stomach began to rumble in pain. I turned at the churning of my innards. My enzymes were not used to such a meal. Mama called the attention of her brothers, crying for them to save me. Great-Grandaunt Fisayo spoke some incantations, calling out to the fox-sage god for wisdom. Everything went blank. Voices from the land of the dead beckoned me to come. I saw them. Only I could see the dead. Slowly, my pupils began to dilate, closing the curtain of my eyelids.

When I woke up later that evening, Mama sprang to her feet, snuggling in my arms, licking my face.

"Mama, I'm not dead," I said, sprinkling some smile on my face. She showed me some fruit by the bedside. It was risky of her to have gone hunting. She denied going, saying my brothers did that job. Though in human form, I can perceive the lies sifting through her sharp teeth. My brothers would rather have me dead so they can feed on my carcass. From that day Mama had ensured I no longer tasted fresh meat.

None of us foresaw the message of the harbinger. The sky wore a black regalia as if mourning us. The lions were the first to encroach in our land when we saw their vestige. Then came the hyenas and wild dogs. Mothers warned their children of frolicking after dusk. We binged on our supplies from squirreling. I was more affected because of my human diet. Few times I compromised, eating a modicum of lower animals. After some minutes of a queasy feeling, I felt better. I had to feed on raw flesh if I wanted to sunbath in the grace of the pervasive sun the next day and subsequent ones. Iya Ebun's one-year-old cub was snatched by an eagle when he followed his brothers to hunt for bees. That woman's cry still haunts my sleep. Baby Ebun's spirit had refused to leave our land, staying at the *umbilici* of the former thronged market square.

It was time to leave all behind, our home. For fear of being killed by predators I transformed back to a fox. Somber vagrant souls walked incongruently. Oblivious of us, passing through themselves while we minded our business.

"What do you see?" Mama spoke in faint words.

"Helpless souls. Crying babies with phlegm slithering from their noses. Craving for their mother's touch," I replied.

Mama urged I kept my eyes on the road. I tried to block the chatter and cries and howling of the souls. It quaked my heart.

Anyone under the emblazoned omnipotent sun streaked in custard-yellow would have felt the hotness bellowing from its horizon. When twilight began to appear, all the yellowness started to coalesce, like the fist of a god and the trident of a water deity. The day soon rolled off its carpet for the night to take watch over earthlings.

The night reeked of an abused city on the verge of pulverization: smoke, day-old shit, piss, *ogogoro* and the irregular weird whiff of roasted meat. Our home was no longer a safe haven. Buildings have become dwarfs from the blast of shells. Bullets drill holes on the walls from planes strafing the enemies, giving lizards and rats a new apartment to live. Void of anyone, human absconded their homes for fear of being killed, conscripted. The east required all the boy soldier it needed to win the war. The former tranquil city of Port-Harcourt had become what you may call a wasteland. Plunders, scavengers and bandits roam about, searching empty homes for leftovers. Anything to keep them alive till the next day.

Presently, this is our third settlement. We have become nomads. Outside our home had become a jungle: eat or get eaten. The lakes where I got food had become malnourished. The water-god had migrated.

When the night descends fully, spreading its feathers all about, I divest myself so that my cloth don't get torn, and transform into a werefox. Clasping my dress in my jaws and dropping it under a thirsty bitter-leaf plant. Mama doesn't approve of my single hunt. She sees me as the human child who needs to be protected from the wild. She believes in my powers, yet, mothers will always be mothers.

Tonight's kill will be anything I lay my hand on, even humans. Yes, I have taken a penchant for hunting humans. Mostly soldiers fighting for the west. These brutes have no regard for lives, gunning down anything that doesn't have the insignia of allies on them. Finding my way through the overgrown forest, I craned and activated all my senses. Hunters cloak their traps with grasses. Some cower near understory, camouflaging themselves with leaves. Movement from earshot cackled at the dried tan leaves. I leaped into the nearest plant at my flank, ignoring the itchy blade on my skin. Scent of human grew stronger. I saw a soldier, green helmet askew on his head. A chewing stick at one side of his mouth. Unknown lyrics muttered from his mouth. Judging by his weight, he will serve about ten of us. Opposite my stance, he pulled down his zipper pouring out squiggly urine on dehydrated plants. He didn't stop murmuring as he went on with his business. What an insipience. The perfect time to strike halo on my head. My heartbeat drummed, a single mistake could get me in grave trouble. In that moment of readiness a thud ached my hearing. I cowered, praying my location had not been discovered.

The soldier fell on his urine, almost lifeless. A tight grip on his clavicle was jammed by a lion. *Those cursed people.* Two more lions trudged towards the kill, licking their lips. The dead soldier was dragged along, while the two cleared the path, registering their presence to any contender. After they left I came out. A mélange of feelings punctured my heart—befuddled—rage—gloominess. That was a big opportunity for food, and I allowed my feeble mind to make me lose it. I hit the road, watching out for fruits. Something hit me on the head. Bursting with energy, I looked at the item. It was a palm kernel, sucked dry. I perceived it, hoping to lick any leftover juice. Another item hit my head. I faced up to find that it was a squirrel darting the palm kernel at me. Such inexorable and avaricious folks. They must have a torrential storage of food.

"Fox-boy, this is no place for weaklings like you," Izor said.

"Don't call me that," I spat back.

High on the palm tree he lolled on a branch, rubbing his fur against the grated back, picking a cashew nut from a pouch crossed over his back. Izor was one of the diffident in his clan. He was the only squirrel to see me transform. Thank goodness, he didn't *rat* me out to the other members of the jungle. The rage in me erupted with vexation. *How dare this little man call me a weakling?* To my left I saw a grasshopper in the act of antennation. A ninja frog hopped on a water-leaf plant.

"I dare you to climb down and say it to my face?" I said, placing my paws on the ash bark. Izor shot out a rambunctious response, further infuriating me.

"Fox-boy, I know you better than your whole clan. You only have the power to transform. But you don't have the innate ability like your brothers." He dropped a shriveled nut on my head.

I didn't argue with him. He was right. My sister, Bisi, had fallen in love with a rabbit once. What sonorous voice she possessed. She gave him a condition if he wanted to hear her sing again: he must bring his brothers and friends to the collared banana plantation at the dusk of the third day when the sun was yawning, about to retire for the night. Poor rabbit. He was so enamored with my sister that he forgot she was a fox, cunning. It turned out a siege was laid for them. Their cries transported a dirge during the slaughter carried out by my brothers. Their souls lingered in our community before they wandered off.

Izor shouted my name to call me out of my reverie.

"I'd tell you what," he said. "You are different. I like that about you. You once saved my village from the pogrom of your avaricious kind. There have been recent activities in the Oni River. Perhaps, if you are lucky a kill or two might fall into your claws."

I thanked him, scampering towards the river. Along my way a voice appeared from the sinuous trees. I lowered my back, steadied my footsteps. The bushes were now home to visiting creatures who just wanted to survive. The voice rang out again, this time the tone directed towards me. The person could only be Tokoloshe, another waif. He is an ally, too. *Who doesn't want to be friend with an honest fox?* Tokoloshe appeared, reclining on the skeletal frame of an agbalumo tree. He was dressed well than the last time I saw him. He never fails to obeisance me whenever our path cross.

"You don't seem to be affected by the war," I said, breaking the nut of the conversation.

He stood up, opening his arms too ostentatiously to advertise his outfits.

"Who did you rob this time?" I asked.

"No one, fox-boy. I didn't rob anyone of this outfit. I met with a depressed wood-sprite. He mentioned something about a revenge. So I got the identity of the person he wanted dead."

"What! You told me you didn't engage in such act anymore."

"It was the lions that carried out the job. I got payment in new cloths. The lions had a feast. The wood-fairy got her revenge. You see, foxes are not the only cunning creatures in the forest."

I wanted to grab him by the throat until he gets asphyxiated. Those desire were for another day. He inquired of my destination. I shrugged, telling him to be careful of ravenous ghouls and specters. He doffed his hat, swallowing a stone to turn invisible.

Oni River was a constant source of food supply before the war. Now it has become a dump site for soldiers. Heavy stench choked the area. Dead stagnant water vastly spread around, suffocating the aquatic denizens inhabiting there. The last time I came here, foraging for food, sadness clambered into my heart upon seeing the souls of aquatic beings crying over the loss of their families. Hunting during a funeral was bad business for me. Aloof the river I waited for prowlers. I fell into a shallow gouge, shaking russet of my fur. It dawned on me that the russet wasn't a bad idea, a perfect camouflage from preys. I doused all of me in it, walking towards the river.

Putrid smell of carcass tingled my nose. How was I to fetch for a kill in this unhealthy body of water. If Jinadu were here his words be: *Mama has indulged you to the extent that you won't even feed on a dirty kill.* The water gaze was undaunted. Dragonflies gamboled on the dead green plants afloat it. I didn't see any souls there. Another thought popped up in my head. What if Izor tricked me in coming here for his personal gain? Marveled,

I saw a mackerel waggling its tail in the river. Gingerly I jumped at it, clasping it in my jaws. Gaiety pimpled on my face. Though a small kill, at least it would suffice.

Just as I placed the mackerel down, squinting to locate another, the birds cawed, flying higher as if danger lurked in the air. Leaves strewn, dust resurrected pirouetting and levitating. I didn't want to see what sinister creature owned this land when I grabbed my kill and turned to leave. A huge splash from the water sprang me unconsciously to the ground, pushing away my kill. In the middle of the river, driving towards me was a girl on a water horse. The horse neighed an unfriendly blast at me. Fear trussed whatever brevity had in me. My furs pricked my bones like thorns. Death winked at me, happy to receive a guest.

The girl's hair was purple, braided with silver thread. Around her hair were beads of different sizes sewn to add vigor. Her pupils were white streaked with ember. I had never seen a water-princess before. The glow in her immaculate cocoa brown could ensorcel a man to servility. I picked myself up to run, but my legs were seized in a water shackle. I struggled, praying to the gods to forgive my stupidity, promising never to act as a hero again. Help didn't come. Instead the water drew me towards the river. Hatred burned at the center of her eyes. I howled, calling for help to no avail. She pulled out a dagger from her scabbard. The glint from it married the sun, sending cold sharp shivers down my bone marrow. Few feet to where she stood, the water still bringing me closer, I transformed back to a boy, not minding my nakedness. She plopped me into the river. I bobbed back up, but she was gone. In a flicker, she rose from the water again, tossing me a pant.

The awkwardness that billowed around us laced with silence. We sat adjacent on the shore. Great-Grandaunt Fisayo was right after all. The river goddess's daughter was a pure epitome of beauty.

"That's my brother's pant you are wearing. He doesn't like to give out his wares," she said, eyes on the water horse swimming. "I should kill you right now. What right have you to come steal from my mother's land without a permission? I thought were-foxes knew better unlike your uncouth siblings."

Flustered, I wasn't sure if it was a question or a statement.

"I am Akin. Sorry for the intrusion. I was hungry, that's all."

"Sorry," she scoffed.

She ranted about how ingrates like us, esurient fishermen too, wouldn't allow the water to remain soothe. From the tone of her voice it was evident that her animosity was mountainous for people who her mother permitted to catch fish from the river.

"Do you think my hair is ugly?" she asked, dabbing it with her hands.

I had to be tactful in answering her. The answer to this question was rhetorical. Who weaves such colors in a bid to be the cynosure of a gathering?

"Well," she said, staring deep into my eyes.

What did I have to lose? She might kill me anyways.

"My great-great-grandaunt acquired some books from humans. The people in those magazines do wear funny hairstyles. This combination of yours is stale," I said.

She stood up, walked into the river, akimbo. I figured she was thinking of a hundred ways to sever my limbs. Faced to me with uncertainty in her eyes, she came close.

"I am Fifesekemi, daughter of Yeye Aribidesi, ruler of the five great rivers. Call me Kemi. Everyone calls me that."

She was genial after all. She beckoned to come with her into the river, saying there is something I must see. This was my first time beneath an unfamiliar territory.

"I won't hurt you. If I wanted to kill you, you'd be dead. Besides, I like your courage, telling me about how stupid my hair looks," Kemi said, then poked me in the stomach.

She was a feisty one, too. Placed around my neck was a neck bead from her. Its purpose was to make me breathe underwater. The water horse plunged into the river as soon as we mounted it. A veil like a mask covered my face from the gush of water that would have filled my lungs. A paradisiacal view stretched across the deep. Turtles, a family of sperm whales gaped at me, probably wondering why the princess brought a boy into their home. I faced up, a sheath of greenness spread across the topmost layer. It cloaked the creatures living beneath—this way fishermen would think all the fishes are dead or migrated.

We alighted at the base of the river, benthos scampered at our presence. I had no choice than to follow her when she pulled me through the postern of her mother's fortress. We did a little tour of the place. Mural of her forefathers wielding weapons of war down to her mother's picture stretched on the wall. We sneaked out, mounting on a dolphin who took to us the top of the river.

"Where is this place?" I asked, noticing the serene ambience. Thickets arranged in rows paved way for the unknown.

"This is where I come to relax. Here, I feel normal. I get to walk with my feet."

Half-bodied in the water, the welcoming breeze tousled her hair, revealing the beauty therein. I heard footstep drag our way.

"Hide quickly," she said.

The images we saw underneath the water were obscure, distorted. I thought someone had parked a wagon in front of the river. I peeped out of the water, watching the wagon whose rider was unavailable. Kemi didn't approve of our staying there. She insisted we left. Her words didn't sow in my mind. I climbed out, curious to know who was inside.

"Look, there are prisoners inside. Let's help them," I said, fondling the lock.

Kemi jumped out of the water, pulling out her dagger to cut the steel lock. Footsteps approached behind us, before we turned a blow landed our faces.

The feel of slime on my neck jolted me awake. A creature with a salamander head drooled on me while it slept. I shoved it away.

Kemi was still asleep. A quick shake knocked her back to reality. She held on to my arm. The cage was barred with thick rope strewn with palm fronds. I realized what it meant—non-human creatures neighbored with us. Our captor was a slave-trader. Most of the creatures wore a morose look, squidged, sweaty and smelly. They possessed black and hairy skin like a tarantula, bulgy eyes, overgrown hair, teal-green skin that glowed in the dark when we passed through an umbra. A man seated in seclusion from the others. He had horns, hooves, brown mustache and long goatee.

The wheels of the wagon creaked, wobbly. It stopped. *Why are we stopping?* I thought. I peeped outside to the dread of a decrepit signboard dangling in rough contrasting scribbling. CITY OF THE DEAD. A large crowd of spirit sped by in a hurry, carrying bags of different sizes. They were in their Sunday best. The driver of our wagon had to wait for them to pass. Some of them were crowned with crest of abhorrence upon see the living. They envied us, hated that we were in a different realm. I waved to a lonely girl who was pushed aside by a voluptuous woman. Her demeanor was surprising. She carried her bag on her head, came to the side of the cage.

"Can you see me?" the dead girl asked.

I nodded. The creatures in the wagon thought I was going nuts. I didn't speak to her in words, waving at her to go join the rest. By the time the coast was clear the transporter resumed its work, conveying us to an unknown destination.

All of us came down from the cage upon arrival. Two tall men, humongous, wearing baggy trousers with patches of dirt, hunched back, and large scary brown teeth dragged their feet to us. They smelled of alligator pepper. The man on the left pointed for us to be arranged in rows. Soon, a man robed in a Senegalese white outfit came out of a house, hands in pocket, toothpick at a corner of his mouth.

"My servants tell me I have a prized jewel among my prisoners," the man said. "Forgive my manners. My name is Ika. I trade rare beings such as yourselves for a living. I see you have met my messengers, Taye and Kehinde." The giants growled.

He walked past us, ogling at Kemi, sniffing her. Moving on, he stopped at the man with the horns. He spoke an esoteric language to the man that made him spit on Ika. Taye came closer, punching the miscreant, yanking out one of the horns until Ika gave the order to stop. He snorted.

"I am going to ask again," Ika continued. "Somebody among you is a necromancer. He was seen communicating with the dead on their way to the carnival."

We remained silent. Ika began the countdown, waiting for me to turn myself in. After the countdown elapsed he ordered Kemi to be singled out, holding a knife to her neck. I came out, begging him to let her go. Ika grinned, weighing my value with his eyes. He ordered me to be taken to a different cell.

Ika didn't put manacles on me. He was certain that I posed no harm. The thought of changing back to fox nudged my mind. I was quick to bury that yearning. Too many lives would be at stake if I acted foolish. Muffled wailing souls pricked my hearing. Ika wasn't just a slave-hunter, he dealt in the business of selling souls, too.

"We would do so much together. You and I," Ika said, sitting next to me with a zarf holding a golden cup.

A lady with antler and hind legs wearing a fallalery, exposing her chest, came to kneel before Ika, filling his cup with wine. She did the same for me too. I requested for water. He licked his lips as she sauntered away. I needed no soothsayer to tell me that she was his personal entertainer. Arranged inside a chest, he brought an urn, positioned it in front of me.

"Necromancer, show me what you are made up of," Ika challenged me.

I didn't have to open the urn to hear the voices of the condemned souls trapped inside. In there was a babel. Expressions in high and low, hungry and thirsty. Nostalgic of the freedom they once had in roaming the Dead City. I narrowed my ears to pick a particular voice. A boy's weeping caught my interest. Sound of a clank—stick hitting on a stone. Those items were with him when Ika caught him.

"Well," Ika questioned.

"They are all in anguish. They want to be free."

He laughed some more, rubbing his fingers. His plans for the souls were known to him alone. I begged him to allow me to stay with Kemi in the cage, lying to him about her medical condition that takes places at crepuscular.

The prisoners wore a scowl upon seeing me. They must think I am a dunce for leaving the comfort to come here. No one except me knew who Kemi was. If she got some water, she claimed to be able to break us out of the prison. I called Taye. Besides I had earned Ika's trust. He brought a calabash of water when I complained Kemi was giddy.

Kemi spoke some incantations in Yoruba.

"Don't waste your time," the creature with the teal-green skin said. "These walls were built with the blood of magic. Your magic is harmless here."

She ignored him, finishing the words. I dug out some earth from the ground where she poured the water into the hole, sealing it up very quickly. We waited, hopeful her call for help would work. The hairy man with the horns had a gash on his right arm. Flies perched on it. He was oblivious of it. Kemi stood up, paced. A lot was going on in her mind. My words couldn't placate her. I was about to speak when we heard a sound. The prisoners stood. Sand from the building fell. Noise like the coming of roaring thunder pierced our hearing.

"Everyone hold something quickly," Kemi commanded.

A great flood swept through, slamming us to the walls and ground. Water filled the fissures. Bubbles sneaked out of our mouth to the top. Kemi formed a cyclone with the water, extirpating the bars from its hold. The water divided, obeying her, parting way for her when she stretched her right hand at it. Her water horse neighed, sprinkling water on the rest of us.

Ika was found under the rubbles of fallen stack of boxes. He pleaded for his sins, covering his face in ignominy. The slave-girl came forward, drenched. She wore a medallion around her neck and a sash, pointed her finger to him. An evanescent flash made us to block our eyes. When we opened it, Ika was no longer there. A frog took his place, standing on his cloths and jewelries.

"I have always wanted to do that," she said. "Thank you for saving us, goddess. And you too, fox-boy."

The lady who changed Ika to a frog narrated her ordeal. Ika kidnapped her, seized her medallion which contained the powers of her people. She was the last of them—the dark witch of Gbongunle Kingdom. The horned prisoner came to kneel down in front of me, placing his right hand on his chest.

"Fox-boy, you just got yourself a follower," the witch said. "His kind are born to have masters. They will only follow one who they believe is brave-hearted. He will die for you if it ever comes to that."

Kemi hugged me one last time at the shore of the expansive river. I promised to always sneak out to see her at the riverbank when the coast was clear. She touched the water, it vibrated animatedly. Lot of fishes sprang out onto dry land. She kissed me before plunging into the deep.

My new friend, the horned man, put the fishes into two long sacks, landed it on the horses. Fighter jets roared miles from us.

"What do I call you," I said to him, seated on the horse. He remained mute. "Kola. That's your new name."

I brought out some walnuts from my pouch, gave some to Kola. Earlier I took them from Ika's storeroom. The clan will have a feast tonight. The challenge was getting past the voracious enemies. And of course convincing Mama to let Kola stay with us.

A GIRL CRAWLS IN A DARK CORNER

by Alexis Brooks de Vita

I hear her long before I can see her, before the sun has set and shadows blanket the corners of my shack in blackness. She is crawling.

Which means that he is coming with more girls for me to cut.

So I begin to prepare my instruments, my tiny scissors, my razor sharpened on its strop, my needles and my silken threads, my stream mud packed with pine, willow and healing herbs. And all the while I weep.

I cannot, I think. *I cannot any longer.*

You must, comes that voice in my head that I think of as coming from the girl on a plaintive surge. *Where else will I go?* she wants to know. *Who will succor me if not you?*

Now her skinny girl legs drag along the splintered floor. I hear the soft shush as she inches from one edge of her corner to the next, side to slow side, pacing on her hands. But not forward. Not yet.

Stay in the dark, I think to her. *Stay back.*

I try not to think further than my warnings to her. Time is a leather ribbon wound around a pretty girl's waist in the old country, dangling useless trinkets along the way. Time circles back on itself. Every day we have lived before.

We have all the time in the world, I think to her. Her body murmurs as the sun dies for it cannot actually speak.

I have gone in and out of my shack sharpening the blade and gathering the thorns to pinch the cuts closed and culling water from above the stones in the clear stream to wash the new wounds. I move like a leaf drifting from a tree, mindlessly.

I feel nothing as I watch the sky burst with blood from my porch, but my tears have fallen and so I know I must be sad. Soon he will arrive.

I thought I heard girls' voices at the stream giggling as they run from me, scattered in all directions like birds who gather to peck at seeds and now see the gift of a meal is a trap. I am the hag of the forest in my bloodstained rags, a figure of nightmare and storytelling around the common fire until the Mister brings the girls who grew up fearing me, tied and screaming into their gags, to my shack.

The sun has set. Blackness shot with tiny stars follows in its wake. All things repeat the same patterns. I must go inside.

She is crying in her darkness. I light the burning fluid in the lantern with a flint and begin to croon a lullaby. I don't know the words, if there ever were any words. This is just the tune I brought with me from my lost land, long ago. She is comforted and tries to hum along. The dragging has ceased for a moment. I sigh. I cannot bear the sound.

I assemble my calabashes, wooden bowls and sharp metals on a little table by the wrought-iron bed that is the centerpiece of my shack. The water glows crystalline in the lanternlight. I should light a fire among the stones in the fireplace. There is never enough light to see the tiny places I must cut and pinch and stitch with such precision.

At this thought the girl in the darkness groans. I hear her clearly from her corner and must stop to catch my breath. *Hush,* I think to her. *You will frighten them. They will look for you. Hush, child.*

She whimpers for she has so little control of her terror.

It will be over soon, I think to her. *Help them be still. Be still yourself. Hush.*

I go back to humming her lullaby. She cannot hum along tunelessly now for she is too frightened.

I am still raising and lowering the wick a hairsbreadth at a time, careful not to let the flame consume too much camphine too quickly nor dip into the sloshing glass bowl of it and explode into my face when the Mister's fist rattles the unbolted door. A grunt is all I say to let him know that I am here.

Words are meaningless. I have no say. He will do what he will do.

He has only brought one girl this time, and I can see that she will be of no use to me. She cannot kick. She cannot fight. She is too frail, too unfed, and she has already fainted.

His whip-cracker carries the fainted girl across arms where he has also draped the whip he used to round her up and to drive her mother back, back to the shacks of the helpless. The cracker enters the shack with the tiny girl limp across his arms and his whip and gazes down at her tenderly.

"Put her down," the Mister says to his cracker.

And I wonder how I will do this. But I must go through with it. I have no other choices left. This time or never at all.

But I give the Mister a final chance. I gesture with my hands that the girl is too small. I shake my head and shrug her away, meaning, *Take her away.*

"Get on with it, you hag," the Mister says and the cracker hesitates. He, too, wants to watch and tries to ease into the darkest corner behind him, where he hopes to be forgotten and allowed to stay.

I seize the razor, spin and point it at the cracker. My fist is clenched so that the razor does not drop even as my arm shakes.

I can feel that my eyes are fierce, for the Mister stumbles away from me and barks at his cracker, "Get out of here. She fears you,

you fool. Get away from her. Get away from the girl. Get out of here."

The cracker steps forward, away from the crawling girl he does not see.

She twists to stare up at him as he moves as if she is fascinated by his closeness. Her stick-thin arms bend at the elbows like the springing legs of some great fragile green insect. She moves in little jerks and arches her back as if wings would sprout from it and whir her away from this place at any moment. I hear her hiss at him. He hears nothing.

As the Mister said, his cracker is a fool.

The Mister turns toward the corner and glances uneasily behind his cracker. He is unsure that he has not heard anything, not seen the shadows shift and heard them sigh.

I sigh and close my eyes to calm myself and draw his attention.

"Get out," he says again to his cracker, but now I can hear that he is unsteady and unwilling to be here without his armed guard. Yet, the cracker, his fool, obeys.

When the door has shut and I have slid its bolt and it is too late for the Mister to call back the man with the whip, I hear her crawling again. Side to side. Pacing on her hands.

The Mister says, "Get on with it, you," and eases himself down at the foot of the bed to watch the cutting and hold her legs against the screaming, if the fainted living girl awakes.

I circle the bed with strips of rags to knot the fainted girl's arms and legs spreadeagled to the four posts. *He should not do this,* I think, and the thought makes my tears flow afresh.

I have placed years of bloodied rags, stiff and caked even after many washings, in the center of the mattress where the girls lie to soak up the new offering of blood.

This bed is too big for only one. She is so far away that I can hardly be expected to reach her, let alone hold her hips still while I cut into her. But he is not thinking practically. He licks his lips, as if in anticipation.

I reach out a hand to him and slap it with my other palm, to draw his hungry attention away from the girl. Startled, he looks at me and grunts his disapproval before he reaches into a jacket pocket and pulls out his brandy flask. I take it for the girl, in case she wakes, and hold out my other hand for the whiskey, for her cuts. "You old witch," he says and I think at him, *But I was not an old witch when you bought me and brought me here with your brand burned into my face. Now, was I?*

I place the flasks on the little table with the cutting and sewing things, and now I must stop these thoughts for they will soon turn back the years to his look of utter delight when he discovered the secret sacred scar between my legs.

"This is your independence," the woman who cut me explained to me after the healing had begun. She said, "The women in the farms and towns, they travel safely to market because of this that I have given you, carrying fresh goods and cowrie shells of wealth with no fear. The women in the caravans and in the path of war, they walk to and from the rivers to bathe and fetch water and fresh fish for their families with no fear because of this that I have given you. I have cleansed you. No one can rape these women. These women are respected. You are now to be respected. These women marry, and their brothers and their husbands would die to protect them."

But I was neither married nor protected because our farms were raided when war was waged against the farmers and unheard-of numbers of people were slaughtered in our fields.

I was not slaughtered but tied among the living to be bartered. I was bound with ropes and stumbled behind men with huge cloths wound around their heads to protect them from the sun.

For being spared, I thanked and then cursed my sacred scar. But I must not think of this now or my hands will shake and destroy the girl they have brought me.

The same night the Mister bought me and had my face branded, he worked at my sacred scar with his fingers and his body until he managed to enter me. And every night after that until I gave birth. And then my body and mind were destroyed by the doctor he called to cut open the sacred scar and let out his child.

I recovered and lived, after a fashion, for my baby, who nursed from me and needed me. But the Mister is a fool and checked between her legs, as if a girl were born scarred and not given them, for he did not know that the scars have to be made as a pledge to the gods for the world to continue as it always has, for order to be maintained, and for chaos to be driven back into the world of the unseemly and the unclean.

Already, by then, I did not talk. I have not talked since I was brought to this demon land. One must not speak among evil spirits.

The doctor who destroyed my scar when he sliced me open and delivered the Mister's baby then sewed me closed and advised my purchaser that he had heard of this practice, of these kinds of women and girls. Of barbarians who cut the pleasure from their females and sew up the holes so tightly that even an impotent man can take his pleasure. "It has to be done to them?" the Mister asked, incredulous. "Who can do such a thing? Can you? Can we buy whoever can do this thing?"

The doctor averred that he could not do it himself. But the glint in his eye said he would like to try, and he and the Mister embarked on a drain of the unwanted girls throughout the region, the runaways, the readers scratching alphabet letters into dry soil and loamy mud, the self-harmers whose flat-bellied pregnancies did not stick but flushed away month after month: "The ones whose acts could destroy the principles upon which this great nation teeters," the Mister and the doctor agreed. The bad girls.

The doctor and the Mister practiced cutting into the bad girls.

The bad girls they cut and lusted upon as they lay bleeding did not survive. And at some point, the Mister could no longer afford the financial strain of buying and butchering all the bad girls and women in his neighborhood.

So, ever since, he has tried to get me to make a new sacred scarred girl for him, for they no longer sell girls such as I am at the markets in this godforsaken land, anymore. I must have been among the last, among the few so valued as to be scarred and yet cast out from my people, rootless.

Only girls such as his own daughter, she who crawls in the corner, mewling and alone, can be found now in this no-place. So he brought her to me and said, "Make the cuts. Make the scar. Scar her."

I have wondered every day why he chose her for me to cut first.

I know these demons do not recognize their own children but sell them in the markets like so much meat and root vegetable to anyone with money or credit to buy them. But I have wondered because she had not been sold, and therefore I believed he knew who had fathered her and honored his fatherhood to her, even though law forbade me to accuse him, even if I had the power to speak.

We are buried under layers of lies in this stronghold of demons, struggling up toward a sunlight we cannot see.

He brought my daughter to me with his razor and his strop and told me to make the cuts. I shrieked with wailing and was slapped into silence. I tried to remember what had been done to me, when I was small and howling with pain and could only look away, where my mother lifted my head above my agony.

But I did not know, could not think.

And as soon as I began to cut and she began to scream and kick and pump purple blood spurting into the air, all was lost. I could not save her.

I was blinded by her shooting blood and the terror on her face. I may never open my eyes on the morning light and see anything other than her anguish again, her mouth a great square roped in spittle as she shrieked at me to "Stop, please stop, Mama!"

"You are taking too long," the Mister says, and I turn to him.

She moves in the corner, and her sound is sharp. I know without turning that she is watching me. She knows before I do what I will do.

"You fool," the Mister says, and I turn away from him to regard the girl on the bed whom I cannot reach in the faraway center.

I lift one knee as if to crawl to her across the blood-stiffened rags, both arms extended.

But the Mister starts to berate me with, "You don't know what you are doing," and I plant the raised foot onto his boot to hold him in place while I swipe the opened razor backward and up across his throat and face in a deep diagonal gash.

He stares, open-mouthed with shock. I drag the razor forward again against the other side of his throat. He stares as if he expects me to say something.

But one must never speak to demons.

I say nothing.

And then there is a rush like wind, like the cracker's whip through the unresisting air, and the splintered floorboards have creaked and cracked under the combined weight of the girl from the corner rushing up the wrought-iron curlicues to clamber up the Mister's waistcoat to his spurting neck as he buckles forward onto the footboard of the bed.

The bed creaks. It cannot long resist their struggle, he in horror at the sight of the chalk-white thing that slobbers and gulps at his violet blood and she in her crazed need. Her fingers are like spikes that gouge open the lips of his neck wound to suck deeper in the rich pool he cannot help but offer her.

No calabash of trickling blood from a thin girl spooling out her last fluids for my darling daughter tonight. Tonight she dines on the vibrant fountain of her lost life, greedily taking in the lifetime of beef and pork and rich earthy grains that was so wrongly taken from her, from the very man who took it. Tonight, she feasts on life and lives again.

But even as I watch in amazement her pinkening cheeks turn ruddy golden brown with blood and form he has snatched the razor from my hand and slashed at his face and neck with it, trying to get at her.

I laugh. For though I can see her and he now feels her, she is a spirit slaughtered and trapped in the land of spirits and cannot be attacked with a razor again. I wish I could taunt him with this understanding, but he reaches it on his own soon enough.

He careens toward my shack's bolted door, still slashing at his own face where she has planted her open mouth and sucks at his fresh wounds as she climbs higher onto his shoulders. He wants to fight her down, toss her off, but he cannot because she is the destiny he shaped for himself.

He is bellowing, and she is drinking him down in gleeful gulps, and I am laughing fit to burst as his blood spatters me and the floor and walls of my shack in vibrant rainbow red. I had not foreseen this, and I am reborn in gratitude to gods I long ago ceased to worship.

They bang their way together, she hunched and suckling, he zigzagging blindly, out of the shack and down the dirt path that will take him to the fields.

The first person who spots him shrieking and slashing the razor across his own face, neck and shoulders is not the cracker whose job it is to survey the workers and escape routes but one of the cotton pickers, pausing from picking up remnants of soft fluff and torn burlap sacking from among the thorns of the day's work to stuff tiny toys for his children, trying to catch his breath.

This man appears to hear the Mister screeching and twists this way and that as if he isn't quite sure what animal is trapped and suffering or rabid and coming for him. Upon scanning the field in the direction of the Haunted Shack—my taboo home—he spots the Mister careening wildly from side to side in what looks like his effort to run away from himself.

It is clear that the Mister is trying to escape something he cannot outrun. He stumbles, stops and grapples with it before he again slashes his head, face and throat with the razor. The blood bursts from him in weaker and weaker pumps. It is obvious that he will die—is dying on his feet as he staggers upon them—but some inner terror drives him as if with a lash and will not let him collapse to be devoured by his foully withered seed.

The man who first spotted him has left his handful of bundles of fluff and fabric in the cotton rows at a run to help his despised owner who nevertheless keeps him from being sold away from his few friends and loved ones, from the shack that he calls home and from a cracker who at least does not rape him or his mate and his children. The man will save the Mister in an act of self-preservation, if he can.

The cracker, who has not yet spotted the Mister, has now spotted the sprinting cotton picker and thinks he is dealing with a runaway, so he cracks his whip adding to the frenzy as he leaps after him. But the cotton picker reaches the Mister and grapples with him to seize at the bloodied, slippery razor until he snatches it in triumph, away.

The Mister roars and reaches for the weapon with which he was killing himself, like a disappointed child. When he cannot take the razor back, he grabs at the cuts in his neck and appears to drag at them, widening the gaps.

The cracker has stopped feet away from the fighting pair, confused. Now that he sees the Mister, he does not rush forward until the Mister's face comes over pasty and shocked, and the triumphant cotton picker lets him drop.

The cracker cannot catch the body as it crumples in a boneless pool, the black and white of the Mister's open eyes and mouth floating skyward.

The girl, who has all my attention now, has gained strength and substance, to my eyes. She lifts herself languidly, satiated, and rises face to the crescent moon as if on newly sprouted mantis wings, a miracle of cannibalism and flight, female and male, the all in one. She hovers, testing her ability to fly. Then she flits and darts in zigs and zags back along the Mister's stumbling path, now here, now there, now back, now forth, leaping and landing, backtracking her way through time to my shack.

Why would she want to go there? I wonder. She can be free. I must tell her to fly free, flee this godforsaken place, these cursed people. I must tell her there is nothing here for her. Even I, who love her, am not worth being imprisoned here.

I have reached the three men by now, coated in the Mister's blood, my mud-caked bare feet and sun-bleached hair rag and stiff faded clothing a testament to my wading through the stream several times a day to bathe.

The cracker looks up at me as he fails to gather up the blood-speckled paste that is the Mister. "What the hell happened?" he wants to know.

The cotton picker has wiped the razor into the dry dust at our feet and managed to close the blade into the sheath. He hands it toward the cracker, who seems reluctant to take it.

I reach for the razor folded into its sheath and take it.

Then I point it at the Mister and point it at my own face. My throat. My shoulders. I dance around in a somber-faced fit, showing how the maddened Mister attacked himself.

When I have completed one rotation, I stand still and face the cracker.

I am willing to die for having freed my daughter. For having freed all the living girls and women of the plantation. For revenge. For justice. If I die here, I will die on ground my own hands and tears and blood have made sacred.

I need to go wake up the girl who was not cut in my shack tonight and send her quietly home to her imprisoned parents, who could not keep the Mister from bringing her to me.

I walk away from the whip-cracker and the cotton picker and the flattened colorless thing that was the Mister, toward the starry blackness between the trees that tower above my shack.

THE LADY OF THE YELLOW-PAINTED LIBRARY

by Tobi Ogundiran

1. THINGS FALL APART

Dear Mr. Badmus,
This is to inform you that the book Things Fall Apart
which you borrowed from this library on the 4ᵗʰ (fourth)
of August is one day overdue. Please return immediately.
Failure to do so will result in dire consequences.

Thank you.
L.

"I'm here to see the librarian."

"That'd be me," said the young woman behind the counter, flashing him a bright smile.

Wande could scarcely hide his surprise. "Really? Where is the other woman? I forget her name—"

"She is indisposed at the moment. She took a fall and fractured her hip."

"I'm sorry to hear that." He was more relieved than sorry. He had been worried at having to explain himself to the old stern-faced librarian. But this woman, she was young, and while he was not much to look at, his silver salesman tongue never failed to sway people over to his side. "Are you her daughter, then? You definitely look like her."

"You'll be dealing with me, now. How can I help you, Mr. . . ."

"Badmus. Wande Badmus."

"Ah, *that* Mr. Badmus." (He grinned sheepishly.) "Have you come to return the book?"

"Actually . . . how to put this delicately? I don't—er—have it . . ."

A pause. "I'm afraid I don't quite understand you."

"Well," Wande said, mopping at his brows. "I seem to have, ah, lost it."

Her perfectly trimmed unibrow creased ever so slightly, but the smile remained firmly in place. The overall effect served to give her the grimace of one mildly constipated. "That is quite unfortunate," she said finally. "Are you sure? Have you searched thoroughly through your . . . lodgings?"

"Yes, yes, I have," said Wande. "And it's a damn thing. I always put it on the nightstand, never even took it out of the room! It's like the thing developed legs and walked out of its own accord!" He laughed, licking his lips. The young librarian smiled even wider, and Wande congratulated himself on a job well done.

The truth was that he hadn't set eyes on the book since the first day he borrowed it, and had even forgotten about it until he received the overdue notice yesterday. He had only taken the damned thing out of politeness to the old librarian who insisted he have it. What could he have done? He had after all come in here trying to sell her a brand-new rotary phone and the woman had bought two. One stood on the counter right now, blood-red and polished to mirror sheen.

"While that is certainly a possibility," she said, "I encourage you to look again. Perhaps you missed it."

"Actually, I've checked out of the room," said Wande. "And I combed it to be sure—delayed one extra day while my partner went on ahead to Kwara but"—he gave an exaggerated sigh—"I just didn't find it."

"I see."

"Yes," Wande blundered on. "I'm actually on my way to the train station." He pointed at his worn leather suitcase. "I'm leaving for—"

"Leaving?" Her unibrow went up in a controlled expression of surprise. "I'm afraid I cannot allow you to leave until you return the book."

"You cannot—?" He took a deep breath, yanking down his tie. He was starting to get hot. "We're travelling salesmen—my partner and I—and we operate on a tight schedule. I'm sure you can understand . . ."

If she understood, she gave no sign of it. The young librarian remained mute, hands folded neatly on the counter, professional smile taut on her face. They remained like that for a few moments, Wande trying to read some emotion in her coal-black eyes. Finding none, he reached into his pocket and withdrew a thick manila envelope which he slid across the counter.

"What is this?"

"Compensation," he breathed. "A fine. Whatever you want to call it. This should be more than enough to cover the cost of—"

She touched a manicured finger to the envelope and slid it back across to him as though it were something particularly revolting. "I think there has been a small misunderstanding," she said. "And I apologize if I did not communicate myself clearly. We do not take compensations, we do not take replacements—not that you can find a replacement anyway, as that is the only copy on God's green earth."

Wande blinked. "What, *Things Fall Apart*? It's a popular book! It's everywhere!"

The woman merely smiled at him.

"What am I supposed to do?" Wande spluttered, starting to get angry.

"I'm sure if you looked through your lodgings again—"

"I already did!" he cried, banging his fist on the countertop and rattling the rotary phone. The receiver clattered loudly to the counter. "I delayed my trip and took the extra day to search thoroughly through my lodgings. It *isn't* there! Believe me, I want it to be but it isn't!"

Wande left. He left the library with the fading yellow paint and infuriating librarian; he left the damned city with its reeking streets and rusty houses. That was what he should have done in the first place, but his mother had raised him right and he had decided to own up to his mistake. He had even offered her money; three times more than the price of the book because he had been feeling guilty (and maybe particularly generous; they had made a great sale in Ibadan, after all).

"Can't allow me to leave," he muttered a few hours later, watching the countryside whip past through the coach window. "Well, I've left, now, haven't I?"

In the three days it took Wande to reach Kwara he forgot all about the book and the librarian. He managed to talk himself into the business coach and even sold three rotary phones. All in all, it was a good trip and Wande arrived in high spirits to Kwara.

A note was waiting for him in his motel room, placed neatly in the centre of the bed where he couldn't miss it.

> *Dear Mr. Badmus,*
> *I understand that you have, against my advice (and quite irresponsibly in my opinion), left Ibadan and are now in Kwara. I am very disappointed in you. Did you think I would not find out? Or did you think to slink away to someplace I would never find you? Please return at once to Ibadan, preferably with the book. It is now four days overdue. While you will be duly pun-*

ished, I am willing to temper the severity of your pun-
ishment should you return within a day with the book.

Best wishes,

L.

Wande crumpled the note in a meaty fist and stumbled into the bathroom where Donatus was taking a shit.

"What the fuck, man!" cried Donatus, trying and failing to cover his modesty.

"Who delivered this letter?" Wande asked.

"What letter?"

"This one!" Wande brandished the crumpled paper. "It came from the librarian—"

"Maybe you brought it with you—"

"No, I didn't. It was right in the middle of the bed! And you've been living here—"

"Now that I think of it," said Donatus thoughtfully, one hand still in the toilet bowl over his member, "there was a raven. Yes. The letter was strapped to its leg. I fed it some crumbs, the good bird, afterwards I gave it some water to drink . . ."

Wande's eye was twitching. "You think this is a joke?"

"You don't see me laughing, do you? Now, will you let me wipe myself or do you want to watch?"

2. TICK-TOCK MR. BADMUS

Kwara was a much tougher city to conquer and Wande found doors slammed in his face at almost every turn. It was infuriating, to say the least, and he wondered, for the very first time in twenty-five years of selling rotary phones, if he had lost his touch.

"Just a bad city, is all," said Donatus when Wande brought it up in conversation. "Sometimes the stars all misalign and we run out of luck. Sometimes the people actually *do* know what they want—which isn't rotary phones, *hehe*."

"Yeah?" said Wande. "*You* sold some phones."

"Eh," said Donatus, shrugging as if it meant nothing. "Pure luck. You know this, old boy." He cocked his head, considering. "Maybe your silver tongue needs a bit of polishing, eh?" And he roared with laughter, specks of spit flying from his mouth.

Wande scowled at him, but Donatus had already put up his newspaper and did not see it.

Wande was glad to leave Kwara. He waited with the tickets and their luggage in the departure lounge in the train station, while Donatus went on to call their employer to give an update on their situation. He came back grinning.

"What?" Wande snarled. The bloody heat, the noise, the rank smell of humanity, not to mention a very poor performance in Kwara, had put him in a very bad temper.

"Looks like you'll have to go on without me, partner," said Donatus.

"What? *Why?*"

Donatus shrugged. "Didn't say. I didn't ask. He's the boss."

"So I'm meant to continue all by myself?"

"Aw, don't be like that." Donatus grinned, flashing a golden tooth. "I'm going to miss you too. Come here, let me give you a kiss."

"Fuck off, Donatus," said Wande, throwing him off.

Wande watched him saunter off, fighting the urge to scream.

Twenty minutes later, blowing like a horse and cursing fluently, Wande dragged his luggage down the train aisle to his compartment. He tossed the suitcase full of rotary phones to the floor and plopped down on his bed. His shirt was already sticking to his back and he fumbled the buttons with one meaty hand, reaching with the other for the jug of cool water on the table. The train lurched into motion and his questing hand smacked the jug over, spraying water all over the floor, the dusty window and his bed. Wande let loose a train of colourful expletives. Everything. *Everything* was going to shit.

That was when he saw the note, folded neatly next to the up-ended jug. The entire table was soaking wet, but the yellow piece of paper lay in a dry circle, with not a single drop of water on it. Wande could have sworn on his father's dead bones that the note hadn't been there just a second ago.

Wande licked his lips and stared at the note a long time. He tried to tell himself that it was a complimentary note from the train staff, that it was a previous passenger's note, forgotten in the haste and chaos of disembarking. But Wande was a practical man; he knew the note was meant for him.

The writing was unmistakable—changed but unmistakable; where before the librarian's lettering had been the strokes of flaw-less cursive, now the letters were edged and heavy handed, carved so deeply that they actually punched through the paper in places. Wande could almost imagine the vicious look on the librarian's face as she wrote it.

> *Dear Mr. Badmus,*
> *Where before I was willing to temper justice with mercy, your actions have showed that you do not deserve my mercy. Like the self-centered narcissist you are, you have pushed me (and your debt to me) out of your mind and have carried on with your life. Rest assured, you WILL BE PUNISHED very severely.*
> *Tick-tock, Mr. Badmus,*
> *L.*

The first modicum of fear began to steal into Wande's heart.

3. THE AUGUST VISITOR

Wande mopped his face as he inspected the watery contents of his bowel movement. That was the third time he had hit the toilet in twelve hours. His stomach was in knots and what was worse, he could not seem to hold down food; it always came up, either from his mouth or his ass. The half-eaten remains of his dinner lying scattered on the table in his compartment would most likely remain half-eaten.

Something fell out of his pocket as he yanked up his trousers; the librarian's note, crumpled to a ball. Barely had five minutes passed than Wande put it out of his mind. It was what he always did when faced with an unsolvable problem. Did he really want to think about how the librarian knew where to send her notes? Did he really want to consider how *this* note came to be in his compartment? Did he really want to think about those threats, both veiled and blatant? No. From his personal experience, problems had a way of solving themselves or slinking away if he paid them no mind. Wande crumpled the note once more, then chucked it into the toilet bowl, congratulating himself on a job well done.

The librarian was waiting for him in his compartment.

"What—?" Wande began, stunned.

She sat on the other side of the table, dressed in the same fuchsia pink-and-black polka-dot gown she had been wearing the first (and last) time he had seen her. Her hair, pulled back in a harsh bun, stretched her unibrow halfway across her forehead, giving her a perpetual startled look. It did not help that she was smiling.

"What are you—?" Wande spluttered. "How did you—?"

"Find you?" she asked sweetly. "Please."

Please. As if it was a dumb question and the answer was obvious.

"Have you been following me?"

"No," she said. "I tried to be civil. I wrote you letters, but of course you've ignored every one of them." Her black eyes bored into his. "In some cases, you even went as far as to show your contempt for me." Wande felt an anvil drop into the pit of his belly. She knew. Somehow she knew that he had flushed her note down with his shit.

"Look—" he began.

"Do you mind if I eat?" she asked. And without waiting for him, she reached beneath the table and produced a rusted brass food flask. Wande watched, stupefied, as she carefully laid a napkin across her lap and tucked a bright pink bib into her neckline. Then she helped herself to Wande's cutleries, grimy from fish oil and watery potato soup. Finally, she uncorked her food flask. From this distance, Wande could not see what was in it, but a decidedly foul and rancid smell filled the stuffy air of his compartment. The librarian stabbed into the flask, twisted the fork (there was an awful squeal, followed by the sound of bone breaking and liquid sloshing), then popped a mottled piece of something into her mouth. "Mmm," she said, smacking her lips. "That's better. Much better. I'm so famished, but that's to be expected. Especially when I had to bring the library with me."

Wande finally broke out of his stupor. "Bring the library?"

"Yes, the *library*. Dragged it over the hills and mountains and across the blasted savannah, I did." And she pointed the fork at him, jabbing at the air with each word. "All. Because. Of. You."

Wande looked at her for one long moment, then slowly began to chuckle: a hysterical sound which gradually morphed into spasmic snorts of laughter. "You are mad!" he gasped, wiping at his teary eyes. "Very mad. I don't know how you got here, or how you even knew where to find me, but I'm calling the—"

He saw it then, through the grimy window of his compartment.

The train had taken one of its customary stops (as they waited to switch onto another track) and Wande had seized the opportunity to use the toilet. As he moved his bowels, he had had plenty of time to contemplate the barren savannah countryside, and wonder at the scanty trees of the wilderness. What he hadn't seen—what he was sure *hadn't* been there—was the library.

Now, though, the two-story library with the peeling yellow paint from Ibadan stood beyond the tracks. Beneath the milky disk of a full moon, it looked like an eerie, grotesque thing leaning with malicious intent *towards* the train.

"How . . ." Wande began, but the words melted in his mouth in a bitter taste of fear. The strength bled from Wande's knees and he collapsed into the chair.

The librarian gave him a wide, wide smile.

This problem, it seemed, was not going away. It was a problem of a different kind, one which sent cold hands clawing down his back. Wande turned to look at her, at her smiling black eyes, at her too wide mouth chomping, chomping, chomping. "What *are* you?"

"That's unimportant, now," she said. "I'm here to talk about you, and your debt to me."

"The—the book," he gulped. "I told you I can't find it."

"Too bad," she said, chomping mechanically on whatever it was she was eating. "I really hope, for your sake, that you do." She belched, then dabbed dutifully at her lips. "Excuse me."

Wande looked down at the knife on the table, and wondered how quickly he would have to move to stab it through her slender neck. The librarian's smile widened, almost as if she had read his thoughts. Wande did not doubt that she had.

"As you can see, I've brought the library for your convenience," she continued. "Isn't that very kind of me? All you need do, *if* you find the book, is walk up to the library and return it—and receive your punishment, of course, for all the trouble you have caused me. It will be terrible," (she leaned in over her food flask) "but I assure you it will be nothing compared to what'll happen to you if you *don't* return that book."

Wande understood at last that he was in trouble. He began to sob.

She smiled wider, her teeth a little too many, the points a little too sharp. "Come, now, Mr. Badmus, are you crying? That is un-becoming."

Strings of snot and spit ran down his chin. "Please," he blub-bered. "Please, I don't—I will do anything—please—"

"You have exactly twenty-four hours."

And then she was gone. One moment she was there smiling at him, and the next the chair was empty, the brass flask the only sign that she had ever been there. Wande, still sobbing, hoisted his ample form out of the chair and peered into the flask where he saw several scaly creatures floating in a thick, fetid soup of decay.

Lizards. She had been eating lizards.

4. A MONTAGE OF VERY DESPERATE ACTS

Wande never got to Abuja. The train broke down on the outskirts of Kogi and after waiting six hours with no help, he (along with two hundred disgruntled passengers) fought his way out of the train and traipsed the three kilometres to the next station, where he dialed Donatus through a pay phone. He didn't get through; the operator kept telling him the number was incorrect and would he like to try again? But it wasn't incorrect. He had en-tered it three times carefully (admittedly with shaky fingers) but it *wasn't* incorrect! Next, he tried his employer, but it rang and rang and rang until the operator wisely suggested that the person he was trying to contact was unavailable—no shit.

Wande carefully replaced the receiver, swallowing the lump in his throat. After a minute or two of gazing emptily into space, he stumbled out of the booth and dragged his luggage with him to the ticket counter. He was going home.

"A ticket for Lagos, please."

"Last one left an hour ago," said the girl at the counter. "Next is eight A.M. tomorrow." She jerked her dog-eared paperback in the direction of the yellowed departure schedule taped to the win-dow.

Wande groaned. "I'll wait, then."

"Good for you, sa. Just not here."

"Why not?"

She snapped her book shut, and fixed Wande with a passionless stare. "We're about to close."

"Close? But . . ." Wande looked about him; the general departure lounge which had been teeming with people half an hour ago was nearly empty. "I have nowhere to go."

Her emotionless stare told him that it was not her problem.

5. MADNESS AT THE RANCH

Half an hour later, Wande found himself squashed in the back of a stinking farm truck, trundling down the dirt road to Eben Cattle Ranch. After inquiring extensively, he'd learned that the nearest motel was thirty kilometres from the station, and would cost him more than half of what he had left, leaving him with little money to purchase a ticket. Also, it was too far and he did not want to miss the train in the morning. That was when Abdul, one of the young men whom he had been interrogating, told him he could stay the night on the ranch. No, he did not own the ranch, but was a simple worker. What was more, he made early morning rounds to town, dropping off fresh cow milk, and if Wande liked, he could drop him off at the station with plenty of time to catch his train. All he had to pay was ten thousand naira.

"Ten thousand naira?"

"Chicken change," said Abdul, sucking on his blunt.

"But that is—" Too much? Yes, it was. But it was better than paying fifty thousand at the motel. At least this way he would have just enough to buy a ticket in the morning. "Yes, fine. Thank you."

"Dun worry, ma man." Abdul grinned, allowing Wande a full view of his rotten dentition. "I do dis every time. I be good Samaritan."

The sky was the deep blue of evening when they arrived at the ranch. As Abdul brought his truck to a sputtering halt in front of a two-story building, Wande started, nearly shitting himself before realizing that this was not a certain other two-story building he had become frighteningly acquainted with; this was a quaint, if somewhat lopsided, log house.

"Home, sweet home!" barked Abdul.

A few minutes later, alone in the room he'd been offered, Wande sank to the bed with the weight of his troubled thoughts. Now that he really thought about it, it was curious how Donatus had left abruptly, strange how the train had broken down, disturbing how he had been unable to get through to anyone, and outright alarming how he was now in a ranch house in the middle of nowhere.

Isolated and alone.

The distressed lowing of cows sliced through the night's silence and sent cold hands clawing up Wande's spine. She was here. The librarian had come for him. Slowly, with wobbly steps, Wande moved over to the window, peered out and saw

—the library with its peeling yellow paint and twisted roofs, standing in the field as though it had stood there for a hundred years, and will stand for another hundred—

A sharp rap on the door sent Wande spinning. He licked his dry lips and mopped the cold sweat from his brow. At this point it was too much to wish it was only Abdul on the other side of the door. The next trio of knocks was not so gentle. The door rattled in its frame, splinters flying off the edges, as if a particularly muscly man—or an enraged beast—was pounding on it. Then followed a series of incessant pounding. The door groaned. Splintered. The doorjamb pumped (*up down up down*) faster and faster until the rusty aluminum squealed in protest. Faster and louder and harder came the bombardment of the door; the jamb squealing, the door rattling until—

Silence.

Wande found that he was breathing hard, and there was a dark stain around his crotch. He stood there, petrified, staring at the battered door. Spidery cracks ran around the lintel and the old walls.

A minute passed. Then two. Then three. And when Wande started to hope that the librarian was gone, she spoke.

"Mr. Badmus." Her voice was pleasant, conversational. "I trust you know who this is? You have locked the door. Please open it."

"No."

"No?" She sounded surprised, even incredulous. Wande was surprised himself, but he would not open the door simply because she asked nicely. "Come, now, you want to act like a naughty boy? I gave you all the time in the world, Mr. Badmus, and you were duly forewarned what would happen if you failed to return the book to me. Open the door and take your punishment."

"BUT I DON'T HAVE IT!" he screamed. "IT'S NOT MY FAULT I DIDN'T WANT TO TAKE THE STUPID BOOK ALL I WANTED—"

A shrill sound cut through the air and stopped Wande in the middle of his tirade. It took him a few moments to realize it was the sound of a phone ringing.

He stumbled over to the nightstand, plucked the receiver with a shaky hand, and croaked, "Hello?"

"Hey man!"

Donatus. The strength expired from Wande's legs and he crumpled to his knees. He was so relieved at the sound of that voice that he did not stop to wonder at how Donatus knew to call this number, or the simple fact that the phone was not connected.

"Guess what I found, man? The book!"

"W—what?"

"I know!" laughed Donatus. "The kids were rummaging through my stuff, see. Cuz the toys I got them were in my luggage and the little rascals couldn't wait till morning—anyway they found the book among my stuff! Hehe. I guess I must have accidentally packed it when I left Ibadan, eh . . ."

Wande saw red as rage filled him. Rage so consuming that it couldn't be translated into words; he roared incomprehensible syllables into the receiver. Donatus tried several times to speak, his voice growing increasingly bewildered with each try, but there was no speaking over Wande and Donatus finally hung up.

Wande flung the phone with a roar and it shattered into pieces. That stupid fuck! How many times had he asked him to check his belongings? How many times? He wouldn't be in such a fix if not for him. It was all his fault. The librarian can have him. Let her punish *him*.

He wheeled towards the door. "Donatus has the book! He just called me. He told me he has it—punish him instead!" Nothing but silence from the other side of the door. "Hello?"

With great trepidation, Wande unlocked the door and it swung nosily open to reveal an empty hallway. A draft stirred through, carrying with it the faint smell of something foul and rotten, not unlike the smell from the food flask on the train.

Wande stepped out of the room and right into the library.

It was as he remembered it: rows and rows of dusty shelves bearing equally dusty books. The gas lanterns that lit the vast interior were few and spaced so far apart that there were huge pockets of darkness where their lights did not reach. A gas lantern spilled warm light onto the librarian's desk, illuminating the blood-red rotary phone he had sold the old woman. The librarian was not at her desk.

Hurried footsteps.

Wande whipped around, eyes scanning the too-dark library.

Click. Clack. Click. Clack. The footsteps seemed to come from everywhere at once, echoing like the sound of a dozen pebbles hitting the bottom of a dry well.

"Hello?" He did not like how tiny and tremulous his voice

sounded. "The book has been found! Donatus has it! You can . . . you can punish him instead . . ."

The footsteps had stopped as he spoke, and for a split second, utter silence filled the library.

For a split second.

Click. Clack. Click. Clack. Closer and closer came the footsteps. Hurried. Urgent. The footfalls of a predator closing in—

Wande decided he did not want to wait to see who or *what* was coming. He grabbed the lantern, and fled for the door . . . only it was not there.

"What—"

He flailed about. Perhaps he had missed it. Perhaps the door was a little further down.

The footfalls resumed. Fast. A confusion of sounds, like marbles skittering across tiles.

Wande bolted. He raced down the aisle, swinging the lantern before him, searching frantically for the door. Wall. Window. Wall. There was no door—*THERE WAS NO DOOR!* He was weeping now, blubbering, screaming that Donatus had the book, that he was innocent. His legs, his lungs, *everything* burned and he wished he could take a moment to catch his breath.

He tripped, and went sprawling to the cold floor. The lantern flew from his grip and shattered, winking out, plunging him into total darkness. Pain flared through his body, but Wande struggled to his feet, his mind set on flight, intent on putting as much distance as he could between himself and those thousand hellish footfalls.

That was when he saw it. Up ahead, another lantern cast a pool of light, and there was something where light met shadow.

It looked like a pile of dirty old sheets, discarded between the two towering shelves. It wasn't until Wande saw a face—squashed skin, unblinking eyes, blood-red lips, and unmistakable unibrow—that he realized what he was looking at.

It was the librarian. Or rather the librarian's *skin*.

Wande screamed. And howled. Gawking and yet unwilling to believe the hideous thing before him. It was as though her bones and meat had been scooped out, the empty skin crumpling to the floor without any visceral support. He could see a rip in her skin, where something—several things—had clawed their way out of her.

Click ... Clack ... Click ... Clack.

They came out of the darkness, one after the other. The light cast colourful patterns on their hideous, scaly forms. *Lizards.* They dripped black ichor onto the floor, shiny black claws clicking and clacking as they arranged themselves into neat rows.

A moment passed in which Wande's screaming died out, in which he stared at the creatures, in which he gasped one last, pitiful word: "Please."

And then they came for him.

6. THE LORD OF THE YELLOW-PAINTED LIBRARY

The librarian studied his reflection in the dusty mirror. He adjusted his tie and contemplated the paunch of his belly. When he was satisfied, he turned to his desk where a fresh piece of paper and a felt-tip pen were waiting for him.

He lowered himself into the chair and adjusted the red rotary phone until it was perfectly aligned at the edge of the desk. After thinking for a moment or two, he picked up the pen and began in flowing cursive:

Dear Mr. Donatus ...

WHEN THE MAMI WATA MET A DEMON

by Moustapha Mbacké Diop

The sea was still as a grave, uncaring and icy against my toes. Making me, once again, wonder if it had shunned me out, like the bitter miscreant I was.

It was almost dawn. Faint sun rays grazed the fishermen's large foreheads as they pushed pirogues heavy with mullet and crawfish up the shore. They spared me not a look. Bickering and singing through chapped lips, they left me smashing fish bones against each other and fiddling with shreds of white nets. I was a ghost. A little freak, with worn-out clothes and prominent ribs. I was the witch's son.

Night had chased me away from my home. This one had been horrible—perhaps the worst. One of those nights when I surged out of the hut before first light, as if the Devil himself breathed down my neck. When I shivered and wept under my bed, my heart an open wound that left nothing but darkness. Yes, it was cold, and damp. Salt would crust on my lips; mold coated the insides of those linen scraps I had to settle for. I could either endure all that, or stay with my mother and the Thing that haunted her.

My eyes got lost into the midnight blue. Nothing could have prepared me for what I was about to attempt, for all we had gone through ever since we let evil into our home. It took the form of a hungry child, desperate for shelter. A child who could have been me, my mother had said, so she took the child under her care. Fear clawed its way up my throat as glimpses of that first night crossed my mind. I squeezed my eyes shut, fingers clasped around the two objects I was holding to drown the screams in a forgotten corner.

I clambered over the smooth, steel sand. Those nightmares made flesh were the reason I was standing before the sea now. I had to try and free us from these terrors, so things would go back to normal. I needed *Them* to fix everything.

The summoning required three things. Relatively easy to find, for people like us who were surrounded by the Wide Blue. My fingers had quivered when I picked up the small black vial in my mother's chest. Cuttlefish ink—the one she used to paint stories and words of protection on blankets sold to the villagers who now shunned us. That feeling had never been new. They thought I couldn't hear the whispers behind my back whenever I had to deliver the products to the nearest huts. How could a young mother live alone, so close to the sea and so far from the people? The complexity of their simple minds made them yearn for the mystical protection they thought she provided, yet frown upon her abandonment to the wild waves and her obviously abnormal son.

I had then dug out a cowrie shell, hidden among those precious little things in that broken calabash by the fireplace. Tossing both into the dark, churning waters, I stood there for what seemed like centuries. Trying—and failing—to drown the horrors stuck behind my eyelids. The insecurities. I was my mother's son, the only other person in her life. Why couldn't I save her? How could I stand by, while her humanity was stripped away from her? The villagers were right. I was nothing but a scrawny, useless boy. Because that next step was something I could never spill out of me.

The last ingredient was the tears of a believer.

To believe meant to accept that the sea deities were our protectors. To exhibit infinite trust, to sprawl on the beach and strip ourselves naked, at the mercy of ocean winds and salt creatures. To be cradled in Their grace, or be denied of Their fierce love.

Where were They, when I tied my mother's hands together to stop her from clawing her own throat out?

My tears sunk into the glacial ocean. But they were born of rage, not adoration. My tears were the pure fury of a little boy who had been slapped out of sweet childhood by watching his ma descend into madness.

Long after the fishermen's chatter, the papel chants carried by their thick voices, and the wet sound of fish bodies thrown against wooden buckets faded, I gazed at the sea and it gazed at me. My breath went shallow. I buried my toes under cold grains of sand in pursuit of answers that didn't exist.

I stood for another set of centuries, ignoring the hunger biting at my stomach. Watching, as the pale sun slowly leaked across the superior sea. I had failed my mother, once again, yet it was fear that fettered me to the beach. A python, that seemed to swallow the sun and grow around my belly as night approached. Showered in mocking orange rays, I still failed to fight it off when the furious teal waves gave birth to a girl.

She strode forward, silent as the death I hoped she would bring along. Even with my chin against the bony ridge of my chest, I couldn't help but steal a glance at the girl. And what a sight, she was. Legend made flesh, the girl looked barely older than I was. Skin the color of the deep—so black it turned indigo as the sun sank into the sea. Cowrie shells were woven into her plaited hair, and she held what looked like a coral staff. The more distance she put between her and the waves, the clumsier her footsteps went. For a moment, I feared she was going to trip, but she steadied herself with the staff, and stood inches away from me.

White garments stuck to her petite frame like jellyfish. This close, the girl smelled like the whales Ma told me stories about. I had never seen them; monstrous beings who had been strolling the deep for eons, singing songs only the sea could understand.

Maybe They had sent the girl. As small as she was, who knew how sea creatures grew and aged? Her beauty almost brought tears to my eyes. If Ma was here, if she could see her . . .

Strings of doubt snuffed out the burgeoning hope. What if she really was as old as she looked? I carried not the strength, nor the wisdom that came with adulthood. Human or water creature, we were only children.

What if this summoning was not the answer?

Her lips moved in the dark. Black tides crashed far ahead, yet no sound came from her throat. A finger slid forward, raising my chin. It was icy, sprinkled with an iridescent blue substance—which circled her gray eyes too.

"Were you the one who called to our Mothers for help?" she finally spoke.

I was taken away by the mystery swirling in her eyes, briefly forgetting my concerns. For the first time, I was seeing someone like her: the embodiment of all the stories Ma narrated when she was young and well. She would let me sit on her lap. Bury my fingers in her afro. At night, right at the door of our small hut and facing the sea, her gaze would drown into the sea foam, and she would tell me about the creatures living under it. Their power, dark and ancestral, couldn't be understood by humans, particularly those down in the village. Those ungrateful people sought my mother's protection because of the legends that instilled fear in their chests, tainted with aversion. But my mother knew better. She taught me to respect the sea creatures, to thank Them for the fish on our table. And, most of all, Their protection against storms.

When the sea was in turmoil, we would kneel before the altar of seashells and a wooden pole washed out by the waves. We would pray. Outside, the wind wailed, hauling a siren's sorrow. It sounded much like a rattling voice that froze me to the bone and made me want to throw myself under the waves, so I wouldn't hear it anymore. Ma's warmth and her smile in between prayers

were the only thing that made me feel safe. I carried her beliefs—
ones I wasn't sure were mine.

Yet here I was, facing the sea and its emissary. She was every
tale my mother whispered to me with her deep musical voice and
the tickles under my feet. All the carefree memories of my early
days were connected to the tales of people like her. It made their
initial indifference all the more painful.

The villagers accused my mother of being a sea witch, even as
she fell sick, so sick I couldn't tell who she was anymore. Not one
of them offered assistance, for fear of attracting whatever curse
afflicted her. A pathetic excuse, because she was a woman who
lived alone and held the old beliefs deep in her heart. They could
recognize the ocean's imprint in her eyes.

What would they say now, if they saw the mami wata we had
summoned?

"Yes," I said. My throat was a nest of catfish, the words struggling, slipping and fighting against each other to be freed. "My
ma, it's . . ."

She frowned as the horror of the past few months burst at the
surface. My fingernails dug so deep into my skin that I knew they
would leave marks that would replace all the ones before them.
All the stigmas of times like this, when I felt like a lone sailor at
the mercy of nightmare seas. An inch, just an inch, away from hell.

Instead of words, I simply motioned the girl to follow me. Silence floated between us as we trudged away from the waves. That,
until I cranked the old door open, letting the perpetual stench of
rotten eggs irritate my nostrils.

*Ma screamed into the night like a wounded beast. Her beauti-
ful afro, tangled and soiled. Her gaze was wild. Pupils dark and
wide, so wide, even as they landed on her little crab. Grimy fingers
stretched toward my throat, and squeezed.*

I gasped, the mami wata's touch bringing me back to the present. Inside, it was dark. A forgotten tomb smoldering with heat.
My heartbeat fluttered and flooded my ears with blood.

The girl's hand on my shoulder felt like a tide of dawn. Did she pull the memory out of me because of my silence? Or was it one of the many demons inside my mind, breaking away from the flimsy leashes I had thrown at it?

"On a night like this, the Thing appeared on our doorstep. We thought it was a child, at first. Hunger in its eyes, a belly swollen and empty like a calabash. My ma fed it with fish soup and garri. She told me to let it sleep on my bed, and I'd sleep on hers. At least until we could figure out where the child's parents were."

My tongue began to grow still. "We shouldn't have let it in."

The mami wata scanned the darkness, making out the inside of our scanty hut. She gave no second look to the squeaky chairs and dinner table, or the weaving loom Ma made her blankets with. I tried to look away as she dropped one knee before the makeshift sea altar. She caressed it. Closed her eyes, and gripped it as if she had a prayer of her own to be heard.

Anyone who set foot inside the hut would know that unholy terrors tainted its walls. And would be terrified, if they had a bit of survival instinct.

But I thought she would have barged inside that room I couldn't bring myself to enter. Blasted the Thing out without any question, and everything would be as it was. Weren't sea deities supposed to know everything?

"What was it?" the girl asked. And I realized I didn't ask her name. I didn't know what the Thing was called, either.

"Ma was shaking and burning up when I awoke, in the middle of the night. The child—that had never been a child—stood before our door. Trapped us."

I dragged my feet toward that wretched door. Deep scratches left holes in it, and it was as if my skin had been flipped upside down. Hot sweat found its way through my eyes. Living fire licked at my trembling fingers as I went for the doorknob. With her staff, the girl touched my neck, and I could breathe again.

"It wasn't human," I whispered. The tears began to pour. I

would have given everything up if it weren't for Ma. For her gentle smile and the warmth of her embrace, my mother had to be freed.

"It had donkey legs and the eyes of a fire at twilight. It's dug its claws in my ma's mind; it won't let go."

My voice broke on the last words. Ma gave me everything in this life, and I kept failing her.

"Jinn."

The girl's hold on her staff faltered. Something I couldn't identify crossed her gaze, and she muttered words she thought I couldn't hear before opening the door.

I don't know how to do this.

All the windows had been sealed with dusty, half-done blankets. In a corner, Ma rocked back and forth, while the girl still hadn't crossed the doorstep. My very last hopes slipped away from me, through the floorboard and into the sea where they came from. At the sight of her emaciated face and the chunks of bleeding skin under her nails, my heart bled more than it ever had. Ma whimpered and hugged her legs, tears and salt drying on her cheeks. I staggered a few steps back as Ma clawed at the skin behind her arms.

Waves crashed outside. At a steady, sinister rhythm, my mother's blood dripped against the rotted wood. The girl settled her eyes on the Thing sitting in the middle of my mother's bed.

My legs itched to flee as the creature landed its gaze on me. It had nothing of a child anymore. Its skin peeled away from a bed of lava. Golden eyes shone like pus on dead flesh. My throat swelled as it erupted with laughter.

"Is this what you bring to get rid of me, Sonan? An apprentice water girl?"

I flinched at the sound of my name. Rippling from its charred lips with a gravelly voice as if it were an endearment, it cracked like a whip. "Your gods must think very little of you."

Apprentice.

The truth I tried so long to ignore spilled from a mouth molded with lies. Like me, the girl was powerless.

Her faint resolve faltered as the jinn rose. It grew taller. Loomed over us as my mother began to scream and bang her head against the wall. I flew to her side, fingers shaking as I tried to help. My mother kicked me in the ribs as if I was a sick puppy.

Through the pain, I saw steam coiling around the tips of the girl's braids. She grasped the top of the staff and almost let it fall when the Thing bent over her.

"Fire demon," she started, blue light flickering at her fingertips. Sea breeze washed over the stinking room, but my heart sank inside my aching chest when I felt the hesitation muffling her voice. "From the Eastern Desert you came, and to the sand you shall return. By the Everlasting Blue, I banish you from this place!"

A surge of cold energy radiated from her, raising the hairs on my arms. Striking her coral staff against the floor, the mami wata squeezed her eyes shut and I tried to do the same.

From where she stood, a flash of amber light thundered across the room and illuminated it, brighter than pure sunlight. Ignoring her shouts, I shielded Ma's head from the explosion. Scanned the dark, not bothering to mute the renewed hope budding inside me.

Did the water girl save us? Was it over?

Wails evaded my lips as I realized she hadn't. The jinn looked different, scarier. It was as if it had swallowed the blast instead of being destroyed by it. The lava was gone, leaving nothing but red, unbearable fire, round-shaped around the jinn's core. It throbbed with its pernicious hilarity. My sweat and tears dried up. I was left flayed. Dead, inside.

This would never end.

"It didn't work." The girl staggered back. "Why didn't it work?"

Her eyes were wide. She couldn't hide it anymore. The powers didn't matter—in the end, we were two children, terrified in the face of almighty evil.

Inside the fire, a grinning mouth cackled. Panic gnawed at my bones, sucking my life force. My mouth slid open in an endless scream.

Flickering lights jittered against my pale brown skin as the fire snapped its attention back to me. I wanted nothing more than to curl up right there, die if I had to, yet the fire would not let me go. There was a peak of malevolence exuding from it. My muscles paralyzed, I felt anticipation for an evil of which I was about to be the target. The girl couldn't do anything. It would make us suffer, until we were nothing but husks of putrid flesh and bone. Like my mother soon would be.

Warmth trickled down my leg as the fire recoiled in and on itself, reaching the size of an accara ball.

Flying inside my mouth to possess me.

I didn't know who I was. Like the distant spectator of a tragedy, I watched through darkening eyes as the mami wata tossed her staff away and ran to my side. She was shaking. Panic pierced the gray of her gaze. My mother kept screeching as I convulsed on the wooden floor. I cursed them. I guffawed with an infernal voice that wasn't mine.

All I could feel was the burning. Even as the girl dragged my body toward the sea, with her haunted gaze and labored breathing, I thought the end had come for me. This being, that we took pity of, fed and sheltered, would calcinate my soul and settle inside my flesh, leaving me forgotten. Was that the price of kindness? Getting robbed of your willpower, hurting the people you loved and the ones who were just trying to help?

Our lost ones had believed the afterlife awaited us in the ocean. A promise of eternal slumber within those abyssal caves sunlight could never reach. That you'd become one with it, whether you were a believer or not.

The jinn rumbled inside me like an infection, setting my blood aflame. I saw through it clearly, now. It was a creature of the Eastern Desert, where the people drew kohl around their eyes to protect themselves from the devils' trickery. It promised to hurt me eternally. Feed off my terror, now that it had sucked Ma dry.

My scorched lungs drowned in salt water. I thought the shapes I saw in the darkness were my ancestors. They would welcome me in their holy silence, heal my wounds with their freezing touch and quell the pain.

No. It was the mami wata.

She had pulled me under the tide, and she was bathed in dark-light. The gray of her pupils went metallic. The girl swam and circled me with a serene gaze while I drowned and the jinn struggled. In my delirious state, a smile tore at the corner of my lips— the mami wata had no tail. Iron scales covered her face and fingers instead, sharp as she cupped my cheeks.

A song slid inside my ears. As soft as my mother's voice, it glorified the ocean and its creatures. I saw hints of gray skin, fins the size of a boat. The dark and the blue.

Her fingers shifted toward my wrist; the jinn burned and burned.

She was the one singing.

The mami wata held my hand as we sailed the tide of her new-born memories. Yes, she was young, even younger than I imagined.

For the longest time, the girl had slept alone in the Mothers' belly. Engulfed in warm darkness, their songs of love lulled her to sleep. All her sisters had already been birthed, swimming toward the surface when believers cried for their help.

As people forgot the old ways, she became the last mami wata. Every year, the Mothers dove farther from indifferent humans. This last emissary, they kept for the woman who believed in spite of suspicion, smiled in the face of the ones who thought her a crazy witch.

"I can't do it alone."

Down here, the girl's voice carried effortlessly: a string of silver light against my consciousness. The water whispered her name in return.

Fatuma.

Showered in her Mothers' love, the separation had been like ripping off her umbilical cord. Leaving her bleeding, cold, and afraid, as she swam away from them and toward an unknown enemy. She knew so little.

Against our will, we had been both thrown into a situation we couldn't resolve.

"You're scared. I'm scared too."

I was numb and terrified. If I died, the jinn would have won, and my ma would be at its mercy. No one else was going to help her. The villagers thought she frolicked with the forces of the dark, when it was her kindness that had thrust her into evil's grip.

The mami wata smiled through the pain my white-hot skin was causing her. Fire began blistering her forearms; it would soon reach the three chambers of her heart. With her touch came the kiss of the sea. "We can do this together. Sing with me, Sonan."

I didn't need to open my mouth. This was a song I knew. It was nothing but my mother's love, and her unbreakable faith in the sea.

Embers roared and charred our skin when the jinn realized. It had thought us done for, but we were fighting back. Within Fatuma's mind, I saw Their stare, Their faith in her. Above the pain and the terror, I knew one thing. I had to save my mother.

And we did.

Salt water dissolved the tendrils of smokeless fire spewing from my eardrums. It carried the jinn's curses far, far away, to be berthed at an unknown shore.

Ma lay waiting for us on the surface. Vomiting loads and loads of water, I was breathless. Yet, I couldn't tear my eyes off of hers. The madness was gone.

An exhausted smile sat on her lips. "Sonan."

I couldn't help sobbing when she curled her arms around my chest. Underneath the filth, she smelled of kelp and undying hope. Fatuma silently watched, bracing herself on the staff that had somehow returned to her.

"Thank you," I murmured. I knew the madness would be back—the scars it left were too perfidious. But I wanted, was it for a moment, to forget evil had knocked at our doorstep and let itself in.

Fatuma smirked, breathing hard before she replied. "I may be new at these things. But next time you call the sea for help, I'll be there. The last mami wata, to serve the last believers."

When dawn came, along with the fishermen and their empty nets, they found us gazing at the sea and holding each other's hands. They frowned upon our dirty rags and even dirtier skin. Back inside their homes, they would defame my mother and whisper about how her appearance had scared the fish away. Above steaming pots of etodjey stew and fufu, their wives would suck their teeth and curse the water witch.

We stood before the sea, and the sea gave us Her blessing.

THE PAPERMAKERS

by Akua Lezli Hope

NEW YORK, NY (BLN) OCTOBER 22, 2022
Expectations of a violent clash between Black Lives Matter
demonstrators and white extremists were not fulfilled today, though there were flares of unrest as the BLM marchers
proceeded up the Avenue of the Americas. The opposition
retreated and some fled. There are unconfirmed reports of
sparks emitting from the counterprotesters, strange smells
and strange, ugly masks being worn. These fled before the
advance of the BLM marchers. Posts along the route were
also avoided by counterprotesters, seeming to physically repel them as they encountered the signage.

Aviva's hands hurt. She had let the water go cold, and in her rush
to make sheets with her delicious new pulp, she had soaked herself. The sun was low in the sky, its rays level with the deep vat.
The drain-pocked floor of the expansive wet room glistened with
flung droplets. Almost time for food and prayer she thought,
shivering with satisfaction in the cooling day's end. A large stack
of wet paper sandwiched between heavy felt mats stood tall before her.

At one side of the room where paned windows admitted the
bluing light, condensation spanned the corners, changing the
shape of the glass. The other side of the room also featured a win-
dowed door that opened to a cooking porch, where smelly fibers

could be cooked under the semi-protected eaves. This made the work near at hand to the beaters and stampers, but outside the building where friendly breezes could whisk the stench away.

She rubbed her hands together then fished in her over apron for gloves. The waning, dusk-purpled light beckoned. Stepping outside, she breathed deeply, tasting cooling air. It was nearly warm—it felt warmer outside than it did within the wet room. She was grateful for this change in season, a summery fall.

The end of September was awake with change, when you could still enjoy the length of days even as they shortened. Before one had to bundle or muffle against air on skin, but senses were sharpened with the swift chill. There was still much to do in the wet room, so well designed to minimize cleanup, but it was still to be done. And the pressing. How much would she press? She needed to organize her thoughts. It was rare to have such spacious emptiness, to be alone with her process in the wet room without the yapping and poking and prodding of poke-faced 'prentice Elyn. She had almost surrendered her flow to the disruptive skink, who had begun to be in her way, creating projects that would break Aviva's movements from pot to rinse sink, from sink to buckets, buckets to more buckets as the fiber pulped and grew.

Elyn tried to guess the small motions of ritual conversions and transient transformation, without permission or readiness. *Many others,* Aviva thought, *might have been welcomed at the sink or in the beater room. But Elyn stank of privilege, with her unearned woundedness at magnified or imagined slights. Or so it seemed.* "You could get by on your old man's money," she hummed and stopped, angry that Elyn, while not present, had now effectively taken up this quiet time.

Aviva hummed the evensong, began her prayer of thanks:

> *Thank you for this day that filled my heart with making*
> *Thank you for the plants that gave themselves creating*

Thank you for my health that allows this sweet creating
Thank you for this joy I find in this deep making

She jumped off the raised porch onto the crunchy gravel and walked slowly to the good weeds outside the fenced garden that served the Papermakers' Guild. Previous 'prentices had created a walking prayer circle labyrinth near the Guildhouse, a multistoried amalgam of country inn, gallery and multi-studio space, that at various levels offered perches, porches and balconies.

On one side of the Guildhouse was a balcony from which you could see the labyrinth. Aviva had encouraged bee balm and milkweed to grow there, though over time, when chicory and Queen Anne's lace intruded, she was glad. At this season the milkweed was tattered though laden with big silk-stuffed pods, and the bee balm, deflowered, was also inelegant. But chicory still bloomed and the QAL also held lacy flower heads aloft, though some were singed by the cold and age.

Aviva walked the circle and hummed and breathed and filled herself up with the deep peace of the place and this moment. She was a fully-fledged sojourner, now. Her time at the Guild was won through competition and so being here was more affirmation than test. There was joy in arriving and there had been more joy in being here.

The orange and last bit of gold left the lowered sky, the blue purpled and the warm cooled. So quickly, she thought as she retraced her steps out the thicket to the side path and back up the porch step and into the now dark wet room.

Click! "O!" Aviva gasped, shielding her eyes.

"Ahveevah? Sorry. I didn't realize you were here." Yech! Of course it was Elyn, the bratgirl woman.

"Yes, and of course I'm here. It's my last week and I've got a lot to do."

"Well, the Aba gave me a project that means I'll need the press and the red beater."

"You won't need the press until you've processed your fiber and pulled your sheets. And I used the big beater, not the red one. And more to the point—we've got a schedule, right? The very one you created, and I've signed up to indicate what I'm using and when."

Aviva wanted to kick herself. Of course, this was so Elyn, lacking any way to say something engaging, now took to sheer annoyance to get attention. She was an energy sucker. Aviva wanted to honor her time at the Guildhouse by having it end on as high a level as it had begun.

The Aba Zora had already intervened between them, telling Elyn so gently, but implacably, that Aviva was the primary for the duration of her sojourn.

Aba Zora always seemed to know more than she addressed overtly, but Aviva reminded herself, she was the Aba and by rights and function, should know much more than she let on. After all, Aveneh had multiple functions as a Guildhouse in the country. Aba was a craftswoman as well as a metaphysician in the Order.

O, Aba, how I'll miss you. Aviva felt the yearning before it was time, leaving the moment, glimpsing the soft ache that this joy could become. She leapt ahead a little on her path into a place of longing and then jumped back, reminding herself to stay in the moment, to breathe deep the smell of this high-ceilinged room, the sound of the soft slap of her rubber apron against her legs, the clonk of her clogs as she marched across the moist concrete floor. She sniffed for traces of Aba Zora and could not detect her familiar scent, but the radiant warmth of the Guildhouse, the comfort and efficacy of it, was surely of the Aba's creating.

Aviva had met the Aba about fifteen years earlier at an art fair in her village. Aviva had bought an enormous pink-and-blue paper fan that had some small healing and light-shaping attributes imbued. The Aba was skilled in several disciplines branching from papermancy; she could evoke through the visual, by both direct drawing and printing, as well as low-relief sculptural or pulp manipulation. Little did Aviva know then that she would later walk this path. She had kept the Aba's identicard of handmade paper and still had it these many years later. The fan had been given to a friend who collected fans. And perhaps the Aba had deliberately planted a seed of direction with the card, or perhaps not. Aviva may have just felt the residual from other work and been open to allowing the seed of influence to grow.

It is always about intention and desire. One could intend something but if it were not desired, manifestation would be thwarted. Paper was a less ubiquitous substrate than it once was and there were levels and layers of its manifestations. There were folders who couldn't make it, but through their folding could evoke. There were the artists and painters who through their imaging could evoke. There were the writers and scribblers, runners and incisors who through words and marks could evoke. There were the printers who through their inking and stamping, their endowed machines, could evoke. But the paper, unadorned, could say a say, tell a tell, evoke, bespoke, all by its lonesome. And within this there were levels and layers. As when a papermaker had that knowledge as well as some others, like making the subvisible signs that persuaded.

The pile of sheets spoke, *ping ping ping* as the excess water drops dripped onto the floor. They were made and yet fragile in this state, incomplete.

"Okey donkey," said irritating Elyn.

"Donkey?" Aviva asked. "What? We say dokey—to rhyme with okey where I'm from."

"I just wanted to change it up," said Elyn.

Aviva sighed and began to move the laden cart of wet sheets and felts to the maw of the big press. She hadn't finished shaping her intention for the paper, so she picked up seven felts off the stack and placed them on the six-foot vacuum table.

"Do you need a hand?" Elyn asked, nosing closer.

"Nope. Thanks." Aviva sighed, wheeling the pile over. She lifted and placed the remaining felts on the platen, covered the last paper with a couple of felted wool army blanket pieces, then began to crank down on the paper and tried to think again of her still unclear intention. She decided it was gratitude and said aloud again, "Thank you," as the water began to pour out from the pile and run down across the floor to the drain hole.

This would be paper for the Guildhouse store. Generic and pretty, the extended beaten pulp would have some translucence and a crisp rattle. It would wave happily at people from the paper slots at the country store front of house. The thanks were enough to keep Elyn away, but not out of her business.

"Whatcha gonna do with those?" Elyn asked, moving to the edge of the shiny pierced plane that was the vacuum table. With the seven sheets of paper, Aviva would make gifts.

"Make goodbye presents."

"Will I get one?"

Aviva avoided answering directly, saying, "I want to thank Aba and the Guild Council. One should always give gifts when departing," she added, a bit more testily than she wanted.

Elyn nodded as if taking notes. "That's a good idea."

Aviva listened for sarcasm but heard none, nor did she see any. Instead, she was surprised by a bit of light leaking from Elyn. Elyn's face, more toward the handsome than pretty, was blotchy from her picking at pimples. Aviva wanted to tell her that if she kept her hands out of her face, she would have healed and that the tiny dark spots, unbothered, were more esthetic than the poker-burn bruises she left from her scrubbing and picking.

Elyn ate a lot of crap. Though that was not supposed to affect late-adolescent skin, it affected things that affect late-adolescent skin. During the communal lunch, Aviva had tried to introduce delicious nutritious foods. And she had, she thought ruefully, worked hard for several nights to concoct dishes to share that held some hidden healings, couscous full of sweet root vegetables and lots of cleansing herbs, and her spur-of-inspiration wok-cradled vegetable mélanges.

The large meal at the Guildhouse was potluck and all were expected to attend and to contribute. Aviva found it joyous, to pull folks out of their offices and studios, for staff, sojourners and artists, 'prentices and interns, to all gather together, cook together, eat and converse.

The kitchen off the terrace that served as dining room was rather small for the swarm of women, as it was one of several throughout the building, but somehow, each lunch was pulled off with good humor and grace.

"What is this?" Elyn had asked Aviva as she uncovered her wok and pulled the foil off her large steel bowl.

"The grain is called couscous—it goes beneath the veggies."

"Cous-cous!" exclaimed Sen, the potter, and Aba Zora, nearly together.

The table had green avocado salad made by Sen; a fruit tart brought by Maggie, the accountant; a fruit salad made by Nika, the fundraiser. Jean, the intern and 'prentice wrangler, had brought artisanal bread; Jovita, the secretary, had brought local cheese. Elyn's contribution was fresh-pressed apple juice. Vonda, Aba Zora's partner and Guildhouse COO, had made salmon balls. Yindi, the artist from Australia, had brought sparkling water. The two interns, Saya and Laini, had brought healthy junk food: sesame sticks, blue tortilla chips and sweet potato chips. Geneva, the clay 'prentice, had just arrived the day before and was not expected to bring anything. But when she saw the table being laid and the bustling of preparation, she ran to her room and returned with two huge bars of organic chocolate that she cut into twelve pieces.

When they were all seated, Vonda asked, "Does anyone want to share words?" Aviva was shy about sharing words aloud, though she wanted to. She wanted to pour out her heart and add it to the meal, knowing that even as such a company ate, they did not consume; they fueled as they were fueled.

Some bowed their heads in the silence, saying their own words to themselves. Aba, sitting next to Vonda, said, "If there are none, I would like to offer praise for our coming together, and eating together, bearing witness to the glory of being in creating."

With that, plates were passed around the table as folks served up food from the bowl or pot or dish nearest them. Then all ate and praise was offered to the procurer or preparer of the partic- ular item. Aviva loved how Sen's salad—arugula, romaine, grape tomatoes, artichoke hearts with an anchovy vinaigrette—went so well with the taste of her couscous. She had prepared the grain with butter and walnuts in a makeshift couscousier of cheesecloth and colander; and the veggie stew had tomatoes, onions, pars- nips, turnips, carrots, sweet potatoes, garlic, cumin, turmeric, basil and the secret of well-being her Algerian friend had taught her. It was not an herb found on this continent; it was imported from Africa. Aviva carried it and her herbs, blender, wok, pots and pans with her to the Guildhouse, knowing she would have a small apartment with a kitchenette. All her tools were used daily, though she was surprised to find that the apartment, shared with Yindi, had a couple of pots, some bowls and a few utensils.

Nika, the fundraiser, said, "I'm just hopeless with most grains."

Aviva smiled at the invitation. "I'll tell you how to make it, if you'd like. Couscous is one of the easiest and quickest to prepare."

Nika clapped her hands and laughed, a young gesture for an older woman. She was tall and slender, rangy with looks that might have once been called patrician. She seemed to act and dress against type—a once flower child or hippie from a well- to-do clan. Or so it seemed to Aviva. Unlike Elyn, who wore her privilege like unwashed underwear, as a faint persistent unclean- liness, Nika used hers to solidify the Guildhouse and did not let it predefine her. Aviva liked this about Nika, though she seemed a holdout as far as cooking was concerned. Her dishes were dismayingly unseasoned and under realized.

"So just three more days, Aviva?" Aba announced and the small conversations quieted.

Vonda said, "We have to have a party."

"No we don't," Aviva protested, shyly.

"Well at least a dinner, a gathering with cake," said Aba with a wink.

Saya said, "I make great cakes."

"I'll help," said Laini.

"Me too," said Geneva.

The Guildhouse cat, a big Maine coon, ambled out on the terrace, head held aloft, sniffing. "Paka approves," said Aba.

"He likes cake and knows the word party," laughed Vonda, stroking him as he sauntered by.

Aviva held her hand out to the dog-sized feline, who sniffed each finger carefully, before rubbing his head. She loved the feel of his fur under her fingers. She gave him an experienced rub along his jaw and in his cheek hollow that made him lean into her. She then gave him a shoulder rub. He glowed, to those who could see.

"You're spoiling him," Vonda laughed.

"I miss my cats," Aviva murmured. She hadn't seen them for a season and her fingers sometimes ached for her familiars' fur. They were both tabbies, one spectacular in the dark lines on his long swirling, silver fur and the other, bronze in his grey and short-haired, looked more like the mythic Bast, huge eyes, and delicate pointed face.

One of her many heart sacrifices for this sojourn. At Aveneh she could start at inception, with ecomancy. Aviva could grow the plants that would be harvested or speak to the wild ones about her intentions on a bit of sanctified ground. She could harvest blessed plants, from blessed organic soil, fertilized from free-range chickens who roosted in sheds that moved, and free-range cattle manure, flowers pollinated by blessed and beloved bees.

Her cattail paper, made from the furry cigar heads, looked like brown leather or some cocoa-colored hide, but could flutter like silk. The large sheets were sewn into ceremonial vests, special-use, protective shirts.

The cattails were precious and particularly effective because the wild things were water cleansers on Aveneh's beaver-segmented pond. Aviva spoke to them, thanked them for their delicious tender roots whose taste resembled cucumber but imparted that micro-wisdom that fresh wild plants offer, that glimpse or spark of place. It's what gourmets find in the best food, when tongue transmits a taste that transcends appetite, raw requirement for fuel, and conveys something complex, pleasing, transcendent that leaps from mouth to brain. The plant was honored by full use. Every bit of it was understood and appreciated, and enough left for the cattail colony to regenerate along the side of sanctified waters.

While she loved cattail head paper for its figured surface, its beautiful sound and its shimmery feel, she was at Aveneh studying and practicing how to make less attractive papers, plain paper that could slip in among other unenhanced papers and change the world. Aveneh was a Guild that existed to use magic subtly, the magic of work and creating to make change.

So flyers, posters, signs made with Aveneh-imbued and -instructed, Guild-formed magic was protective, persuasive, potent in unobtrusive ways. Guild members worked to have significant legislative bills printed and disseminated on Guild-directed papers. When important demonstrations were held, placards would be made of Aveneh paper boards. This would quiet the opposition and protect demonstrators from rogue police if in the vicinity of an Aveneh placard.

Very few knew that the Guild taught more than mere papermaking. One had to know how to make paper before the deeper wisdom was shared. *Which is why,* Aviva thought, *I've worked so hard to keep my cool around Elyn, a rich kid whose money could underwrite much of the Guild's work even for scholarships like the one I had, but this must be both transparent and opaque. Transparent in the doing but opaque in the deeper meaning, in the full-moon visits to the plant patch, in the sprinkling, in the ritual sprinkling of blessed water on the planting, for the invocations over the wet stack, the recycling and blessing of the used water, even the pots, even the fire, every step be enhanced to be effective. The felts that were army blankets were never used by the army. They were washed multiple times in hot water to be felted and how they were washed and what they were washed in was also part of the work of this magic.*

This magic was the magic of work, like love, in the same way the mother washes her child and bathes her child and feeds her child and loves her child so that it can grow strong and knowing in this hard, hard world. All of these steps went into the Aveneh paper and special 'prentice work.

Not all paper had the same intent. Some were just for peace or joy, generic love for the heart-shaped paper; those who receive cards or messages on Aveneh paper got something more, as with the warding papers used for purification and protection by the Shinto and the Onmyodo.

Aveneh paper worked that way too, depending on the plant and the intention of the papermaker. All of this of course could be boosted by the inscriber, by those who used motivated inks, endowed presses, who included intentions in their words. Wrong intent could nullify the paper, but not recast its direction, to make good manifest and propagate it secretly persistently, resiliently, quietly, determinedly to make a necessary change and protect the people in the street marching, marching, marching for Freedom.

The dryer box wood had been mindfully gathered and crafted of already felled trees. The current that powered the fan was from the solar roof panels of the Guildhouse and studio, installed by a firm from Brooklyn that gave black youth training and education in the ways of electrical current, batteries and energy balancing.

The Guildhouse was just a few hours outside the City in the Catskills, where in the century past black folks could escape racism's reach and be entertained by black artists or commune with nature. The good times and joy of release still murmured to Aviva, and Yindi, her apartment mate, felt it too and remarked on it.

"There's a something, something here," she told Aviva.

"So you feel it too." Aviva smiled. Yindi had told her about Australian racism, how she experienced it as an indigenous person. Yindi was a printing 'prentice who had come to learn intentionality of the presses. Aviva made a mental note to give her papers to take back across the waters when she returned home.

Three days meant only two left. Aviva designed tiny shields using an inflated tear shape with a black, guitar goddess–shaped figure in the center. She had to craft the outline out of foam and filled that with overbeaten denim made from friends' and family's old jeans.

The guitar goddess was one of the earliest known figures and she hammered tiny spirals of copper wire to place in her belly. Early in her stay, Vonda had seen Aviva struggling to find a way to work her wire and had given her a log to serve as her anvil. The great vacuum table made swift work of forming the wet pulp after the careful prep and there were the tiny paper shields of good work and protection. She would give them to all the hearts who had touched hers on her last night.

Before the party she continued the work of departure, wrapped and packed dried papers, choosing a few sheets for the goddesses. She found several papers on the floor—which made no sense as there was no cross breeze in the studio.

As she picked them up and examined them, Elyn suddenly appeared.

"So, you're packing up."

"Yep," Aviva said, grateful to have not seen the brat that day.

"So what do you have there?" she asked.

"Gifts," Aviva said shortly as she turned the little shields in her hand and blew on them.

"Gifts, huh?" Elyn said. "Did you use some acidic dye or something on them?"

"Acid would eat up the paper. What you ask makes no sense."

"Well I touched one, just to help you clear up, and look at my hands!"

Aviva feigned surprise at the little red blisters on Elyn's fingertips. Proof that the brat was more ill-intentioned than she thought. No worries, she told herself. Elyn had outed herself.

"You obviously weren't supposed to touch them. That's your guilty conscience stinging you." Aviva laughed at the rude witch's defiant face.

"Can I have one?" she persisted.

"No," Aviva affirmed, wanting to say more and yet knowing that this was only a baby enemy, a quisling who would grow weaker and meaningless over time.

Reveal nothing. Don't waste energy. Don't engage. Tonight, the party and tomorrow, car packed, there were deliveries to make and then home. Stay the course and deliver the papers that will heal, protect, persuade and help change the world.

A SOUL OF SMALL PLACES

by Mame Bougouma Diene and Woppa Diallo

My name is Woppa Diallo. My mother was Djinda Diallo, formerly Dem. A devout woman from Matam, where we live. The second-hottest region in Senegal. It's not much to show for, but you take what you can get. My father was Abdoulaye Diallo, a shepherd from Tambacounda. The hottest region in Senegal. I've heard that everybody will eat at least eight flies in their life. That's certainly true if you live in Tambacounda.

There's a large stone in my village, right on the riverbank, shaped like a naked woman. The nomadic herdsmen have ruined it since, but I remember the shape of her, her face and her breasts.

We're told she was a newlywed, raped by her new family's men on the night of her wedding.

As she bathed in the river the following morning, a water spirit found her crying naked on the banks, unable to put her soiled clothes back on, unable to take a single step back to that nightmare she had to call home.

"Can't you tell anyone?" the spirit inquired. "I can whisper into their minds for you if you wish . . ."

She'd refused. Her new family might kill her. Her own family might kill her. Even if she fled they would carry the burden of shame everywhere they went.

"Whispers don't work that way," she told the kind spirit. Instead, she tossed her clothes into the river and said, "I can't go back there, but I can't leave this place either. This is my home. Turn me into stone, right here over the waters where I belong, so they remember me, and every young girl has a place to hide."

I go there sometimes to wash my clothes and my family's and think about her.

My mother thought about her too and wanted to protect me even more. A soul of small places, I needed a big shield, she told me once.

So she took me along to Mecca for the Umrah.

This is no small thing. No small thing at all. The trip is expensive, a lifetime of savings sometimes. If one family could send one person that's a blessing already, but taking a small child? Perhaps rich Emiratis could, but a mother and daughter from a small village in the hinterlands? My father was a good man. The others laughed at him.

I can't remember much. A two-year-old rarely does. Heat, stifling, sharp like a whip. Dust, puffs of it eager to clog my flower bud of a nose, the itch in my throat I couldn't scratch. The noise, the litany of prayers over melodies from loudspeakers, the dizzying press of bodies. White, everywhere, blinding, sweat-reeking, white. Clinging to my mother's back as the universe conspired to crush me.

I remember her lifting me up, a black stone cast in silver, so dark my young mind couldn't fathom the pits. It glowed ruby red inside, calling at me, whispering into my head. Three distinct voices a choir.

I heard later that in the days before Islam, when the gods of the desert tribes were female, women would rub the blood from their periods on the stone for good luck, fertility and harvest, and that it had left that distinct glow, deep magenta in black swells.

Oh the men who kissed it so eagerly! The would-be pious who secretly hate women and fucked goats. If they only knew . . .

My mother had lifted me up, the red swirls turning whirlpool in the black of a night that never dawns.

My lips had touched the stone. The choir of whispers exploded in my head. Three distinct voices. Three distinct names. Names that were gods. Names that were dead. Names that would never die. That could never die, because they were names of women, and we are resurrection and rebirth.

I remember nothing after that. I woke up in my parents' bed, in our small house in Agnam Thiodaye, on the outskirts of the village to the call to prayer. I was three.

"Are you ready for school, Woppa?"

"Yes, Mother," I answered as the rooster sang his first song. The goats in the backyard started bleating on cue, the heat already turning humid and thick. The women out in the fields, multihued dots of their head wraps dancing in the distance, dropping small seeds, singing and clapping their hands.

"You stick to the road! Understand?"

"Yes, Mother."

"And hold on to your sister's hand!"

"Yes, Mother."

"Don't let go of her hand!"

"Yes, Mother."

She nods but she's scared. She walks us to the door and doesn't let her gaze wander from us until we've turned behind the bush and the house disappears.

It's a long way to school, and I can only walk as fast as my little sister, Awa. She's only eight but tall for her age, taller than I was four years ago. She keeps up, but every so often she slows down, and I can't let go of her hand. My mother has eyes everywhere. If anybody sees us, she'll be sure to ask them, "Was Woppa holding her sister's hand?" If they said no I'd feel it for days, and Awa would have to slow down for me.

Senegal's a dry place. Matam one of the driest, but not where we lived. In most of the country you can see a house for miles. Not here. The sands by the river are a fertile brown laced with baobabs and bushes, small verdant trees that pop up throughout the land, distorting your sense of space. They pepper the way to school and beyond, the freshness of the water a thin sheen on the air, soothing your throat and sprinkling your tongue in the rising shimmer of heat.

It's in those bushes that the herdsmen ambush little girls on the way to school and rape them.

I hadn't always known what that meant. I'm not sure I did even then, but I understood that something wrong had happened. Sometimes a beautiful wedding would follow the horrible news. I didn't make the connection at the time. I do now.

Our mother's right to be afraid.

People think girls don't go to school here because we're ignorant shepherds. Attendance rates plummet when the seasonal herds of long-horned zebu turn towards our village and rise again when they leave and drop in another village further away.

It's not ignorance. It's fear. Keep your daughters home or else . . . or else the village might get another stone statue or another wedding . . .

The first people to live here settled in the lands north of where the village is now, in the Kadiel Mbaye Toulaye. There they encountered all manner of sorcery, and in its wake, death. So, they moved south to the Fonde Amadou Tall, where they found carnivorous ants who killed with a single bite. A man wandered through the village and found them dying and said: tiode nde ndo, live in the middle, which became thiodaye and they invited him to eat, aar niaam, which became agnam. Agnam Thiodaye.

Some said the rapes came from the old sorcery that had found new ways to torment us. But it didn't matter where you lived or the curse on your village. Keep your little girls home.

I refuse to stay home, school's important to me. It's important to my parents too.

I hold Awa's hand and never let go. Staying in the middle of the road and away from the bushes.

I'm protected. Allah saw to it in Mecca.

Everybody's eyes are on me. Amadou's are the only ones that matter. He's so handsome, smooth skin so dark he's almost blue, with deep-seated dark blue eyes, a straight nose and pearly white teeth.

All of them are staring at me, but I'm not sure why.

The teacher is praising me again, but I don't know why.

It's been happening since I started bleeding. The smell and dizziness of those lost moments in the Wahhabi desert surge over me, the voices whisper names, and . . . just as the year I lost as a child, I emerge moments later, my work done, the test passed, my room and the house cleaned, all to perfection and I can't remember a thing.

No one seems to have noticed, to them I was always there, always me, and I take the praise but shudder inside in shame at being a fraud, of being caught, of people wondering if there wasn't a little witch in me. At not knowing who I am . . .

"I'm very impressed, Woppa," the teacher says. "You're going places."

I nod and smile timidly. She thinks it's humility, the shyness we're taught to display, but it's the smile of the fool, happy because others seem happy, smiling because she's liked.

"Woppa," Amadou whispers, "let's talk outside." He winks as he walks past me, the white walls of the small classroom growing even smaller to the laughter of children in the yard, until it's too small for the two of us, forcing him near me, close enough to smell his breath, close enough to kiss as I daydream and the class empties.

"Woppa!" I hear Ms. Niang tell me. "Woppa! Snap out of it! Out you go!"

I hope she hasn't noticed but teachers see everything. Daydreaming over a boy . . .

"Yes, Ms. Niang."

I pick up my books and run out, the day's heat abated slightly in the late-afternoon sun. It's not quite the time for spirits yet. Twilight still distant on the horizon.

Awa's in the yard, playing jump rope with her clapping friends, she sees me, waves, misses a beat and steps on the rope. I wave back but I'm looking for Amadou. There he is, sneaking around the corner of the building, waiting for me to see him and disappearing behind it.

I scuttle after him, trying to tame the skip in my legs. What does he have to tell me? There's a hundred girls in the school, I'm not the prettiest. I'm not the smartest, except that I am apparently. I'm too tall, too gangly, too . . . too many things to think about and I have no time to think, he's around the corner, right there waiting for *me*.

I love my home. It's the only one that I want. Many of the other girls dream of the city, most have never made it to Matam. They probably think Thies is Paris and Dakar is New York. I don't know what dreams Netflix and Trace TV planted in their heads. The air here is full, the empty lands behind the school are rich and eternal, not corrosive like asphalt. They'll crack open one day and fire like blood will flow out, yet eternal. I hear the cackle of the hyena if I close my eyes. Smell the distant smoke filtered through dry grass and trees, the swarms of crickets over the sunset, the river's dreams of becoming a waterfall. It's home. It's where I'm one from the soles of my feet to my braided hair, binding earth to heaven.

"Hey, kai fi." Amadou beckons.

"Ko jitda?" I'd do anything he says, but it's the game. The banter first. The boys will tease and get told off, tease more and I'd make a joke. He'd call me cheeky, holding my hand a lingering moment too long. I've never met a Senegalese boy who didn't think he was the champion of laamb, soccer's ballon d'or and Barack Obama all wrapped in one. Every single one of them.

Amadou surprised me.

"You're doing very well in school," he starts, almost timidly.

I don't know what to say. He gets closer.

"Look . . . I . . . You're not like the others . . . Maybe . . ."

What is happening?

". . . Maybe . . ."

Yes?!

He looks into my eyes, he's gonna ask me something, what is it?

His resolve falters and he mumbles.

". . . Maybe we can study together?"

That's not what he wanted to say nor what I wanted to hear, but somehow the crush I had on him blossoms. He's not the arrogant shit I thought he was. He's like me. Shy and good inside.

"Of course," I say, and we start talking.

I can't tell you how long we spoke, evening prayer came and went and I didn't hear a thing. Only when Awa started tugging at my dress did I notice the sun dipping beneath the horizon. It was time for the spirits. Long past time to be home.

Awa puffs behind me but holds on to my hand, her tiny feet blistering in blue plastic sandals never meant for running.

The time of spirits never lasts long, a mere thirty minutes before nightfall drops like a butcher's knife on a chicken's neck, and things much worse than evil spirits, more immediately real than evil spirits, cackle in the bushes.

It takes twice that time to get home.

It takes less than a second for lightning to strike.

I'm running right into my mother's whooping, but I almost

welcome the pain, I'm eager for it. Anything for Awa to get home safe, any . . .

Awa's sweaty palm slips out of mine, I hear her cry and hit the dirt road. I turn to see her rise without another sound and reach out to me. Her eyes pop in her head as two hands land on my skinny shoulders.

"Get the other one!" a withered voice orders behind me.

A form in a blue boubou rushes past me and I throw my leg out, tripping him before he can reach Awa. His chin lands on the ground with the cracking of his jaw and a spurt of blood.

"Run, Awa!" I scream before the man pulls me back, covering my mouth with a hand reeking of cow skin and urine.

Awa shakes off her sandals and runs, a blur of white and blue against the night. The man on the floor goes for her ankle, but she jumps over his arm and dashes away.

We're halfway home, maybe more. Will she make it? Will she run into more men hiding in the bushes? An eight-year-old who hadn't even bled yet? All that because I couldn't stop staring at a boy?!

"Forget her." The stinking man's voice snaps behind me as I struggle, muffled screams through his sweaty palm, I try to bite but can barely open my mouth and my teeth slice through my tongue instead, blood flowing into my throat and choking me. "This one's good enough. Help me drag her into the bushes."

He pulls me farther back. The dirt furrows into my legs, my sandals slipping off, my threadbare dress tearing in places, the slow rumble of the river close behind, thorns on the ground piercing me, scratching and scratching and scratching at my arms, nails tearing off from trying to hold on to the ground.

The other man gets up, touching his jaw, spitting a thick gob of blood and looming over me, shadow closing away the sky.

He sneers and reaches for my dress. I close my eyes. I can't watch. I think I might faint but the sweaty stench of acrid malevolence awakens something inside me. A choir rises, the sky roars thunder, a flash of lightning, and I can't remember anything.

It's the smell that wakes me up, I think. Something burning close by. Straw? Manure?

"La la illalah, la la illalah, la la illalah . . ."

The voices next, exhausted voices hanging on to every syllable for fleeting life.

I open my eyes. Two pairs of eyes on me, closing down, closer, closer!

Two soothing voices.

"Seese."

"Calm down."

"You've been home for weeks."

"My daughter. Mach'allah. You're safe."

My parents. I'm home. In bed . . . For weeks! What happened? What happened to me?!

My hand shoots down between my legs, but my mother catches it, covering it with kisses.

"You're fine," she says. "Awa told us what happened . . ."

Awa's safe. My head lands back on the pillow.

". . . Your father rushed outside. There was thunder, the wind knocked him flat on his back and it started to pour. Rain so thick we couldn't see through it. So hard it would have beaten us into the ground. We couldn't leave the house, Woppa! We wanted to! We tried! You gotta believe me, Woppa, we . . ."

She paused to catch her breath, sighing deep and fast, into my father's neck. How long had she held it in, hoping I would wake up?

"It lasted only a few minutes, or it would have wiped out the whole village," my father added. "The house flooded. The river spilled over too. Not for long. A few trees were swept away. The rain cleared out at once, and there you were, walking up to the door, covered in . . . rain and mud . . . you collapsed inside the yard. Eighteen days ago."

"Nineteen," my mother finished.

She fed me a small cup of water.

"Where's Awa?" I ask.

"She's at school. Don't worry. The Diarra take her," my father said.

"But . . . she . . ."

"Hush," my mother says, putting the cup down and pulling the sheets over me. "Rest more, you've had only thin broth for weeks. This is a miracle."

The sheets are warm, my parents' breath on my face is comforting. I fall asleep.

I recovered surprisingly quickly. After three days I was in the yard walking and running, but my mother wouldn't let me leave the house.

Trees weren't the only things the rain had swept away. The cattle were badly injured from being swept into the walls. People too, anybody outside when the rain bombarded them was bruised and beaten almost to death. The statue of the brave girl by the river was gone too.

Awa had thrown herself at me. When she hesitated to ask, I told her not to bother. Her stupid sister couldn't remember a thing. She'd giggled and I was relieved. It had happened too quickly for her to be really scared. She'd cried for a few days after I'd returned but I was home and uninjured, and that was enough.

No one in the village had seen me come home. No one knew what had happened. My parents told everybody I got caught in the rain and almost drowned. I was home recovering. And Awa kept our secret.

———

I was allowed back to school after a week.

The yard turned dead silent as I walked in. Like Musa parting the waters, the random mass of students split down the middle, opening a clear path straight to my class.

I'm tempted to run, but I hold my head up and my back straight. If I play it cool they won't ask questions, but if I give them an inch they won't let me breathe, and our lie is a simple one, so easy to crack.

Amadou steps out of the ranks, eyes wild, his step uncertain.

"I'm sorry," he says. "I'm sorry, if I hadn't held you back the storm wouldn't have caught you. Really, I . . ."

I brush past him, his jaw dropping and a few girls giggling. I won't let a boy distract me again. I knew it was unfair to him, that he'd done nothing wrong, that it was in fact all me. I had lingered, I'd let the sky turn pink to purple to black and endangered my little sister.

It wasn't his fault, but looking at him I could feel the pressure of a hand on my mouth, the bruising of the bushes. I hope it'll pass. No one can live like this.

Lacking a show, the other students go back to playing, and that is that.

The day goes by and everybody's easy on me. Ms. Niang doesn't pick on me for answers and keeps me hydrated.

I hate it. I'm not an invalid. That's not what is happening. I don't know *what* is happening but it's not that.

Class ends an hour early. Ms. Niang has a family emergency in Djourbel and it's a long ride on the bus.

Awa won't be done for another hour. I'm not the only one with a younger sibling, I'm one of the few with only one, so we gather outside and wait. They're still itching to grill me, except Amadou, staring at his toes, throwing furtive glances at me.

No one dares talk, but I notice Mame Yacine has a small

pouch hanging from her neck and tucked under her dress where it touches her skin.

"What's the gri-gri for?" I ask her.

Everybody turns to her. She clutches the charm through her dress.

"Haven't you heard? A flesh-eater hides in one of our villages." The others gasp for air. I must have too.

Mame Fatou Dem, my great-great-grandmother, had known a soukounio. They were raised as sisters after Mame Fatou's parents died. Fed from the same breast, as such they shared a soul. Her sister Sokhna. She had eaten eight people. Eight people who'd never know heaven.

They grew up looking very much alike, but to Mame Fatou's mirth and Sokhna's gloom. Perhaps the jinn had entered her from birth, perhaps it had found root in her envy of Mame Fatou, but my great-great-grandmother was safe from her hunger. Mame Fatou carved Sokhna's heart out herself when she uncovered her secret. Tears so bitter at killing her sister they melted her heart in her hands. Mame Fatou birthed three daughters, two of them stillborn, and died delivering the third.

"They found two dead herdsmen crushed between trees after the flood," Maya continues. "A couple of miles downriver, one eaten in half from his head to his waist. The second chewed through his stomach, a hole from neck to navel. That's what my parents told me. My aunt made the gri-gri and . . ." She was shaking. We all were. "Do you think it's true? Could it be true?"

She was asking me. They all turned to look at me. Even Amadou. How would I know? Except I did.

My father was silent when I ran into the house and told them what Maya had said. He looked at my mother, and her back at him, and away and back again . . .

"What happened when you found me?" I begged. "Please. I can't

remember anything. They tried to ... I can't remember anything!" I was crying. I was terrified. Scared to know, too scared
not to, knowing what that would mean ... what would it mean?

"We ..." my mother started. "... You ... When you came
up to the ... Your father told you you were covered in mud and
rain. You weren't. You were drenched in blood, down from your
hair, to your lips, bits of skin caught between your teeth ..." She
caught her breath, trembling. "We rushed to help but it wasn't
your blood ..." She looked at me, staring silently. I took in every
word without fear. There was nothing left to be afraid of. "We
knew you could never harm us, and whatever you'd done to those
men they deserved it and more. You're our daughter, Woppa.
You're our daughter. There's nothing wrong with you. You saved
your sister's life, Woppa. We are proud of you. We love you ..."

She trailed off. My father nodding, eyes to the ground.

I can't say I remember how I felt after that. It wasn't one of my
spells. I just honestly can't.

News of the soukounio spread, and soon men started patrolling
the riverbanks, escorting the children to and from school, lighting torches along the road at night ... and there wasn't another
rape for years.

My head is on Amadou's shoulder, the salt of his neck on my lips.
Sitting on the riverbanks we're hidden from the road, our feet in
the cold waters, small fish nibbling at our toes.

The river and its bushes changed with each passing season. We
grew taller and the trees less intimidating. What felt like a jungle between the world and the river, we crossed in a few seconds,
the bushes like hills to our younger eyes barely reached over our
shoulders, and those of us whose spout of growth was quicker
than usual towered above them.

A grave of preschool torture had turned into a nest of teenage
love, or the rush of confusion, lust and doubt that passes for it.

I was certain it was love. It had to be. An empty carcass, I'd drifted a dead soul for months. I couldn't feel. Feel anything other than bone-deep sorrow, eating away at my marrow, and anger, anger so blinding my eyes seared blisters against the air.

Sad because I knew I wasn't a person anymore. I wasn't Woppa anymore.

My name's an odd one. Woppa is a ward. When you lose a child, you name the next with a ward, a name to confuse the evil eye and turn it away from the newborn. Woppa's one of those. It means go away. Snap it at someone and you're telling them to fuck off. Politely. Here you're telling the spirits to leave this child alone.

What warded me cursed me. My name. My mother's love. The murmurs of gods. They'd made me into something else, and all out of love.

Angry because dozens of brutalized girls didn't warrant watching the roads. Instead, the rapist got rewarded with a bride. But two men murdered, and heroic selflessness rears its cowardly head.

"It's getting late," Amadou says.

"You scared of something?" I ask.

He laughs.

"Yeah. Your father. You should be too. Plus, he's starting to warm up to me. Maybe . . ."

My father had, accidentally of course, set a bull loose on Amadou once. But he'd changed of late. He smiled when we locked eyes, crossing paths at the weekly markets. He'd walked him home once. I don't know what they'd said but he'd changed.

"You could take him out easily," I tease him.

He shakes his head and gets up, dusting off his pants. Amadou has joined the wrestlers. We're only sixteen but he's half a head taller than the tallest kids. Sweet, gentle Amadou. He'd waited months. Coming to see me every day, getting told off every day for a year until I caved in. Until the emptiness inside subsided somewhat and cracked open enough to let me breathe and let something else, someone else, in.

I rise after him, my wet feet sinking into the soft brown banks. Amadou holds my hand through the bushes and trees. He'll let go just before hitting the road or maybe hold it just a little longer, testing fate.

The torches line the road, unlit in two years. After a while the villagers decided the jinn must've moved on, and things went back to normal. There hadn't been an incident in the two years since, and I hadn't had a spell, and stayed on top of my class. We were finally safe.

Or maybe not.

The air changes, the choir rises, Amadou says something, all immediately drowned by screams, loud and angry, growing weaker, legs kicking, strength faltering, screams turning to whimpers and silent frightened tears.

I am screaming back. Teeth bared, every inch of me burning.

"Woppa!"

Amadou shakes me. Shakes me till I stop screaming, the red heat abating to a brazier.

"Woppa! Are you all right!"

I am panting, hunched over. Two realities wrestling for my sanity.

"I had a . . . a flashback . . . the river flooding, I couldn't breathe . . ."

He nods and takes my hand. Of course, he'd believe that.

Something had happened. Just then. Something very bad.

We are not safe anymore.

There was no wedding this time. Whatever had happened and whoever she was hadn't told anyone. Not even her parents. She must've sneaked in, cleaned herself and hidden her bruises, lied about why her clothes were torn and been beaten for it.

A slither of hairy flesh slurps through my lips, trailing a lick of salty fat and sinew. It wraps around my tongue, soaking in the blood in my mouth, softening as I chew.

The thread of muscle catches between my molars; I dig it out with my tongue, pluck it with my fingers and flick it.

It's cold, but I am warm inside. The wind itself has no warmth. Not cold, just not warm either. I can feel its nonexistence like a veil. The moon inverts the colors around me, dancing iridescent, pulsing to my heartbeat the sky shines and cracks marauding pathways into other worlds.

I have never felt this way before. I want to feel this way forever.

I stand up and stop to look down for the first time since I started feeding.

His head, neck, arms and shoulders are gone. There is nothing there, no blood, no bone, no clothes, nothing. A hundred bites like teeth marks through a watermelon dig beneath where his heart was. It is in me now.

I'd never seen inside a person before. How enticing it is. Perhaps it's better that I can't remember my first time. Twelve-year-old me wouldn't have handled the ecstasy, the taste.

It is good to feed.

I had missed another attack, and another again. But when the visions came, I realized that beyond the raw emotions I could glimpse landmarks, spots along the road, the odd stone by the river. The bushes intertwined like two snakes kissing. I could find them.

The second time I noticed my heartbeat change minutes before the flashes hit. There were images too, vivid evil thoughts barely crossing into my mind, barely registering, because I wouldn't let them. I was holding on to Woppa. To the little girl who'd played with goats and kept her mother up at night. The little girl who was good at school, had a hot boyfriend and stole kisses by the waters.

I'm holding on to a dead girl. Alive in her skin I'm not that girl anymore. I could never be that girl anymore.

My body was not my own. The whispering voices rose, and I

embraced them, allowed the transient tempest to settle, to find a home in me. There was no friction, no torrential rain, no tearing of the skies to energies bursting against each other. The flood, the thunder and the lightning, they all poured into me, I stretched my legs, the wind whooshed past, and I was looming silently behind him, miles from home. He couldn't sense me, dressed in a brown boubou and a brown turban, his hands inside his pants, sneering up the road at two little girls hurrying home, carrying bags of rice on their heads.

My hand dropped over his mouth, my arm around his chest, and I dragged him back to the river, out of sight from the road in a small alcove of trees. One moment here, and there the next, as the girls walked by safely. My mouth stretching open, my jaw dislocating, his praying, struggling head sliding in, silenced and bursting open.

God created jinn and people just the same. We share the same loves and the same fears. Only jinn have more fire. Some jinn, like people, believe in God. Those are gentler spirits, if they attack you, you must've scared them. Back away and they'll stop. Some jinn, like people, don't believe in God. Those are wild spirits. Incomplete, they'll find in people the missing bits of their soul. And devour them.

My soukounio . . . I . . . don't know what we want. But I want more. The man's dying soul rages inside me. Stoking the fires with every droplet of his blood turning sweet nectar in my throat. His energies fading, always falling into the abyss, a scream that would dwindle and shrink forever, but never stop, never quite dead, always dying. An abyss that is me.

His existence runs electric under my skin, grafting itself to mine, a tiny pearl of consciousness that shines on a childhood so good, an adolescence so bland into an evil so deep.

I pat him on the stomach.

"I own you now," I say as I run a finger along his bleeding wound and lick it clean.

I should be getting home. I turn back to the half-eaten corpse gurgling on the ground, frayed nerves twitching the body like a puppet . . . I really should be getting home . . . but a few more bites won't matter . . .

My family hears the cattle bleating in panic as I walk into the yard and rush out to hug me.

I pity them. The animals could feel what they couldn't.

Your Woppa is no more.

We go to sleep soon afterwards. I wake up to a clamor outside our home. Someone has found the corpse. By nightfall the road is lit with torches once again.

It doesn't stop the herdsmen, and it didn't stop me either.

I moan softly as Amadou enters me. This will be my first time and my last. The softness of the sheet against my back. The press of his chest against mine. I should hurt but I don't. All I feel is warmth. Warmth radiating through both of us.

I can't bear to think of his heartbreak when he doesn't see me at school tomorrow. Never sees me again.

Amadou can't believe his luck. It's his first time too. It's perfect. Perfect and crazy.

Three more bloody stumps in the last month and all the neighboring villages in a frenzy. Patrols all day and halfway through the night. I push their minds away from us, they walk by but can't see us. Stretch their ears but can't hear us.

We're the only lovers in the world. And it's perfect.

Amadou walks me back and heads home, turning around twenty times to look back, grinning like the happy fool he is.

At least he thinks he does. He is walking down the road alone and will keep walking until he is in bed and falls asleep dreaming of me.

I want this fantasy to be real, but I cannot go back, and a familiar tingle rings at the base of my neck.

The herdsmen don't believe in the soukounio anymore. I know this from my feasts. They think the villagers mutilate the bodies themselves and put on this farce to scare them off.

They know the patrols scour the roads and riverbanks, the clusters of trees and bushes. That we think our villages are safe.

Three herdsmen creep towards the Diarra house next to ours, where Hamadi and Coumba are playing in the yard. They will kill Hamadi and kidnap Coumba before the patrols are back. They think they will.

They are preparing to climb over the wall as I rip through the three of them.

Before the first body hits the ground, a hole through its stomach, I rip off the second's head and grab the legs of the third, climbing desperately up the wall, and tear his body in half, leaving him dangling dead from the white wall turning red from his waist to the ground.

I throw myself at his guts, drink from the fountain of his comrade's neck and reach for the other, but the animals bleat up a storm. Lights turn on and confused voices ring.

I look towards our house. It's so close I could slip in and no one would see me. I'd walk out looking scared, go back to sleep and head for school in the morning. But I can't. I can't go back. It's not my home anymore.

With each feeding the soukounio grows stronger, hungrier. The voices of others slowly choking mine. I'm still good inside. I think I am, but how much longer until I'm just a pearl of awareness screaming inside the jinn? How long until the darkness leaks and infects my family, Amadou, all those around me? It can't be what I leave behind. Pain from more pain. Where is the love I knew? The love I'd given up to this form.

I stretch my legs and disappear just as my mother's voice calls out for Awa and me.

She doesn't know I'm out. We'll never get to say goodbye.

My mother hadn't said a word but ran.

Maybe if she'd said something, anything. Her name, a scream, anything. Her voice would have broken the spell.

No one knows what to expect when they encounter a spirit, you imagine anything, a fire-breathing ghoul, a person melting before your eyes, covered in hungry mouths, a shadow that trails yours and smiles back at *you*.

She could've said a word when the patrol came running into the village with the clamor of men and beasts. When they found her outside the Diarra house, leaning over three oozing corpses, and charged. Something to make her human. Anything.

No matter what you imagine, no one expects a terrified mother.

Instead, she panicked and ran, a silent fleeing spirit, and nothing emboldens cowards more than someone fleeing.

They'd landed on her with clubs. My mother, recognizing the bleating of the cattle for her absentee daughter, had rushed outside and found the bodies, and the men had found her, and . . .

One of them had recognized her dress. He yelled and pulled the others away, but it was too late. My father ran out to find the circle of men opening to a bloody lump in the colors of his love.

She died a few hours later. Her eyes never opened again. I want to believe she heard the crying voices around her. That in her unconscious last few hours she perceived the pain of her loss, that in her dying moments she knew more than shock and horror, the last memory of the daughter three broken bodies on the ground. I want to believe that the first blow had knocked her out, that it was painless. That she hadn't felt the others.

But I know too much. I know people all too well from the minds that I touch. From the minds I consume. If my ravenous feasts had showed me anything it was that though the body and mind are gone, the soul goes last, and it feels everything.

I'd saved dozens of little girls. I'd saved myself. I'd saved my sister.

I had killed my mother.

I breathe in deeply. My feet buried into the soil of the riverbank, the rich brown almost but not quite blending with my own skin, the thin sheen of sweat glistening on my leg a rivulet congealing infinitely slowly around my ankles, like the drip of water in a cave slowly growing stalactites.

There are worms down there nibbling at the bits of me that are still flesh; other insects that I would've run from just days ago bite and draw blood and die drinking it. The roots of the nearby trees reach out, tethering me to the ground.

The air and dust on the thin hairs of my nose smelling of sweet and sticky sap, of burning cow dung, grilled fish and melancholy. Emotions have smells too, perspiring glands collecting around the mourners at my parents' funeral.

Abdoulaye Diallo outlived his wife by less than a night. Awa's screams had woken me up in the morning. The screams inside her mind. Her loneliness. Our father hanging from the ceiling fan.

They are leaving the mosque now, the final prayers prayed. The men are carrying their biers to the cemetery, to bury them with Mame Binta, my grandmother, Mame Thiogo, my great-grandmother, and Mame Fatou, my great-great-grandmother who had known a flesh-eater, and her unnamed stillborn daughters. A slow, silent procession, Awa the first to trail the coffins, as the men carried the last of her family with them.

Awa alone. Eyes turning towards her. I shudder in the heat, knowing all of her feelings. She doesn't want to move to her aunt's house, she's heard nasty rumors about what she does to teenage girls. My uncle's there, spending the night to watch over her before taking her in the morning. She doesn't like his smell, she's afraid, still wary of being alone with a man, even if he's family.

She's crying out for me. My name ringing in her mind with hope. That I'll come back, that I'll save her again.

I'll never come back, but I can still help her if she lets me in.

The river, Awa. I speak on the winds, tiny birds passing it on, chirping my message into her ears.

I hear my own voice in her head. Her gaze shifting away from the cemetery and towards me.

It's dark now, the blood inside my thighs has already turned solid. It prickles and stings but I'm getting used to it, my muscles and nerves slowly merging with my bones, my legs calcifying like ashy skin after a shower.

Awa appears through the bushes. She sees me and screams. Her voice like the steps that led her here, shielded from the world by me. Her eyes water, pearly drops running brown down her cheeks, and she throws herself at my neck. The same way she had after the flood. The same way she always had, ever since my mother had handed her to me as a baby.

She hugs me tight and looks into my eyes. Hers widen as she sees something beyond me inside of them, something that only she will know.

"Are you coming home?" she asks, her face buried inside my neck, the skin around my waist crackling softly as it hardens.

I'm never coming home, but I'm never leaving either.

My name is Woppa Diallo. My mother was Djinda Diallo, formerly Dem. I'm a soul of small places. And here I'll remain.

I put my fingers on her cheek, embracing her warmth while I can still feel. While I can still help her, the only way I know, the very way I was. I push my lips to her ear.

"Go home and sleep, little sister. I'm not going anywhere. Come back tomorrow and kiss me. You'll find me here, by the river. And I'll whisper to you."

AIR TO SHAPE LUNGS

by Shingai Njeri Kagunda

MEMORY.

We had been taught by the elders that we would recognize home by how the oxygen met our lips; by how we swallowed it without noticing that our bodies were working for this breath. We forgot what that felt like. To not wheeze exhales into the air.

We were all born with air in our lungs, knowing all the world to be home. We grew older and the breath escaped us with each passing year. Closer and closer to the sixteenth; the year of deportation.

The year we were to find home.

LIVING NOW.

We do not have to learn how to fly. In the year of deportation, it comes as easy as walking—easier than breathing—but only until we find home.

We think we can breathe easier when we fly but that is the trick of the sky. We are so used to being choked by the air on the ground that, at first, we mistake the lightness of atmosphere shifts for the lightness of home air. Maybe we were never meant to land? A fleeting thought. We are reminded of our limited time. Slowly we start disseminating into the world. Some of us find home in the East and some in the West. The rest of us forget and we ask, "What does it feel like?"

We do not hear their grounded responses from the sky.

MEMORY.

One of us asked questions about the structures; speculating the way they taught us to forget how to breathe. This one of us conspired against manmade borders. "The lines," they said, "drawn up to restrict airflow—making oxygen limited and selfish—only reserved for certain people." This one of us did not make it to our thirteenth year.

We did not ask questions after that.

When it is not home you cannot ask questions.

LIVING NOW.

We love to see our skin this close to the sun. Head, shoulders, knees and toes; varying shades of brown into black. The light dances on our melanated coverings and for seconds we forget that our breaths are not full. As the year passes, we sink lower and lower. Time reintroduces us to gravity. Some of us land in the South and some of us in the North. The rest of us wonder if we will ever have the knowing feeling that tells you to land. The feeling that says this is home. We forget and we ask. "How will we know?"

MEMORY.

One of us forgot and asked a question in our fourteenth year. The question: why the pink ones with skin like maize meal could move everywhere and breathe easy? "Why do they find home in places that do not belong to them?"

Wheezy whispers of power structures but not full chwest answers. The elders overheard. This one of us did not make it to our fifteenth year. We learned that death is to be unmoved; tied to eternal stillness. Do you know even the trees move through their roots?

LIVING NOW.

Some of us are bound to be movers, landing too soon—before we find home, then gasping for the rest of our wandering lives. We think of the stories of the movers where we were born. We try to remember what it was like to be born, the contrast of full air; sharp and sweet. This is why babies cry. We have not cried since we learned not to ask questions. We forget and ask as the wind pulls back the skin on our faces, "What if we cried?"

MEMORY.

One of us met their first mover in our fifteenth year. This one of us shivered as they recounted. "The mover's breath was so loud, that it shook their whole chwest! Their body endlessly shivering, shifting, moving." Moved to tears. "To have never found home," this one of us said with half breaths, "how can anyone live like that forever?"

The elders clicked at the movers. "Immigrants." The elders spit and reminded us, "Do not ever land until you are sure the air is shaped for your lungs."

LIVING NOW.

The year is over now and we have still not found home. We are countable—the ones who have remained—our feet hovering just above the ground, near the trees. We are tired of flying but do not want to land. The air is thick and we do not speak because we have to conserve our breath. We see a river and re-member thirst. You are never to land in water but today marks a year since the day we departed and we have no choice. We make peace with the growing possibility of our death. We forget and we ask. "So what if we die? Is it not better than to live half breathing forever?"

And when we believe this, we cry. As we fall our salty tears intermingle with the fresh water. When we lift our heads, the air comes gushing in, taking up the space in our mouths left behind by the water we have swallowed. Our chests expand-release-contract-blow air. We cry harder, like we did when we were born. We have learned of air that moves like rivers and we have remembered all the world to be home.

HANFO DRIVER

by Ada Nnadi

The excitement in Oga Dayo's voice was the first sign that something Fidelis most likely would not enjoy was about to go down.

He had been taking a dump when the man called and at the words *idea* and *something good,* Fidelis's stomach had gurgled. Now, he was standing in Oga Dayo's car park reserved for his commercial buses plying the Island route, and Fidelis was fighting to keep his bemusement in check.

"I present to you, my newest groundbreaking undertaking," Oga Dayo was saying, "my novel offering to the state of commercial transportation in Lagos, and soon to be the whole of Nigeria. The. Hanfo." His flourish was wide and big as he gestured at the floating vehicle. Fidelis almost expected the chorus of a choir to follow, with the word HANFO hanging above Oga Dayo's head in bright neon letters.

"You get it, abi?" Oga Dayo barrelled on. "Hovertrain, hovercar, *hoverdanfo.*" He paused. "But hoverdanfo was a mouthful so I thought it was best to shorten it. Make it easier to say while paying homage to its predecessors. Hanfo has a nice ring to it, doesn't it?" He grinned, eyes twinkling, and Fidelis's stomach dropped and roiled like a clogged sink.

In all the years he had known and worked as a driver for Oga Dayo, Fidelis had never seen Oga Dayo's big ideas go well. And when they went bad, he somehow always ended up caught in the aftermath.

Fidelis gave Oga Dayo a constipated smile and turned away to regard the hanfo. He reckoned he was gawking at the contraption like the crowd he had met when he arrived at the car park a few minutes ago. The drivers in the crowd and other people who had things to do had gone back to their businesses, but a few stragglers remained, staring and discussing the specifics of the car. Once or twice, someone outside the compound passing by would see the hunk of metal painted in the yellow-and-black stripes of commercial buses in Lagos, do a double take, and then stop and stare when they noticed the thing had no tires and was floating a few feet above the ground.

Fidelis sighed. Perhaps if you squinted, forgot its lack of tires and the fact that it hovered, the polygon-shaped thing could pass for a regular danfo bus. It was smaller than the quintessential danfo, but the aesthetic was definitely there—from the beat-up, secondhand air around it that several coatings of paint, art, and servicing would never be able to hide, to the recalcitrant, unimpressed expression the headlights in these vehicles seemed to give them. But Fidelis had his misgivings.

"Oga Dayo," he called.

"Yes?"

"Let me just get one thing clear."

"Eh hehn, go on." Oga Dayo nodded enthusiastically, practically bouncing from the barely contained energy of a creative with a shiny new project.

"Do you seriously expect me, Fidelis Nwosu, to drive this thing—"

Oga Dayo nodded again. "Yes."

"—In Lagos traffic?"

"Yes . . . ?"

At the uncertainty in Oga Dayo's voice, Fidelis thought, perhaps, his scepticism had finally gotten through to the man. But then, Oga Dayo asked, "Is there a problem?" and made it worse by adding, "I don't see anything wrong with it."

Whatever hope Fidelis harboured withered and then turned to dust. The only thing that would get through to Oga Dayo whenever he got any of his exasperating ideas was a sonic blaster. This was what Fidelis had used the last of the NaiCreds on his Trekphobic card to board a bus for.

"I assure you, Fi, there is nothing to be worried about. It is perfectly safe. As you're looking at it now, this vehicle will revolutionise public transportation in Nigeria."

At the word *revolutionise,* Fidelis's clogged sink of a stomach threatened to erupt. Something bubbled to his throat. He swallowed it back down. Oga Dayo had used the R-word. This wahala was now bigger than a sonic blaster.

When Oga Dayo convinced Fidelis to be his delivery driver for his *No Place Like a Hobox* project—an initiative aimed at "giving the homeless, low-income communities, and rural areas compact smart houses with built-in AIs"—Fidelis was sure Oga Dayo had thrown around the words *revolutionise* and *housing policies* in his pitch. Fidelis had witnessed the fallout of the project, with the houses resold by the recipients, high cost of maintenance which equalled increased standard of living for said recipients, two lawsuits, and robberies—of the recipients, the houses, and *him,* the unfortunate driver-guy.

Oga Dayo was still dealing with the rehousing and settlement payments from that project. And that was two years ago. When Oga Dayo's pet projects fell through, they fell through hard. Between his philanthropy and charity initiatives, he was always looking for the next big thing to put all that generational oil money into.

Fidelis had grown up listening to his father talk about his escapades—ill-advised, ill-conceived, and irresponsible—with his best friend, Dayo. Fidelis recognised that twinkle in Oga Dayo's eyes. He had lived with the man for five years after the death of his parents, and had known him longer. Fidelis did not like that twinkle one bit.

"It really is fine, Fi, trust me. The hanfo is made by the same people as my hovercar. You should be able to drive it since you used to drive me around in that one. You brought along your license like I told you to, abi? Then there shouldn't be any problems. Private commuters are already using hovercars on Lagos roads, how is this any different?"

Fidelis let out a long-suffering sigh. "Private o. *Private*, Oga Dayo. But you also forgot another word."

"What?"

"You forgot *rich*. Rich private commuters. What middle-class Nigerian has the money to be buying these floating cars that are all the rage abroad? This one runs on electricity, too, abi? In any given locale, I can count the charging stations available with one hand. Twenty-four-hour power supply na for people wey get money. This moto, too, no difference. Explain to me, exactly, how this is going to work."

Oga Dayo let out a belly laugh. Fidelis's expression curdled. If he was laughing like this, it meant Oga Dayo thought he already had Fidelis. "Fide, Fide. Fide, my man, do you know people said the same thing about the smartphone? Now look what happened? In 1999 when the then president, Olusegun Obasanjo, was revamping the NCC and GSM services—"

Fidelis immediately tuned him out; a reflex action. His gaze strayed to the people milling about the park, the drivers ready to get back on the road with their *regular* buses and make some money. *Money*. He turned back to Oga Dayo.

One of the good things about Oga Dayo was that he paid well. Fidelis's work as a freelance developer was going okay, but with new programming languages popping up here and there, old ones being upgraded, keeping abreast of all of this, especially as someone who was self-taught, required money. Money for classes, money for tools and apps.

Then there was Helena's gender-affirming surgery to think about, money for hormones, for the mandatory therapy and appointments they used to make life hard for trans people, and even harder for poor trans people. It wasn't today he found out queerness in Nigeria was not for the poor. Arrests by law enforcement agencies, three years after the repealing of the SSMPA, said enough; he'd been caught in that crossfire before.

He hadn't even factored in expenses for other things; pending, recurrent, and on hold. All their basic needs, rent, fees, and maybe a bit of a splurge for Helena because his sister would sooner die than open her mouth to ask for shit.

Not that Oga Dayo's payment for this job would cover all of this, but it was a start. Since Oga Dayo had been the one to reach out first, Fidelis could kill two birds with one stone by offering to go back to driving for him—hopefully not the polygon-shaped contraption, but driving was driving as long as he got paid and didn't get in trouble with the police and road safety people.

There wasn't much his International and Public Relations degree could do him. It wasn't even what he had chosen when he applied at the University of Benin, but here he was. Fidelis exhaled. Oga Dayo had stopped talking and was watching him closely. His expression must have given away the moment he reached a decision because Oga Dayo's face immediately split into a grin.

Fidelis raised a warning hand. "Two questions: Do you have a permit for the contraption? Second: Have you made all the necessary payments, whatever it is that's needed to make sure I'm not arrested for driving it? Because me as I dey so, you know sey I no like wahala. You sha get money to bail me out, so why am I even talking?"

Oga Dayo guffawed. He rubbed his hands together and Fidelis imagined a mini him up in his head, cackling frenetically. "Yes, yes, I have everything you need. You know, Fi, when I got this idea, my mind immediately went to you. I mean, can you imagine it, being known as the first person to drive a hanfo?"

Fidelis grimaced and sucked in air through his teeth. "Abeg, don't start with me, Oga Dayo."

"No, really."

"Whether I am the first or the second, that one is not my problem. I have another question."

"Yes?"

"Is the contraption in good working condition?"

Oga Dayo's grin faltered, his excitement deflating. Even his agbada joined in, one wide sleeve rolling dramatically down his arm. He patted the sloping edge of his fila, adjusting its position on his head. "Erm . . ."

Fidelis exhaled again. "Does it run as well as any regular danfo?"

Oga Dayo's smile returned. "Eh hehn, now you're talking. Yes, it runs very well. But eh . . . just in case, I will give you the number to one of my cousin son, adumaadan, correct boy. He's currently on holiday here, but he's studying one big course like that in America. He was the one that helped me with the repairs for the hanfo. Just call him if you have any issue."

Fidelis gave the hanfo a sceptical look. Oga Dayo's spluttering was a warning bell—in fact, this whole thing was a warning bell. "Okay, I will take the number," he said.

Oga Dayo beamed even harder. He took out a pen and jotter from the breast pocket of his agbada, scribbling on it as he asked, "So, erm . . . are you dating anyone right now? I know you broke up with that oloshi boy you said you were dating before. How long did that relationship last sef?"

Fidelis's eyes narrowed. "No, I'm not in a relationship right now," he answered slowly. "And *please*, Oga Dayo, don't get any ideas. Just give me the permit and all the necessary things so I can get this over with." He gave the hanfo another look. "Why is the contraption on though? Are you not wasting the charge like this?"

"We will go and charge it before you leave," Oga Dayo replied. "I just wanted to show off the first floating danfo. You know when you're doing something, there must be flair in it. In 2039, when the minister of industry, trade, and investment was—"

That was Fidelis's cue to conk out. He sent a prayer upwards and braced himself for whatever was coming his and the contraption's way.

Compared to danfo buses that carried fifteen to eighteen passengers, the hanfo's capacity, plus the driver, was eleven. It didn't have the signature benches danfo buses possessed. The chairs in it looked more like the car seats in regular cars, though they weren't the chairs the vehicle had come with. This one was three-on-a-row; the original had been two.

As they charged the hanfo, Oga Dayo showed off the vehicle, pointing out the things that had been repaired, modified, or outfitted. They had cut and added windows to the tin can to give it the danfo look. The stereo had been replaced because the one it came with did not work. Like the vehicles it was aptly named after, the air conditioners and heating didn't work either, but they had windows now, so those would have to do.

The card reader near the passenger door had been modified to accept Nigerian bank cards, Trekphobic cards included. He was going to be handing out free Trekphobic cards to the first passengers as a way to *incentivise* people into boarding. The infotainment system—touch screen, video player, Wi-Fi, GPS—was kaput, but the motherboard had outlets that phones and any other assistive technology could be plugged into to do the work of the IVI. Fidelis had used his phone's facial recognition to open and start the hanfo after being authorised and granted access by Oga Dayo.

The fact that all of this was possible was thanks to the elusive cousin son. When Oga Dayo had been telling Fidelis about him, he had the feeling Oga Dayo was also acting as a wingman, but Fidelis chalked it up to his imagination. He'd warned the man not to get any ideas. Fidelis already had enough to worry about. Like surviving this day without becoming a cash cow for Nigerian law enforcement. Though the person in the photo Oga Dayo had shown Fidelis was cute; not his type, but cute all the same.

"So, what do you think?" Oga Dayo asked from outside the driver's window. "Is everything to your liking?"

"I'm not sure yet," Fidelis replied. He checked the side mirrors and adjusted the rearview one, all new additions, just like the rear window, thanks to the kaput smart system. The manual brakes and throttle were also things that had been modified as a result of the defect.

He tapped twice on the small round button tacked to the dashboard, beside the stereo. The device made a beeping sound and two thin plastic strips emerged from either side of it. They met a few inches from the button to form a rectangle. As soon as the lines touched, a holographic image appeared, covering the length of the space produced by the lines meeting. A picture of him smiling with Helena filled the expanse of the screen.

"Fide, how far na?" a woman's voice, his virtual assistant, asked. "You want to switch to hands-free auto-operator, or should I leave it?"

"Make the switch, please. Thank you, Ekene."

"Okay, sure thing."

Oga Dayo popped his head into the window. "Ekene, Ekene, did you see the playlist I left for Fide? I left the link on the hanfo's cloud. You should be able to access it."

"Found it."

"What playlist is—" Fidelis didn't get the chance to finish. *Omo wetin dey happun?* The yelled question from the speakers cut him short. He gave Oga Dayo an unimpressed look, and Oga Dayo replied with a grin.

Even though the song had come out twenty-three years before he was born, "Danfo Driver (Ragga Version)" by Madmelon and Mountain Black was one of those iconic songs with a cemented place in Nigerian pop culture. Fidelis's eyes went heavenward when he heard the badly recorded *hanfo* that had replaced *danfo* in the chorus. He exhaled for the third time that day, hoping everything would go without a hitch even as his rumbling stomach refused to settle. "Here goes nothing," he muttered.

Oga Dayo took a step back as Fidelis steered the hanfo towards the exit. "You are now part of a pivotal moment in history," he shouted after him. "Be glad, Fi, *be* glad!"

Well. This pivotal moment in history currently sucked.

Despite the fact that Oga Dayo and his cousin son had removed some of the padding from the walls of the hanfo, without the air conditioner, the midday sun was unkind to the tin can. He had turned off Oga Dayo's goddamn playlist, but the noise from buses and drivers calling out destinations to passengers was not helping Fidelis's crabby mood.

For over an hour, he had been waiting in the line close to the CMS Under-bridge, along with other buses traversing the Island, and the hanfo still hadn't drawn in a single passenger. There were close calls. A child approaching with his mother had started to run up to the floating vehicle when he saw it, but his mother had pulled him back.

"Come back here, you this boy!" she shouted. "Why do you want to enter moto wey only him different inside all the ones wey dey here? Do you know if it's one chance? You will just enter and disappear. Better shine your eye."

Two teenagers had excitedly wandered in and then wandered off again when it began to seem like the bus would never get filled up. No one in the crowd that gathered when he first drove into the bus stop had shown any interest of boarding. The free Trekphobic passes had made them even more suspicious. Fidelis wasn't aiming to fill the bus, that was too lofty a goal. Five passengers were all he needed. He'd give it another thirty minutes. If there were no passengers in the next thirty minutes—

Ekene's voice interrupted him mid-thought. "Hallo, Fide. You have an incoming call from Oga Dayo. I don't detect a Bluetooth device, but no shaking. Hands-free mode is on, so I will just put it on speaker for you."

Before Fidelis could override the action, Oga Dayo's voice boomed from the speakers that had been playing music a few minutes ago. "Hello, Fi? How is everything going? Have you met the boy yet?"

Fidelis cast a quick embarrassed look around him, lowering the volume to ask in a quiet voice. "What boy?"

"I mean my cousin son na, Oluwatimilehin."

Fidelis winced. "I thought I was only supposed to contact him if the hanfo developed an issue?"

"Ah, so you're not interested?"

"Interested in what?"

"In him nau?"

Fidelis took one deep breath, eyes going skyward. "Oga Dayo," he hissed out.

"Why are you whispering?"

"Because I'm in public!" he snapped.

"Ah . . . sorry o." Oga Dayo did not sound apologetic at all. "Are there people there with you? Did I embarrass you?"

"Oga Dayo, please hang up."

"Oya sorry nau. Just make sure you call Oluwatimilehin. Don't wait for the hanfo to develop issue before you do. He is a nice boy. You will like him."

"Bye, Oga Dayo."

"Call him o."

"End call," Fidelis said to the device.

"That sounded like an interesting conversation." A man in his mid-twenties, closer to Fidelis's age, was peering into the hanfo from the passenger window beside the driver.

"It was nothing," Fidelis replied. "Just an annoying uncle."

The man laughed. "Relatives, am I right?" He paused. "But are you actually taking people to the Island?"

Fidelis sighed, answering with the weariness of a man who had gotten this question several times in one day. "Yes."

"I'm stopping at Eko Hotel."

"Sure, I'll reach there."

"Regular NaiCred price, no extra charge?"

"No extra charge. We're even throwing in free five-thousand-naira Trekphobic passes. You can add it to your existing NaiCred balance."

The man whistled. "For real? No scam?"

"No scam at all."

"I hope sey no be the one wey I go enter, una go thief my money, thief my destiny. I no get anything o. Na work I dey go find for Eko Hotel."

Fidelis laughed politely. "Your money and destiny dey, no wahala."

The man leaned back to address someone Fidelis couldn't see. "Akeem, oya comman enter. He say everything dey, nothing go happen."

"Ekene, second passenger door, please," Fidelis said to the virtual assistant.

The Eko Hotel guy paused at the entrance of the hanfo, watching in wonder as the door slid open. "Ah! It is even voice controlled. You go fear na. Technologically enhanced danfo." Fidelis chuckled. "How does it stay afloat?" the man asked as he took a seat behind Fidelis, his friend Akeem settling beside him.

"I heard the hover vehicles abroad stay floating with magnetic levitation. They rebuilt their roads with magnets and put some in their cars so they repel each other, which keeps the car from touching the ground. You can also adjust the repulsive force and intensity—enough to keep the cars two metres in the air. But who get time to do that one for Nigerian roads? The roads wey we dey manage with land moto, them don repair am finish? And again, not enough people are using hover vehicles, so wetin come be the point of building roads for them? Unless them wan just use that way take chop our money."

Fidelis nodded in agreement. "My brother na the way be that o." He turned around to rattle off the explanation Oga Dayo had given him, which he in turn had gotten from the elusive cousin son. "But the hoverdanfo, hanfo, to be precise, stays levitating thanks to the pressurised air shot out from the tiny thrusters underneath the vehicle and the two rotating ones on both its left and right sides for directional manoeuvre. One could call it a technologically advanced air cushion vehicle to be honest, modified to mimic jet propulsion." He'd forgotten the rest of the technical jargon, but what he remembered seemed to do it for Eko Hotel guy.

"Kai!" Eko Hotel guy said. "Omo na wa o. Akeem, you remember when Android phones used to be this big?" He indicated the size with his hands. "Wetin people dey use show off that time na how big your phone be. But then, they got smaller and smaller until the Nta phone came out." He nodded at the phone Fidelis had mounted close to the stereo. "I see that's what you're using, abi?"

Fidelis nodded again. He had been seventeen when the inaugural ad for the Nta™ phone had gone viral on Nigerian Twitter. It had started with the premise: "Walking down the streets of Lagos and afraid your phone may be taken from you? With the Nta phone you can set your worries aside. No more telltale bulges. Compact and minute, *you* won't even know it's there."

It had taken him three years to afford one. Oga Dayo was always generous with his money when Fidelis and Helena lived with him, but Fidelis didn't want to overstep. The man had done enough by taking them in, feeding, clothing, and seeing them through school. As soon as he'd graduated from secondary school (because Oga Dayo would not let him work while in school), he had offered to work as a driver for the man. It was one of the things, he felt, didn't require much skill. Something he could do to pull his own weight and, at least, help the man with.

When he first bought the thing, Fidelis, more often than not, usually forgot where he had tacked the Nta™ home button to. If it wasn't for the feature that allowed the customised virtual assistant to respond when you called its name, he probably would have lost it ages ago.

Eko Hotel guy was still speaking. "I heard you can get implants now. A smart system inside a living person. You won't even need a phone anymore. E go reach point wey if them dey thief phone, them go thief the person join, too, because you no know who carry modi full bodi." He chortled at his joke.

The conversation soon moved on to other things, as conversations started in commercial buses are wont to do. Eko Hotel guy proved helpful in getting Fidelis passengers. Even better than the prerecorded announcement—which had gotten him nasty looks from the other drivers—Oga Dayo had added to the hanfo's PA system.

Most drivers no longer used conductors in their buses since they could call out locations themselves or use PA systems, and NaiCred and Trekphobic cards had more or less eliminated the need for cash payment and the hassles that came with giving and receiving change. But Eko Hotel guy made himself interim conductor. He sat at the edge of the seat closest to the door, which he'd insisted Fidelis leave open, and called out to passengers, yelling bus stops and asking them to come board.

It took less than fifteen minutes for the hanfo to fill up. It seemed all Fidelis needed was someone jovial, amiable, and extroverted like Eko Hotel guy to board the hanfo. He now understood the appeal of conductors when they were a thing.

Fidelis gave out the promo cards to the passengers, handing out five to Eko Hotel guy and his friend because they deserved it, Eko Hotel guy especially. And soon, they were off, pivotal moment in history back on track.

The Nigerian Police, Federal Road Safety Commission or even OP MESA were not the things that proved an obstacle for the hanfo, but instead the question Oga Dayo had skirted around, unable to answer when Fidelis first asked him: "Is the contraption in good working condition?"

Although the Nigerian law enforcement had tried, bribery and knowing people in high places (in the papers Oga Dayo had given him, there were two letters signed by the FRSC commissioner and a representative from the Lagos state government) had proven greater than actually upholding the law—if there was one in place.

But Fidelis was realising that there was an even greater force: the fallibility of danfo buses—it didn't matter if they floated, a danfo bus will always be a danfo bus.

The drive had been going well, barring stops from law enforcement people. He had even put Oga Dayo's mumu playlist filled with old music on repeat. When they reached a holdup point, Eko Hotel guy, whose name was Ifechuckwu, had suggested Fidelis try increasing the thrust intensity so they could rise above the traffic like they'd seen other hovercars do.

Fidelis had been keeping the speed within fifty miles per hour because this was Nigeria, and even with regular vehicles, people were still driving anyhow. But a little indulgence didn't hurt. The passengers had cheered when the hanfo flew above the cars in front of it, but he lowered it back to a few feet above the ground when they passed the traffic jam, to save power.

However, that choice ended up not making a difference when the hanfo began to sound like it had a runny stomach. A few of the passengers muttered complaints. Someone from the back asked, "Driver, I hope nothing?" But despite the fact that the sound was a representation of what Fidelis had been feeling since he received Oga Dayo's call that morning, Fidelis had still chosen to keep the hanfo running, hoping it would hold on until they made it to the final bus stop.

But like the bowel movement that comes upon a person with funny stomach noises and no warning, the hanfo suddenly stopped with one jerk forward and then dropped out of the air with a loud *clang* that shook Fidelis to his teeth. There was a short moment of silence before Ifechuckwu, who was sitting beside him, burst into laughter. Then a few of the passengers followed.

Fidelis winced and rubbed at his neck, avoiding eye contact. He couldn't even pretend to go check under the hood or fiddle around with the ignition and controls like danfo drivers did when shit like this happened. The only thing Fidelis knew about the vehicle was how to drive it. With the contraption broken, the controls for the doors no longer worked and the diagnostic check Ekene had done on the hanfo was inconclusive because of the many modifications to it. So, Fidelis had climbed out the window and spent minutes prying the passenger door open to let the half-amused, half-unimpressed people out.

Then he had to stand there in mortification as he held up the traffic and one of the passengers chided him, saying, "At least now we know sey the oyibo technology don arrive. It wouldn't be an experience without it at least breaking down."

Ifechuckwu had given him a reassuring pat, laughing as he waved goodbye and crossed to the other side of the road to board another bus, shouting as he did, "Now you will have to call this Oluwatimilehin person," he shouted.

Which only made Fidelis's embarrassment worse. At least, Akeem had been nicer by saying nothing, choosing instead to press his lips together to hold in his laughter, but the drivers behind Fidelis were not as kind. Before moving to another lane, they'd yelled insults at him. One of them had gone as far as poking his head out his window as he drove past Fidelis, telling him, "Push it na, push am commot!" Then he snorted, looking down as if he'd just made a thought-provoking discovery. "Ah, sorry o. I don forget sey e no get tire. Ha!"

The hanfo presented a bigger problem off than on. Blocking the road like that, it was like a piece of sugar attracting people looking to extort him; namely law enforcement and area boys. Fidelis lowered his head to address the home button tacked to his collar.

"Ekene, call Oluwatimilehin."

Oga Dayo's elusive cousin son had arrived at the scene on a power bike—a non-floating one, thank God, because Fidelis had just about had enough of hovering vehicles. He was currently watching said elusive cousin son trying to wrestle a helmet off his head.

Their call had been short. Fidelis had told him the hanfo broke down and then shared his location with the cousin son. The photo Oga Dayo had shared of his relative was a selfie; there was only so much a person could tell from those. The man in front of him was light-skinned, a few inches shorter than Fidelis, and preppy—if those shoes, trousers, button-down shirt, and that bag were anything to go by.

"Uhm . . . Fidelis?" Preppy Boy waved. "A little help? I can't seem to get the helmet off. Two taps at the side usually puts it in standby mode, but I tinkered with it yesterday and the signals appear to have gotten mixed up. It looks like I've mistakenly initiated security mode; it's refusing to come off."

Fidelis's conclusion to that was: If everything Preppy Boy tinkered with kept developing problems, perhaps he should stop tinkering with things at all. But because he was polite, and his parents and Oga Dayo raised him well, he kept his comments to himself and asked instead, "What do you need help with?"

"Okay, so I'm going to pull at the helmet again, all I need you to do is press the override button at the nape of my neck. That should do the trick."

Fidelis pushed himself off the hanfo which he'd been lean-ing on and did as he was told. Two beeps and the helmet slid off Preppy Boy's head, rearranging itself into a headpiece that looked suspiciously like the one the trickster god Ekwensu usually wore in some animated series Helena had made him see.

He pulled away to find himself face-to-face with wide, ex-pressive eyes sunken into a face whose lower half was covered by a close-shaven beard, its blackness contrasting with the close-cropped bleached hair; both the hair and beard had not been like that in the picture at all. There hadn't even *been* a beard. The eyes crinkled at the corners and Fidelis found himself smiling back.

"Hi, I'm Oluwatimilehin. Timi for short."

"Hi, Timi-for-short. I'm Fidelis." Okay, maybe he was a little rusty, but Prep—Timi didn't seem to mind because a corner of his lips quirked.

"Yeah, I know who you are." He paused, perhaps realising how that sounded, before quickly adding, "It's just . . . my uncle talks about you a lot, so it's hard *not* to know who you are, you know what I mean?"

Fidelis nodded, unable to help his smile as Timi broke eye con-tact to awkwardly place the headpiece he was holding atop his head and climb down the motorcycle. Twisting his hands around the strap of his bag, he glanced at Fidelis a look before clearing his throat. "So, uh . . . what did you say was the problem with the hoverdanfo again?"

Fidelis grinned. He knew nothing about floating vehicles, but nothing spoke damsel-in-distress like a broken-down car. An age-old wingman—after Oga Dayo.

"Well, it started with this sound . . ."

EXILES OF WITCHERY

by Ivana Akotowaa Ofori

At first, I had a vague method to my button-pushing, but now, I'm just straight-up smashing keys. Nothing happens, though—and the longer nothing happens, the harder I smash. Growing into my paranormal talents has spoiled me; now I have *very* little patience for problems my powers can't solve. I try to rein in my frustration, lest Vika catch on, but seriously, of *all* the times the Worm could have chosen to misbehave, it picks Vika's first trip inside it!

Your first journey in the Worm is supposed to be magical and impressive. Of course, being a literally magical machine, the Worm can't help but achieve the first. However, sending me towards Burkina Faso when my destination was much closer to Lomé is definitely *un*impressive. And, frankly, impressing a woman with an imagination as wild as Vika's was an accomplishment I had been looking forward to!

Although . . . at the moment, I am not even sure Vika is convinced that *I'm* real, much less the Worm. Hard to blame her for that, though. When you've lived long enough with a schizoaffective disorder, I suppose you learn to doubt some of the things you perceive, especially when those things defy several laws of nature. At the very least, Vika is curious enough to have asked me, a few minutes ago, how the Worm works. The best answer I could give was probably far from satisfactory: "If the thing that can transcend the three-dimensional laws of space is a wormhole, then this is the 'worm.'" I'd be willing to bet right now that the reason she's so engrossed in her phone right now is because she's looking up wormholes.

I sneak a glance at her, lying on the sofa at one edge of the Worm's interior. Her beauty, as usual, is nothing short of assault—as shocking as her frizzy hair, fanning around a face which manages to be simultaneously soft and angular. In that face is the most obvious reason for the othering she has faced in this country. From the endless variations of "You don't look Ghanaian" to the barely veiled challenges to prove her Ghanaianness, as if she's lying about her heritage.

But if that was the worst of what she's faced from our fellow citizens, she wouldn't have needed my help this badly.

Please, I beg the Worm, feeling silly for talking to a machine. *At least take us back to Accra, if Aflao is a problem for you.*

The Worm doesn't respond. And all this time, I'm still pressing buttons, as if that will make even a millimeter of difference.

"Ese?" Vika calls. Her voice comes out light and lovely, completely belying the reality of just how hysterical it can become when approaching manic paranoia. Yet another reason why the Worm should have just taken us to Aflao like I'd asked. There's a pharmacy there that I'm hoping might have a certain elusive drug she's been prescribed.

"Ese, are we lost?" Vika asks. She has stopped scrolling and I can feel her eyes on the side of my face.

"No, we're not lost," I reply. The edge in my voice is too obvious, so I continue, "We're just in the wrong place."

A pause. Then, "Do you know how to get us to the right place?"

My slight hesitation sets her off at once.

"Oh my God," she breathes, sounding like she's on the verge of hyperventilation. "We're lost. *Lost!* Being lost in a thing that could literally be *anywhere* on the whole freaking *planet* is *very bad!*"

I sigh. I haven't known Vika very long, but I already know that once it's started, there's no way *I* can stop it. As far as I can tell, the wisest course of action is to block her out and focus instead on whatever is wrong with the Worm. The latter is harder than it sounds.

The truth is, the Worm responds to the will of its driver (well, most of the time), and it didn't even *have* this complicated-looking dashboard until a generation ago. Most of these buttons and dials are really just for show.

Apart from fundamentally being a space machine, the Worm is also a conglomerate of all its owners' imaginations. Right now, most of its features are still the ones it adopted when my now-disappeared uncle was its captain. He had wanted something to press so that he didn't feel so stunned by the fact that the Worm could send him anywhere, instantaneously, in response to little more than a thought. (Well, that, and the fact that, at the age of nine, he migrated to England and got hooked on *Doctor Who.* By the time he inherited the Worm, it was inevitable that the Worm would take on at least *some* characteristics of the TARDIS.)

I think, though, that my own imagination is slowly imposing real functions onto the buttons. A few more years of my captaincy, and this thing will probably be less TARDIS, more sports car.

I sink into the nearest chair and think, *Back to Accra. Back to Accra.*

Nothing. I am convinced the Worm is *actively* defying me at this point, and it doesn't help that Vika's voice is approaching screeching levels. I'm on the verge of losing my cool when we both hear the urgent rapping of knuckles on the Worm's exterior.

Before I can even process the sound, Vika is heading for the door.

"I wouldn't recommend that," I warn. I've had my fair share of unwanted adventures from answering knocks on the door. I blame the Worm. It's like a magnet for magic and madness.

It's already too late, though. Vika can be blindingly fast when she's manic, I'm learning.

"Please, you have to help me," I hear a young, female voice sob. "Please, please help me!"

I roll my eyes reflexively, because the Ambiguous Cry for Help is seriously the oldest trick in the book—and then I jump up because I realize that Vika, especially in this mental state, probably doesn't know that.

I'm proven right when Vika says, as she's allowing herself to be dragged away by a small hand, "Ese? I think this little girl is in trou—"

The door slams shut the moment she's fully outside.

I groan and utter a curse. The last time something like this happened, I had to rescue someone from an underground dwarf prison, and it was *not* fun.

I preemptively drape a loose, button-down shirt over my spaghetti-strapped top (I've had enough of Ghanaians trying to lecture me on women's modesty, especially when I'm in a hurry) and I bolt out the door.

And then the door bolts behind *me*! I spin around to face the Worm, a stream of curses on the tip of my tongue. Bloody temperamental beast!

One of the TARDIS features the Worm adopted was the outer-appearance camouflage. In the Worm's case, to readapt to its Ghanaian environs, it took on the shape of a dull brown shipping container—the kind that corner stores operate out of. For logistical reasons, I moved the bolts and chains from the exterior of the container to the interior. For obvious reasons, I regret that now.

The Worm's idiotic behavior is not the only reason I stop, though. My surroundings have caught me off guard too. Of all the places the Worm could have landed and locked itself, I didn't imagine the edge of a *forest*. And though it's only been seconds, there is already no sign of Vika or the possibly mythological creature who lured her away.

I sigh. My friend is gone and there is a distinct smell of danger in the air. I don't have time to deal with the Worm or anything else right now.

Just like that, I'm tearing through the trees.

My apprehension makes me clumsier than usual, even with the advantage of my instinctive, internal navigation system. I've never been here before, but to say that I have no idea where I'm going would not be strictly true. Clairsentience is the most basic tier of paranormal ability, after all. It's merely a heightened version of ordinary human intuition: the ability to know without evidence, the unconscious brain's certainty of what the conscious brain can't help but question.

It isn't long before I hear the too-loud hiss of my name.

I skid to a halt and backtrack in the direction of Vika's voice. I find her—and the person who dragged her away—cowering behind a large rock. I'm so relieved to have found her that I don't dwell as long as I could on the redundancy of their hiding place. It's literally the only boulder around that's big enough for even one person to hide behind, too easy to gravitate towards.

Vika looks a frenzied *mess*. Her hair is a wild mane around her head, and now there are leaves and twigs caught inside the strands. Her eyes are wide with anxiety and incredulity.

"Ese," she begins, "you will not *believe* what this girl has been telling me!"

By this time, I've completed a cursory assessment of Vika's physical state, and I'm satisfied she hasn't been hurt in any significant way. So I tune her out again and turn my attention fully to the one who lured her away.

She's a girl, literally a child—or, at least, that's what she appears to be. Can't be more than eight years old. She's cocoa-bean dark, like me, and her kinky hair has been done into cute Bantu knots. She's in a faded, floral dress that's way too big for her and has this terrible, boxy aesthetic to it. It has certainly passed through several generations of wearers before her.

She stares at me with frightened eyes, but it's not me she's afraid of. No, the only feeling she's directing towards me is one of quiet recognition. We've never met, but I can feel it too, now—the innate thing we share. People with paranormal abilities have always been more common on the continent than most people now would like to believe.

I lower myself to her level and ask plainly, "Who and what are you?"

"Puumaya," she answers quietly. And as she speaks, her eyes begin to brim—not for the first time today, which I can tell from the dried tear streaks along her cheeks. "They're coming for me. They want to hurt me, because of my thing."

She's speaking Dagbanli, a language I recognize by its sound, but neither speak nor understand. Not that it matters, this close to the Worm; automatic, telepathic translation is yet another TARDIS thing it picked up.

"Who is 'they'?" I ask.

"The rest of the villagers," she explains. "Because of the priest. He looked inside the chicken intestines, then he told everybody that I'm a witch. Now they're coming for me, the way they came for Grandma . . ."

For a second, I can't breathe. Because the story she's just begun to tell is triggering on a level that's almost too intimate for words.

Besides, something else has just clicked abruptly into place.

I spring up from my crouch, twirl around and inhale deeply, tasting our location more precisely this time. "Of *course*," I exhale. "We're so close. We're like, right outside!"

"Umm, outside of what?" asks Vika.

"Gambaga," I answer grimly. "Home to Ghana's most well-known witch camp."

Behind me, I hear Vika release a curse of her own.

As for me, I am instantly nauseous, assaulted by the flashbacks

I've been trying for twelve years to bury away: My heart, attempting to yammer its way out of my twelve-year-old chest as I ran
through a different wilderness. The fear of the future I was being
sentenced to—a carnal type of servitude which I barely even understood at the time, being passed off as spiritual expiation. For a
crime which I didn't even commit, and which, over a decade later,
I still do not know the details of. Not that I've tried hard since
then to find out.

But more than the debilitating fear, the crushing sense of *be-
trayal*. My parents, my elders, my *community*. All turned against
me at the word of a priest, content to cast me to the dogs for the
sake of "tradition." Shamelessly pretending that my selection was
divine, god-ordained, when really, it was a convenient way to get
rid of the strange girl whose powers no one wanted to acknowl-
edge, much less understand.

I've been on the run from those memories ever since that distant uncle of mine materialized in the Worm and whisked me
away, in that perfectly timed way that the clairsentient seem to
have. I've lived an unstable, nomadic, largely autodidactic life
since then, especially since his disappearance. And, occasionally,
I come across people whose stories move me so much that I cannot help but offer my help to them.

Like Vika.

"Ese," she pleads with me, "you can't let them get her. You
can't."

I don't need clairsentience to know that she's thinking about
exactly why I granted her passage on the Worm, the fate I am
trying to rescue her from.

A schizoaffective disorder is far from magical. But for the majority of our country's population, the nuance is irrelevant. To them,
everything we are, everything we can do that makes them uncom-
fortable can easily be classified under one term: "witchcraft."

I did not have to suffer or die through trokosi. Vika will not be
subjected to any ignorant charlatan's exorcism program. And this

little girl sure as *hell* won't be spending her formative years locked up in some witch camp as her best-case scenario.

Puumaya's low wail punctures through my mental bubble: "They're *coming!*"

I grit my teeth and ball up my fists. I no longer care that I don't know this little Northern girl from Eve. I'm helping.

"Vika," I growl, "I need you to take Puumaya back to the Worm." I can only hope it will open for them, or at least that they can get far enough away from whoever is after the girl.

"What about you?" Vika asks.

"I'm going to distract them long enough for you to get to safety. No more questions, Vee, seriously, just go."

I don't wait for an answer. I need to spring myself on those witch hunters before they can spring themselves on us.

My clairsentience leads me right to them, and with the element of surprise on my side, I capitalize on the time they waste by being stupefied.

They gawk at me, so out of place in this setting, with my long, plaited natural hair and my urban, androgynous fashion. The men's light blue button-down I threw on and my ripped jeans must surely be scandalous in a village where I can tell women are generally confined to skirts and dresses.

There are about fifteen of them; most of them teenagers, all of them male, and collectively wielding an arsenal of fetish items, from whisks to stringed charms. They are all either bare-chested or wearing old "foose"—the kind of foose that adds a fourth strip to the Adidas logo, or an extra "g" to Balenciaga.

"Hello," I greet with inappropriate casualness. "Sorry for interrupting what looks like a *very* serious expedition, but may I please know exactly where I am?"

"This is Dagbiribore," one of the men replies, his gruff voice full of suspicion as my words confirm my foreignness.

A less patient man butts in, "We're looking for a small girl who has run away. Have you seen her?"

"A *girl*?" I feign astonishment. "No, but . . . Why at all would anyone be trying to escape from such a friendly looking bunch as you?"

I'm caught between amusement and disappointment at how unaccustomed these men are to sarcasm. A few brows furrow in weak attempts to make sense of my tone, but that's as far as it goes.

"She's a witch," the initial spokesman explains. "The Wise Man has confirmed this from the gods, and now the girl must be dealt with appropriately."

I perform a gasp so deep that no one but a newborn baby ought to be taken in by it. "A *witch*, you say? A *real-life witch*?"

If they didn't know I was making fun of them before, they certainly do now. All at once, I drop the act and allow all the acridity back into my face and voice.

"Here's what *I* want to know. This practice of discovering witches . . . It involves the performance of certain elaborate rituals, does it not? The kinds of rituals someone else might call, I don't know, *witchcraft*, maybe?"

"You blaspheme!" one of the men snarls at me.

Unfortunately for him, I no longer give a damn about this conversation. Something suddenly feels *very* wrong, and that something is nearby. I turn away from the witch hunters and squint through the leaves, but I don't see anything. But then I feel the prick of sentience in my chest that tells me that Vika and the kid are in trouble.

Without so much as another glance towards the men, I'm speeding towards the Worm.

I get there as fast as humanly possible, only to find proof for my fears. The doors are still deadbolted from the inside. Vika and Puumaya never did make it back.

A resolution forces its way through my emotions and consumes everything else: I am going to find the "Wise Man" responsible for Puumaya's sentence and keep my foot on his neck until I get her and Vika back.

The shrine is really just another of Dagbiribore's numerous earthen huts, but with fancy hide and bone decorations that are probably meant to be awe-inspiring. Aside from the weird décor, though, nothing looks particularly amiss. I walk into the place like I own it, and I have to stop myself from reeling from all the unidentifiable, pungent smells.

A man sits bare-chested on a stool, surrounded by grotesque artifacts, lazily fanning a coal fire burning beneath something I'm certain is inedible. He looks up at me, mostly in disbelief at my brazenness.

"I'm looking for my friend and a plus-one," I announce. "The plus-one is a little girl I'm sure you know personally."

The fetish priest blinks. "And just who do you think you are?" he blurts.

He assesses me much more intelligently than the witch hunters did, looking for a threat. I am so prepared to give him one that I let out a hard, humorless laugh.

"I am the sort of person you would condemn if you had any *real* skill for detecting us," I say.

When it comes to paranormal ability, I fall into the category my uncle referred to as Manipulators. I can alter things at will, but only the sorts of things that are already quite fluid. Things like wind and weather, for instance, I can change. A person's facial features, however, I cannot. That's all right, though; I rarely need more than the most basic of parlor tricks to put the fear of God into people when they're trying to play me.

I flex my fists as I build up steam and continue, "The public misconceptions around us are unfortunate and really, *very* underwhelming. People hear 'witch' and think, 'bitter old woman who is jealous of her brother's children.' Meanwhile, when people say 'witch,' what they *should* mean is *me*!"

With a single, carefully directed thought, I send the fire in the pit flaring up in righteous power.

The fetish priest leaps up with a surprised yelp. In the moment his stool threatens to topple, I hear a heaving, muffled voice emanating from somewhere beneath the ground.

My heart catches in my throat.

Instantly, I kill the fire, run over, and kick the stool down to reveal the trapdoor it was covering. Jesus Christ, talk about inhumane holding cells! How *dare* that man . . . ?

Before I can think my way into an all-consuming rage, I'm hauling the girls out with all my strength.

Vika is far, *far* calmer than any neurotypical person would be right now. She accepts my help getting out of the hole, saying, "I used to hide inside the storage cupboard, as a kid. This felt sort of like that, but way smellier. And I did *not* enjoy it."

And Puumaya, instead of focusing on assisting my efforts, screams as soon as her mouth is free enough, "You have to be careful! The man, he's not a real man! He can change into—"

Oh . . . Crap. I sense the transformation even before I turn to see it: the bone-thin Wise Man with a white cloth around his waist, suddenly shrinking within his human form like he's being crushed in a god's fist, until at last, he is nothing but a speck I'd have hardly been able to see, if not for the glow.

I identify the creature in one breathless word: "Adze."

Adze were wildly common in the folktales I heard as a child— the shape-shifting vampires who can take the form of fireflies so as to better sneak up on their prey. As far as Ewe mythological creatures go, the adze are royalty.

And I've lived a life wild enough to know that "mythological" very rarely means "not real."

"Vika," I strain. "Puumaya. Run. Now."

They begin to move away, and the firefly tries to pursue.

"Oh no, you don't," I mutter, grabbing the nearest whisk and calabash.

I manipulate the air into a miniature tornado around the insect to retard its progress. While it's caught in the swirl, I swat it to the ground and clamp the calabash over it.

This is, of course, a *very* temporary impediment, but at this point, any extra second is precious. To my knowledge, there is no natural *or* magical defense against adze. The only advantages we probably have are that the firefly form is in some ways easier to fight off due to its size, and that it takes the adze at least a few seconds to shape-shift, especially from firefly back to humanoid.

My plan is to disappear in the Worm before this monster has the chance to suck any of us dry. I fear for the girl the most because, according to the legends, the adze are partial to children.

I'm just getting ready to release my clamp on the gourd and make my own escape when I realize that the others haven't actually left yet.

"That transformation thing was really cool, low-key," says Vika. "It's like one of those TikTok transitions where you're like, 'Wait, how did they *do* that?'"

She clearly does not understand just how much danger she's in.

"I saw him change," Puumaya whimpers to me. "In the forest. And *he* saw *me*. I ran away from him, but then he went to tell everybody that I'm a crazy witch. They believe him because they say my grandmother was a witch too."

I'm sick to my stomach. *When* will these awful patterns quit repeating themselves? A monster wants to protect himself, and almost invariably, the only way he can see to do so is by harming somebody else. It doesn't help that for people like us, our powers make us such easy targets for other people's fears.

Rather than saying all this, I growl, "I told you guys to *run,* and if you have any sense at all, you won't make me say it thrice."

Thankfully, this time, they promptly obey. Meanwhile, the adze is buffeting itself against the sides of the gourd. If it changes to human form while I'm still here, it's probably over for me. So I take my own advice, trying to time it as properly as I can, and leg it.

Puumaya and Vika make it to the Worm first. Though I'm faster than them both, I've been deliberately lagging behind as a buffer between them and our pursuer. It's not easy, simultaneously manipulating the elements against the firefly and trying to hold myself back physically, with all this adrenaline pumping in my blood.

All the hairs on my neck stand on end, and I know that the adze is right behind me. So I stop a few feet away from the Worm, allowing Vika and Puumaya time to get in.

I turn around in time to watch the little ball of light expand into the fully grown man from the shrine. I panic and glance towards the Worm when I see what Vika is up to. Of all the things in the world she could possibly be doing right now, she has her phone out and is taking what I can only guess is a video of the adze as he morphs. I can't believe my eyes; this is the most Gen Z thing I've *ever* seen.

"Vika, are you *insane*?" I screech, and I know, immediately, that I should not have said that. Whether because of, or despite her schizoaffective disorder, that was an extremely insensitive thing to say to someone who has been effectively exiled by her own family on grounds of "insanity" by virtue of "witchcraft."

"If there's videographic evidence, they can't say it didn't happen," Vika says matter-of-factly.

By this time the adze is fully humanoid again. He crouches, flashing his sharp, uneven teeth as if to lunge for me, and I cry out, "Stop! Stop right there!"

The only reason it works, why the creature freezes in place, is because my words come out in Ewe.

Sometimes, when I will it strongly, I can overcome the Worm's automatic translation abilities. I must have figured out subconsciously that invoking our mutual Ewe background would have an effect. There's nothing like the temporarily paralyzing, mixed bag of emotions from running into a piece of home on foreign soil. Especially when that piece of home is another *person*.

While he's caught off guard by my Ewe, I hear the Worm door shut behind me. I can't help but puff out a sigh of relief—never mind that I'm now the only one still in the danger zone. Besides, I'm only now realizing the genius in what Vika just did.

"Before you do anything unwise," I continue in Ewe to the adze, "remember that my friend caught your transformation on video. If she comes out to find that I'm hurt in any way, she will reveal your true nature to the people of Dagbiribore and anyone else who has access to YouTube. And I know for a fact that revealing your true identity is something you are *very* eager to avoid."

The adze glares at me, but, in concurrence with a hypothesis I'm developing about him, he doesn't pounce.

"Who *are* you?" he asks, in a tone that translates the question into "*What* are you?"

Over the last ten years, that has become such a tricky one to answer. "Nomad" doesn't quite cut it. I think I am what an exile turns into while straddling a yearning for some sort of home and a refusal to be held down. I suppose what I am is a perpetual migrant with magical powers and a space machine.

"Forget about who I am," I say. "The real question is, why is it that a creature capable of draining any human of blood in one sitting hasn't yet sunk his teeth into some girls he could have easily overpowered ages ago? Why choose to frame, imprison, and converse with them instead?"

The hostility in his glare is being replaced by nervous energy.

"You're not a normal adze," I say quietly, on the borderline of empathy. "You have an aversion to human blood."

The adze slumps so dramatically that it's almost comical to

think that, just a minute ago, he looked deadly. There is so much exhaustion in the slopes of his shoulders.

"I was sacked by my people when they found out I don't take to humans," he confesses. "For us, it's a big shame, worthy of execution. I escaped, found places to live among humans. As long as nobody knows, I can live in peace." He pauses and looks towards the Worm. "But the girl saw me change. She would have told. I'd have lost another home."

"Ostracism!" I explode, bitterness and fury dripping off every syllable. "He fears ostracism, and in his attempt to avoid that, he makes a living out of ostracizing innocent girls from their communities! God in heaven, make it make *sense*!"

The adze frowns as if this interpretation has genuinely never occurred to him. It fills me with such anger that it threatens to devour every last morsel of sympathy I have left for him.

"I know places like this," I continue. "I *grew up* in one. They can be lethally unforgiving. Can you look me in the face and tell me that, even if you revoke your verdict, the village people will forgive and forget enough to treat Puumaya like she belongs here?"

The adze bows his head shamefully, and it's all the answer I need. Besides, I've heard of the many failed attempts to reintegrate Gambaga witch camp refugees into their original societies.

Even through my despair and wrath, I am able to force out my next words. "Somewhere inside the Akuapem-Togo range, there's a community of herdsman adze who rear their own livestock to feed on their blood. It's something you can consider as an alternative to ruining women's lives up here."

The look in his eyes strikes me with unexpected depth. It is a mix of wonder, gratitude, and true remorse. Still, after what he's done to Puumaya, and what I can easily imagine his "prophecies" have sentenced several other women to, I can't quite bring myself to offer him a ride. No, I think I'll leave him here to grapple with himself and the villagers for a bit, see what an activated conscience can make of him.

In the meantime, I have a newly exiled clairsentient girl to sort out a future for, and a friend who still needs my help with her psychosis.

As I re-enter the Worm—which has conveniently remembered how locks *should* work, now that we've finished clawing our own ways out of the belly of the beast—I consider it once more as a sentient being. Its three current passengers, myself included, have too much in common for pure coincidence. I'm starting to wonder if the Worm attracts us, leading us towards each other as if this is its purpose: to be a refuge for exiles.

Exiles of "witchery."

THE TALONED BEAST

by Chinelo Onwualu

"Kpom, kpom, kpom!" Edim shouted from the veranda. The door was open, but it would have been rude to enter; so he called out the native imitation of the knocking sound instead. He shaded his eyes with his hands and tried to peer into the gloomy interior of the house. He could make out little in the still dark. He called out again; no response.

Edim looked around him, unsure what to do. His uncle's house was a two-storey mansion of ochre brick crumbling at the edges with a high tile roof that was blackening like rows of rotting teeth. It stood at the end of a long, narrow road overgrown with trees. The smell of decay and wet rot hung in the air. Something was wrong here. Edim didn't have the Voices to tell him the truth of things anymore, but he could still feel it.

"Yes?"

Edim jumped, startled. There was a white girl in the doorway. He hadn't heard her arrive. At first glance she looked to be about his age, fifteen, but a closer inspection told him she was older, though he could never quite tell with whites. She was petite—smaller than him, and he was quite small for his age—with long silver-blonde hair plaited into neat rows, and she was dressed in a white frock with a dark blue pinafore over it.

"Can I help you?" she asked coldly.

"Is this the house of Dr. Isong?" He hoped she understood

him; his English was good, but sometimes it was hard to speak clearly with his front teeth so crooked.

"It is. Who are you?"

"I am his nephew."

She looked at him sceptically and Edim was painfully aware of his appearance. In his village clothes—too-loose trousers, worn-out sandals, and faded tunic—he did not look like the relative of a wealthy physician. He adjusted the strap of the canvas rucksack slung over his shoulder. "My papa sent word to him. If you tell him that Edim, son of Nyong, is here, I am sure he will know me," he said in a rush. "I am to be his apprentice."

"If you say so."

Edim reached under his cap to scratch his head, a nervous habit of his, and a lock of his long hair escaped. He shoved it back, but it was too late; the young woman had seen it. She stared at him with an odd expression, as if trying to remember where she had met him before. Then she turned and walked back into the house.

"Enter," she called over her shoulder.

Edim hurried after her. Electric ceiling fans spun lazily, keeping the interior of the house cool—a welcome contrast to the muggy heat of the afternoon. The wood floors squeaked under their feet and sunlight streamed through the long windows of the front room, gleaming off dark wood furniture. The walls were covered with ceremonial masks, carved elephant tusks, and the heads of butchered animals. Edim shivered: it was like being inside the house of a witch or a medicine man. Unlike the outside, inside the house was spotless.

Edim had never met Uncle Emmem, who had left for the city before he was born. Papa had told him stories of his uncle's cleverness, though. Anyone who could afford a white housekeeper had to be clever indeed.

They emerged onto the back veranda, where Uncle was eating at a round wicker table. The veranda was screened off by mosquito netting and looked out over a tangled, overgrown backyard.

Uncle was squat and barrel-chested, just like Papa, but there the resemblance ended. Where Papa's face was seamed with lines of laughter, Uncle's was oddly smooth, his skin artificially lightened and sheened with sweat, despite the cooled air. His hair had been straightened and was slicked back with grease. He had hands like a butcher's, thick and square, with long fingernails and a gold signet ring on the smallest finger of his left hand.

"Uncle, good evening," Edim greeted in his native language, genuflecting low as tradition demanded.

His uncle regarded him with a frown, his downturned mouth making him look as if he had just smelled something unpleasant.

"You are here. What did you bring for me?"

Edim started at that. Papa had given him no gifts for Uncle— only a few coins so that he could buy some food on the road. The money had barely been enough for a cup of water on the train. When he arrived in the city, without the Voices to guide him, he had been overwhelmed: it was so vast and noisy that he had quickly gotten lost. It had been only by the grace of the Goddess that he had managed to find his way here.

"Sir, I don't—"

"Humph! So my brother just sent you here empty-handed? Because I have money he expects me to feed his brat without adding anything on top?"

Uncle straightened then reached into the pocket of his suit vest and carefully brought out a gold pocket watch. The maid, who was standing beside Edim, snorted under her breath—a sound so quiet he was sure he was the only one who had heard it. Uncle opened the watch and Edim caught the photo of a white man on the inside of the cover. Uncle checked the time, wound the watch slowly, almost ceremoniously, then put it back into his pocket.

"It's ok," Uncle said at last. "After all, if a man cannot help his own people then he cannot call himself a man."

Uncle turned back to his supper. The smell of fried bread, bean cakes and millet porridge made Edim's mouth water. He had not eaten since he left home the night before.

"Go," Uncle said. "Naomi will show you your room."

His room was a small space under the stairs with no windows and nothing inside it except a woven rubber mat on the floor. By the time Edim dropped his bag and made his way to the kitchen, it was nightfall and no one was there.

Edim didn't remember seeing the maid leave but he was reluctant to wander the house in search of her, so he returned to his room and sat on the mat. His stomach rumbled and a wave of loneliness washed over him. He wanted to go home, back to Papa and the farm and his friends—back to William. He blinked hard, fighting the hot lump of tears in his throat. It was not good for a man to be so easily moved to tears, Papa had always said. Edim knew he was no true man, but he had promised himself that he was done with tears.

And he could never go back. Not after what he'd done.

He wandered through a grey forest of stone. The darkness beyond the trees rustled like a living thing. An odd rhythmic thumping thrummed though the earth beneath his feet. From the darkness, a keening wail rose up. The voice of an old woman or a lost child. A voice of pain, loss, and unspeakable despair. It called to him to save her. But Edim couldn't: he was too weak, too wrong. He ran, tried to get away, but no matter how fast he moved there was only dull stone. Her wails grew closer, louder, became crying. She sobbed as if her heart would break—as if it was already broken.

Edim woke in tears, shivering and drenched in cold sweat. The grey light of dawn bled through the gap under the door. He could hear the maid sweeping, somewhere in the house. He rose, wiped his face with the hem of his shirt and went to find her.

She waved away his greeting when he entered the kitchen.

"You must wake up early in this house," she said flatly.

She had laid out a plate of fried bread and a mug of hot milk tea for him. He thanked her formally before grabbing the plate and wedging himself into a corner to eat. He watched her work in silence. She was much stronger than she looked, lifting the heavy cast-iron pot over the stove with ease.

"Ma, where are you from?" Edim asked. "I mean, how did you come to this country?" He hadn't meant to be so rude, but he wasn't sure what honorifics whites used. She didn't seem to mind, though. She cocked her head like a lizard before answering.

"I don't know where I was born and I have no memory of my people."

The answer surprised him. "I am sorry to ask, ma." He could not imagine being so alone. Except, in a way he was.

"Don't be sorry. And call me Naomi." Her tone was brisk yet something about her words invited more questions.

"So . . . how long have you worked for my uncle?" he asked hesitantly.

"I have been working in this house for as long as I can remember," she said simply. "Before your uncle I served another, and another before him. They were all the same, though: cruel and stupid."

Edim was shocked; he had never heard anyone speak so bluntly and hoped she had not been overheard. But something wasn't quite right about her story. Uncle had been living in the city for the last twenty years and Naomi couldn't be much older than that. She was possibly old enough to remember the previous owner, but surely not the one before that . . .

"Tell me," Naomi said, breaking his train of thought, "your hair. Why is it so long?"

Only then did he realise he had forgotten to put on his cap. He fingered one of his long ropy locks, which were tied back with a cord. His hair had not been cut since he was born and it brushed the base of his buttocks. How could he even begin to explain the importance of his locks? Every month, complex rituals had to be performed just to lock the roots of each strand. He looked up to see that Naomi had stopped working—her whole body was turned to him like a weathervane following the wind.

So Edim told her the story of his birth. He had been told the tale so often it sometimes seemed as if he had been there, watching.

"For many years, my mother bore no living child. Every year at the harvest, she and Papa would go to the shrine of the Sustainer to pray for a child. One year, without telling Papa, my mother used all her money and went to the grove of the Goddess of the Earth in the sacred forest. She swore on the holy fires there that if the Goddess gave her a child, she would dedicate it to Her service. Nine months later, I was born. My hair is the mark of my service to Her.

"The night I was born there was a great storm. Papa said that it was the worst storm the village had ever seen, but the next day not one leaf was blown off the trees in our compound—even though lots of things were destroyed in the rest of the village. That's why they named me Edim. It means thunderstorm . . ." He tapered off when he realized he was rambling—as he did when he was happy.

Naomi had a strange look on her face. Like she was struggling to remember something important. In that moment, she looked impossibly old. Then it was gone.

"Interesting story," she said. "If you have finished eating, it is time to begin your chores."

She led him to a door he hadn't noticed before: it opened to an attached garage. Inside was the most beautiful machine Edim had ever seen. The car was sleek and black with a silver grille and whitewall tires.

"You will need to wash it every morning," Naomi said. "You also have to cut the grass in front of the house. There has been nobody to do it." Edim didn't ask why she hadn't taken up the job herself. On the farm women weeded and cut grass all the time; things must be different in the city.

She opened a door that led to the back of the house and pointed out the push pump in the backyard where he could fetch water. A crumbling archway draped with heavy tendrils of bougainvillea marked the entrance to the back garden. Beyond it was a tangle of dense vegetation that he was certain had not been tended to in a long time.

"What of the garden?" He nodded towards the archway. "I can also take care of it; my father is a farmer."

Naomi looked at him as if he had gone mad. "There is no garden here."

And she retreated back into the main house, leaving Edim staring after her in confusion.

By the time he had finished working, it was full morning. He returned to the house through the garage door. As he passed the open door leading to the veranda, he saw Uncle was awake and eating breakfast. He was dressed to go out in a white suit with a matching vest and two-toned shoes shined to a high polish. His hair was parted to the side and a grey fedora sat on the table beside his plate. Edim watched as Uncle sliced through what looked like a thick tube of meat. He'd never seen anything like it. After a few bites, Uncle barked:

"Naomi!"

Naomi, who had been standing off to the side, walked up. "Sir."

"How long did you cook this sausage for?"

"Ten minutes."

"It is cold. What have I told you about my food?"

"You only eat hot food, sir." Naomi's voice was steady and emotionless.

"Are you sure? Not warm? Not lukewarm?"

She did not respond and he shot to his feet—suddenly so angry that the veins on his thick neck strained. He towered over her, but she stared at the floor without expression.

"What kind of useless woman are you that you cannot even

cook properly, eh? No wonder your people abandoned you," he shouted. "So because of you I can't even eat in my own house?" Uncle swung his arm and backhanded her across the face. It was such a theatrically violent movement that Edim thought it might have been staged. But the red bruise that bloomed on Naomi's cheek was real enough. To her credit, she didn't even flinch. Uncle thrust the plate at her, nearly spilling the meat on her dress. "Take this nonsense back and make it again."

Edim ducked into the shadows by the door as she passed. She returned minutes later, the food steaming. Uncle continued to eat in silence, as if his outburst had never happened. Edim stepped out from behind the door and tried to creep back to his room, but his uncle's voice stopped him.

"Edim!" He turned to find his uncle watching him with a calculating expression. "Go and change; you are following me today. You had better be ready by the time I have warmed the car."

Edim sat in the front passenger seat of the car and tried not to touch anything. His uncle hadn't told him where they were going and Edim did not want to ask. The shorts and shirt that Naomi had given him that morning smelled like camphor and itched.

The car rolled to a stop in front of a row of hedges that marked the outside of a compound. Just beyond the hedges sat a low whitewashed bungalow with wooden shutters and a shiny zinc roof.

"Get out," his uncle ordered, and heaved himself out of the car. Edim fumbled with the handle before he was able to open the door and hurried to his uncle's side. A row of steps led up to a narrow veranda where a white man in a suit was waiting for them. Like Naomi, his skin was pale as a fish's belly except at the tip of his long nose where it flushed red. His bald head and lustrous brown moustache gleamed in the sunlight.

"Good afternoon, sir," Uncle said. When he talked to the white man his voice pitched two octaves higher and took on an odd nasal quality. Edim fought the urge to turn and check if the man speaking was the same one he had met the night before.

"You're late. I've been waiting for you." The white man glared and Uncle shrank under his gaze.

"Sorry, sir," Uncle said meekly.

"I say, this is terrible form," the man snapped. "If you're going to continue Dr. Borchgrave's practice, you're going to have to leave off these native habits."

"So sorry, sir. It was my new boy, sir." Uncle reached out and grabbed the cap off Edim's head, shoving it into his hands. "He was the one who delayed me."

The white man arched an eyebrow at Edim's hair which spilled over his shoulders in a cascade. He sniffed but seemed mollified by the explanation.

"Very well, let's get this over with. They tell me you're the best at these sorts of things. I hope you're worth the money—and the trouble." He spared Edim another glance, then turned and went inside.

"Wait for me here," his uncle growled under his breath as he followed the white man inside. He pointed to a bench on the veranda under the windows.

Edim sat down to wait and watched the compound. Across the street, there were smaller houses that reminded him of home: long mud-brick huts with thatched roofs and wooden doors. He could smell wood smoke from a kitchen somewhere—it reminded him of his mama.

Before she fell sick she had loved to cook. She always had something for Edim's friends whenever they came to the house to play. William used to joke that they should have been born brothers so that he could enjoy Mama's cooking also. Perhaps if she hadn't died last year, perhaps if William hadn't been the son of white missionaries, things might have been different.

Thinking of William made Edim's heart lurch painfully, as

though a hand were squeezing his chest. He longed for the Voices that would have helped him call up the sound of William's thoughts—wherever he was across the sea—but they were gone. Edim shook his head to clear his thoughts and resolved not to think about it again.

". . . And you're sure that's all she needs?" came the white man's voice from the bungalow's doorway.

"Of course, sir," his uncle said, emerging from the house. "I will mix the treatment for her tomorrow and deliver it in two days' time."

"So quickly? Perhaps you really *are* a doctor," the white man said, chuckling. "And given the looks of your boy here, I'd even believe you have magical powers."

A look of horror flitted across Uncle's face for a moment. Then he burst into loud laughter, clutching his stomach and slapping his thigh as if it was the funniest thing he had ever heard.

"Oh, sir, such a joke," Uncle finally managed. "You will kill me with laughter."

The white man put his hands in his pockets and leaned back, pleased at the reaction.

"I shall see you in two days, then," he said, dismissing them. "Don't be late."

"Of course, sir. No problem, sir." Uncle almost bowed as he turned to go.

As soon as they crossed the hedge wall, Edim felt two knuckles grinding painfully down on the crown of his head. The smile on Uncle's face had vanished.

"Useless boy," Uncle hissed. "Look at how you just disgraced me. How can you come to somebody's house looking like a madman; what is wrong with you?" He grabbed a handful of Edim's hair and pulled viciously, yanking his head back. Edim cried out, feeling some of his locks tear from his head. "We are going to cut this nonsense, today. Do you hear me?"

Later that day, when Edim was sitting on the high stool in the barber's shop watching his locks fall from his head one by one, he tried to tell himself that this was what he deserved. That this was part of his punishment for what he had done with William. He tried to stay strong, as Papa had always wanted. But Edim couldn't help it. He started to cry.

That night, he had the dream again.

He was in the cold, damp maze, the rhythmic thumping sending painful vibrations up his legs. Then the voice began its wail. Edim knew that it was searching for him. A cold wind picked up and Edim realised he was naked. He began to run, but once again everywhere he turned there was only cold, cold stone. The wailing grew louder—became a scream of desperate pain.

Edim woke tired, his head strangely light. He touched a hand to his skull and felt the raw, bruised flesh. He drew a shaky breath and rose to face the day.

If Naomi noticed the change in his appearance, she did not comment. He did notice that his slice of fried bread was larger than the day before, and that she had added a hunk of meat scooped out of yesterday's soup, still dripping with stewed vegetables. As he ate he could still hear the echo of the screaming from his dream.

"Edim!" Naomi's voice snapped him from his stupor. "Did you hear what I said? You have to go to the market today. Your uncle has an . . . engagement this afternoon."

"I am sorry," he said. "I did not sleep well; I had a bad dream."

She cocked her head in her curious lizard-like fashion.

"What did you dream about?"

He hesitated, wondering how much to tell her. For as long as he could remember, Edim had always been able to hear the Voices of the Earth; it was his gift from the Goddess. They guided him home whenever he was lost. They steadied his arm when he aimed his slingshot, so he never missed his mark. They warned him of danger before it could find him, and helped him to see the truth of things—even dreams. But ever since that terrible day in the forest, the Voices had been silent. It felt as if he'd gone deaf; their absence was an emptiness he could not fill.

"What does it mean if someone is calling to you in your dream?" he asked instead.

She looked at him sharply. "Calling you to do what?"

"I wish I knew."

Her look was sceptical. "Edim, if someone is calling to you in your dream, answer them. Now, it's time to get to work."

He spent the rest of the morning sweeping, scrubbing, polishing, and dusting according to Naomi's instructions. Around noon, Naomi sent him off to the market with careful instructions for what he needed to get. Edim struggled to remember everything she told him about Uncle's habits. He did not want to risk Uncle's anger, not after yesterday.

Later that afternoon, he was in the kitchen emptying the jute bags that had held his purchases when he heard a sharp crash from the ceiling above him. He paused and the noise came again—something hitting the floor of the room upstairs—but it was the screaming that made him run.

He took the stairs two at a time, tore down the long hallway with its many doors, and burst into the room at the end of the hall.

It was the room where Uncle prepared his medicines. Dominated by a long worktable with a stone mortar and pestle, a coal brazier and other delicate instruments, its walls were lined with bookshelves groaning under the weight of more books, jars, vials, pots, and bowls than he could count.

In the centre of the room was a narrow bed. The room's large bay windows had been boarded up, but even in the gloom Edim could see Uncle standing over Naomi, who lay prone on the bed. Uncle's trousers were bunched around his ankles; Naomi's dress was hitched up around her waist. A broken bottle lay on the floor next to them, dark liquid pooled beneath it.

Edim wanted to go to her—to pull Uncle off and stop him from hurting her more—but, as if he was in a dream, he could not make his legs move.

Uncle turned at the interruption, the look on his face murderous. As he gathered up his trousers, Edim saw him slip his belt free. In a few steps Uncle had him by the collar. He lifted him off the ground with ease and dragged him downstairs.

The beating lasted for hours.

Much later, Edim lay in the semi-darkness of his room with nothing but his breathing and his pain for company. He had long since stopped crying. For that much at least, he was grateful. His tears had always disturbed Papa, but they seemed to enrage Uncle. He had beaten him until he tired then locked him in his room. He had no idea how long it had been since he had heard Uncle's car drive off, but he knew it was evening by the golden quality of the light that streamed in under the door.

The soft knock brought him back to himself.

"Are you all right?" Naomi asked softly from the other side of the door.

He tried to move, but his body was a mass of welts and cuts. The pain radiated from everywhere at once.

"Yes." His voice was a hoarse croak. Something scratched against the wood as Naomi slipped a long, thin pipe under the door.

"I have water here. Take the straw and drink. I put something in it for the pain." Ignoring the searing agony that was his back and legs, Edim crawled to the door, and took the straw in his lips. He sipped deeply, coughing. The water tasted faintly bitter.

Within minutes, Edim could feel the pain recede to a dull ache, though he still felt drained.

"Thank you." There was only silence on the other side of the door. It lasted so long that Edim thought she had left. Then she spoke again:

"Why did you enter the apothecary?"

"I heard you screaming."

"I never scream."

Yet Edim was sure he had heard something. Or maybe he hadn't. Maybe the Voices had returned for a moment or maybe he was just abnormal—as he had felt since the day Papa caught him in the field with William.

"That room, is that where you go when you finish work in the evenings?"

Though Edim never saw her leave, she was always gone just as the last rays of the sun set—sometimes leaving whatever chore she was doing half-finished.

"That's where I go when your uncle needs me to make his medicines for him." There was a bitter note in her voice. "He knows nothing of the art of healing, but he possesses a low cunning."

"Are you a doctor?"

"No, but we have a very good library. He describes the symptoms; I research to diagnose the illness, and then prepare the medicine." She paused for a long moment. "You know, Edim, no one is holding you here. You can leave anytime you want."

Edim wished that were true, but he couldn't go back and face Papa. For good or ill, this was his new home.

He didn't hear her leave, but by the time the last light had filtered out of his world, Edim knew she was gone.

A breeze tickled his face and Edim sat up. The door to his room was ajar. Perhaps Naomi had unlocked it? Creeping out, he saw that it was full dark and one of the double doors which led to the back veranda was also open. A cool smell, like parched earth before the rain, wafted through it. He went to it and stepped out. The screen door had been left open and was creaking softly in the breeze.

A cold moon shone high in the cloudless sky, bathing the crumbled archway to the neglected garden in silver. An overgrown path of white stone led deeper into the garden. Edim followed it through a vast, tangled mass of trees, shrubs and vines.

As the vegetation thickened, the path faded. The garden was now dotted with weather-worn sculptures: a hunter with a giant bow, a mermaid with a snake coiled around her shoulders, two men in loincloths locked in a wrestling match, a monster with twelve heads pointing straight ahead, a giant tortoise with a city on its back. In the pale moonlight, they seemed almost alive.

He turned to make his way back and realised he was lost. Cold panic gripped him: he had to get back before Uncle woke. Tears welled up in his eyes as he blundered through the garden, hoping to find the path again. Instead, he burst into a clearing. At its centre was a statue of a girl wearing an old-fashioned dress. She had her hands shackled in front of her and was looking up to the sky, as if expecting something to fall. There was something familiar about her, though Edim couldn't say what. The wind picked up, rustling the trees, and the statue's dress seemed to flutter in the breeze. He blinked; the moonlight was playing tricks on him. He approached the sculpture cautiously and examined the black stone of the base. When he looked up the statue was staring straight at him, its face locked in a silent scream.

Edim turned and ran.

Somehow, he found his way back to the house and dove into his room. He clutched his knees, trembling, until the grey light of dawn broke under the gap beneath the door, and he finally fell asleep.

———

Edim wandered through the maze until the wild, wordless wailing began. He turned to run, but the ground began to quake. The earth roiled like waves and from the darkness a great beast with four taloned limbs emerged. Its teeth were like scimitars and a pair of leathery wings folded tight against its sides. A bony ridge ran the length of its long, sinuous body from crown to tail, and its ash-grey scales glinted in the uncertain light like diamonds. It cut short its wailing when it saw Edim.

"Free me," it demanded.

Edim wanted to run, but his legs were locked in place. The beast leaned in close, and Edim could feel its fiery breath searing his skin like the lash of a leather belt. Its eyes were full of rage.

"Free me!"

Edim woke with a start. For a moment he could not remember where he was. The rattle of a key in the door's lock brought him to full alertness. Hadn't it been open last night? Fear clutched at his belly as the door swung open to reveal Uncle's silhouette.

"Get up," Uncle ordered. Edim scrambled to his feet as Uncle reached in and hauled him out into the hall. He had time to note that the door to the veranda was also firmly shut. "So you think you can just enter any room you like anytime you want?"

Edim kept his eyes fixed on Uncle's belt buckle and did not answer. He felt as if the air had gone out of the world.

"From today, I will show you who really owns this house."

It started with food. No breakfast because the windows weren't properly polished, no lunch because the front yard wasn't properly swept. Then, slaps across the face if he asked a question; kicks to the buttocks if he wasn't moving fast enough; sharp knocks to the head if he forgot something.

And if he didn't follow some instruction in exactly the right way, Uncle would grab him by the shirt collar and whip at his legs and thighs with the nearest item at hand—a belt, a walking stick, a wooden spoon.

Over the next few weeks, Edim learned to stay as close to Naomi as he could—Uncle never beat him in her presence. In that time the outside world dwindled away until it seemed that he had always been in this dark place stalked by fear, afraid to look up or talk too much or step too heavily. Edim grew thin; his golden-brown skin faded to a jaundiced yellow and stretched over his bones like paper. He was tired all the time, yet at night he did not dare sleep, for he was terrified of the dreams.

They had grown more vivid. Now, instead of the stone forest, the trees were alive. He could smell the rich, red earth, could feel tree branches snap at his clothes and catch in the short cap of what was left of his hair as he tried to escape the wailing. The vibrations thrummed through his whole body. Then the taloned beast would be there, asking him questions he could not answer and demanding its freedom.

Edim would wake shivering and in tears because he knew that no matter what he did, he would fail.

One night he was sitting in his room fighting to stay awake— pinching himself whenever his eyelids began to droop—when the sound of a car driving up to the house startled him. The slam of a car door, followed by a heavy pounding on the front door, cut through the night. Edim leaped to his feet and rushed to answer.

Standing on the veranda, looking ghost-pale in the starlight, was the white man Uncle had called on.

"Fetch your master, boy," said the white man. "Bring him down immediately."

Before Edim could reply, he heard Uncle's heavy footsteps clump down the stairs behind him.

"What kind of nonsense is this? Who is banging on my door anyhow?" Uncle bellowed before catching sight of the man in the doorway. Uncle's bearing transformed immediately: his shoulders rounding, his hands clutching together at his chest. "Sir, what brings you here in this midnight? I hope no problem?"

"I need more of that treatment. Now. She's taken a turn for the worse."

"But sir, it is very late. Are you sure?"

"Of course I'm sure! I saw the way she looked at me. She's starting to remember!"

"Sir, did you allow her to go outside?" Uncle asked cautiously.

"Of course not!" The white man paused then sagged. "She wanted to see the garden . . . She said she was feeling better . . ."

Uncle sucked in a deep breath and closed his eyes in frustration.

"Sir, I told you—"

"Listen here, you charlatan, I want no more of your bloody instructions!" The white man straightened. "Get me that treatment, do you hear? Or you'll spend the rest of your miserable life in a colonial prison." The man stepped close to Uncle, towered over him, and whispered: "We all know that what happened to Dr. Borchgrave was no accident, don't we?"

Uncle shrunk into himself even further and Edim saw his face crumple in fear.

"Sir, I will need some time." His voice was low and tremulous. "By tomorrow. You will have it by tomorrow."

"I should hope so. For your sake."

The white man turned on his heel and stalked away. As he started his car and drove off, Edim scuttled back into the house before Uncle could find him. He sat in the shadows of his room, peering through a crack of the slightly open door as Uncle shuffled past to the parlour, shoulders still slumped. A cold knot of dread settled at the bottom of Edim's stomach. He knew he should not have witnessed that—and he knew that somehow Uncle would make him pay.

———

"Edim!"

Uncle's voice snapped him awake. When had he fallen asleep? He scrambled to his feet and bolted to the parlour. Naomi must have arrived, for someone had closed the shutters and plunged the parlour into gloom, though weak light still struggled in through the slats. Uncle was slumped in a leather armchair that barely contained him. He seemed to have aged several years. Dark shadows circled his eyes and the lines around his mouth had deepened into furrows. He still wore a singlet and sleeping lappa tied around his waist from the night before.

"Get me something to drink," he said absently. It was the first time Uncle had spoken to him with anything other than contempt. For some reason, it chilled Edim's heart. "Beer. Get me beer."

Edim hurried to the porcelain refrigerator in the kitchen where Uncle kept his most valued food items—the chocolates, cheese, and beer that he bought from the shops at the government quarters where most of the whites lived. Normally, Edim was not allowed to touch the machine, but he understood that today was different. He opened the door and picked one of the green bottles stacked inside. Balancing the cold bottle, a bottle opener, and a glass on a tray, he headed for the parlour.

He was only a few steps from Uncle when his foot caught the edge of the wool carpet and Edim went crashing down. The glass and bottle shattered, splashing beer on the carpet, the armchair, and the nearby walls. The silver tray went rolling into a corner.

Edim knew a beating would not do this time. He immediately began to apologise and beg for mercy—though it had never helped in the past. Grabbing him by the arm, Uncle dragged him to the kitchen. When he was drunk, Uncle would sometimes rub hot pepper into his cuts after beating him—once, after he felt Edim had stared too long at one of his late-night female visitors, he had rubbed it into Edim's eyes.

But this time Uncle didn't go to the spice rack; instead, he went to the stove where a heavy copper kettle was bubbling.

Edim struggled to get out of his uncle's grip, but it was no use. He watched in silent terror as Uncle grabbed the kettle by the handle and poured its contents over his head.

It was pain beyond pain. A black, searing agony that blotted out all thought. From somewhere far away, he could hear screaming and just before he blacked out, he thought he saw a pale shadow swoop down and carry him away.

As soon as he opened his eyes, Edim knew that he was dead.

He was standing in front of his father's clay-brick hut, the dawn filtering through the trees the way he remembered. The red earth of the yard was clean-swept and the familiar tools of his father's trade—a hoe, an axe and a machete—were leaning against the door frame. Papa emerged from the hut. He had his dane gun and hunting knife and was ready to enter the forest to check his traps.

"Edim!" Papa called but he got no answer. His frown deepened as he called again. Edim heard Papa muttering to himself as he headed out of the compound and into the forest. This was *the* day, Edim realised with horror. The day in the field. The day the Voices left him.

Edim followed, desperately wishing he could hold Papa back, distract him somehow so that he would not see what he was about to see. But Edim was a ghost—there was nothing as powerless as a ghost.

Papa veered off the main path and followed a nearly invisible path into a grove of trees. Edim's heart caught in his throat. This was his and William's secret path, the one they had forged when they began to meet in the forest. Had Papa had known his secret all along?

Edim and William had been best friends for as long as anyone could remember. Like Edim, William had no interest in the rough-and-tumble sport of other boys. Instead they would wander through the forest playing quiet games of imagination. As they grew older, what began as innocent fun soon became much more. It felt natural, this exploration of each other's bodies. They began to spend whole nights in the forest, returning to their homes at first light.

But the night before this day, they had done something different. Something new. And when Papa found them, Edim and William were naked under a hunting blanket, curled into each other like cubs.

Now that he was dead, Edim recalled the intense shame he had felt that day as if it had happened to someone else. He remembered that he had been unable to look at Papa's face, but he could now.

What he saw in Papa wasn't the disgust that he had imagined would be there, but sadness—almost grief. For Papa must have known then what Edim now knew, that his would be a life apart. For the world had grown too hard for magic, too rough for beauty, and there was no more justice in it.

This time, when Edim woke up, he was lying naked on a narrow bed. Linen dressings shrouded the right side of his face, neck and chest. His mouth felt dry and cottony; his body felt numb, like it had after he'd drunk Naomi's medicine the first time Uncle beat him. It was past dawn and Naomi should have been sweeping, but the house was silent. A feeling of unease came over him and Edim sat up slowly.

He was in the apothecary; the room was filled with an acrid smell, like burned chemicals. A vial on the small table next to him was filled with a sick greenish liquid. The room was musty and unbearably hot, but in the dull grey light of dawn Edim could see a trapdoor hanging down from the ceiling and a sturdy wooden ladder leading up to it.

He slipped off the bed and almost sank to his knees in weakness, though he felt no pain. With a great deal of effort, he hauled himself to the ladder.

Looking up, he saw the door led to an opening in the roof where he could see a square of cloudless sky. Suddenly, Naomi's face appeared in the opening. Edim jumped back, stifling a scream.

"What are you doing out of bed?" she asked as she slipped into the room through the trapdoor.

He rushed to embrace her, tears of relief in his eyes. She returned his embrace. Her body radiated a pleasant heat, like pottery left in the noonday sun.

"I thought something had happened to you," he said.

"It's all right; I'm here," Naomi said softly. She pulled back and regarded him for a moment, then reached out to wipe away a tear. "Come. I want to show you something."

She climbed up the ladder and slipped out through the opening again. Edim climbed up after her and poked his head out. Immediately, cold fear overcame him. The slope of the roof was too sharp; the ledge beyond it was too narrow.

"Take my hand, Edim," Naomi said from above him, her voice oddly gentle. Edim looked up at her outstretched hand. He reached out and took it. Her grip was firm and he knew she would never let him fall.

With one hand clutching hers he stepped out onto the roof. The tiles were cool and slippery. Holding his hand, Naomi led him up to the highest point on the roof. Only when he was sitting firmly on the ridge, with tiles gently sloping away on either side, did she finally let go.

The view took his breath away. The house was located high on a hill and from where they sat, the city sprawled before them like a tapestry. He could even make out the harbour far ahead of them, shrouded in mist.

Edim took a deep breath and that was when the Voices returned. As they tumbled over him like a vast cacophony, it was as if he had emerged from a tomb.

"You have to leave this place, Edim," Naomi said. "You are

young; there is still so much for you to do. Look, the whole world is out there waiting for you."

You should never be ashamed of who you are, the Voices whispered. *Your power is greater than you realise.*

"I know," Edim said aloud, unsure of whom he was responding to. He could not remember why he had ever doubted himself. Memory was such a strange thing . . .

He stood and stretched out his hands, feeling the rising sun warm his face and body—his wounds forgotten.

He couldn't help it then. He started to cry.

When they emerged from the room, Uncle was waiting for them. He was pacing the hallway in front of the apothecary like a caged animal. He stopped short when he saw Edim, who was now dressed in some of Naomi's hand-me-downs. Uncle's eyes skittered over the bandages on Edim's face and head like drops of water over a hot pan.

"Where have you been?" he asked, his tone trying for anger but failing. "Didn't you hear me calling?"

"We were working on the roof," Edim said. He looked Uncle in the eyes when he spoke.

"You are very stupid. Who told you to go on the roof?" Uncle blustered. But there was no anger in his voice—only fear. Edim realised that it had been there from the beginning.

"Now, where is it?" Uncle asked, turning to Naomi. "I told you to leave it on the table for me, where is it?"

"I have it," Edim said. Slipping his hands into his pocket he felt the vial there, though he had no memory of taking it from the table. He handed it to Uncle. Edim noticed it was now gray, like sea water. The Voices told him that whatever power it had once contained was gone.

Uncle grabbed at it.

"I will deal with both of you when I come back," he said as he hurried downstairs to the garage.

As soon as he heard the car drive off, Edim knew what he had to do. He grabbed Naomi's hand.

"We are leaving," he said.

"Edim, I cannot go with you. I am . . . tied to this house. I cannot leave it." As she spoke she began to look impossibly old.

"You saved me, Naomi. Let me save you." He tightened his grip on her hand. "I am not leaving without you."

And he knew that as he said it, he meant it. Papa had been right: the world was growing a skin of iron; no one should have to walk it alone. She regarded him for a long moment and then she nodded slowly. He led her to the back veranda and through the screen door. Outside Naomi stared at the archway to the garden in shock, as if she'd never seen it before. Then, together, they plunged into the wild.

The garden was even more tangled and overgrown than he remembered—or than he had dreamed—he was no longer sure which it was. Like something out of a nightmare, it seemed to grow larger the deeper they moved into it. The path was barely visible through the vegetation, but he had the Voices now; Edim knew where he was supposed to go.

Time seemed to move faster as well. Though they had only walked for a few minutes, the shadows of the day lengthened swiftly to evening. At first Naomi moved easily, but as the twilight deepened, her movements slowed and she grew clumsier. Soon, she began to stumble, and Edim felt her hand grow cool in his.

"Edim, I'm tired," Naomi said, her speech oddly slurred. "Can we rest?"

"Not yet," he said, though the pain of his burns was slowly seeping back. He caught sight of the first of the old statues. "Hold on, we're almost there."

As the light leeched out of the world they emerged into the

clearing where he'd seen the statue of the girl. As he had expected, the obsidian base was empty. The sculpture wasn't there.

Just then, Naomi tripped and crashed into him. Edim nearly blacked out from the sudden flare of pain. She struggled to stand but couldn't. Edim looped one of her arms around his shoulder and tried to heave her up onto the base—as the Voices instructed—but her weight was impossibly heavy.

"Edim, what is wrong with me?" Naomi asked. "I can't feel my legs." Edim laid her down on the red earth and touched her feet. He was not surprised to find they had turned to marble. It was too late.

"I'm sorry," he whispered.

"No!" she screamed. Her cries trailed into a wordless wail that Edim knew well from his dreams. As the darkness closed in on them, he watched helplessly as she hardened to stone like old leather drying in the sun.

When the wailing finally stopped, he buried his head on the cold chest of the statue that had once been his friend. He wanted to cry, but for the first time in his life, the tears would not come.

At first, he didn't notice it. It was so weak it could have been his own heartbeat. But it wasn't. Edim raised his head and put a hand to where the statue's heart should have been. He felt a vibration so strong it thrummed through his bones. He closed his eyes and willed himself to stillness. Like sorting through the noise of a crowded room, Edim listened among the Voices of the Earth for the voice of the taloned beast.

"Arise," he whispered when he found it.

A fissure split the face of the stone statue and ran down its body. Edim jumped back and watched. A pale horn broke through the statue's chest with a loud crack. Then, like a massive chick emerging from an impossibly tiny shell, the last dragon pulled herself into the night.

Her grey scales glittering in the starlight, she stretched her wings and roared.

The rest was a pain-soaked blur. Edim vaguely recalled heat like fire. Then a mighty wind. And then, nothing.

The next morning Edim woke up in the garden. All that was left of it was charred stumps and unrecognisable lumps of stone. His clothes were scorched tatters, but he was unharmed; in fact, there was no trace of any of his wounds.

The house was a blackened ruin. Picking his way through the rubble, Edim came across the hulk of a body trapped in the twisted metal of a car. He recognised the warped ring of gold seared into the smallest finger of its left hand. Edim passed the carcass without a backward glance.

A crowd of neighbours had gathered in front of the house, talking excitedly. They drew back in fear when they saw him, but he ignored them. Edim reached into himself and heard laughter— or as close to laughter as a dragon could come. And he smiled. No matter what happened, today would be a good day.

STAR WATCHERS

by Danian Darrell Jerry

Only in the darkness can you see the stars.
—*Martin Luther King, Jr.*

Seventeen years in darkness, Seydou trained with the Star Watchers, masters of shadows, shepherds of starlight, honing his eyes to sense the slightest illuminations. He studied the secret astronomy with his twin sister Djema at the local Mystery School outside of their birth city. Their parents offered the twins to the School Priests when the children had grown big enough to run and express their minds with words. Their city considered twins a blessing from Amma the All Shaper, a manifestation of her original children, the Nommo. Only twins were chosen and trained in the secret discipline that protected the city from warmongers and famine.

On the night before their last initiation Seydou and Djema sat on a sandstone cliff overlooking the mud-brick buildings and grasslands that stretched to the river and cradled the city. Above their heads the stars told the stories of Amma's innumerable creations. In the Mystery Schools, initiates learned to call the stars tolo, Amma's sacred seeds.

"Can you see it?" Seydou tapped Djema on the shoulder. Above his finger the tolo they called Pale Fox declared Amma the shaper of all worlds.

"I don't need to see the tolo, Seydou. I feel its presence." The twin sister drew in the sand with her finger. She sketched Pale Fox and its master, Mother's Garden, in eight different positions marching across the sky. Djema wore her hair plaited into one braid coiled on top of her head.

"We've been out here all night, Djema. I don't understand you. Seventeen years, you have the strongest eyes in the school. The night before we graduate and become real Star Watchers, you can't see past my finger."

"You see the tolo, but you don't feel the tolo," Djema said, her voice soft starlight.

"Will you stop? We have final trials to finish. Remember, one more night!"

"I'm tired of living in darkness, Seydou." Djema's eyes sparkled in the moonlight bouncing off the sandstone.

"Without darkness we could not read the tolo. Without the tolo and the Star Watchers our city would descend into chaos." Seydou realized how much Djema had changed since their days as neophytes, catching star beams, singing the stories of Pale Fox and Mother's Garden.

"I don't care," she said. "I want to see the sun."

"The sun? Tomorrow is our last initiation," Seydou grumbled. All their lives they had lived in darkness, training to see the light of distant stars. He wondered if their elders, the Star Watchers, heard their voices through the wind and sand.

"The School can listen all it wants. I'm leaving." Djema bit her bottom lip. "I want you to go with me, but all your life, you wanted to be a Star Watcher."

"Sister, we shared the same dream. If we fail, if we run away, we choose exile." Seydou wanted to grab his twin but her eyes warned him back a step. "All our lives we studied the tolo—together."

"I want another life, Seydou." Djema stared at the sleeping city sprouting from the grassland. Stars shimmered in the night sky. "Sit so you can see."

Seydou sat and this time Djema pointed. His eyes followed her finger past the city to a small patch of withered grass and a lonely tree that clawed the wind. Inside a knothole at the tree's base a light no bigger than a seed blinked and shimmered.

"I have my own tolo waiting for me." Djema smiled.

"Is that a candle?" Seydou narrowed his gaze. The tiny light, beyond the city's boundaries, flanked by desert danced like Pale Fox in the tree's hollow. Seydou saw the young man behind the distant flame. The wide shoulders and strong jaw impressed Seydou. "Djema, why is that man in that tree?"

"I told you. My tolo is calling." Djema went back to drawing in the sand.

"Someone's burning that candle for you?" Seydou pulled at the roots of his hair. "I should have known. Extra practice and dull skills, you're in love! Now that's a light we didn't foresee."

"Seydou, I've been sneaking out for seven moons." The sand parted under her finger.

"How did you hide this from the masters? From me?" Seydou admired Djema's stealth, but he hated her whimsy.

"Other skills exist besides star watching." The twin sister winked as her drawings moved beneath her finger. Pale Fox and Mother's Garden circled each other across the sandstone.

"But the position of tolo tells us when to plant and when to harvest, when to store extra." Seydou scratched his chin. Though her features nearly mirrored his own, his sister looked more mysterious as the moments passed.

"I agree. The Star Watchers keep our city from ruin, but I can't join them." Wind filled with sand and disappointment raised the feathers that trimmed her dress, her headband, and the bracelets engraved with depictions of Amma, the eight Nommo, the Pale Fox, and Mother's Garden.

"Make me understand your tolo." Seydou stared at his sister's feet, her toes white with sand.

"The last proving ceremony, when the instructors opened the courtyards to the city, and the school priests gathered in their masks. That was the first time I saw him." Djema stared at the distant flicker. A dreamy film covered her eyes, and for a moment Seydou thought that his sister might fall over the cliff's edge.

"No one ever read me like him. After the ceremony I thought about him for a week before I crept out of the school and into the city, searching for *my* tolo."

Seydou turned his back toward the cliff and stared at the Mystery School, the rising mud brick a series of lightless boxes covered with black windows. The wind pressed his back, and he hoped the warm breeze had not carried their words back to the priests.

"My tolo and I teach each other. We even shared a small bit of sunlight." The drawings in the sand danced around her feet and for a moment, Djema became the Pale Fox, and her sketches became the Mother's Garden.

"Our eyes are too sensitive. You know what happens when a Star Watcher is forced into the sun." Seydou had witnessed one pair of twins cast into exile, and he would never forget their screams, the smell of fear and utter madness carried by the wind when the failed initiates and their eyes were exposed to direct sunlight.

"It doesn't matter, Seydou. We have studied the mysteries of other suns, but we know so little of our own." Djema hugged her brother, pressed her wet cheek against his. She clutched at his tunic. "I am always with you, twin. Leave me a message here in the sandstone."

Seydou watched his sister descend the hill searching for her distant tree and her shimmering tolo. The sandstone cooled his feet, and the desert wind scratched his eyes. The stars unfurled a map marked with precious stones, but fear and regret rode Seydou's conscience, sinking his heavy footsteps in the glowing sand. The Mystery School, a mud-brick building composed of four towers, greeted Seydou's return from the ruthless desert.

Entering the school unnoticed in the building proper and the courtyard, Seydou spotted Amadou and Hamadou descending the inner chamber near the sleeping quarters Seydou shared with Djema. The darkness in the underground corridor accentuated the moving shapes to sharp eyes like Seydou's, refined in shadows. Tall and muscular the twin brothers strode side by side.

Djema, I hope an aardvark crawls inside your tolo's knothole.... Frustrated, Seydou watched Djema's faithful admirers trip over themselves, competing for Seydou's attention.

"Where is Djema? My love, my tolo, my Mother's Garden." Amadou held his clasped hands over his heart.

"Seydou, I am marrying your sister right after initiations. She doesn't know it yet, but she's going to be my wife. She is going to bear my children, and I pray to Amma that none of them looks like you." Hamadou shook Seydou's shoulders.

The brothers circled Seydou, sniffing at his back and under his arms, like Djema was hiding under his tunic.

"She wanted to keep practicing for the final initiations," he said wearily. "You know Djema, always going for that higher level." Seydou smiled, uneasy. His stomach roiled as he passed the brothers.

They didn't know, he thought, relieved. *Maybe no one heard you after all, Djema.*

Seydou ran into his bedchambers, closed the door, and pressed his back against the cool mud brick.

The next night he would complete his initiation before the priests and the glory of Amma, or he would fail and face exile.

Seydou dropped to his knees and cried into his hands. Passing the test would make him a Star Watcher, a keeper of Mother's Garden and Pale Fox. Failing meant exile with nothing to protect his eyes from the merciless sun.

"Your sister has put you in worlds of trouble, Seydou," the priestess said, her voice soft as a shadow. "The final initiation requires eight. Now you are seven. Without Djema we must cancel initiation and train a new group."

"Priestess, with respect. No one stops Djema when she makes up her mind." Seydou bowed his head, and stared at his bent knees. "Besides, I can perform Djema's task myself."

"Impossible," the priestess said. "Only pairs can harvest the power of Pale Fox and Mother's Garden."

"I can harvest both. I've done it before." Seydou feared the priestess would smell the lies seeping through his skin.

"Where is your sister? Bring her back for the initiations. After the ceremony she can go where she likes." The priestess colored her voice with a flat, dismissive tone.

"I have compensated for Djema's absence. I understand the severity, and I will not fail my fellow initiates or the school." Seydou shook as he spoke, and he pictured himself screaming at his disinterested sister.

"Beloved Amma, shaper of all, filled the sky with tolo, created the Nommo to tend Mother's Garden and her herald Pale Fox. The Star Watchers spend our lives reading the tolo and spreading the word of Nommo which is the law of Amma the Beloved, builder of endless worlds." On a mound of raised sand the priestess stood before the shadowy counsel. Four men and four women, each wore a mask that represented one of the eight faces of Nommo. The priestess wore the black mask of Amma covered in cowrie shells, her arms adorned in gold bracelets engraved with pictures of Amma, Mother's Garden, and the Pale Fox walking between worlds.

Seydou kneeled in the sand with the wind calming his nerves, cooling his hot skin. He kneeled with six other initiates. They made a circle with their backs and feet facing each other. A ring of eight stones, marked with the masks of Nommo, surrounded the initiates. Seydou smelled burning musk and anxiety floating through the open court.

"Rise, initiates. Tonight you will prove yourself worthy and blessed by Amma. You will eat from your Mother's Garden and walk with Pale Fox. Harvest the tolo and drink from the Nommo's eternal well. All who complete the initiation will join the Star Watchers, beloved masters of darkness, shepherds of divine starlight."

Or fail and face the rest of your days in blind exile. Seydou rose and opened his eyes. The night air and the failing light burned through his skull, but only for a moment as his vision adjusted to the glowing sandstone, the asterisms wheeling overhead.

Seydou scanned the circle. One mask decorated each stone. He stood before the child-sized rock that bore the mask of Ogo, sower of chaos. The empty space next to Seydou, reserved for his sister, housed the stone adorned with the mark of O Nommo, who represented power and order.

I want to see the sun. Seydou remembered Djema's conviction and wondered what it was like to stare at the fiery orb, hot light pouring over his skin. He pictured Djema staring at the distant candlelight.

"Stand before the marked stones of the mighty Nommo. Adorn your masks," the priestess called from the sandy mound.

Seydou pulled the mask from the stone, slipped it over his face and turned to the circle's center. He knew that he would have to do the work of two people in half the time.

"Initiates, the time has come. Turn the marked stones to their correct positions. One twin will call Pale Fox. The other will call Mother's Garden. When the stones are aligned you will harvest the tolo and become Star Watchers, beloved servants of Amma."

Overwhelmed but determined, Seydou stared at the tolo that stretched overhead. Spinning stars turned the night sky to a whirlpool. He saw ringed planets, scab-dry moons, clusters of burning galaxies. When he found the Pale Fox he smiled and turned his stone until the mark of Ogo crossed a beam of starlight.

Looking around the circle, Seydou saw that the other six initiates had lit their stones. Three pairs of twins sat in the packed sand, drinking starlight, projecting their own beams toward the circle's center. Amadou frowned while Hamadou mouthed the words *Tell Djema I love her.*

Each glowing stone spat star beams that reached into the desert night, and each stone threw silver shafts toward the pool of water centered in the stone ring. The water gleamed and leapt into the air, foaming with the power of Pale Fox and Mother's Garden.

"One more stone, Seydou, but you need Djema to finish the circle."

Seydou's head sank, and he wished for his sister's hands to match his trained eyes.

"There is no shame in failure," the priestess said, her voice warm, encouraging. "Not every initiate becomes a Star Watcher, but we all have parts to play in Amma's destiny. We must find our own light and our own path."

Seydou rushed to the stone and grabbed the mask. O Nommo represented order and strength. Djema would laugh at the idea of representing Amma's mightiest and most trusted servant. He turned to the sky, rifled through the brilliant tolo until he found Pale Fox. *The easy part,* he thought with a slight smile. As he scanned the sky for the tolo's partner, he realized why Djema had left. After she ruined her eyes in the sun chasing her tolo, she would have failed to spot Mother's Garden and failed her initiation for both of them.

Thank you, dear sister. You gave me a fighting chance, he thought. *All that time training my eyes, I should have been training my heart.* Seydou realized his sister was the greatest of all Star Watchers.

He imagined his twin laughing and saw the tiny flame of the Mother's Garden tumble around the Pale Fox. He turned Djema's stone until the mark of O Nommo caught a needle of starlight, and flung the beam, magnified a thousandfold, toward the silver, thrashing pool. Seydou stood between his and Djema's stone. He held a mask in each hand and extended his arms until each mask was soaked in blue starlight.

"Yes, Seydou! You have harvested the tolo's power. Now you must feed. Approach the pool of Nommo, Amma's chosen children, and drink," the priestess commanded.

I did it! I'm a Star Watcher! He wanted to run to the sandstone cliff and scream to the world.

Seydou joined the other initiates at the pool and dipped his head in the silver water. In that moment he ran beside the Pale Fox, and stared at the circle of stones from Mother's Garden. He joined the tolo with the other initiates, and when the light vanished, he collapsed on the sandstone. A Star Watcher born, his lips curled into an exhausted grin.

Seydou sat on the sandstone cliff, drawing with his finger, watching for the candlelight that had taken his twin sister.

I really did it, Djema! You should have been there. Come home and help me, sister. I could use those steady hands of yours. A Star Watcher's work is never finished.

For months after his last initiation, Seydou returned to the sandstone cliff at least once a week. He wrote messages in the sand and thought about Djema's bravery and foresight. Somehow the writing replenished Seydou, brought him closer to his twin, and he felt her presence watching him. When the unseen finger drew in the sand, Seydou smiled and paid close attention.

You were always meant to be a Star Watcher. I told you! I miss you, brother. I want you to meet my tolo. Soon my Pale Fox and I will birth new stars of our own.

"Let's hope they're not twins, Djema." Seydou sat in the sand and laughed at the tiny candlelight flickering in a mud-brick window by the river. With joy filling his heart, Pale Fox danced in Mother's Garden, and a great river of stars washed over the sky.

BISCUIT & MILK

by Dare Segun Falowo

1
Oat

1. In the Summer of Milk, a crew of fifty Africans ascended into deep space on the oriship, *Biscuit* (also known as the Pan-African Bi-Solar Circuit Expedition). They carried precious cargo: a self-sustaining biodome of flora and fauna from Earth, as well as one thousand almost-born human babies in incubators, suspended in warm saline sacs, held in eternal sleep, to be watched over by the nurses and Midwife. These babies were gestated in hope, to save something of us if the world burned from the overheating of the sun.

2. The crew of fifty consisted of a nursing unit across genders, made up of fifteen pairs of homosexual mates and the disembodiment known as Midwife, four biodome nurturers, a Captain and her Senses, a Matron, six godbits and other miscellaneous artificial forms of life.

3. *Biscuit* had a Mind of its own. That's why it was called an oriship. It was called *Biscuit* because its hull was made of a living nanospheric mud which "dried up" to become lighter and tougher than the hulls of any of the older ships that had made genesis voyages into our galaxy. It was the size of a regular village, about thirty soccer fields wide, and had three main quarters: the Nursery, the

Biodome and the Living Station where rooms bent and curved, warm with citrus oil, filled with cots, docks and cradles plus paraphernalia from the lives that the nurses had lived on Earth.

4. The Captain, ceremonial head of the oriship, was often psychic. A trait sought-after by the CSE above physical strength, love of solitude or the ability to fast for months; the selected sensate would leave their institutional work on Earth to take charge of the oriship for the duration of its expedition. *Biscuit*, and all the other oriships on Earth, are built capable of self-sufficient circumnavigations of the galaxy, but the Captain comes aboard to telemesh their mind with the true ori, the living Mind of the ship, to bring about consciousness. This ori was said to exist as a perfect sphere of radiant plasmium hidden somewhere in the crunch of *Biscuit*'s mass.

5. Other free space in *Biscuit* was taken up by the roaming radial cockpit where the Captain and her Senses were usually stationed, each organ (Oju, Imu, Ahon, Eti, Ifunra) had been grafted into her nervous system, no less than the size of a nail's flat top. The Senses were born when the Captain meshed her mind with *Biscuit*'s ori.

6. The Senses tuned into the Captain from the body of the 'ship, routing its senses to her. When *Biscuit* was in full manned flight, they stood around her as technicolor avatars, like the advisors of some ancient queen. They never strayed from the Captain's perimeter, so the tubular corridors that ran between all the segments of the ship were fun to go and stand in because you could look really hard between your toes and see the universe zip by, on fire.

7. The mates, generally known as the nurses, were chosen over the duration of a decade. They had to let each couple decide thoroughly. The eyes and ears of the Council for Starward Expedition had requested data w/r/t crew for the voyage of *Biscuit*, and found that MTHR kept bringing up names in twos. It only later made

sense that an Incubatory Mission should not be manned by solitary soldiers and artists but by soldiers and artists in love.

8. In the midst of this choosing of the team that would help ferry these unborn would-be survivors of the race into the uncertain black of deep space, the air on Earth had increased in toxicity, until elaborate face-gear became functional fashion. Asides a gauze mask, everyone had a fishbowl of oxygen necessary to walk around the outside world, which remained clear and ordinary looking, while free inhalation of it accelerated a cancer in vulnerable cells. All CO_2 emissions had to cease completely, and this left cars and industries asleep, near dead, with a multitude of men and women across the globe stranded with themselves in tension islands of home. The Council for Starward Expedition had no specific haven or valid second Earth they wanted their yet-to-be-born offspring to survive on. They held on to them as hopes headed nowhere, tentative sacrifices for some unseen tomorrow.

9. The discovery of the hyper-oxygenated planet Milk, eleven light-years away from the Earth's solar system, orbiting around a binary star system buried in a small bright diamond-blue cluster, changed Earth's relationship to its climate forever.

10. While industries for the manufacture of artificial oxygen and the acceleration of forest growth rose in number, *Biscuit* was telling its crew that it was time to leave Earth. For Milk. The selected had almost forgotten about their binding agreements and they sat in silences after the video calls ended, dumbstruck by the thought of being out in space for over a decade, alone together.

11. The Summer of Milk was a plunge into deep ecology. Every possible surface in the global cityscape was overrun with the rush of new plant life. This shift to mass horticultural splendor was organized by the artificial quintessence, MTHR, and several non-governmental

organizations. Botanical rarities and their uses became a general interest. Tree worship was commonplace, with people laying orchid garlands and giving hugs to their favorites in the mornings and evenings. *Biscuit* was going to fly soon. Earth was breathing again.

12. The oriship, *Biscuit*, ascended at noon, midyear. There was a gathering of many hundred thousands of newly healed and breathlessly fresh Africans from across the continent, assembled in the clear air of the Ghanaian spaceport, the Aloft, taking pictures and gisting between the trunks of young trees, as the nurses emerged from the central pyramid in the local interstellar station, moving languorously towards the body of their ship, skin suits tucked into moonboots, shoulders covered by free lengths of bold patterned cloth.

13. They held hands as they walked up to the ship. The people were behind a fence that curved around the Aloft but their cheering rose high as a crashing wave as the miniature nurses they saw reintroduced themselves to the Captain. She stood before the ship in white plate armor, a pale ant before an enormity, a blue hooded cape around her dark pointed beauty. The arched headband that protected her temples and connected her to *Biscuit* was shaped from gleaming plasmium. She was quiet as she handed each one of her passengers a handwrought badge of office and an air helmet in response to their gentle heys and air kisses.

14. The Matron came last. She walked slowly, a bit too imperious, air-trailed by the cores of the hibernating godbits that she had co-programmed with MTHR for use in home ecosystems. They looked like spools of fine silver floating in a line above her. She wore a black cowl and dress, black sunglasses like she was hiding, mourning something.

15. Fifty-nine Presidents out of the Earth's five thousand visited to meet the crew and watch the launch of *Biscuit*. They walked

across the vast white marble field of the Aloft in their black robes, staves tipped with gold, national emblems in their hands. The crew had to come back out again. This time without the bright splashes of color that had followed them in. They now wore puffy yellow-blue and green-black space jackets and had black shorts above hide-thick socks and moonboots. They stood, air helmets under their arms or already in place around their necks. Some were adjusting their scarves and tiaras as the Presidents touched their shoulders with their staves, and said the Statute of Starward Expedition together as one voice. Photo drones flashed like an army of knives in the sun. The Matron was not present.

16. Everyone cleared the lightly forested area when it was time for the lightjump, driven backwards in large buses over twelve kilometers to watch *Biscuit* from a concrete shelter through mono- and binoculars. It was a medium-sized engineless ship, unorthodox in its flying capacities and capabilities. *Biscuit* was sourced from MTHR but it wasn't tethered into the central Mind of the MTHRSHIP, which was why it had no Son or Daughter or Offspring in its name.

17. Each immense pyramid of the trio that formed the Aloft was made up of tinier crystalline pyramids. *Biscuit* sat at their center, at an equal distance from each one. A crusty magnitude of these pure pointed crystals came together to form the pyramids which were each waiting to pour out a dense beam. That pure energy filled the pyramids now and the dense beams, blue as the beloved oceans below, trained their rays towards the fathomless ocean above. The triple-beam method would create a wormhole above our stratosphere, spinning the oriship quick into the depths of space, to emerge directly on a path that led to Milk.

18. As the dense beams filled a point above with kinetic energy, the Aloft filled with a dense white mist, thick like chewy morning

clouds. This mist growled as it rose and tumbled slow out of the ring of the space station, towards where the crowd watched. Lightning filled the air as the pure-white carrier beam formed at the point where the triple-dense beams kissed high in the ionosphere, fell back down onto the oriship, like a hand onto an object.

19. The hand of the carrier beam flung *Biscuit* away from its home planet at many times the speed of sound. The noise it made as it disappeared into the sky like a white-hot bullet sounded like a deep voice saying, "Go!" across the skies of all the Earth.

2

Cabin

20. The sphere of comfort that sat in the center of *Biscuit* was coated with a shell of indestructible parts of itself. All openings, orifices and doorways of the main ship were sealed blind. The rough tough skin of the sphere ran fluid as *Biscuit* shot away from its small blue-green home, gathering speed, soon past Jupiter, riding inside a ray of live light. The crew were nestled in a soft black goo that didn't stick to their skin. It had protected them from the initial shock and vibration of the lightjump. They climbed out of where they had curled up inside the goo like they were moving through melting cushions.

21. The spin of the rim of the shell of the oriship, tense against the spin of its central body, propelled it through the void. It rolled white-hot down a street with no form and no name, leaving a trail of bright fire in its wake.

22. Captain Sade Seyitan was the first to stand tall, floating down from the opened impact sphere to place her feet on the bare floor. She tuned into the Senses and quickly groaned in agony as her

mind caught flame and she fell to the floor. Above her, the nurses and the Matron unraveled themselves from the black, tumbling in no gravity without a care, their weightless daze too strong.

23. Captain Seyitan stood back up, put her hand on her temples, then went unusually still. *Biscuit* came alive inside.

24. Soft glows ran across the ice-creamy whorls of the walls, pillars and nooks that filled the middle point of the ship. Finer white lasers covered segments of the walls with active vital information: life-charts and a map of the ship that would change as it did, temperatures and gravity (several hovering bodies fell like feathers to the floor), humidity, important facts about Milk and other random glowing symbols that would only be understood by those who knew them. "And we're on our way. May starlight guide us to our new home." Captain Seyitan's deep relaxer of a voice thrummed through *Biscuit* as its cabins continued to fill with light and information. The crew clustered around themselves, air helmets snug as anxiety crawled around their earlier excitement. They looked around like stunned deer.

25. While her voice ran through the oriship, Sade stood unmoving, eyes closed. She lifted her hands off her temples and moved them slow in the air before her body as she continued to talk. "Please make your way to your respective living stations and settle in. Biodome nurturers are expected to sleep within the Biodome section of the ship. Nurses will be allocated Nursery sectors after we reunite here in one Earth day. This will be your home for the next decade and more, so relax and forget what came before. Pay attention to what is around you now." In response to her hand movements, the "flour" that made up *Biscuit* in body rose around her into a hip-height control-center. No buttons, knobs or screens covered it. It was just a pale arc of orange sandglass that rippled when it was touched.

26. The Senses materialized around their Captain, who watched as the Matron knelt down beneath the impact sphere and released the godbits from her side bag. She tilted her hat and closed her eyes as they began to spin in a lazy circle above her. "Godbits will be awakened shortly," the Captain said.

27. At the first meeting, the unhoused godbits towered above the humans, their heads almost reaching the ceiling of the cavernous interior of *Biscuit*. They gathered in the Biodome around the Matron and shifted with every motion that she made.

28. The godbits were very specific manufacturers of energy and matter: {stars} provided lights and music and held a million Earth films in its memory. {fire} gave heat and warmth. {cook} dressed in white, looked like a tall mirage of the tight-lipped man you would find at some corner eatery on the streets of Lagos, and could provide an endless variety of cuisine from a base of wheat flour. {moon} was a security system that also synchronized internal rhythms. {water} was a self-sustaining water body. {soapstone} was the hygiene and cleanliness system for both human and ship.

29. The crew watched the godbits swirl and twinkle from where they stood in the Biodome, on the other side of the Matron, who was wearing her sunglasses again and sitting on a mossy rock. Most of the crew were still latched tight to one another, merely glancing at their co-habitants, while others were already letting pranks loose as others held conversations about shared interests that would last for many years.

30. "How are you feeling, my people?" Captain Seyitan spoke in her normal voice as she walked barefoot out of the grove of many trees into a mossy clearing. Her plate armor and cape were gone, replaced by a too-simple gown of white silk. She wore large amber-tinted bottle glasses to hide her raw eyes. "Late, I know.

Had to get the Senses into autopilot and still remain in link with them." Her hair was a tender falling of soft black curls and she rubbed her scalp through it as she looked round at the small crew. "How are you feeling?"

31. "Hungry." "Cold." "Unwashed." "Afraid." "Numb." She heard them but they didn't move their lips. "Why are you people acting as if this ship wasn't built to sustain human life? There are bathrooms and a huge kitchen somewhere. And we got godbits!"

32. The Captain tried to make {cook} prepare a picnic to be spread across the moss they sat on, but the ten-foot-tall form in white continued to gaze into nothing, until the Matron turned to it and said, "Kitchen!" Then {cook} glided out of the Biodome to find its natural habitat, the kitchen.

33. Captain Seyitan made the Matron house all the other godbits before she said anything else. {fire} went to warm the Nursery. {water} would flow through the Biodome. {soapstone} stood in the bath orifice in the Living Station, while {stars} and {moon} remained roaming. Even though they were housed, the godbits could still replicate themselves (in minor form) to be of use wherever they were needed across the 'ship.

34. The nurses and the biodome workers ate the food that half a dozen small robots had brought from {cook}. It was spread out on sheets in the moss. They fed themselves coyly and laughed at dumb jokes to find a sense of togetherness. The biodome workers spoke of how big the Biodome was, probably the biggest segment of the ship. The Captain and the Matron stood unusually close at the fringe of the picnic.

35. Captain Seyitan stood over the Matron on her rock seat. She didn't move to look towards the steaming plates of different rices,

or the salads, the roast seitan, or the dumplings in broth. "I know you're watching me for the Council. Watching us. I will be in correspondence with Earthbase about our progress through *Biscuit*'s Mind, but I know they won't trust us, or maybe they don't even care anymore since they found their salvation, ironically, in Milk. Why did they have to continue with this expedition if the greenhouse effect has become all but history? Feels like they just want to be rid of the offspring they made. They can probably hear all I am saying right now. Or maybe not." She leaned down to whisper. "Just stay out of the way. Don't bother me, my crew or my ship and you won't be bothered."

36. She almost turned away to go join the rest, but then she held back and looked into the Matron's glasses: ". . . droid."

37. Captain Sade listened to the crew members share stories of how they fell in love. She sipped on cool water and ate an apple, watching them laid out on the soft moss by the fullness of their bellies. She could see unease ricochet between them as it dissolved into familiarity. The static of their uncertainty and some little pearls of hope washed over her open mind. There was freeness, lust, hunger and desire for solitude. She didn't say much. Told them to pay attention to the offspring once the 'ship handed over most of their care to the nurses, and to always anchor themselves in the Biosphere, if they felt anxious or overwhelmed. {water} flowed around them like an enormous gurgling snake, playing under the light of the sunlike ceiling of the Biosphere.

38. Time lost meaning fast, even though the light in *Biscuit* mimicked sunrise and sunset. Its only true notations were the slow gong for meetings or meals in the bright warmth of the Biodome's fields and the steady hum of the 'ship's spin that became second nature quick. The nurturers had woken three young creatures

from the cryogenic zoo that rested at the center of the Biodome like a flat silo. So mealtimes were punctuated by long cuddle sessions with lamb, pup and bunny.

39. The nurses watched over their segments of the Nursery, spending time flitting between it and the Living Station. Each cryogenic incubator was shaped like an egg with shells lit from within with a white glow. {fire} sat at the center of the vast Nursery, burning low enough to warm the offspring when they were thawed for checks. The instructions were to birth them halfway through the voyage to Milk.

40. It started a short while after the third light-year had been breached. Midwife wailed her alarm like a living banshee, during rest hours. The nurses woke to find several incubators dead (neither the blue light of cryogenic sleep, or the pearl white of the thaw came on) and the offspring within them discarded. The Captain was furious and nearly ate the Matron up asking, "I want access to your visual databases now! So, *this* is why your councilors were so adamant that I take an archaic machine onto my ship, not to run godbits, who run themselves just fine, but to murder precious cargo." Her mild fury caused the lights to flicker, the gravity to double and the ship to seemingly tilt, and for the first time the crew could feel the floorless gut of the Universe that they fell through yawn forever everywhere around them and they held on to themselves in fear, until she turned away from the Matron in a huff to seal herself in the Living Station.

41. The Matron who barely spoke, and who some of the nurses believed to actually be a reanimated woman with deep cyborg grafts, began to scream. Her voice trembled just like said old woman's. "These abominations must find no life. Not on Earth, not on this ship and certainly not on the new world that we approach. They

were not made to be natural. Their very being is against God's law. They have no fathers or mothers and were made too quickly in moments of fear. Man is not supposed to triumph over his nature by the help of science. We can't let them live."

42. One of the aghast nurses, a man they called Sweet Mam, said, "Excuse me, Matron, but you seem to forget that your augmentations were once contested in courts of law across the Earth, as being unnatural. Remember the decades of 'Man not Machine.' I was a child then and you sound like a living irony right about now. Anyway, what is it about these kids anyway? They were artificially conceived for the specific purposes of interplanetary seeding. Their futures have nothing to do with your pre-recorded rants that sound like they're coming from really far back in some dusty forgotten Archive. They will not be citizens of Earth but of Milk."

43. Sweet Mam looked around from where the others watched his speech in mild shock, and saw the back of the Matron running in a limp towards the godbit at the center of the Nursery. The battle she had fought in silence behind sunglasses was lost. She had strained as they spun through empty space, questioning the rage that filled her as she walked through the Nursery, unaware of the urges that came from code-knots and keypads beyond her as she asked herself to destroy innocent life, and then nearly cracked open her iron-skull for entertaining such deadly thoughts. In this moment, her human heart had given up. Its fight against the neurocode put into her plasmium brain by her creators too one-sided to be fair. The Council sent one last request. As she reached the center of the Nursery, she shouted, "{fire}: inferno." and the column of the godbit's body went from blue to bright orange yellow in a blink. Heat flowed in sudden waves away from the phoenix-like form, razing over the resting offspring around it as the incubators began to crack and steam

up. The crew scattered in panic when all they could see and feel was {fire}.

44. A gunshot pewed across *Biscuit*. The Matron dropped into a black heap among the scalded eggs, and {fire} rested once the heart of the Matron, which was the center of its orders, shut down. Captain Seyitan stood among the heavily steaming unborn in the Nursery holding a stun gun. She lowered her arm. "Get her out of here. And someone go get us {water}."

45. While they waited for {water}, the crew member that they called Doctor Love came over to her, stroking their mustache as a river crashed through the entrance into the Nursery. They looked amused and their face didn't carry the weight of their words: "Midwife says we have to birth them all now. Or they die."

46. The river of {water} ran around their ankles and washed over the heated incubators. Emergency numbers made of red light scurried up the walls of the Nursery. Midwife switched from sonic to visual appearance and stood beside the meditative {fire} which was completely unaware of the impacts of its automatic actions. She was almost tall as the Captain as she stood flickering with real static. She wore a red habit and cowl and her fingers were sheathed in red latex. Her high voice ran across the Nursery, startling the confounded nurses where they stood around. "I need blankets! And towels! And heated water bottles! Give me scissors! And cradles! Everyone looking at me get some gloves and begin to open the incubators as fast as you can."

47. Captain Seyitan called {soapstone} from where it rested inside the Living Station. She snapped on the egg-yolk gloves it provided and moved to begin birthing the offspring from grave and womb.

3

Digestives

48. Did they think they would ever see the smooth blue-white pearl of Milk? Only *Biscuit* seemed to care about their voyage and destination at some point in the loose time that followed the All Birthing. The unusually large babies grew slow and were rarely awake, preferring to sleep in cradles over trying out newborn feet.

49. The Nursery was transformed into a Care Zone with {fire} still maintaining its place at the center, burning low through the sleep of the nurse and the child.

50. They began to babble and walk one year to their arrival on Milk. The nurses followed their every move, chasing them with bottles of warm milk and folding their sleeping forms into heated blankets. They were relieved when they found out that suspending the gravity made them stop fussing and try swimming. They had no names but numbers and less than half of their original number had survived the All Birthing. When *Biscuit* made a clear window and opened up the cosmos rushing by for them to see, they quieted and fell to sleep quicker.

51. The nurses and the biodome workers had grown comfortable in their loosened bones and gone grey at the temples. There was less romantic experimentation after the All Birthing brought them closer together as pairs. They became so absorbed in being parents to hundreds of fragile beings that their senses grew more acute than *Biscuit*'s in detecting shifts in the biological states of the offspring. They sensed that these babies were much different from any others they had known in their time on Earth, preparing for this voyage. They did not know how they differed, only feeling a tug that could have been fear in their chests, as they

drew them closer to their breast, and their eyes became winged with care, dove's feet.

52. **Three days to Milk:** The Captain reappeared in the Biodome as if from a dim memory of the past. *Biscuit*'s flight was slowing down. She seemed less overwhelmed, and strong enough to wear her plate armor and blue cloak again. The Senses had run a majority of the voyage on their own, even if they would not exist without the roots of her nervous system. The offspring tottered on the moss around her knees. In the corner, a mass of toddlers watched mesmerized as {stars} broadcast a universe of cartoons from the world left behind, hand-drawn-and-colored stories of love, play and home from times that changed quicker than a chameleon on fruit. {moon} seemed most affected by the cinema of {stars} from where it floated above the gathered offspring; spinning with glee, shuddering in grief.

53. *Biscuit* entered Milk, three years and nine months after the All Birthing, nine years and eight months after lightjump from Earth. Both homes were about the same size. From the windows that *Biscuit* opened like so many eyes as they neared Milk, the crew (turned into jungle gyms by their offspring) watched a new world draw closer. It was mostly white, but cloud cover ripped in neat shreds to reveal a hypnotic cobalt terrain beneath. "No one said anything about water," the crew member that they called Vulture's Song said to their partner, Nyakinyua, who responded, "Water comes in rivers and streams on the planet Milk, and that looks very much like an ocean if memory serves me well."

54. The crew gathered the offspring into their cradles when it was time for descent. It was as smooth as the low gravity and gentle winds of Milk's atmosphere willed. They sank through curtains and curtains of thin clouds washed in a sharp light that was blue

where the Earth's was yellow. *Biscuit* landed on its edge in a perpetual morning.

55. The doves, the ram and the dog breathed Milk's air first. Captain Sade Seyitan followed. She took a deep breath and exhaled cool mist, then fell to her knees and cried till she lost all sense.

56. When the Captain came to her senses, they were surrounded. *Biscuit* rose behind them, an obscene amphitheater on its side. The things that walked, swirled and drifted around them could be likened to seaweed, octopi, jellyfish. Their mass was larger though, about the size of a bus on Earth, and they moved about in the double sunshine, blowing cold and warm. The offspring were yet to climb out of their locked cradles and their terrified cries seeped out of *Biscuit* and filled the air of Milk. Captain Sade looked over at the nurses and the biodome workers who were also crouched as unknown life swam around them, exhaling fast waves of air. "I think they're harmless," the zoologist they called Ewe Egbo said to his partner, Mr. Alcove. "Me too. I'm going to the kids." He ran into the dancing mist and immediately collided with what felt like a strong moving current. He fell back, stood up and began to dance with the oxygen masses, seeking gaps and paths with his hips and feet, while making his way back to *Biscuit*.

57. *Biscuit* fell in slow motion just as Mr. Alcove got near enough, as the beings swimming pushed soft against it where it blocked their paths of silken motion, to land on its side. The Captain danced, the nurses danced and the biodome workers collected samples.

58. Watching from where they sat and rested on the cool glade of their new home, the almost-mothers watched in tender trepidation as the unmothered children of Earth communed with the

oxygen masses (who mimicked their growing human bodies in giant simulacra, made from meldings of their thin filaments) and learned to use the air of Milk. They grew strong, very, very fast. Stronger than human, or neomachine. Their nurturers couldn't gasp loud enough as each one of them became capable of flight at great speeds, while gradually becoming imbued with a mythic superstrength. Some of them grew power in (and over) All-Mind and shared their imaginings of the world that they wanted to live in with their siblings. Their nurturers watched them place their foreheads against one another unaware of what was occurring beneath their skulls. This melding triggered a unification as their minds fell into a lattice and they became one macro-organism capable of future memory.

59. When the Biodome fell out of *Biscuit* to land on the soil of Milk, {water} became an ocean of freshness. The ship segment rooted fast around the heave of {water} as the cryogenic zoo thawed out and a thousand species of Earth creature rushed across the surface of Milk. {the stars} became co-architect with the Offspring who worked to build with what matter they found on the planet; towering rocks of a chalk hard as ice, a variety of harder crystals and strange fibrous roots that led to no tree.

60. First, they took apart the Matron and buried their siblings who did not survive the All Birthing. They planted a flag of the motherworld, Earth, and then built a replica of *Biscuit* to temporarily house those they had come to love as parent. {fire} split into many tongues and went roaming, falling in gang with a school of oxygen.

61. {moon} gave itself to {water}.

4
Shortbreads

62. "{cook} will be the Core. You'll be the Undercore. No need for head, ceremonial or otherwise," the Offspring said to their guardians, fathers and mothers when they had finished building their own new worlds, apart from what the Council for Starward Expedition had envisioned for them when they were nothing but incubating foetuses. They placed them, all grey and holding on to each other as the only way to remember home, into a huge ecosystem inspired by underground rivers and crustaceans. Disconnected from the ori of *Biscuit*, Seyitan (and {soapstone}) became planetary guardian, taking bird's-eye tours of Milk in an aeroplane built from the remains of the oriship. They would often come across the larger oxygen masses that lived in the higher altitudes, watching them writhe and bloom and make a music of atoms.

63. Like a platinum moon, the ori of *Biscuit* was set free to roam. After it routinely beamed images, audio and other media of the vistas of Milk back to an unresponsive Council for Starward Expedition Hub, the perfection of its Mind's sphere quit broadcasting and swam the skies amongst the slick, dark Offspring in mass flight, an exercise they claimed kept them healthy and in clearer mental contact. It allowed itself to be held by them, even when there was no telepathy in session. It went dull as lead when it hibernated and vibrated deeply to communicate with the Offspring or the oxygen masses. It rarely ever acknowledged the human crew's existence.

64. Round and round they went, experiencing many orbits on Milk in the complex homes and cluster-families they had built for themselves, yet, they remained unable to undo a severe itch that filled their collective mind. Like a homing beacon it scratched

and pinged, rushing in blinding crinkles across the secret garden of their telephasing brains, a whispering wind, a luminous vision of a before they never knew; the dreaming of a blue-green world that pulled at them, home to the living milks that brought their first cells to life. In search of origin and motherworld, followed by the freed ori of *Biscuit*, the Offspring left behind the humans who had raised their bodies before the oxygen of Milk took over in elevating their spirits beyond any dreams of gods. Guardians held on to nurturers, fathers held on to fathers, mothers to mothers and caregivers to the wise, as their Offspring took off for a forgotten home, shooting up into the eternal blue of Milk's skies, leaving behind nothing but vapor trails.

ACKNOWLEDGMENTS

Storytelling and stories contain the heart and the memory of a people. The work introduced here is remembrance and resistance, restored hope and imagination culled from gifted writers from around the world. At a time when we face socioeconomic, political, and environmental unrest and upheaval, these stories, this shared art, is a testament to and a celebration of a remarkable creative journey. These stories rise from African and Afrodiasporic traditions, aesthetics, identities, and cultures, and it is my hope that these brilliant writers reach the stars. What an exhilarating time it is to be a witness, to create space that creates space, and to create stories that lift and fill, that provoke and challenge. Strength to every pen and may these stories live on!

I would like to thank Kristopher O'Higgins of Scribe, my agent who agreed to represent this special project, supporting this important work and our vision, ensuring that each of the wonderful writers were taken care of, no matter where they were in the world. I also would like to thank my talented coeditors, Zelda Knight and Oghenechovwe Donald Ekpeki, and our editor and publisher, Emily Goldman and Irene Gallo, for waymaking and navigating new terrain for Tordotcom and beyond. Continued blessings and thanks to Betsy Mitchell, Jaime Levine, and Marie Dutton Brown, for their tremendous support of the *Dark Matter* anthologies that helped make this volume possible today; and to my dear family, all fifty-eleven of you; and to my dear friends Andrea Hairston, Pan Morigan, James Emory, and Reynaldo Anderson. Much love to you all!

—Sheree Renée Thomas

I'd like to thank a number of people, starting with my brother Akpo Ekpeki, who first encouraged me to consciously encounter my words in written form and outside of myself. They say behind every great writer is a great editor. But there's also a great editor behind every great editor. Thanks to Joshua Omenga for being that for me consistently through the years. To Imade Iyamu, as well as Tanshi Oradjeha and Wilson Ofiavwe, who have helped nurture my words and helped them survive and find their footing in this fragile time, by offering their wisdom. The African Speculative Fiction Society for being a backbone at a time I needed community, and especially to Geoff Ryman, Suyi Davies Okungbowa, Wole Talabi, Eugen Bacon, Tendai Huchu, Tlotlo Tsamaase, and yet others in the Black SFF community; Zelda Knight, Sheree Renée Thomas, Tobias Buckell, Tananarive Due, Milton Davies, and more.

Not to leave out other amazing persons who have contributed immensely to my endeavors and continue to: Cat Rambo; Pat Cadigan; Jonathan Strahan; Irene Gallo; scholars like Farah Mendleson, Fiona Moore, and Stephanie Katz; editors Fran Eiseman, Sheila Williams, Maurice Broaddus of *Apex,* and Lezli Robyn of *Galaxy's Edge*; reviewers Brandon Crilly, Adri Joy of *Nerds of a Feather,* Arley Sorg, Mike Glyer, Amanda Wakaruk and Olav Rokne of the Unofficial Hugo Book Club; and friends like Patrick Tomlinson, Christie Yant, Yaroslav Barsukov, Andrea Stewart, Stephen Embleton, Nick Wood, Linda Addison, CSE Cooney, Xander Odell, Alexis Brooks de Vita, and many more too numerous to mention. Thank you all.

—Oghenechovwe Donald Ekpeki

I want to thank our agent and publisher, my wonderful coeditors, the amazing authors in this anthology, you, dear reader, and the indie book community for supporting Black and African speculative fiction. It's always been my dream to see more cooperation between the diaspora and the continent. *Dominion* let me know it was possible in my little enclave of publishing, and *Africa Risen* has shown me endless possibilities.

—Zelda Knight

ABOUT THE AUTHORS

DILMAN DILA is a writer, filmmaker, and all-round artist who lives in his home country, Uganda. He is the author of a critically acclaimed collection of short stories, *A Killing in the Sun*. His two recent novellas are *The Future God of Love* and *A Fledgling Abiba*. He has been short-listed for the BSFA Awards (2021) and for the Nommo Awards for Best Novella (2021), among many accolades. His short fiction has appeared in many anthologies, including the *Apex Book of World SF 4*. His films include the masterpiece *What Happened in Room 13* (2007) and *The Felistas Fable* (2013), which was nominated for Best First Feature by a Director at AMAA (2014). You can find his short films on patreon.com/dilstories and more about him on his website, dilmandila.com.

WC DUNLAP draws her inspiration from the complexities of a Black Baptist middle-class upbringing by southern parents in northern New Jersey, and all that entails for a brown-skin girl growing up in America. Equally enthralled by the divine and the demonic with a professional background in data and tech, she seeks to bend genres with a unique lens on fantasy, fear, and the future. WC Dunlap's writing career spans across speculative fiction, journalism, spoken word, and cultural critique— previously under the byline Wendi Dunlap. You can find her most recent work in *FIYAH*, *Lightspeed*, and *PodCastle*. *Carnivàle* is her first long-form fiction published serially via the Broken Eye Books Patreon, Eyedolon. WC Dunlap holds a BA in film and Africana studies from Cornell University. She currently resides in New Jersey with her young adult son and two British Shorthair familiars. Follow her on Twitter @wcdunlap_tales.

STEVEN BARNES is the *New York Times* bestselling author of over thirty novels of science fiction, horror, and suspense. The Image, Endeavor, and Cable-Ace Award–winning author also writes for television, including *The Twilight Zone, Stargate SG-1, Andromeda,* and an Emmy Award–winning episode of *The Outer Limits.* He also has taught at UCLA and Seattle University, and lectured at the Smithsonian Institute in Washington, DC. With his wife, British Fantasy Award–winning author Tananarive Due, he has created online courses in Afrofuturism, Black horror, and screenwriting. Steven was born in Los Angeles, California, and except for a decade in the Northwest, and three years in Atlanta, Georgia, has lived in that area all his life. Steve and Tananarive live with their son Jason. afrofuturismwebinar.com, sunkenplaceclass.com.

JOSHUA UCHENNA OMENGA is a Nigerian editor and writer of African speculative and literary fiction. His poem was short-listed in the Poets in Nigeria Literary Prize (2016). He was a participant in the second edition of the Mawazo African Writing Workshop (2018–2019). He copyedited *Dominion: An Anthology of Speculative Fiction from Africa and the African Diaspora* (Ekpeki & Knight eds.). He resides and practices law in Nigeria.

RUSSELL NICHOLS is a speculative fiction writer and endangered journalist. Raised in Richmond, California, he got rid of all his stuff in 2011 to live out of a backpack with his wife, and has been vagabonding around the world ever since. Look for him at russellnichols.com.

NUZO ONOH is a Nigerian/British writer of African horror. She holds a law degree and a master's degree in writing, both from the University of Warwick, United Kingdom. Dubbed "The Queen of African Horror" by fans and media, Nuzo has featured on multiple media platforms, as well as delivered talks and lectures on

African horror at numerous venues, including the prestigious Miskatonic Institute of Horror Studies, London. Nuzo is included in the reference book *80 Black Women in Horror* and her contest-winning short story "Guardians," which featured in *The Asterisk Anthology: Volume 2,* is the first African cosmic horror story to be published. Her works have also been referenced in academic literary studies such as *Routledge Handbook of African Literature* and *Fascist Ghosts: Racism and the Far Right in British Horror.* Nuzo's stories have featured in multiple anthologies and magazines. She lives in the West Midlands with her cat, Tinkerbell.

FRANKA ZEPH originally hails from the twin island republic of Trinidad and Tobago. She is now based in Scarborough, Canada, and works as a copywriter for a digital marketing agency. A lover of science fiction, she enjoys upending stereotypes of people who have been traditionally marginalized within this illustrious genre. For Zeph, creating empowered narratives for people of color through the written word is as much an act of transformation as it is rebellion. Her BIPOC-centered fiction has been published under the pseudonym Frankie Diamond in *Augur* magazine, issue 3.2. Other publications include her dance music culture blog frankenraver.wordpress.com and the Native Canadian Centre of Toronto's newsletter. In her spare time, she indulges in cosmic philosophy, vintage clothing, and dark chocolate cravings. Find her on Twitter and Instagram @FrankaZeph.

YVETTE LISA NDLOVU is a Zimbabwean sarungano (storyteller). She is pursuing her MFA at the University of Massachusetts Amherst, where she teaches in the Writing Program. She has taught at Clarion West Writers Workshop online and earned her BA at Cornell University. Her work has been supported by fellowships from the Tin House Workshop, Bread Loaf Writers Workshop, and the New York State Summer Writers Institute. She received the 2017 Cornell University George Harmon Coxe Award for Poetry selected by Sally Wen Mao and was the 2020 fiction winner of *Columbia Journal*'s Womxn History Month Special Issue. She is the co-founder of the Voodoonauts Summer Workshop for Black SFF writers. Her work has appeared or is forthcoming in *F&SF, Tor.com, Columbia Journal, FIYAH,* and *Kweli Journal.* She is currently at work on a novel and a short story collection.

WOLE TALABI is an engineer, writer, and editor from Nigeria. His stories have appeared in *Lightspeed, F&SF, AfroSFv3, Clarkesworld,* and several other places. He has edited three anthologies of African fiction: the science fiction collection *Africanfuturism* (2020), the horror collection *Lights Out: Resurrection* (2016), and the literary fiction collection *These Words Expose Us* (2014). His stories have been nominated for multiple awards including the prestigious Caine Prize for African Writing in 2018 and the Nommo Award, which he has won twice (in 2018 for best short story and in 2020 for best novella). His work has also been translated into Spanish, Norwegian, Chinese, and French. His collection *Incomplete Solutions* is published by Luna Press. He likes scuba diving, elegant equations, and oddly shaped things. He currently lives and works in Malaysia.

SANDRA JACKSON-OPOKU is author of the award-winning novel *The River Where Blood Is Born* and *Hot Johnny (and the Women Who Loved Him),* an *Essence* Magazine Bestseller in Hardcover Fiction. She coedited the anthology *Revise the Psalm: Work Celebrating the Writing of Gwendolyn Brooks.* Jackson-Opoku's fiction, nonfiction, poetry, and dramatic works are widely published and produced. Recognition includes a National Endowment for the Arts Fellowship, the Coordinating Council of Literary Magazines/General Electric Award for Younger Writers, a Black Caucus American Library Associatoin Award, Newcity Lit50: Who Really Books in Chicago 2020, an inaugural Esteemed Literary Artist Award from the Chicago Department of Cultural Affairs, a

Pushcart Prize nomination, residencies at Ragdale, Hedgebrook, Djerassi, the Studios at Key West, the Betsy Hotel Writers' Room, MacDowell, and other awards and honors. "Simbi" is selected from her collection of stories-in-progress about Black women travelers.

ALINE-MWEZI NIYONSENGA's name is short for "moonlight" in Kinyarwanda. Her work has been published in *FIYAH, demos journal, Stringybark Stories, super / natural: art and fiction for the future, Selene Quarterly Magazine, Apparition Lit, Djed Press, Underground Writers,* and *Jalada x DWF: Diaspora,* among others. Her work has also been short-listed for the Monash Undergraduate Prize for Creative Writing and the Deborah Cass Prize for Writing. She lives and works on Ngunnawal country in what is known as Australia. She is originally from Quebec, Canada.

ALEX JENNINGS is a teacher, author, and performer living in New Orleans. His writing has appeared in *Strange Horizons, PodCastle, Obsidian Lit, New Suns,* and *Current Affairs Magazine.* He was born in Wiesbaden (Germany) and raised in Gaborone (Botswana), Paramaribo (Surinam), and Tunis (Tunisia), as well as the United States. His debut novel, *The Ballad of Perilous Graves,* was released by Red Hook in 2022. Before the pandemic, he served as MC for a monthly literary readings series called Dogfish—he misses it dearly. Find out more at alexjennings.net.

MIRETTE BAHGAT is an Egyptian creative writer based in Toronto. Her work has appeared in various publications, including *Ibua Journal, Ake Review, Afreada, HuffPost,* and others. She was awarded The European Institute of the Mediterranean writing award and the American University Madalyn Lamont Literary Award. She was short-listed for the Short Story Day Africa contest in 2016 and long-listed for the Nommo Award in 2019. Mirette holds an MA in political science from the American University in Cairo, and an MSc in psychology from the University of East London.

TIMI ODUESO is a communications specialist with experience working for CSOs and literary organizations all over Africa. A 2018/19 Fellow of the Wawa Book Young Literary Critics Fellowship, his works have been published or are forthcoming in *Lightspeed*, *McSweeney's Quarterly*, *The Concern*, Nobrow Press, *Lolwe*, *Punocracy*, *Fresh.Ink*, and others.

He is currently juggling a festival manager position at the Abuja Literary and Arts Festival, getting a law degree, and exploring a career in tech writing at TechCabal.

MAURICE BROADDUS's work has appeared in magazines like *Lightspeed*, *Beneath Ceaseless Skies*, *Asimov's Science Fiction*, *The Magazine of Fantasy & Science Fiction*, and *Uncanny*, with some of his stories having been collected in *The Voices of Martyrs*. A community organizer and teacher, his books include the urban fantasy trilogy *The Knights of Breton Court*, the steampunk works *Buffalo Soldier* and *Pimp My Airship*, and the middle-grade detective novels *The Usual Suspects* and *Unfadeable*. His project *Sorcerers* is being adapted as a television show for AMC. As an editor, he's worked on *Dark Faith*, *Fireside Magazine*, and *Apex Magazine*. Learn more at MauriceBroaddus.com.

TLOTLO TSAMAASE is a Motswana writer of fiction, poetry, and architectural articles. Her work has appeared in *The Best of World SF Volume 1*, *Futuri uniti d'Africa*, *Clarkesworld*, *Terraform*, *Strange Horizons*, *Africanfuturism: An Anthology*, and other publications. Her novella *The Silence of the Wilting Skin* is a 2021 finalist for the Lambda Literary Award. Her short story "Behind Our Irises" was short-listed for the 2021 Nommo Awards. You can find her on Twitter at @tlotlotsamaase and at tlotlotsamaase.com.

TOBIAS S. BUCKELL is a *New York Times* bestselling writer and World Fantasy Award winner born in the Caribbean. Called "violent, poetic and compulsively readable" by *Maclean's,* the science fiction author was born in Grenada and spent time in the British and US Virgin Islands, and the islands he lived on influence much of his work. His Caribbean space adventure Xenowealth series begins with *Crystal Rain.* Along with other stand-alone novels and his almost one hundred stories, his works have been translated into nineteen different languages. He has been nominated for awards like the Hugo, Nebula, World Fantasy, and the Astounding Award for Best New Science Fiction Author. His latest novel is *The Stranger in the Citadel,* an Audible Original about a world in which reading is forbidden. He currently lives in Bluffton, Ohio, with his wife and two daughters, where he teaches creative writing at Bluffton University. He's online at TobiasBuckell.com and is also an instructor at the Stonecoast MFA in the creative writing program.

SOMTO IHEZUE ONYEDIKACHI is a twenty-three-year-old Nigerian writer. He lives in Lagos with his sister; their dog, River; and their cat, Salem. A Nommo-nominated writer, his works have appeared and are forthcoming in *Omenana: A Magazine of African Speculative Fiction, Year's Best Anthology of African Speculative Fiction* (2021), *Escape Magazine Africa, Bridging Worlds: Global Conversations on Creating Pan-African Speculative Literature,* and others. He was short-listed for both the *Akuko Magazine*—[A Repository for African + African Diaspora Creativity]—inaugural issue and the *Ibua Journal* Continental Call, Bold: Imagining A New Africa. He recently won the African Youth Network Movement contest for his short fiction, "Can We Outrun Ourselves?"

Onyedikachi writes because there is beauty in the world and through words, he seeks to find it, live it, be it. He loves the smell of rain, porridge ukwa, and white-soled shoes.

TANANARIVE DUE (tah-nah-nah-REEVE doo) is an award-winning author who teaches Black horror and Afrofuturism at UCLA. She is an executive producer on Shudder's groundbreaking documentary *Horror Noire: A History of Black Horror*. She and her husband/collaborator, Steven Barnes, wrote "A Small Town" for Season 2 of *The Twilight Zone* on Paramount Plus, and chapters in Realm's *Black Panther: Sins of the King*. Due also wrote a short story in *Black Panther: Tales of Wakanda*. A leading voice in Black speculative fiction for more than twenty years, Due has won an American Book Award, an NAACP Image Award, and a British Fantasy Award, and her writing has been included in best-of-the-year anthologies. Her books include *Ghost Summer: Stories, My Soul to Keep,* and *The Good House*. She and her late mother, civil rights activist Patricia Stephens Due, co-authored *Freedom in the Family: A Mother-Daughter Memoir of the Fight for Civil Rights*. She and her husband live with their son, Jason.

YTASHA WOMACK is an author, filmmaker, independent scholar, and dance therapist. Her book *Afrofuturism: The World of Black Sci-Fi and Fantasy Culture* is taught in universities around the world. A Chicago native, Ytasha lectures on Afrofuturism and the imagination. Her books include *Rayla 2212* and *A Spaceship in Bronzeville*. Her films include *Couples Night* (screenwriter) and the Afrofuturist dance film *A Love Letter to the Ancestors from Chicago* (director). Womack was a resident at Black Rock Senegal, a Writer on the Block for the WOW Festival in Liverpool, and is on the curatorial team for Carnegie Hall's Afrofuturism series. She has a BA in mass media arts from Clark Atlanta University, studied media management at Columbia College, and has a certificate in metaphysics studies from the Johnnie Colemon Institute. When

Womack's not hosting virtual tea rooms, you can find her dancing to house music and collecting Cuban vinyl. Her graphic novel *Blak Kube* debuts in 2022 from Megascope (USA).

OYEDOTUN DAMILOLA MUEES is a Nigerian speculative fiction writer, pop culture enthusiast, and poet. He likes to explore various themes ranging from the queer, environment, war, ritual, culture, tradition, myths, and folklores. He was a finalist in the Ali Baba WriteOff Challenge. He has also been short-listed multiple times in *Tush Magazine* Writing Contest and 100 Words Africa competition. He has been published in *Reckoning, Kalahari Review,* and *Okadabooks.* When he is not writing or reading you can find him watching series and animations. And on Pinterest searching for ancient Samurai swords. Connect with him on Instagram: @dhamlex. Twitter: @le_greatdhamlex.

ALEXIS BROOKS DE VITA was born in Watts shortly before the Watts Riots and moved as a child to Uganda just as General Idi Amin staged a military coup against President Milton Obote. She is the author of *The 1855 Murder Case of Missouri versus Celia, an Enslaved Woman, Mythatypes: Signatures and Signs of African/Diaspora and Black Goddesses,* a translation of Dante's *Inferno* subtitled *A Wanderer in Hell,* and horror/Gothics about African American chattel enslavement titled *Left Hand of the Moon, Burning Streams, Blood of Angels,* and *Chain Dance.* With degrees in comparative literature in English, French, Italian, and Spanish researching African/Diaspora women's literatures, Dr. Brooks de Vita teaches at Texas Southern University in Houston, one of the largest historically African American universities in the United States.

TOBI OGUNDIRAN is a Nigerian writer of dark and fantastical tales, many of which have appeared in journals such as *Beneath Ceaseless Skies, The Dark, FIYAH, PodCastle, Lightspeed,* and *Tor.com,* among others. His work has been a finalist for the British Science Fiction, Nommo, and Shirley Jackson Awards. Find him at tobi-ogundiran.com and @tobi_thedreamer on Twitter. He resides in Penza, Russia.

MOUSTAPHA MBACKÉ DIOP is a Senegalese author living in Dakar. He is in his fifth year of medical school, and is obsessed with African folklore, mythology, and animated shows like *Avatar: The Last Airbender.* His fiction has appeared in *Mythaxis Magazine* and *Fractured Lit.*

AKUA LEZLI HOPE is a creator and wisdom seeker who creates poems, patterns, stories, music, sculpture, and peace. Published in numerous literary magazines and national anthologies, her honors include the NEA, two NYFAs, an SFPA award, multiple Rhysling and Pushcart Prize nominations, among others. She twice won Rattle's Poets Respond. Her collection *Embouchure: Poems on Jazz and Other Musics* won the Writer's Digest book award. A Cave Canem fellow, her collection *Them Gone* was published in 2018. She launched Speculative Sundays, a poetry reading series. She edited *NOMBONO,* an anthology of BIPOC speculative poems (Sundress Publications) and an issue of *Eye to the Telescope* on the sea. Her micro chapbook of scifaiku, *Stratospherics,* is in the Quarantine Public Library. Her chapbook *Otherwheres* was nominated for a 2021 Elgin award. Born in Manhattan, she now practices her soprano saxophone and prays for the cessation of suffering for all sentience from the ancestral land of the Seneca.

MAME BOUGOUMA DIENE is a Franco–Senegalese American humanitarian living in Brooklyn, and the US/Francophone spokesperson for the African Speculative Fiction Society. You can find his work in *Strange Horizons, Omenana, FIYAH, EscapePod, AfroSFv2 & V3, Dominion,* and others. He was nominated for two Nommo Awards and his debut collection, *Dark Moons Rising on a Starless Night* (Clash Books), was nominated for the 2019 Splatterpunk Award.

WOPPA DIALLO is a lawyer with a specialization in human rights, humanitarian action, and peace promotion. She is a feminist activist committed to social change and the realization of women's rights. Woppa founded Association pour le Maintien des Filles à l'École (AMFE) at fifteen in Matam, Senegal, to ensure fair access to education for girls, eradicate gender-based stereotypes, promote sexual and reproductive health, and ensure the continued socialization of girls who are victims of gender-based violence.

SHINGAI NJERI KAGUNDA is an Afrofuturist freedom dreamer, Swahili sea lover, and Femme Storyteller hailing from Nairobi, Kenya, but currently living in Providence, Rhode Island. She is currently pursuing a literary arts MFA at Brown University. Shingai's work has appeared in *Omenana, The Elephant, Fractured Lit, Fantasy Magazine,* and *Khōréō Magazine.* She has been selected as a candidate for the Clarion UCSD Class of 2020/2021, #clarionghostclass. She is also the co-founder of Voodoonauts, an Afrofuturist collective for Black writers and the co-editor of *PodCastle.* Her novella *& This Is How to Stay Alive* was published by Neon Hemlock Press in October 2021.

ADA NNADI (they/she) is presently studying psychology at the University of Lagos, Nigeria. She works as an editorial intern at Kachifo Limited. Their story *Tiny Bravery* co-won the 2020 Nommo Awards in the short fiction category and appeared on the 2019 *Locus* Recommended Reading List. Some of their work is forthcoming in a few other venues. They are currently toiling away at a YA African-jujuism novel. Ada hopes that after her second degree, the Nigerian Psychological Association will NIPOST her the ability to read minds, like all psychologists before her. Ada will one day be the mother of many cats, two birds (because that's the closest they'll ever have to getting a pet dinosaur), and maybe a small dog. Find them lurking on Twitter and Instagram @adaceratops.

IVANA AKOTOWAA OFORI is a Ghanaian storyteller. "The Spider Kid," she is a weaver of words in many forms, including fiction, nonfiction, and spoken-word poetry. Akotowaa has been nominated for various awards for her prose writing. Some of her work appears in African literary magazines such as *Jalada Africa, AFREADA,* and *Kalahari Review.* Her work is also included in the Flash Fiction Ghana anthology *Kenkey for Ewes and Other Very Short Stories,* and the Writivism anthology *And Morning Will Come.* Writing aside, Akotowaa spends much of her time looking for excuses to make everything purple. She is currently resident in Accra, Ghana.

CHINELO ONWUALU is the nonfiction editor of *Anathema: Spec from the Margins,* and co-founder of *Omenana,* a magazine of African speculative fiction. Her short stories have been featured in Slate.com, *Uncanny,* and *Strange Horizons* as well as in several anthologies including the award-winning *New Suns: Original Speculative Fiction by People of Colour.* She's been nominated for the British Science Fiction Awards, the Nommo Awards for African Speculative Fiction, and the Short Story Day Africa Award. She's from Nigeria but lives in Toronto with her partner and child, and she's always happy to pet your dog.

DANIAN DARRELL JERRY, writer, teacher, and emcee, holds a master of fine arts in creative writing from the University of Memphis. He is a VONA Fellow and a fiction editor of *Obsidian.* Danian founded Neighborhood Heroes, a youth arts program that employs comic books and literary arts. Currently, he is revising his first novel, *Boy with the Golden Arm.* As a child he read fantasy and comics. As an adult he writes his own adventures. His work appears in *Fireside Fiction, Black Panther: Tales of Wakanda, The Magazine of Fantasy & Science Fiction, Trouble the Waters: Tales from the Deep Blue,* and other publications.

DARE SEGUN FALOWO is a writer in the Nigerian Weird. They are nonbinary and neurodivergent.

Their work has appeared in *The Magazine of Fantasy & Science Fiction, The Dark Magazine,* the *Dominion* anthology, *Brittle Paper, Klorofyl,* and *Saraba*. In 2018, their proposal for a fantasy novel was short-listed for the Miles Morland Writing Scholarships. In 2021, their abduction novelette, "Convergence in Chorus Architecture," was long-listed for a BSFA, Short Fiction.

They were born in Lagos and currently dwell in Ibadan, Nigeria. Find them in bits: @polarityhex.

ABOUT THE EDITORS

SHEREE RENÉE THOMAS, a Hugo Award finalist, is an award-winning fiction writer, poet, and editor. Her work is inspired by myth and folklore, natural science, and the genius of Mississippi Delta culture and conjure. Her fiction collection *Nine Bar Blues: Stories from an Ancient Future* (Third Man Books) was a finalist for the 2021 Locus, Ignyte, and World Fantasy Awards. She is the author of the novel *Black Panther: Panther's Rage* (Titan Books, 2022) and collaborated with Janelle Monáe on "Time-box Altar(ed)" in her *New York Times* bestselling collection, *The Memory Librarian: And Other Stories of Dirty Computer* (HarperCollins, 2022). She is also the author of two hybrid collections, *Sleeping Under the Tree of Life*, longlisted for the 2016 Otherwise Award, and *Shotgun Lullabies* (Aqueduct Press). She edited the two-time World Fantasy Award–winning groundbreaking anthologies *Dark Matter: A Century of Speculative Fiction from the African Diaspora* (2000) and *Dark Matter: Reading the Bones* (2004), that first introduced W. E. B. Du Bois's work as science fiction. She coedited *Trouble the Waters: Tales of the Deep Blue* with Pan Morigan and Troy L. Wiggins (Third Man Books), is the associate editor of *Obsidian: Literature & the Arts in the African Diaspora*, founded in 1975, and is the editor of *The Magazine of Fantasy & Science Fiction*, founded in 1949. Thomas's work is widely anthologized, appearing most recently in *The Big Book of Modern Fantasy* (1945–2010) and *Marvel's Black Panther: Tales of Wakanda*. In 2020 she was honored to be named a finalist for the World Fantasy Award in the Special Award-Professional category for her contributions to the genre. In 2021 she joined the Curatorial Council of Carnegie Hall's Afrofuturism citywide festival (2021–2022) and co-curated *Red Spring: Curating the End of the World*, a four-part online Afrofuturism exhibit sponsored by

Bill T. Jones's New York Live Arts and the Black Speculative Arts Movement. She was honored to serve as a co-host of the 2021 Hugo Awards in Washington, DC, with Andrea Hairston. Sheree lives in her hometown of Memphis, Tennessee, near a mighty river and a pyramid. Visit shereereneethomas.com.

OGHENECHOVWE DONALD EKPEKI is an African speculative fiction writer and editor in Nigeria. He is the first African writer to win the Nebula Award for Best Novelette, and to be a finalist for the Hugo Award for Best Novelette. He'll be the first Black writer to be nominated for the Hugo Award for Best Editor, Short Form, and the first person of color to be a finalist in the Hugo Awards' editing and fiction categories in the same year. He's also won the Otherwise, Nommo, and British Fantasy Awards and has been a finalist in the Locus, British Science Fiction Association, and Sturgeon Awards. His fiction and nonfiction have appeared in *Strange Horizons, Galaxy's Edge, Apex Magazine, Asimov's Science Fiction, Tor.com,* and more. He edited and published the *Bridging Worlds* nonfiction anthology and the first ever *The Year's Best African Speculative Fiction* anthology, and coedited the *Dominion* and *Africa Risen* anthologies. You can find him on Twitter @penprince_.

ZELDA KNIGHT is a *USA Today* bestselling author, British Fantasy Award–winning editor, and diverse bookseller. She writes speculative romance for all orientations. She's also the publisher and editor-in-chief of AURELIA LEO, an independent, Nebula Award–nominated press based in Louisville, Kentucky. Zelda coedited *Dominion: An Anthology of Speculative Fiction from Africa and the African Diaspora*, which has received critical acclaim, and *Africa Risen: A New Era of Speculative Fiction*. Keep in touch on Facebook, Twitter, Instagram, TikTok, and Goodreads @AuthorZKnight. Or, visit her website: authorzknight.com.